## *Dark Rose*

Mike Lunnon-Wood was born in Africa and educated in Australia and New Zealand. Based in the Middle East for ten years, he now lives in Sussex and has a young son.

# MIKE LUNNON-WOOD

---

# DARK ROSE

**HarperCollins**Publishers

HarperCollins*Publishers*
77–85 Fulham Palace Road,
Hammersmith, London W6 8JB

A Paperback Original 1996

3   5   7   9   8   6   4   2

A catalogue record for this book
is available from the British Library

ISBN 0 00 647591 4

Set in Linotron Meridien
at The Spartan Press Ltd,
Lymington, Hants

Printed and bound in Great Britain by
Caledonian International Book Manufacturing Ltd, Glasgow

*For my son Piers
and for Vicky, mine own High Queen of the Celts.
When Irish eyes are smiling . . .*

# ACKNOWLEDGEMENTS

There were many people who helped me with this book, but some deserve more than just my thanks. Firstly, my brother, Squadron Leader Tony Lunnon-Wood, who explained modern air warfare, Commander Crabtree RN and the wardroom of HMS *Nottingham*, in particular the Principal Warfare Officer, Lieutenant Bennet RN, who spent many hours helping me understand how modern sailors fight their warships. Lastly and perhaps most of all the very senior army officer, who must remain anonymous, who read the entire manuscript, tried with infinite patience to explain to me the way the British army actually functions and corrected my work.

Any mistakes are mine, not theirs.

# THE CHARACTERS

## *The Irish*

| | |
|---|---|
| PROF KIERNAN | University professor, head of the resistance |
| DR PETER MORRIS | University academic, deputy head of the resistance |
| MILLIE MORRIS | his wife |
| PAT O'SULLIVAN | resistance leader south-west |
| RORY MCMAHON | resistance leader central |
| JOSEPH O'REILLY | resistance leader north-west |
| BRIGET VILLIERS | resistance leader south-east |
| COLIN MAHONEY | Taoiseach of the Republic of Ireland |
| MAEVE O'DONNELL | resistance leader |
| TONY O'MALLEY | Irish entrepreneur, resistance planner |
| JOHN LA TOUCHE | young resistance fighter |
| DAVID O'CONNELL | as above |
| AISLING MCLOUD | resistance member, Aiden Scott's lover |
| KELLY FAMILY | Moira, Simon, Sarah, Mary, David, Sue and Sinead, a family living in Dublin |
| LT EAMON KAVANAGH | captain of the Irish Navy Ship *Kathleen* |
| MARY JOHNSON | President of the Republic of Ireland |
| CMDT ANDRE HYLAND | commandant (major) in the Irish Defence Force |

## Celts

| | |
|---|---|
| ROBERT DUGAN | captain in the Black Watch |
| AIDEN SCOTT | captain, 22nd Special Air Service Regiment |
| BUSBY GROGAN | 22nd Special Air Service Intelligence officer |
| SALLY RICHARDS | department head, MI6 |
| PETER TILBY | Irish specialist, MI6 |
| GORDON PERSSE | as above |
| ARNOLD CLEAVES | financial expert, MI6 |
| PETER MAYNOUTH | Middle East expert, MI6 |
| PETRA WALLIS | Deputy Director General, MI6 |
| SIR JAMES 'SANDY' MARSHALL | Head of Liaison, Operation 'Dark Rose' |
| MAJOR GENERAL EDWARD STEWART | Officer Commanding, Operation 'Dark Rose' and Commander, 'Celt Force' |
| SIR HUW TRISTAN-CARTER | British Ambassador to the United Nations |

## Invaders

| | |
|---|---|
| ALI JASSEM | Palestinian fighter, commander south |
| MOHAMMED BASSAM | Palestinian fighter |
| KHALIL ASHRAWI | Palestinian leader of New Irish Emergency Council in Ireland |
| GENERAL MUSTAFA SAAD | officer commanding Libyan forces in Ireland |

O, the Erne shall run red,
  With redundance of blood,
The earth shall rock beneath our tread
  And flames wrap hill and wood,
And gun-peal and slogan-cry
  Wake many a glen serene,
Ere you shall fade, ere you shall die,
  My Dark Rosaleen!
  My own Rosaleen!
The Judgement Hour must first be nigh,
Ere you can fade, ere you can die,
  My Dark Rosaleen!

'Dark Rosaleen',
anonymous sixteenth-century poem
translated from the Irish by
J. C. Mangan (1803–49)

# PROLOGUE

## 1992 Amman, Jordan

The worry beads were sweaty in his hand. The air was hot and thick with smoke, the air-conditioning having given up an hour ago. The historic meeting that had gone on for sixteen hours would be over soon. In the room, senior members of Fatah, the mainstream of the Palestinian Liberation Organization, were sitting opposite delegates from the militant breakaway Popular Front for the Liberation of Palestine.

Only days before, Yasser Arafat and George Habash had agreed to put aside their differences, to join forces to concentrate on the struggle. One Palestine for the Palestinian people. All Palestine.

The men in the room were the best and the brightest that Palestine had ever produced. Bankers, lawyers and strategic planners who at last could bring their skills to the struggle.

He watched the men at the table. His role would come later when these men, modern financial magicians had woven their illusion.

He was a fighter. For now he would wait. His time would come. He hoped it would not. They said the west wouldn't fight for it. It would just be talk, more empty nothings from the United Nations, but he would have to be ready, he and his men. To hold what they had even though it would be bought and paid for.

# 1

## *Ireland, autumn 1994*

The kidnappings were executed with precision. The sequence began with the son of the prime minister, the Taoiseach. He was taken with military efficiency as he left the family home, a man staying by the phone box after the car carrying him had been driven away, down the main road, actually past the Gardai at the gates to his family home, to explain what had happened and what his parents had to do to ensure his safe return. Within four hours nine other children and young people, all close relatives of senior Irish politicians and civil servants, had been taken. They were to be the first of more than 150 in the following three weeks. They were considered necessary.

It had begun with money. The finance men had been working for months now. Wielding money instead of guns they found ways to pressure other people, using the preparations that had been under way for years.

Large investments in banks and building societies, carefully shielded behind layers of holding companies, were leveraged to force the debts of many into crisis. The money, in vast amounts, was used to buy up the mortgages and company loans of targeted individuals and they were approached and told in no uncertain terms that a life's work would be in overnight ruin if they asked awkward questions. They were to follow instructions, accept contracts for work for which they would be paid and say nothing to anyone.

In most cases it was just a matter of looking the other

way, but in a few instances the intent was outright co-operation and threats were made. One man, a senior Garda officer, was told his son, already walking with one plastic leg, would lose the other if he didn't do as he was told. To prove the point they showed him photographs, dreadful images of things they were prepared to do, and finally, as if the man needed more convincing, before leaving they killed the family dog. When the money or threats wouldn't be enough and they needed real leverage they took someone close. Kidnapping.

The perpetrators melted into the scenery. As tourists, visiting businessmen and language students they disappeared in the cities and their subterfuge was good enough. Those that noticed the strange faces shrugged it off and happily took their money for rooms, meals, supplies and services. This was modern Europe, the place of open borders, progressive thinking, welcoming to visitors with money in their pockets and these visitors were not just tourists, they were investors. They were buying businesses, spending money, employing people where there was no work a year ago. It became easy not to notice the increase in numbers, or the fact that they were mostly men. To a person who had been out of work for two years, it didn't matter from whose hand top wages were paid. Foreigners had been investing in Ireland for years.

Some ordinary people did notice, and those with suspicions who asked questions at the table or in the pub were reminded that investment was investment and people had work now. This was the much talked-of global village, the way of things to come, where an internationally owned company based in Liechtenstein could buy up land and buildings and extend a factory in Ireland and put in their own management team who, the rumours said, had worked similar magic in Spain and Morocco. Highly paid PR consultants made sure the stories were used in papers and not even they knew that the same papers were now partially owned by the awesome financial empire that had spread its tentacles throughout Irish commerce, industry and society.

## March 1995

In Ireland those who had seen through the charade, that were in a position to act, were hamstrung by blackmail and threats.

The change in Ireland, the surge in investment, in reality only the tip of the iceberg, had been noticed by others, some of them Irish living abroad.

One was Peter Morris, a university lecturer working in New York. Morris was young, in his mid-thirties, tall, lean, and normally seen wearing his mock tortoiseshell reading glasses. He found that if he took them off, he invariably left them somewhere and the safest place for them was on his nose. That cold March evening he was attending a function for professional Irish expatriates hosted by their most famous alumnus, Tony O'Malley. Morris, in spite of his purely academic background, genuinely liked the tough, canny O'Malley who had made a vast fortune in fast-moving consumer goods, his most famous product a tomato sauce that could be bought in almost every country in the world. He was a generous philanthropist, putting fifty students a year through universities, and his interest was genuine. He personally interviewed the applicants, chose the ones he would fund and then watched their progress with interest. What pleased Morris was that they were not all business students. He had taught eight students on O'Malley scholarships in his own field, political science, and he had to approve the man's choices. They were all bright, aggressive, enquiring, hard-working people, and not all of average college age: three had been mature students.

The two men talked at the function and it was Morris

who raised the investment issue with the stocky, energetic business mogul.

'Don't knock it, Peter,' O'Malley had replied with a grin. 'Investment is essential in any business community. In spite of all you academics would have us think, the free-market thinking of the European Community does work sometimes.'

Morris, a man used to viewing things from a detached, academic and purely objective viewpoint, wasn't convinced, but let the subject change to the final game of the Five Nations rugby tournament between Ireland and Scotland to be played the following day.

Moira Kelly stood at the sink in her kitchen and rinsed her hands under the tap. The soda bread, part of a Friday evening family ritual was out of the oven and cooling on the racks under the window. The kitchen was warm. Outside the temperature was struggling to stay above freezing and the central heating had been on since three that afternoon. She wanted it nice when they arrived. She had six children and now only the youngest two were still at home. Sinead, the baby at fourteen, was still at school and Sue, nineteen years old, was studying at UCD. David, twenty-one, had moved into his own flat last year and was in his second year of what she hoped would be a long career with the civil service. David and Sue looked like her, tall, slender, fair-haired. Some people thought they were twins and once when she had showed someone a picture of herself in her youth, they had thought it was Sue. She hoped David would be happy with the civil service. Hoped because she knew he was bored already, bored with the dreary, grey, status quo thinking of the people he worked with. He was seeing a nice girl, a choice she approved of and she took comfort from the fact that she knew his father, God rest his soul, would have also liked her.

He had been dead three years now and she still missed him sometimes, in spite of the fact that she was never sure if she ever loved him. He was a solid provider, an essentially decent man, but occasionally given to the drink, and when he drank he became violent. The children learned to recognize it early and made sure they were elsewhere, but once the eldest of the six, Simon, had come home to find them at it. He had pulled his father off and they fought, two men, father and son, and Simon had prevailed. It couldn't end fast enough for Moira, the thought of her son being hurt, almost as important as the noise they were making and what would the neighbours think? He had been contrite and apologetic the next day as usual, promising never to do it again, but nursing loose teeth and viewing his eldest son with new respect.

Simon would be over later, with his wife and children. Simon was big and heavy like his father, but gentle, gentle as a lamb, and he never touched a drink. Sarah would be coming too. Sarah had married a fellow from Cork who was assistant manager at a factory out near the airport.

The old table could take ten round it at a push and she finished rinsing her hands and faced the mountain of vegetables that needed preparing. Sue would be home in a minute and would help as usual. She was a good girl and while dinner was in the oven they would walk up to Father O'Leary's church with Sinead and take communion together.

Later that evening, Sarah's husband Alan was proudly telling them all of his promotion at the factory. He was now the boss and rather pleased with developments, extolling the virtues of his board of directors, only one of whom he had ever met, as far-sighted, generous men. Ireland needed investors like that he said. Simon, bored with the talk, began to play with his two boys in front of the fire, Sinead in pigtails forgetting her pubescent seriousness, piling in to the game as Sue captured it all on the new video camera. The tape would be sent to America to where Mary, on holiday, was staying with cousins in Boston. Simon was pleased. He had tickets for the rugby match at Lansdowne Road for tomorrow. Ireland and Scotland would be a good game and this was for the Triple Crown. The other ticket was for David. It would be a good day out.

The next morning a young woman by the name of Maeve O'Donnell walked with friends down one of the long pathways inside Trinity College. Maeve was a student at University College Dublin but her two friends were at Trinity and comfortable within the old hallowed walls of the famous university. One of them pointed at a figure walking towards them.

'That's Prof. Kiernan,' he said softly, the respect in his voice obvious. Maeve looked at him with interest as he approached them. His jacket was old and hung off his shoulders and little half-lens glasses hung off the end of his nose. Books and files were tucked under one arm and threatened to spill out at any moment. It all seemed very precarious and Maeve smiled. He was what she expected as Ireland's premier historian. Fusty, dusty, uncaring about trivia, an air of academic brilliance seeped from him as he strode towards them. She had heard there were students that took history not because they were interested in the subject but because he would be lecturing.

Kiernan for his part noticed the three students. They were typical of those he had been educating for forty-five years, young, smart, challenging, rebellious in the best possible way, channelling their energies into work and play with equal vigour, but with one exception. Even in a country famous for its beautiful women, the child in the centre was startling. Clear bright eyes, skin the colour of cream, cheeks rosy in the frosty start of the day, thick dark brown hair cascading down her back. She carried a violin case not in her hand but across her front, a slightly defensive posture – odd, he thought, as she walked and chatted amicably with her two companions.

Later that morning he saw them again sitting against a shop window in Grafton Street, one lad playing pipes, the other the violin she had been carrying. She stood between them singing as passers-by threw money into the violin case. Her voice was, to his delight and as he had hoped, clear and strong and beautiful and he smiled to himself as he hurried down the side road. He had to buy flowers and get home for an early lunch and then make his way out to Lansdowne Road. He had tickets for the rugby. As a lifetime member of the Irish Rugby Football Union he had debenture tickets for every home game.

Two of the men who would be playing rugby that afternoon were making their preparations. The first, Andre Hyland, was an Irish Defence Force officer, but his thoughts were not on his job. They were on the game. He was a centre. Big and very fast with a side-step that had fooled many, much of the Irish back line hopes rested on whether he and Simon Gagen could work the dummies and draw their opposite numbers and clear the wingers to run. The Hastings brothers were both playing for Scotland and they had their centre hope in the line, too. Robert Dugan, also an army officer, from the Black Watch, had powered out of nowhere into the Scotland side three years before. Winning his fifteenth cap today he was fast, very fast indeed.

For Dugan in his hotel room sorting his kit, the butterflies rising in his stomach, it was going to be a good game, and with England on a by, and Wales playing in France for the wooden spoon, most of the British Isles would be watching. He silently prayed not to fumble or screw up. The piss-taking in his regimental mess was bad enough at the best of times, but if he cocked up and cost

Scotland the Triple Crown it would be unbearable.

Two people who would have loved to have found tickets for the game, Eamon Kavanagh and his girlfriend Briget Villiers, had been disappointed. Kavanagh, at sea on his Irish Navy patrol boat, had left the task of finding seats to Briget and she went at the mission with the same tenacious ferocity that she did everything. She was, Kavanagh thought, the most desirable woman he had ever known and he loved her completely. Small, blonde, with crisp blue eyes, she took no crap from anyone and when he was ashore on leave the time spent in her bed made up for the nights at sea when he missed her terribly. The only tickets she had found were from a tout and five times the list price so she refused and instead bought in things to eat in front of the television.

The game was exciting. Both forward packs, almost equal in weight, fought for possession in maul, line-out and scrum, recycling the ball fluidly for their backs. By half-time the score was in Ireland's favour, only one point separating them. Dugan, his face bloodied in a ruck, was standing deep, his eyes on Hyland his opposite, when the ball came out of the maul and the backs began to move, classical running rugby, the ball moving down the line as players drew their opposites barely feet ahead of the huge forward packs. Dugan fed the ball to his winger and dropped back to support, and seconds later the wing, actually falling to a tackle from the Irish fullback, fed the ball back. It bounced awkwardly but Dugan side-stepped, scooped it up and, seeing the gap, tore through it with the searing pace he was famous for. The crowd came to its feet. This was what they had come to see. The fast Scots centre was moving like a hare down the line, and only paces behind him and closing to intercept on an angle but well clear of the pack the Irish centre, Andre Hyland, chasing like a greyhound, behind him both wingers joining the pace.

Forty thousand voices bellowed, yelled and screamed encouragement and the two players, one in a deep blue jersey and the other in vivid green, raced the closing yards for the line. Hyland, his heart bursting in his chest, could feel he was near enough and dived, catching Dugan by one ankle as they fell together into the cold mud towards the line, Dugan's hand holding the ball, reaching out. It was far enough and as a dozen players arrived to drive the play, the nearer Scots raising their hands in delight, the referee lifted one arm and blew his whistle. It wasn't another Scots player that pulled the bloodied, filthy, elated Dugan to his feet. It was the Irishman Hyland and the crowd loved the gesture.

At his home in leafy southern England, Edward Stewart watched the game on television in his study. His wife brought him a cup of tea. 'How's it going?' she asked.

'Irish deserve to win it,' he snapped. 'Other than young Dugan's run they've played a better game.'

She smiled. He was an Irishman, born in Ulster, and the statement was a delight, but he was also a fair man and would not begrudge the Scots their victory if they won. The better team on the day. Edward Stewart was a career officer in the British army and had met the young Robert Dugan only three weekends before. He liked him and he could run like a cheetah, but he wasn't going to save this game. His judgement was proved correct as the Irish pushed back over the line to score and regain the lead.

The final minutes were unremarkable and another man who had been watching it from one eye in his London hotel suite looked back at the papers on the desk. Khalil Ashrawi was the other face of modern Palestine. In his fifties, urbane, articulate, smooth, cultured, sophisticated, he was by profession an investment banker and in his career had worked for two of the biggest names on Wall Street before moving his home and his contacts to Switzerland to head a new Arab-owned bank with

11

headquarters in Zurich. His suits were made by bespoke tailors, his shoes hand-made, and his shirts ordered by the dozen from a shirtmaker in Clapham. He had spent his life as a corporate raider, investing clients' money, channelling resources, the architect of fortunes and of all the high points in his long career, he felt that this project was his crowning glory. It used every ounce of their experience, every resource they could muster, every contact they had made, and it was finally coming to an end. They had just bought a country from right under the noses of its people, its shareholders. It was the most audacious financial endeavour in modern history and it would change the world they lived in.

He looked at his watch. A meeting was in progress and he was awaiting news from his people. In a second chair on the other side of the suite a younger man was watching. This was Ali Jassem. Younger than Ashrawi, in his mid-thirties, he wasn't a figures man but a far more practical individual, a fighter for the cause. One of their top-rank commanders, he was in theoretical command of a brigade of fighters, five thousand people, men and women, some as young as eighteen, scattered across occupied Palestine, the Lebanon, Jordan, Syria, Algeria and western Europe, and he was here to collect his orders. But that would not be until later that night, after the meeting in Tripoli, and for now he watched the screen, waiting patiently for the football results. Rugby was okay, but football was his passion – he was an Aston Villa fan.

Barely a mile away in Kensington a young woman was briefing her uncle and three of his colleagues. They were Ashrawi's people and Mona de Cruz was pleased. She had isolated her target and was confident of results.

It was a month after the rugby game when Mary Kelly, home from America and working in her studio, answered a knock at the door. He was big, in his early thirties and good-looking.

'You do paintings I hear. I want to get one done.'

'Yes, I do. You're Andre Hyland, aren't you?'

'Yes,' he replied with a grin.

'Ah! The toast of the country. I am honoured.' Her tone was slightly mocking. 'Come in. What would you like done?'

'My Mum. I have a photo or two.' He rubbed his neck, flicking something off. 'Can you do a portrait of a photo? It's meant to be a surprise. Sorry,' he added with a grin, rubbing his neck again. 'Just had a haircut and the bloody stuff is everywhere.'

'Suits ya,' she said, in a parody of the north Liffey accent. He laughed out loud and she walked across to the big table and took an apple from a bowl and bit into it. 'Want one?'

'Thanks. I will.' She threw one and he caught it. 'So can you do it from photos?'

She nodded. 'Let's have a look then.' She normally hated working from photos, but she had decided to go back to the States for a few weeks in the summer and needed all the work she could get.

## July 1995

It was a nineteen-year-old civil engineering student who first raised the alarm, drew outside attention to the first invasion of western Europe by outsiders since the Turkish siege of Vienna was broken by a mixed rescue force of Germans, Prussians and Poles in 1683.

David O'Connell sat in a car parked on Merrion Road outside the British Embassy with two other men waiting for the arrival of a diplomat at the Dublin mission. The security was tight, with Gardai at five points round the building, shatterproof windows and large concrete bollards keeping vehicles a minimum five metres from the thick walls. That didn't concern them. They weren't trying to breach it, just trying to see the elusive Howard Mellows.

Mellows was listed as a grade three diplomat with full Foreign Office accreditation, but the two men surmised that someone in the British Embassy was responsible for security and intelligence gathering and if it wasn't Mellows then he would know who they should talk to.

'We should have gone to the Americans again,' O'Connell said. He was sitting in the front passenger seat, his red sweater in contrast to the old jeans he wore.

'Jesus, Davey! We should be having a pint is what we should be doing, not sitting out here like a couple of melodramatic fools,' his friend replied.

'You agreed,' David said. 'You agreed with me!'

'Shut up,' said the man in the back. He was their senior by a few years and the older brother of Robert, the driver. Kevin was also a reporter for one of the Dublin papers and had met Howard Mellows twice before, so he had agreed to get them into his office. 'Let's go,' he said, regretting his offer for the hundredth time as he opened the door.

The pair in front got out and David, clutching a heavy brown envelope, followed the brothers across the street and up the Georgian steps to the main doors of the embassy.

Ten minutes later they were with Mellows in his office and as the diplomat looked to the reporter to begin, David O'Connell stepped forward.

'Mr Mellows, we really need to see whoever is responsible for intelligence gathering. If that's you then . . .' he trailed away under Mellows's direct gaze, pleased nevertheless with the professional sound of it all.

'This is an embassy,' Mellows said, smiling. 'We have a consular section and another dealing in commercial affairs.

Contrary to popular belief, we don't have dozens of James Bonds hidden about the place.'

David O'Connell was not going to be put off that easily.

'Look, we understand you have to say certain things. Give us five minutes of your time.' He pushed his glasses up his nose and in the same fluid move tucked an unruly hank of his hair back behind his ear. 'If I can convince you that I have something worthy then you can pass it on to the . . . appropriate authorities.'

Mellows was thinking fast. This could be a set-up. There was a reporter present, and two youngsters asking to see a spy in the British Embassy in a friendly and neutral European republic, an EU member nation.

'I don't think you understand,' he began before the reporter interrupted.

'Look. Let's cut the shit. I killed the Davenport story for you. You owe me one. This is no joke. No clever journalistic probe. It's deadly serious. Hear them out. That's all I am asking.'

Mellows thought for a second, and then leaned forward and pushed the intercom switch on his desk. He suspected there was a Security and Intelligence Service staffer in the building, but even he wasn't sure if they had one since the cut-backs in the seventies, and if so, who it was. First blood in most missions usually went to the military attaché and he suspected it was passed on from there to the real individual who was known only to the ambassador, the first attaché and the military liaison filter. If there wasn't one, it would go through to London and Century House.

'Miss Gailbraith. Ask Wing Commander Parks to join us, please, and then no calls for half an hour.' He let his finger slide from the box. 'The Wing Commander is as near as I can find for you. He will know who to talk to in London. Once he gets here you have until my phone rings.'

Parks was a portly, smiling chap with a briar pipe and eyes like everyone's favourite grandfather. He also had a brain like a steel trap. Sitting on the edge of Mellows's desk he stuffed his pipe and finally looked up.

'Now what's all this about then?' he asked, striking a match.

They were there for fifteen minutes and then politely shown the door by the diplomat, whose expression was that of a man who had just had his time wasted.

That evening as the two students sat in the small upstairs flat they had borrowed from a friend in Rathmines, the remnants of a takeaway pizza on the table, there was a knock at the door.

David O'Connell opened it and a slim man of middle years, middle height and very middle appearance stood on the dark landing, the only light coming from the open door.

'David O'Connell?'

'Yes?'

'You met a colleague of mine this morning. Air force chap called Parks.' The visitor smiled. 'I wonder if we could have a chat?'

'Who are you?'

'Someone very interested in what you had to say . . . may I come in?'

'They weren't,' David responded.

'But I am,' the visitor said evenly.

Four hours later the visitor leaned back on the hard kitchen chair. He had questioned the two boys solidly, looking over the pictures, drawings and notes they had reluctantly left at the embassy that morning which he had produced from a battered old leather bag as they sat down.

'How long did it take you to put this together?' he asked.

'Three months, on and off. Lots of weekends. We would find one site and then compare,' David replied. 'Every time we found more, bigger . . . '

'Why haven't you gone to the papers with this?'

'Dunno,' Robert said. 'I guess they'd laugh at us, just not believe us because the bubble might burst.'

It was plausible, the visitor thought. The bubble of jobs and money and a future for all. Something Ireland had not been able to give her people since before the famine and even then under the shadow of absentee landlords and an English king.

'Why us?'

'Synergy,' Robert, a history student, said firmly. 'Experience. You are an island people like us. You have been invaded like us and more often than not by the same invaders, the Vikings, the French.'

The small man looked at him steadily and listened.

'Britain has a defence mentality,' Robert continued, 'this century throwing back the Nazis and being prepared to do the same to the USSR in the last decades. You will understand, and what threatens us today may threaten you tomorrow. Ireland is a poor country. Certainly the poorest and smallest in the EC . . . except for Portugal,' he qualified. 'We haven't had a defence worth anything for about three hundred years. We rely on neutrality, Saint Patrick and a few nuns. We will need help.' He paused. 'We'll go to the Americans if we have to, but we thought that it might be better coming from you.'

'Crap,' the man replied. 'The truth, please.'

David studied him for a moment.

'We tried the Americans. They told us to piss off. Didn't believe us. Some lightweight in a cheap suit with a big toothy grin. Kept looking at his watch like he had somewhere else to go,' he finished, his tone a little bitter.

The man smiled. That was far more plausible. 'You know what you are suggesting, don't you? That some fairly highly placed people in the government know about this, are covering it up, allowing it to happen, greasing the wheels.'

'Or have no choice but to keep their mouths shut. We

don't have the resources to establish that, so that must remain supposition,' David replied. 'But either way, someone knows about it and has done nothing to stop it. That's why we have come to you.'

## North West Frontier Province, Pakistan

The man lay in the dry rocks high above the steep, winding road. Below him the heat shimmered upward and he pulled the beige square of fabric further over his head then lifted the big Zeiss binoculars back to his eyes.

Two hundred metres down the rocky, boulder-strewn slope below him other men lay in wait. There were sixteen of them, locals, their traditional sheepskin waistcoats discarded in the heat and just their headgear identifying them as Pathan hill tribesmen. They carried a motley collection of weapons, many with Soviet Kalashnikovs, one with a locally made variant, another with a vintage Lee Enfield. Several weapons the watcher could not identify, but there were none of the usual ancient bolt actions of dubious heritage that one usually saw. All he was sure of was that they were copies of Soviet bloc equipment.

Guns were inexpensive here and every man carried one.

Despite what the Pakistani government said, this far west there was no law. Even in Sind there were no-go areas at night, with heavy police patrols during daylight, but up here west of Peshawar the police and army never ventured. This was hill country where allegiance was to tribal leaders and family and the Pathans and Afghan tribesmen bowed to none but their own. The border between the two countries was scarcely recognized by anyone who mattered, and completely ignored by the locals who had survived for centuries herding goats, trading guns and contraband, robbing travellers and each other.

These men below were not simple dacoits, bandits. They

were the men of Gulam Khan and nothing moved through this pass, not man, nor beast nor trade goods, without paying tribute.

Normally this band would consist of no more than five or six of Gulam Khan's men, but today was different and the watcher high above them smiled to himself as he lowered the glasses and inched back into his shadowed hideaway.

Aiden Scott had been here for two days. Two days of waiting. Among the guns and Russian military equipment, heroin and hashish passed through these mountains to the markets and buyers who waited in the rough no man's land of gunsmiths, smugglers and drug dealers on the western edge of Peshawar. There dealers could buy rough brown heroin by the kilogram, laid out like fruit on stands in a dozen shops along one street. The American DEA people, in spite of the Pakistani government's claims of full support, were powerless to stop the flow.

This operation would halt it through this pass for a while at least.

The set-up had taken weeks, weeks of convincing Gulam Khan that the Afghan connections were in fact dishonourable and meant to betray him. They were not even *mujahedin*, fighters of a holy war. They were simply drug runners and they were not to be trusted.

Serendipity played her part when in the final hours of the campaign a nephew of Khan's was killed in a road crash. Scott had managed to convince him that the death had been no accident and had been engineered by the Afghans.

His attachment as a junior military attaché to the British Embassy in Islamabad was informal. Aiden Scott was a serving officer in one of the more unusual elements of the British army and his brief from his masters was broad enough to allow him almost complete freedom to act as he saw fit as long as objectives were met. Originally from the

Parachute Regiment, he was on secondment to 'A' Squadron of the 22nd Special Air Service Regiment and this was his seventh month in Pakistan as part of a shadowy assistance programme.

He sat back under the shade of the overhang and sipped water from his bottle, careful even with the nearest men two hundred metres away to keep the contents from sloshing. He looked at the clear plastic one-litre bottle. American special forces issue bottles had baffles built into the interior and the sort of soft plastic straw cyclists used. You could shake one of them inches from your ear and hear nothing. The little things made the difference. Like the sandals on his feet and the contact lenses. His clothing was that of the locals. A *khamis* shirt that dropped back and front down to the knees, and *shalwai*, the baggy pyjama-type pants worn throughout the region. A filthy Arab *ghuttra* wound round his neck dropped over his shoulder and on his head he wore the round woollen hat of the Pathan. Brown contact lenses disguised his bright blue eyes and with his dark hair and swarthy unshaven face he looked every inch as much part of the land as the men below. Even his height at six foot two inches wasn't a problem here. Many of the locals were tall, wiry individuals. He pulled the camouflage cloth over his head again and inched back out into the sunlight.

He swung the glasses round to the right and looked back up the pass.

They were coming. Five men picking their way round the path leading two laden donkeys, the leader a thin, hook-nosed man with a curly black beard and an assault rifle.

Here we go, Scott thought. Come on my little beauties. He dropped his gaze to the band gathered below. He was delighted with the sight. They were now split into two groups, six out on the path, weapons held casually looking for all the world like the regular reception group at the handover point, while the remaining ten had settled deeper in the rocks, weapons out and fingers on triggers. This was the frontier as it had always been. Deceit and subterfuge at best and at worst an ambush in the narrow killing ground between the steep walls of the ravine.

Greetings were called by the arrivals but, sensing that they were not as welcome as usual, they moved forward silently.

Iqbal, one of Khan's trusted lieutenants and leader of this group today, stepped forward. He was a slight man and, bearded and silent in the afternoon light, he seemed to qualify for his reputation for absolute nerve. Accusations were hurled and seconds later, donkeys braying and men going for cover, a fierce fire-fight developed.

For Scott the outcome was never in doubt. He doubted that Iqbal had ever studied tactics, but with his numerically superior force in ambush he was following the classic thinking of never dividing your force and never attacking until you can overwhelm your enemy.

One of the Afghans, some deep instinct flashing a warning, had swung up his rifle and the men concealed in the rocks had cut him down. Thirty seconds later it was all over. Three of the five lay dead or dying on the path. One sat huddled on the reverse side of a rock, bleeding heavily, shaking as his body went into deep shock, and the last was silent, face down in the dust, the back of his head all over the rock face above him. One donkey struggled to stand under its load of heroin, bleeding from a dozen wounds in its neck, and the other had run fifty yards down the path and stopped seemingly unhurt.

Scott moved back from his vantage point into the shadows of the overhang and began silently gathering up his meagre equipment. The mission had been a success, but there was no jubilation. There was also no remorse. He had simply capitalized on the natural distrust and aggression of both parties.

He waited. Below, Khan's men had stripped the bodies of anything useful and pulled the corpses into the rocks beside the trail. One of them shot the injured donkey and finally they loaded both lots of heroin on the remaining beast and moved off eastwards, down the trail, as darkness began to fall.

Scott was ten minutes behind them, but moving slowly and carefully in case they stopped, a rough sleeveless sheepskin coat keeping the chill of the night at bay, and his rifle slung over his shoulder like any other man in the mountains.

Twelve hours later he was back in the small bungalow he shared with an American DEA agent in a middle-class suburb of Peshawar, his four-wheel-drive parked beside the house.

'Message came in for you a couple of hours ago,' the American said. 'Your people want you back in Muree.'

'Alther?' Scott asked.

'No. You have been up there too long boy,' he drawled, his Texan accent strong. 'Alther is in Islamabad. It was Parker. Humourless little shit . . '

'Two hours ago?' Scott looked down at his watch. It was just after five A M. Parker was the number three in the embassy, a career diplomat. If he was involved it was something out of the ordinary.

'Yeah. Something's going down,' the American said drily, lifting a tea bag from a chipped cup and slinging it expertly across the kitchen into the sink. 'Why else would he be missing his beauty sleep?'

He thought about it for a second or two and decided to leave immediately without phoning in. He could be at the summer quarters of the British High Commission in Muree by lunchtime. A cigarette hanging from his lips, he began to throw his few things into a bag.

The drive was a nerve-racking journey of hairpin bends, avoiding the overloaded Bedford trucks and buses, their sides festooned in raucous paintings with garish stainless steel prows over the cabs like Spanish galleons. Weaving through the heavies in the traffic that roared its way up the mountain road were Japanese pickups with fifteen, eighteen or twenty people loaded into the rear, and weaving through those little 50cc motorbikes with entire families aboard, tiny children sitting on the petrol tanks, duelling with fate. Twelve miles outside Muree a laden motorbike had been overtaking a bus on a bend and had gone under a truck coming the other way. A pathetic bundle of blood, clothing and black hair was all that remained of the small child who had been sitting in front of her father on the saddle. A crowd had gathered, people coming from stopped vehicles and rough roadside dwellings to gawk at the four bodies and talk about the will of God. Half an hour later he was in Muree's narrow twisting streets cut into the mountainside. They were as crowded and confused as usual and he arrived at the British High Commission just before noon.

'Get cleaned up. You have been recalled,' Parker said, looking up from his desk, a flimsy in his hand. 'The London flight from Islamabad.' He was a prematurely balding individual who had been passed over for promotion three times and now knew he was stuck as number three in a Third World backwater.

'What's up?'

'Don't know, don't care,' Parker snapped, pulling his spectacles off and rubbing them vigorously with a handkerchief, 'but I'll tell you this much. I don't appreciate being woken in the middle of the bloody night to track you down. It's really not on, you know. Alther should have done this himself.'

'He's away,' Scott said sensibly.

'I'll have you know,' Parker responded pompously, 'I don't like this kind of irregular behaviour.'

He was talking, Scott knew, about the mixed role that he filled, assisting the American DEA people, intelligence gathering and once providing some information that everyone knew could only have come from a robbery of the office of a government minister.

Scott walked to the windows and looked out over the valley below. It was a scene of real beauty, steep mountainsides and evergreens, more like Austria or Switzerland than Pakistan. Scott was tired. Suddenly he wanted to go back to Europe, to somewhere where it rained and where grass grew. Where you could eat without getting dysentery, somewhere where they cared about little children and didn't make them ride on petrol tanks. He had had enough of Pakistan and he had had enough of people like Parker.

'Perhaps you would rather the High Commissioner did it?' he said softly. People who knew Aiden Scott knew the signs. When he talked softly the iron was beginning to show. Parker didn't know him.

'I didn't mean that,' he said testily.

'No you didn't. You are the junior here and you know it . . .' he paused as Parker leapt to his feet, all pomp and bluster '. . . and don't even think about threatening me. I am not employed by the Foreign Office. I am a soldier. If you don't like it, tough shit.'

## Hereford, England

The house, an ugly post-war bungalow, was set far enough back from the road to have some privacy. The farm had long since been bought up by the Ministry of Defence and that left the house in isolation. Because it was no more than six miles from the 22nd Special Air Service regiment's home base and training facility it was finally put to use as a meeting venue and occasional guest house, useful for those who would be dealing with people from the regiment and who wanted to avoid being seen in the town.

It was easy to get to, but while the visitors came from the main road the SAS men drove up the back roads from Bradbury lines. This morning there were two cars parked behind the house when Scott pulled his Land Rover to a halt.

He was welcomed by his briefing officer who stood in the kitchen doorway, a mug of tea in his hand.

''Morning, Aiden.'

Scott smiled. He liked Busby Grogan. They had done the intelligence course at Ashford together and the stocky little Welshman always had a ready store of jokes to liven up the inevitable boredom of army life.

'Step this way, my little cherub. Cup of tea before you meet our visitors?'

'Thanks,' Scott replied.

He took the proffered cup and followed Grogan down the dark hall to the living room. There were three people waiting. The first, a scholarly type in his fifties, complete with cravat and bifocal spectacles sat with studied nonchalance in one of the two armchairs. The other man was a little younger with a neat fair pencil moustache the exact colour of his hair. His watery blue eyes peered from above red cheeks and he stood smoking in the curve of the bay window. The last was a heavy-set woman in her thirties. Her face was well made-up and the lines round her eyes showed she was quick to smile, which she did as Scott entered, holding out her hand.

'You must be Captain Scott. I am Sally Richards,' she pointed to the other two, 'Peter Tilby,' the man in the chair waved a hand, 'and Gordon Persse fouling the atmosphere with that disgusting cigarette. We are from Century House.'

'George Smileys one and all,' Grogan said with a grin.

'Hardly,' Sally said, still in full flood. 'Actually, Persse is our man in Dublin.'

She paused then and looked Scott straight in the eyes.

'We have a little problem, Aiden – can I call you Aiden? Good,' she went on, not waiting for a reply. 'We want you to go to Ireland. The Republic. Not your old stamping ground in the Armagh bandit country. You did rather well there didn't you?' she added cheerfully, like a school teacher. '. . . Anyway, the Republic. Guinness and cows and butter-fresh girls. Settle your bum in the place and have a good look around. Things going on. We need to know what.' She stopped and looked at him. 'Now then, Queen and country aside, serving officer and all that, do you have a problem in principle, with the prospect of working there? We need to know we aren't briefing the wrong chap.'

Scott could see his file on the table. They knew all there was to know. His mother was Irish, her family from Birr in County Offaly. She had met and married his father in London, but for her Ireland was always home and every summer Scott and his two sisters spent time there. He was brought up on Irish history, the language, reading the great Irish writers and fishing on the Shannon with his uncles. He had barely escaped Trinity for Sandhurst, but for him Ireland was a decent place where God was God and salmon were to be caught fresh from the river, where the Guinness was black and sweet and people had the time to stop and talk to each other.

'No more than you,' he replied.

'Good,' she said, 'because we believe something sinister is going on there. Not good for our sweet Kathleen, no, not good at all.'

She walked across to the bay window. 'Out of there, Gordon. Why don't you show our gallant captain the holiday snaps?'

Persse stubbed out his cigarette as she pulled the curtains and moved over to a slide projector set up on the table.

The projector beam threw a square on the far wall and Persse sat back on the edge of the table, the machine's control in his hand.

'Two weeks ago three people walked into the embassy at Falls Gate. This kid, one David O'Connell . . .' an image went up on the wall, 'and his mate Robert Hargadon.' The image changed. 'They were accompanied by Robert's older brother who pulled a favour to get them through the door.' The third face went up on the wall.

'The younger two are both at Limerick University, O'Connell is doing civil engineering and Hargadon history. It was O'Connell who noticed it first. He was comparing external works drawings as part of his final year and things just didn't compute. There were structures planned, foundations laid for buildings and support areas that had no finished drawings he could source. Odd things like sealed surface car-parks in funny places, and reinforced post holes along the perimeters. Like this . . .' an image appeared on the wall. A view of a bitumen-covered oblong area with access roads and then the image changed to a close-up of one of the corners where precast concrete slabs joined forming a hollow square countersunk into the ground.

'In the centre of this area there is a toilet block, gents and ladies, all very nice complete with signs. The same sealed area also has a major power delivery cable to an underground junction point at the western corner. This site is equidistant between two small towns. Young O'Connell has his view. He is a bit sceptical about all the new investment. Was this one of the new projects? Why now? Why here? So Hargadon did a title search. Recent change of ownership. The same story repeated in a dozen other locations. A bit of lateral thinking, a bit of adding up the numbers and good deal of healthy scepticism of Greeks bearing gifts. And back to the pictures with a felt-tip pen and a "what if" session.'

Persse pressed the forward button on the remote and up on the screen the image changed.

'We have a group working on the ownership details,'

Tilby said from his seat, 'but it's very complex and getting more so. If anyone thought that the Maxwell companies or BCCI were structured to make things difficult to trace, then this series of corporations has gone on to greater things.'

'Sorry,' Scott said, 'I'm not with you.' His mind had been taking in the image on the wall, the holes left by the pipes sunk into concrete now filled with high steel posts and the wire strung between them. The drawings made it look possible. A small team of men could convert the car-park into a secure area, complete with fences, wire and watch towers in a day.

'We took one of these developments and did what young Hargadon did. A title search. Easy enough to find the registered owner. But then who is the real owner? This one example led us through the Cayman Islands, Bermuda, the Dutch Antilles, New York and then it disappears somewhere between Liechtenstein and Switzerland. A web of seventeen companies that finally hit the wall with some professional directors in Liechtenstein who are paid out of Zurich. The point is, Captain Scott, someone is going to a lot of trouble to conceal the real ownership.'

'Major Grogan will give what little else we have,' Sally Richards said. 'Go over and see what you think is happening while the whizz kids in London start tracking the ownership bits.'

'Can I contact O'Connell?'

'Yes,' Persse said. 'He offered to take someone back to each place.'

When the MI6 people had packed up and gone Grogan sat down with Scott at the pine kitchen table and they began to work through the material, four buff files laid out on the table. Scott took no notes, trained as he was like all intelligence officers to commit to memory whatever details were necessary.

He was a typical Special Air Service officer only in that

he was an outstanding soldier. He was a loner, completely objective driven, disciplined and spartan in his tastes. A keen outdoors man, his idea of a fun weekend was climbing down wet caves, or walking alone through the hills with nothing but a pocketful of chocolate and a space blanket. Immensely knowledgeable about flora and fauna, he was sometimes roped into running sections of the survival courses that dealt with what fungus, berries or shoots a man could eat and live to fight another day.

Technically he was, like all his colleagues, an excellent all-rounder. He had completed all the courses including boat section, mountain warfare, intelligence, communications and helicopters. The only one he hadn't liked was the mountain warfare course. He loved the hills and the heather, but he disliked snow and he hated ice. When he finished that he was promptly posted to Bosnia and spent the winter of 1993 living in the forest watching Serb positions – in deep snow. He had done six months in Bosnia, the last three with very limited contact with the UNPRO-FOR peacekeepers. His only regular contact was with Muslim fighters who sometimes saw him as a visible demonstration of the west's willingness to help, and brought him food from the aid drops, sometimes as an impotent nuisance; then they were sullen and threatening. He was glad to be pulled out when the time came. That experience on the back of two tours of Northern Ireland, his Irish blood and speaking the language made him, as far as Major Grogan was concerned, the perfect choice for this job in the Republic.

Two hours later he finally sat back with David O'Connell's altered photograph.

'If he's right then, conceptually, this is incredible,' Scott said. 'But this . . .' he finished, waving the photograph.

'You thinking what I am thinking?' Grogan asked. They were now both looking at David O'Connell's drawing, the felt-tip pen lines depicting control points and fences.

'I think so. The civvies automatically think of military camps. But no one builds camps like this, not since the first plane dropped the first bomb. Armies are mobile. This is a . . .'

'Detention centre?' Grogan asked.

'I was going to say gulag.'

'A do-it-yourself detention centre. Who would want to build the foundations for camps in a modern European country?' Grogan asked out loud.

'That's for Century House,' Scott said. 'We are simply to appraise the physical situation and report back. Yes?'

'And see what else you can dig up,' Grogan said. 'Whoever did this has got other stuff under way or my mum's a matelot.'

Scott arrived in the Republic of Ireland two days later. There was no subterfuge necessary. Flights from Heathrow's Terminal One flew direct into Dublin and with the diplomatic protocols that existed no passports were required by nationals of either country. He took a taxi into the city where he knew a car was waiting. He had never spent much time in Dublin. The city's North Side was alien ground to him. He had only been there once, a few years before, to have a look at a second-hand piano for his aunt and he had vivid memories of the visit. The South Side was more familiar and he knew his way from the Liffey back through the city's southern limits to Blackrock where he had done his share of courting the black-haired, blue-eyed, creamy-skinned beauties that Ireland was famous for.

The car was in the basement of the Conrad Hotel. He loaded his bags and drove up the ramp on to the street heading for the Limerick road. There he would contact David O'Connell and visit some of the sites. That finished he would move on to the family home in Birr. A couple of days there would allow him time to settle in and begin to think like a local again, absorb the issues, listen to the talk round the dinner table and the feel the mood in the pubs.

The address given for the young man was his parents' house, so Scott waited till he saw him leave and, after comparing the photograph he had been given, he got out and followed for a few minutes. He was pleased with what he saw. O'Connell was tall and wiry, his hair long but clean and the oilskin jacket he wore was much patched. He walked with confidence, the cold wind snapping at his trouser legs. Once no one was about Scott increased his pace until he was walking alongside.

'Hello David. Got a minute?'

The young man stopped and brushed his hair from his eyes.

'Hello . . .' his eyes studied Scott's face, but not recognizing him he said, 'Sorry, you have me at a disadvantage.'

'You took some nice pictures of a parking lot,' Scott said.

'Oh . . . yes . . . you are from the Brit Embassy?'

'Not quite. We need to talk.'

'I'm on my way into town to meet some people. Can we do it later?'

'If you like. There used to be a pub over on the airport road about four miles out of the town. O'Malley's.'

'It's still there,' O'Connell said.

'Good. Eight tonight?'

'I don't have a car,' the student replied honestly.

'No problem. I'll pick you up here, then. Same time.'

O'Connell nodded and launched straight in. 'You think we are right then?'

Scott studied him for a second or two before replying carefully, 'We think you have stumbled into something. You said "we". How many are there of you?'

'Started with just me and Robert. But now there's about nine of us who have talked, think the same.'

'You talk about it a lot?' Scott asked.

O'Connell grinned. 'I'm not a complete dickhead. If we are correct, then walls have ears, right?'

'Right,' Scott said, 'but you've already mentioned eight of your friends and you don't know me from Adam.'

'Oh. I see. Point taken. Keep it shut anyway.'

'Eight o'clock then,' Scott said.

When Scott arrived just before eight O'Connell was waiting on the footpath, a small bag in his hand. He answered Scott's raised eyebrow.

'You will want to see the sites. I thought I would bring a few things.' Then as the car moved off he said, 'Take the left up here. We are going to my friend's flat. We have some stuff to show you. In the morning we can start with Bunratty.'

'Who will be there?' Scott asked, his eyes on the road.

'Aisling. A couple of others perhaps. She shares with two other girls. Why?'

Scott pulled over and stopped the car. 'Listen, David. If you are right and something sinister is going on then it's big. Very big. Lots at risk. Now we want to see if we can help. But that becomes impossible if everyone knows why I am here, so don't start introducing me to people. I don't exist. We never met. You don't know who the fuck I am. Do you understand?'

'Yes . . . sorry,' he replied earnestly. 'Look, do you want me to stop seeing these people?'

'For the next few days, anyway.'

'What are you? I mean you want to see these sites. Are you an engineer?'

'No,' Scott replied.

David didn't pursue it, just sat in the passenger seat and directed Scott to the flat. When they arrived he jumped out and ran in, coming out a minute later.

'They are out till late,' he said. 'It's just Aisling.'

Scott nodded and climbed out of the car, following the student through the door and up the steep, narrow wooden stairs to the first-floor flat.

Aisling was a tall, slender girl with huge wide blue eyes. Her brunette hair was tied back and she wore rimless spectacles, jeans, sweatshirt and the sort of sensible slippers that one's mother bought for the winter. She wore no make-up and there was a smudge of something on her cheek. She stood in the door, arms folded, looking as though she would brook no nonsense from anyone, suspicious and wary, her eyes taking Scott in.

'Ash, this is . . . Mr . . .' David trailed off, realizing he didn't know the name of the man he was introducing.

'Hello,' Scott said. She didn't offer her hand so he didn't either and they just stood looking at each other, David becoming increasingly uncomfortable.

'You have something on your cheek,' Scott said smiling.

Her expression faltered and she quickly raised the back of her hand to her face.

'Other side,' he murmured, pointing it out.

The hand moved across. 'I've been doing the brass,' she said justifying the smudge, but her tone saying what's it to you anyway.

Finally she looked him in the face again and said with the beginnings of an impish grin, 'You'd better come in now. I'll stick the kettle on.'

Newspapers had been laid out and on them a tin of Brasso and a pile of rags stood beside a big copper and brass sauté pan on the kitchen table. She cleared the newspaper and cleaning gear off the surface, pushing the pan down to the end to make room as David arrived from down the hall with a cardboard box.

## New York, August

Dr Peter Morris smiled at the newcomer and lifted his small bag of groceries off the bar stool to allow the man to sit down.

He was a tall man, bony rather than heavy, with large hands and long curly blond hair. He looked through the tortoiseshell-rimmed spectacles, the kind fancied by young city types trying to look learned, and went back to his paper. With Morris the academic effect was genuine and reinforced by the shapeless old tweed jacket, baggy trousers and fine English brogue shoes.

Millie was still at work, and he was charged with bringing home something to eat, hence the shopping bag now at his feet. It contained microwave pizza, green salad in a silver foil take-out tray and a pre-portioned garlic bread.

O'Dwyers was the neighbourhood bar. The fact that it was Irish in name and decor was for Morris, who viewed his nationality as an almost private affair, a little embarrassing because they had completely overdone the shamrock leaves and heavy woodwork. There was never a bar in Ireland that looked like this, unless it was purpose built for the American tourists, the homogeneous global Paddy coming home to search out his roots. Even the natural soft brogue accents of the Irish staff had been coarsened into a Hollywood parody for the sake of the local customers who expected all Irish to be kissing blarney stones as they applied for green cards and a job with the NYPD.

When he first discovered the place he thought that the overkill was a result of the misplaced enthusiasm of the Polish-American owner, but there were so many others like it in New York that it was not only intended, but might well be part of a franchise operation.

He lifted his drink to his lips, looking straight ahead, not wanting conversation, not tonight. The man beside him looked around the other drinkers, searching for eye contact as if he might want to talk and Morris concentrated on the newspaper. The paper was Irish, the previous Sunday's *Independent* and a story caught his eye. Another big project announced, this time a computer peripherals plant to be opened in Cork, with jobs for seven hundred people.

The change in Ireland in the last two years was incredible. He flicked over the pages to the situations vacant section and scanned the columns. No recession evident. There were jobs for management, technical, sales, production, something for everyone and anyone who wanted work and yet he was uneasy. He was a political scientist and the discipline demanded an in-depth understanding of the factors that drove national economies. The two topics were inextricably interrelated as many a politician had found out. Here reading the Irish papers there was no evident recession and yet there seemed to be no substance to the macro-economics. The growth and the boom were unsupported by demand from markets, either domestic or international. Something didn't make sense and he had taken no comfort from Tony O'Malley's indifference at their meeting back in March. He folded the paper, slipped it into his shopping bag and finished his drink. He wasn't looking forward to going back to an empty apartment and so took the walk at a gentle pace. This time tomorrow they would be back in Dublin and by the end of the week he would be back in his old chair at Trinity College. They were looking forward to getting home, Millie too, now that University College had offered her a job. She was a research chemist and a good one. Although she preferred the laboratory, her doctorate qualified her to lecture and she had accepted UCD's offer to teach final year students.

New York had been fun and exciting in the first few months. It was a city unlike any other, cosmopolitan, vibrant, decadent, unforgiving of the weak, and hospitable all at once. The streets were a subculture all their own, the food, the noise, the people there twenty-four hours a day, every day of the year.

So different from Dublin, with her sleepy streets and quiet Sundays. Dublin, where to teach in a fine university was the culmination of a career and so unlike to the American system where it was simply a step into research or the big dollar lecture circuit. He took the stairs two at a time up to the loft, his light coat flapping at his knees.

He pushed the key into the lock and swung the door back, remembering the first time he had seen it and smiling at the memory. When he arrived in New York he had begun searching for somewhere to live and naïvely expected to be able to afford something a decent size, like Edward Woodward in *The Equalizer*, a spacious, gracious apartment in an elegant old brownstone, with polished wooden floors and big windows. He had never realized that most New Yorkers who lived on Manhattan Island had apartments so small they needed fold-down beds simply to have room to walk around and paid huge rents for the privilege. That was unless they were the millionaires who lived either side of Central Park.

Appalled, he had kept looking and one day had struck gold. He had met a zany black woman, all noisy earrings and tribal prints, who owned and ran a successful design company. She was moving to the West Coast to set up there and offered to sub-let her loft to Morris.

He dropped the bag on the kitchen counter, the thump echoing round the now bare walls. The boxes were there, four tea-chests that held two years of their lives, the results of endless hours spent in secondhand bookshops and the markets in the Village.

All that remained unpacked was his big sound system, an indulgence he knew he could never have afforded if he had not left Ireland. The Kenwood units powered a set of B&W speakers and, selecting a compact disc from the handful left on top of the nearest tea-chest, he filled the room with the voice of Luciano Pavarotti.

His cat ambled over to rub a greeting against his legs. He

opened a tin of food and, scraping some out on to a saucer, put it down on the floor. He had found it bleeding after being hit by a car on the street, scared and missing an ear from alley fights. A vet had saved it and, stuck with the ungrateful animal, Morris had brought it home and they declared a truce. It would be going to a new home in the morning. If the old tom was confused and unsettled by the changes, not so the big grey parrot whose cage stood suspended on a hook from the ceiling. Shithead belonged to the woman who owned the loft and part of the tenancy deal was that Morris take care of the bird. It had a selection of offensive words it trotted out whenever guests arrived, its favourite being its own name. The owner would be back in New York the following week and until then one of the people living downstairs was going to look after the bird.

Morris opened his last bottle of Pomerol and, taking a glass and the bottle, sat down on the bare floorboards in the middle of the room, his back against one of the tea-chests, and poured himself a glass of the wine.

The cat finished his meal and walked across the room towards Morris, his nonchalant gait saying much to the parrot up in his cage. Morris smiled. When the cat first arrived he had made repeated attempts to get to the parrot, but the bars beat him every time. Now in defeat he would no longer even acknowledge the bird's presence, even when the butt of four-letter abuse from the parrot who knew he was safe behind the bars.

When the song had finished Morris changed the disc, looking in the tea-chest for something livelier and settling on Gipsy Kings, then sat on the floor again with the remnants of the wine and the newspaper. He liked the big brassy sound of the European band, and playing what he thought was a fairly mean acoustic guitar himself he loved the gutsy performance they gave. He had been introduced to them the year before by a friend, sitting huddled in a tent at the base of Mount McKinley, waiting for a blizzard to blow over. Ice climbing by day, the cold nerve and the surge of adrenalin as the crampons and axe held over a sheer seven-hundred-foot drop, and the blissful exhaustion of the nights, muted music coming from the tiny tape deck and cups of chocolate laced with rum the French way.

He flicked open the paper again and was looking at the first pages when Millie's key turned in the lock.

'Hi,' she called, the greeting a hollow echoey sound around the walls.

He held up the bottle. 'Grab yourself a glass, in the box there, pizza in twenty minutes.'

'Ah! But you're a grand lad,' she said, bending to kiss his cheek, her accent gently mocking him and his County Clare background, 'but what would the boys in Kilrush be thinking with you being after cooking for your woman now?'

'Fuck 'em all. If they knew the woman they would be taking cookery classes,' he said cheerfully, waving the bottle.

'You are so gallant, kind sir.'

She sat beside him on the floor, the bottle between them and sipped from her glass.

'Oh goody. A paper!'

'I'll get the food. Read it and tell me what you think.'

'What am I looking for?' she asked, knowing he wouldn't say as the words left her mouth.

Patrick O'Sullivan shifted the straw in his mouth and walked big and sure-footed across the wet floor in his new rubber boots. They had arrived through the mail the morning before and today his feet were dry and warm. The two rows of animals patiently standing while the milking machines worked, and the others out in the yard awaiting their turn, represented his livelihood and his pride. The best milking herd in County Kerry. Shamus Kelly may have taken the prize but he knew. His were the best. Two hundred and ten prime Friesians. Once he knew every one, but now there were too many. He stopped beside one old cow and ran his hand down the scar on her back.

She had fallen by a fence down in the bottom field three years ago and when trying to regain her feet had torn her skin on a nail that protruded from a fence post. One of the Murphy boys had seen it, telephoned and had Katriona call for him. He had stood in the rain and stitched the wound with a sail needle and good catgut and when the vet had come later he had complimented him on the workmanship. That evening young Shaun, only nine, had scrubbed the milking sheds till they gleamed while he stood, his pipe in his mouth and watched. It was punishment for the nail that he had not driven home and so caused harm to a fine milking animal.

Katriona had not approved, but a boy must learn the value of a good cow and the consequences of a job only half done, he had said to her. It must be right, he had said to the boy. It must always be right. If it's not, then make it so.

They had been blessed with five healthy children. The girls looked like their mother, tall and strong with the promise of the same wide-hipped fertility as the land they farmed. The two boys were like their grandfather, bright and laughing. Shaun, now twelve, had a liking for engines and his brother was at the University. Katriona had wanted one for the priesthood, but he had put his foot down. They could do exactly what they wished with their lives as long as they were happy and what they did was right. These were the nineties, Europe meshed in a common community, the old Soviet bear dead, opportunities abounded for young people and he had never met a happy priest.

He stopped and fished his pipe from his pocket as his two men began to work their way down the lines, pulling cups from pink udders, the cows backing out of the stalls and ambling down the concrete bay back to the field.

He no longer had to bend to the task and when he did so it was because he wanted to. He was a wealthy man now. The original herd had expanded tenfold, and he had bought the neighbouring farm when it had come on the market six years ago. He had new equipment, the loans from the bank were manageable and the co-operative he had formed with two other local men to process cheese and cream was paying dividends. A thousand pounds paid to a Dublin consultant for some research, a pretty name and picture on the old-world-looking jars and they had a nice little boutique creamery that the tourists loved. 'Kerry's Dingle Cream' was now attracting interest and an American gentlemen was wanting sole import rights. The young lad running the place, a marketing graduate of Limerick University, was doing a grand job. He even had pair of young country girls wearing nineteenth-century frocks and shawls selling at the counter. Katriona said they looked like floosies, but never mind that he thought. Next year they would expand a little and sell hand-made shawls, same as the girls wore, linen tablecloths and Phil Coulter cassettes.

He smiled to himself. Because he made his living off the land people assumed he was a backward country hick, a cultchie. He cultivated the impression wherever he could. But he could read a balance sheet with the best of them, discuss international affairs, the failure of junk bonds or anything else. He was the new generation of Irish farmer, a well-travelled, well-educated, ambitious small business-man. His family parked three cars outside the house and enjoyed a decent holiday every year. They had been to Florida last summer and loved it. The year before had been Thailand.

If they only knew from whence we came he mused. The filth and squalor of two rooms with mud floors only fifty years ago. The thin children with chilblains and nothing in their hearts but hope. Men with their backs bent over in the fields digging some other man's ground while the rain fell. The lucky ones got away to America or Liverpool. Now the Americans come back a generation or two on, seeking the old country. The romance of peat smoke or a fiddle player and pints of Guinness or Murphy's. For O'Sullivan burning peat in the fire was only romantic when you could turn off the electric light and snuggle up on a shag pile carpet, knowing the central heating was on anyway. And if you really listened to the words of the fiddler's song they were lyrics born of deprivation and despair, of broken families, loved ones taken by toil and tuberculosis, lifetimes of effort simply to keep potatoes on the table and a fire in the hearth.

But, as he often said, if it's romance they want it's romance they'll get, and if we can make a shilling or two then that'll be grand.

He was something of a enigma to many of the locals, because they knew that the image of a straw-sucking, rubber-booted dairyman, this country yokel, was a façade concealing something far more complex. No one had ever got one past Pat O'Sullivan, not local or traveller. He was as sharp as a knife, and it was said that it was just as well he was fair and a just man, because if he chose to walk the dark road he would be a very dangerous man indeed. Sure they said, and wasn't it Pat O'Sullivan who sent the tinkers on their way when Mrs Boyne's dog had been poisoned? They agreed and supped their pints, for any man who standing alone could move the gypsy-like travellers on, had something special about him and no mistaking it. There had been other incidents over the years when the man had shown his mettle, and with the priest's warning ringing in his ears and the Gardai looking the other way, he had shown that he was a formidable enemy.

Puffing his pipe he walked the row as the next group of animals moved down the herringbone shed. The sun was

41

well up now and breakfast would soon be on the kitchen table, the youngest getting ready for school. Katriona would drive her down in the new car, a brand new Range Rover. Not quite in keeping with the farmer image, but it would turn their bloody heads he thought and he laughed out loud. For Patrick O'Sullivan life was pretty good. Not perfect, but pretty good. The only problem was the cottage. Katriona's people had left her twelve acres and an old stone three-room house down on the Dingle peninsula at Clogher. They went down there some weekends in the summer, or used to. The council had forced a sale on them. The price was fair, good even, but they hadn't wanted to sell. It was Katriona's last link with her parents and the sentimental value exceeded any amount the council had offered. Fergus McKenzie who had the next place along had phoned last night. They were putting up something on the rocky paddocks behind the cottage, and putting them up in what appeared to be an unseemly hurry considering the ink on the exchange agreements was barely dry. After breakfast he was going to drive down there and have a look. Have a look at what was so bloody important as to have his wife crying on her pillow.

He was there by ten, and pulled the car over to a rest on the side of the road down into the bay. Behind him was the hillside, shrouded in cloud and below was the sea. Out on the southern end of the curved shoreline was the cottage, and he could see the structures that old Fergus had spoken of. Tall masts stood up from the ground, not quite high enough to need anti-collision beacons, but certainly high enough to require guy wires back to the ground at three points. There were also lower structures with wires that extended parallel to the ground between upright poles like a high fence line. A shorter, sturdier structure supported a satellite dish.

His elbow resting on the window frame, he ran a rough hand across his unshaven jaw, his dark eyes narrowing and accentuating the deep crow's feet at their corners as he took it all in.

He had been a keen electronics buff in his youth and he knew what he was looking at. This was a multi-band receiving station and the towers were hooked up to transmitters. Somewhere not far away was the communications centre. Maybe even in the cottage. Its three rooms could be big enough. He looked back at the towers and aerials and a dry smile crossed his face. Some men could never read the land. They had been walking across it. Had it not occurred to them that there was a reason why no trees grew here, why only the hardy bracken survived on the hillside? They had certainly never wintered here he thought, or they would know the first winter storm that came off the Atlantic would tear their precious equipment away as if it were no more than an old woman's washing, the same winds and seas that had smashed big ships to pieces on the rocks many times over the years.

Typical of the council to fuck this up he thought. Serve them right. But, he mused as he started the engine, what on earth would the council want with a communications station? Maybe it wasn't theirs. But if not theirs, then whose? And whoever had built the towers would be moving them after the first storm and then forcing Katriona to sell would have been unnecessary, and for Patrick O'Sullivan that wasn't right. Not with her crying on her pillow. It just wasn't right.

# 2

The meeting was in the depths of Century House, and for a full update briefing for the Deputy Director General of the Secret Intelligence Service everyone was in early.

Sally Richards stood, a sheaf of files under one arm and a Styrofoam cup presented in the other hand to one of the analysts who had the coffee pot.

'Yes please,' she said. 'I hate these bloody foam cups. What's the matter with china, for God's sake?'

'Someone has to wash it, I suppose,' the man said. It was the sort of sensible answer born of reasonable thinking she detested first thing in the morning.

'Oh shut up,' she replied. The man smiled. This was acceptance.

Peter Tilby loomed beside her. 'Think nothing of her bad manners, my good fellow, and pour me a cup. I'm so parched I could drink British Rail tea.'

'You have always displayed the habits of your pedestrian working-class background,' she retaliated.

Tilby, who went to Eton and Cambridge, was anything but working class.

'My, my, we are positively venomous today. Once our Pet arrives you two vipers can have at it and I shall retire to the gents' bogs and read the graffiti.'

'You will not. You will remain here and be suitably ingratiating. If you are a good boy I shall let you into the ladies to read seventy-two verses of Eskimo Nell afterwards.'

'Oh, goody. Shall I kiss her arse before she sits down or wait till she's leaving?'

'Really, Peter, if you want to get ahead you will have to learn to do it while she is seated.'

They had been up until three that morning sifting and collating the reports, both the raw material and the typed conclusions from the various people working on the team. Persse, relegated by his tobacco habit to the hallway, ignored the exchange and stood smoking a cigarette. Richards, as head of the Commercial desk had been given this problem because of its location. The Service had no Irish desk, not since the Second World War, and Commercial, normally charged with keeping a watchful eye on the big foreign banks and trading conglomerates, seemed the best choice, both under the new structure and considering the nature of the enquiry. She had worked with Tilby, who, coincidentally, was the best they could muster in the way of an Irish specialist, so long they were almost an institution and the acid repartee, to those that knew them, was a demonstration of real friendship. They were achingly formal to newcomers or outsiders and Persse himself had only been admitted to the close group after four years on the job.

Also ignoring the talk was Arnold Cleaves. He was the much respected money man. Tagged Head of Finance, he reported to Sally Richards and he sat at the circular table, a pile of papers and overhead projector acetates in front of him, polishing his glasses with a crisp white handkerchief. Head of Finance in Century House was not the internal treasury and cost control function the name suggested. When the service had turned its attention from the withering Soviet bloc to protecting the nation's international trade, Arnold Cleaves had been headhunted from a mysterious division of the World Bank who in turn had wooed him from Ernst & Young. His speciality was international finance with particular strengths in the nasty end of it. The word was that Arnold Cleaves had been calling for the Bank of England to look into the Bank of Credit and

Commerce International a full five years before the institution collapsed under the weight of its massive frauds.

Now with a small team of bright youngsters and a network of contacts that spread across the world's financial markets, major banks and discreet offices in Zurich, he could track deals and unmask villains, either individual or collective. Cleaves had proved that there were respected nations with seats in the UN that took white-collar crime to new levels.

The evidence was often such that it would not stand up in a court of law, but to the Secret Intelligence Service, who were less concerned with legal niceties, there was no smoke without fire. When only one bunch had the matches and the motive and guilt had been established, the information was then passed to those who could make the best use of it. Occasionally they were asked to redress the problem and, with no questions asked, their operating methods could be as underhand as the methods of those they were targeting.

Arnold Cleaves and his tiny team had been looking into the Irish ownership issues for three weeks and canteen snippets said that he was unhappy with progress, so unhappy that he had everyone working late every day.

Sally Richards, her cup balanced on a stiff green file, pulled out the chair to his right. She liked Arnold Cleaves. He had the rare ability in an expert to be able to explain his field in the most basic terms, enabling everyone to understand it. He had given her a brief lesson the week before because she simply hadn't believed it possible.

'You can't just buy chunks of a country,' she had said. 'It's unbelievable!'

'Oh, but you can,' Cleaves had smiled back. It was a tight, disciplined expression, like his thought processes. 'The Japanese have made huge investments on the American West Coast, they have also bought large tracts of Australia, mostly as golf courses and resorts. Corporations

46

buy land in other countries constantly. Most countries have a reporting structure, a method of policing or at least understanding exactly what foreign investment is taking place within their borders. This is open Europe. Think about it. With enough money you could buy up most of London and people would be lining up to take your marks, francs, dollars or whatever. Using the right structures and smokescreens you could do it without being noticed, like a hostile takeover of a company. Suddenly one day everyone sits up and takes notice because one collection of individuals, or group, working to a common agenda, has amassed a majority shareholding. You simply find it unbelievable because it's never been done to a country. With enough money you can buy anything. It happens all the time in business.'

Now she sat down beside him, careful to keep her coffee away from his notes.

'So, Arnold, found anything new since yesterday? Going to make Mummy's day and expose the grand plot to all?'

'No,' he said firmly. 'I will leave that to you and the others of your ilk gifted with a view of the big picture.' He lifted his big head and fixed her in his gaze. 'But this I will tell you. Trying to unravel this in three weeks would be like trying to guess an Agatha Christie ending after reading three pages taken at random from the middle of the book.'

'How long?' she asked, going straight to the point. Her people could not put the pieces together until they had them, and the basis of this whole issue was financial. The twice-weekly updates she received from Cleaves indicated there was progress, but it was slow. Too slow.

'A couple of months maybe. If I'm left alone and not asked to attend meetings where I have nothing new to offer. It's wasting my time.'

'You are here, my precious, because I can't even balance

my cheque book, let alone explain how things like this are done. The DDG, bless her little iron heart, likes to be properly briefed.'

Persse ambled in. A few seconds later a woman entered: Petra Wallis the Deputy Director General. She was in her fifties, slim, hair neatly done, and if she seemed slightly school-marmish in appearance that was where any hint of dusty academia stopped. She was a clear thinker, utterly ruthless where her beloved service was concerned. Totally dedicated, she was a career officer, one of the old school who frowned on those casual enough to call their organization 'the firm' or even worse, 'Six'. The old MI6 tag had finally fallen away in the seventies, but for some reason was still used by the press. She particularly disliked Sally Richards's flippant use of the term 'Dr Barnardo's'.

If Petra Wallis was the heir apparent, then Sally Richards was the young pretender, and both were highly regarded by Sir Adrian Corning, the Director General.

The DDG took a chair at the bottom of the table as the last few who stood round the coffee trolley found somewhere to sit and raised an eyebrow, looking around to see who would start. Richards leaned forward.

'Where have we got to, then?' Wallis asked.

'With the actual ownership issues, not far enough,' Richards replied, 'but a couple of other things have come to light that could well be related. The first,' she pushed the papers away and began to speak without notes, 'is a series of recent investments in the Republic and while we haven't managed to trace them back to actuals, in four cases, we have got as far as the same small bank in Zurich. It probably won't end there, in fact Arnold believes there may be another three or four layers, but the coincidence is too strong to ignore. The second point is that seven members of the Dáil, seven so far, and I stress *so far* because we have only just moved into this area of enquiry, as well as five very senior civil servants have recently had their mortgages and in some cases personal loans bought by some outfit called Manxretro. For that read persons unknown. Same in the Senate. We have found three there.'

'So these people are now exposed to debt recall?' Wallis said immediately. Richards was impressed. She had to have Cleaves explain it to her when he had advised of the loan purchase.

'Yes. Considerable amounts of money. Whoever is doing this hasn't bothered with small stuff. Only when they could really get someone by the short and curlies.'

Wallis's expression didn't alter, but everyone in the room knew how she felt about what she termed canteen language.

'I didn't think it was possible to buy a mortgage on the open market,' she responded.

Cleaves looked up. 'You can buy any paper, any debt if you pay enough. And don't forget that people who can muster capital to fund deals like these people probably have equity in someone that has muscle in the original lending institution anyway.'

'The third and most disturbing issue,' Richards continued, 'is something really sinister. The PM and the Minister of Justice both have teenage children. Neither have been seen in recent months. A story has been circulating that they are abroad, in the Justice Minister's case in America, but even with some favours called in at the FBI we have been unable to establish whereabouts. The PM's wife hasn't been out much lately, but here is a picture taken three days ago.'

Wallis took the eight by ten inch glossy print. It showed a woman, her face worn by pain, sleepless nights and worry.

'I took it,' Persse said. 'She's only forty-six. She looks sixty there.'

'Conclusion?' Wallis passed the photograph back, knowing what was going to be said, her expression rigid. She had four children of her own and understood, as only a parent could, the cause of despair and the pain that was etched across the woman's face.

'The kid has been snatched.'

'How many others?'

'We're working on it. There are well over a hundred members in the Dáil. Double that for the Senate and civil servants senior enough to benefit a conspiracy with their forced silence. Most of them have children or someone close that would make them vulnerable. Even if they haven't actually been taken the word would be passed. The example made. The precedent set.'

'Who is behind it?'

'We don't know. Not yet. We have a man on the ground there now, been there three weeks. Between him and our people working the scam from this end something will break soon.'

'Is he ours or a local?'

'Ours, sort of.' Richards hesitated. 'Well . . . borrowed from Hereford, actually.'

'What do you need?' Wallis asked, ignoring the reference to borrowed resources from the army.

'Heads here. Assets there. I want the bloody place thick with good guys. Then we'll have the strength on the ground to do some good.'

'Start recruiting and take who you want on the active list here. I'll get sign-off. Next full meeting will be three days from now. It's time the MoD and Cabinet Committee were involved. Be prepared to brief C in one hour.'

'C' was Sir Adrian Corning.

'Isn't he with the Minister this morning?' Richards asked.

As Director General Sir Adrian Corning reported only to the Foreign Secretary and the Prime Minister and such meetings were called rarely.

'Sod the Minister!' she said frostily. 'Someone is in the process of invading a country on our doorstep.'

'Invading?' someone questioned, implying that the word was a bit strong.

'That's what it looks like to me,' Wallis snapped. 'It's more subtle than most, it's brilliantly planned and so far its execution has been flawless. You don't need a blitzkrieg or a horde of Visigoths for it to be an invasion!' She stood up, her bifocal glasses in her hand. 'Find out who – and soon!'

Aiden Scott sat at the table and watched the passers-by through the window. He was waiting to meet a cousin, a detective in the Dublin Garda. As far as the family were concerned he had left the army and was now taking some leave prior to setting up his own security company. He didn't like lying to them, but it was easier that way. Birr was a small place: the neighbours, who all knew he was in the British army, had heard he was home within an hour of his arrival and the rest of the small community knew by nightfall. His cousins came calling, and just before dark a huge frame had loomed in the back door. It was Big Rory, Scott's boyhood friend.

'Jaysus, if it's not the weary traveller,' he said, his huge hairy hand extended and a wide genuine grin spreading across his equally hairy cheeks. He was a big man, fully six feet five in his bare feet, and as Scott stood his mother again marvelled at the sight the pair of them made. One tall, lean and sinewy and the other even taller, huge and heavy like a great oak. 'Hello, Rory. It's good to see you.' Scott took the offered hand and shook it indicating the seat at the table where the teapot steamed invitingly.

'Rory McMahon. Boots off in my kitchen,' Scott's mother warned as she reached for more cups from the cupboard. She reinforced the warning with a glare and the big man grinned like a little boy and slipped off his boots in the doorway as he had done a thousand times over the years.

As she poured she remembered the first time Aiden had brought him home. They were ten or eleven years old, Aiden very much the half-English summer visitor and Rory already master of the river banks and the wet peaty meadows.

They swapped worlds that year, Aiden entrancing Rory with his model stationary steam engine. They lit the piece of cotton wool soaked in methylated spirits that heated the tiny boiler and eventually, lying on the kitchen floor they would watch the silver wheel begin to turn, its little piston thrashing with satisfying hisses and chuffing noises. Later they would wrap rubber bands from Mr Madden's store round the big flat drivewheel and try to power little drills, drive shafts and once a propeller that had fallen from someone's balsa wood ME 109. It spun, chopping the air just like a real one until its design got the better of it and it went flying off into Mrs Scott's leg. They both got a cuff round the ear for that and were banished into the garden for the remainder of the day.

Rory in turn showed Aiden where the birds nested on the river bank, where they could fish without the warden catching them, and on borrowed bicycles they had ridden together down the Shannon to its secret places to eat the sweet stolen apples, throw rocks into the deep, still pools and explore in an old clinker-built dinghy.

Each summer they were reunited and each summer they had grown, each in his own way through the gawky early teenage years of confusion, shyness and rampant hormones. Aiden at school in England had access to mildly pornographic magazines that could never be found in Ireland and four given to Rory were later sold, much thumbed, to other boys in the village and the profits used to buy a bottle of cheap sherry. They sat down at the river as they had always done, drank the sherry, got drunk and later shared the first of several sessions bent over, throwing up, while they learned their limits. Mary, a local girl the priest despaired over, was an early scarlet woman and their first foray into the world of real flesh. A big, healthy country girl, she had happily hoisted her skirts in a disused cowshed and Aiden, four years her junior, sitting on his haunches by the light of his torch, mesmerized by the heavy white thighs and the dark cleft the smooth columns rose up to, was first. Big Rory stood outside in the dark keeping guard, his heart racing with the excitement, his mouth dry with anticipation and a considerable bulge in his jeans.

Along with the significant events of those years came inevitable conflicts, but they never affected the friendship for long and each holiday when they were old enough they invariably found work together.

Sandhurst for Aiden and university for Rory, the pressures of work and ten years of army postings, finally broke the summer cycle but the bonds were still there. Rory, now the local vet, had married a girl from Roscrea and was the father of three children.

'How long are you back for?' Rory asked taking the cup and saucer from Mrs Scott. 'You'll be coming over for dinner tomorrow night? Sue says it's not up for discussion as you have godsons to meet again.'

'A few days at least,' Scott answered. 'And tell her I'd love to.'

They spent the evening reminiscing, pints of Guinness before them, and it was late when Scott finally said, 'But what about all the money there is about, Rory? Seems like plenty of work available?'

'There is,' his friend answered. 'Big investments in the last couple of years. Lots of mortgage money around. Interest rates are low. Factories all over the place. New plant. Lots of building work.'

'Any round here?' he asked casually.

Rory had known him too long to be fooled for a second.

'Some.' He sipped his drink, the tan-coloured head leaving a line of fine foam across his moustache, his eyes never leaving Scott's for a second. 'But you're not after building work now, are you Aiden?'

'No, Rory, I'm not,' Scott answered honestly and, aware of the people next to them in the booths either side, he finished, 'but we can talk about it tomorrow.'

Moira Kelly was baking. It was what she did. The soda bread was a family thing, baked Fridays, enough to last through till Monday, but the cakes and biscuits were her real passion and when Father O'Leary asked her to bake for the church sale she did so with real pleasure, turning out the 'home mades', using classic tried and true recipes. There were fruit cakes, chocolate cakes so rich with real Cadbury's Bournville they were almost the colour of roasted coffee beans, Madeira cakes, scones, custard kisses and biscuits made with treacle and dried fruit. Mary had gone up to the shop for bananas and they would soon be finished. It was nice to have Mary home she thought. In America for the World Cup, she had followed Jack's army of supporters and when the football was over she had gone back to the cousins in Boston. She lifted the biscuits from the oven. Back only a few weeks and seeing a young man already. She had not brought this new young man home yet, but that was not unusual. Her choice of boyfriends was not ideal. Musicians, not real musicians, pianists or even the players of traditional Irish music, but young laughing men with long hair who played electric guitars in the clubs and bars. She had gone out with an artist once and after that, God forbid, a traveller, not a tinker, but a new age hippie type with dreadlocks who sold crystals and friendship bracelets from a tray in the park.

The door slammed and Mary walked through to the kitchen, a big bag of over-ripe bananas in her hand.

'That's grand, pet,' Moira said, taking them. Now they could finish the last cake, a banana cake, the recipe taken from the Australian *Woman's Weekly* twenty-odd years ago, and sent to her by her sister in Melbourne.

Mary glanced at her watch as she began peeling bananas. She had promised to meet him at six, and the last bus that would get her there in time was at five thirty-seven. She wondered again just what to tell her mum and when. Sam was nice. Dark, swarthy, with perfect clear white teeth, and an American accent laid over his native Persian. Mum wouldn't like that at all. Not Irish, not Catholic, not even Christian. He was born Muslim, but said he didn't bother with that any more, his smile melting her as it always did. He was there doing English, although she wasn't sure why. He spoke it very well, and to improve it she thought, he didn't need a language school, just prac-tice. She looked at herself in the small mirror on the wall under the clock. Her hair was long, raggedy and tied back in a loose pony-tail with a purple elasticized crushed velvet tie. Her one extravagance was the small rimless glasses perched on her nose, the nose that she thought was bulbous, and her skin seemed pale and blotchy. Her hands were always stained with paint and she had heavy thighs, cellulite threatening to appear at any second. Her mother had once shocked her by saying men don't find shape unattractive, so don't fuss, pet. Saddlebags on a girl's thighs, she had said, it's the natural shape of a woman and they like something to get a hold of. This statement from her strait-laced Catholic mother, pillar of the church visitors' group and head of the family, had made her uncomfortable for a moment or two; she had never viewed her mother as a person who would know what men like to get a hold of, but it served to bring them closer. Maybe she was right. Sam did seem to like her. But what does he see in me, she asked herself? He was so exotic. His colouring and his accent and his manners were so unlike the Irish guys she normally met and he always seemed to have money in his pocket and that made a change. The last boyfriend was always broke and she ended up paying for the infrequent evenings out. She began to hurry. It was five-fifteen.

The man she was meeting finished off his work, lit a cigarette and leaned back in his chair. One usually ten-minute briefing for his area commander and he could relax for the rest of the day. He was looking forward to the evening. Being sent to Dublin had been a real bonus. As an intelligence officer he had long hoped for a posting to a western country, and was now actually quite pleased this was his first. If he had been attached to an active group in the past then, believed compromised, he would have been taken off the list for this posting and this job had to be the best yet. It meant two or three hours a day at most, in the back offices of the bogus finance company, sifting informa-tion, monitoring his sectors and preparing an evening report for his superiors. The mornings were his to spend at the language school that was his cover and he was even enjoying that. The best of all was, however, Mary.

When he met her, knowing she was an artist and there-fore unconventional in the Irish sense, and knowing the attraction of the new, he knew he could woo her. It hadn't taken long before he was in her bed. She was so different from the girls of his homeland. Their strict Muslim or Orthodox Christian upbringing made them prudish and unexciting, but Mary, with her creamy skin, full womanly body and healthy appetites, was like a dream. It wasn't her appetite for sex, but everything. She even ate fruit with a gusto that a Muslim girl would find immodest and sinful. He remembered her last night, sitting naked on her bed, her wide mouth smiling at him, her eyes laughing, as she bit into a peach, the juice running down her chin, on to her breasts, and her laugh as he leant forward to taste it. She was smart too. They talked politics, talked about her feelings for family, home, Ireland, her art and all throughout he found that most stimulating thing of all, passion. She had passion. For everything. He was becoming fond of her, he thought. No. It had gone beyond fondness. She was now the single thing he looked forward to and that he knew could become a problem for him in time. Sometime and sometime soon he would have to stop seeing her and end it for both their sakes. His boss was not on to it yet, thank God. Ali Jassem, commander south-west, was a complete professional and he frowned on those who had immersed themselves into local society too deeply, or struck up relationships that could be dangerous.

Ali Jassem, in a borrowed office two doors down, looked at his watch. The daily briefing was almost on. He always insisted it began on time and invariably he was present. Young Sam Abdul Jawad was the duty officer today. Ali liked him. Smart kid. He looked out of the window and the falling rain and remembered the heat of Jordan, the day he had attended the first meeting with Khalil Ashrawi in Amman. My God, he thought, that was three years ago. Seems like just yesterday. The planners, the bankers and lawyers, the strategists who had put together the most audacious buy-out in history at their last planning meeting. Now it was done and his role was about to commence. They kept saying they won't fight for it. They will have no mandate and we have powerful friends. It will, after all, be ours. Bought and paid for. We will negotiate and we will win. For Palestine. Not just Gaza and the West Bank. All Palestine. It was hot in the room. The air-conditioning had failed and he sat sweating, his worry beads in his hand, at the head of the table. Brought before them. They had said don't worry. It won't come to a real fight, but we expect some sporadic violence. Can you deal with that? He had nodded. The locals he could deal with, he replied but what of the west?

Don't worry about them was the reply. They will negotiate. Talk. This will be an internal Irish problem. There
was a knock at the door. That would be Sam.

The briefing began, details of the day's events as they
affected the area. Saad the Libyan would be arriving the
following day. As a wealthy Arab he would be fishing
somewhere for the time being. The briefing finished and
Sam stood up, obviously keen to go. Silly little sod, Ali
thought. He is screwing something and is thinking with his
dick. No that was unkind. Sam was a thinker, a lover, a
poet and a patriot. If he was seeing someone then it
wouldn't be just to slake his lust. He made a mental note to
check up on the situation. Young men will be young men
he thought and sometimes they need protecting from
themselves.

At Century House there were now seventy people in the
new section on the second floor. Every magazine, period-
ical, newspaper and publication was being scanned for
whatever they would reveal. Some teams were now looking for what Persse called the 'blinding flashes of the
obvious'. The detail buried in company reports, or veiled
comments buried in the back pages of some country paper.
The little titbits that meant something only if you knew
what you were looking for.

Other teams were looking for what the trade called
assets. Local people who could be recruited, trained and
used. If they were right, recruiting would never be easier.
Selection was the problem. Choosing the right people for
each stage.

Persse briefed them. 'Avoid those well known for their
strong views. Avoid those who are known to agitate. They
would be the first to be noticed. They will have been
flagged for arrest already. They will be picked up the
moment the covers come off. If not, they can come in later.
Choose people we can develop. People who have so far

managed to avoid being singled out by the media, but have local respect. Look for nice, normal people who somehow, with subtlety, have demonstrated some courage, some willingness to stand up for what they believe in. People with respect from those that know them.'

They waded through hundreds of sources from local papers to the minutes of local council meetings in every town in the country to hours of video tape. The searchers went both to the core of Irish conventional society, the lists of priests, the holy brothers and the convents, and to the fringe sectors. The North Side of Dublin would give them people who were used to keeping secrets, people like petty criminals and prostitutes, people who had been living on 'the stroke', drawing social security payments and dole for years, while holding down other jobs where they could and paying no taxes. The likelihood that these people had noticed anything amiss was slight. They were preoccupied with the simple task of putting food on the table and paying the rent. They would be unlikely to question too deeply the background or real reasons for the mini-boom in the job market, but once informed and recruited they would prove a rich resource.

The one singular powerful element of Irish society they could not directly get to was the family. Conventional intelligence thinking said that you never recruit family. They provide the cover, the background. They should never know. But this was not conventional and they knew that the resistance would be made up of families. Irish blood was thick.

For now the names would be collated, measured against criteria and the results judged by a computer. Those thought best suited to the function, and there would be no more than twenty in the entire country, would be approached by Persse or Tilby and an attempt to recruit made over several visits.

The name at the top of the list was possibly vulnerable

because he was an academic and they were always rounded up first, but knowing the deep respect that the Irish have for their scholars, and the ready network of current and ex-students, Dr Peter Morris would be approached immediately. He had only recently arrived back from an extended trip abroad and he might have even noticed something himself, the way you notice that a friend has put on weight, when those who see him every day haven't.

There were already nine SIS people in Ireland and a further thirteen to arrive in the next few days. They were all very uncomfortable. The Secret Intelligence Service normally had one staffer in any country. In a large mission there might be two and in only four countries were there three intelligence staff. Big teams were unnecessary. They could all be supplemented. Resources could be drafted in at a few hours' notice, but that was rare. The local function based in the country simply got on with the job of gathering information and running their networks, their cells. Traditionally, in the old Iron Curtain countries of the Warsaw Pact, they took years to put together. Here they were trying to do it in weeks.

But here they were not selecting people with access to military data, or the files of government ministries. They were trying to put together cells that would form a resistance network. The spies would be found later. Even so Tilby was unhappy. It flew in the face of all their experience and as he waited for Scott in the Terenure house with the other three members of his team, he paced the floor.

Scott was disappointed. The rendezvous with the cousin in the Dublin police had been cancelled. But Rory had been helpful. The issue explained, he had been able to fill in the local details for Scott. He would be good, Scott thought. He was measured, calm and with real nerve under pressure. He was also respected locally and could move about in the

60

course of his profession. Scott had spent the last few days in Birr, talking to the locals, spending time with people who would matter. The old man on the river had been a find. He had been fishing and they had got talking. He drove a bus in Kilkenny and was down for a few days' holiday. Rory had found him. Recently he had been doing trips to a place not far from Clonmel on the road to Mitchelstown.

'It's a flying school,' he said. 'Funny place to learn to fly. One of them said that they usually go to Florida. I have cousins there. Anyway, seems they want experience at flying in cloud or something. That's what the lad said. Nice boy. Mo was his name.'

'Go there often?' Scott asked casually.

'Every week for months now. Must have delivered hundreds of them. They must have loads of money.'

'Why do you say that?'

'I come back empty. They are paying for the round trip, and I came back empty every time. Mind you, they may be using another company I suppose.'

Scott arrived at the Dublin house just before three o'clock. Persse was pleased to see him because Robert Hargadon's brother, the journalist who had first got the two students into the British Embassy, was due soon and he wanted this meeting out of the way.

Scott sipped a cup of coffee as he brought Persse up to date, finishing with the flying school titbit.

'No one goes somewhere to learn to fly in bad weather. You do that on simulators. Hundreds of people? RAF Linton-on-Ouse only has about fifty going through at any given stage. I want to go and have a look.'

'Don't be away too long. The ambassador is seeing the PM here tomorrow. He is going to corner him. Ask the question, if he can get him away from anywhere that might be wired. A walk in the garden or something.'

'Just hope they don't have directional surveillance mikes,' Scott said drily.

'We have briefed him, but he is a diplomat which makes him bereft of any common sense,' Persse responded. 'Anyway, we may want you to get in and talk to him in his residence. Dark of night and all that.'

'Break in?' Scott looked up.

'You've done it before.'

'You have, too,' Scott said, not knowing but guessing correctly.

'I'm too fucking old for that burglar shit,' Persse muttered, lighting another cigarette. 'Be back tomorrow night will you? If nothing else, the ambassador is going to give him a recognition device. You'll have the other half when you go in.'

Tilby ambled in. 'Ah, our forgotten soldier. How are things on your tour of Irish construction sites?'

'I'm going down to Clonmel. Have a look at something. I'll fill you in when I get back.'

'Just phone,' Tilby said, pointing to a cellular telephone on the dining-room table. 'This must be the last time you come here.'

Scott looked at him.

'They haven't told you yet? Typical army. You'll be staying on, old chap. When this whole thing breaks you will be staying behind. Chindits and all that.'

Scott shrugged. It was typical that some civilian should know before him.

'Where do we meet?' he asked picking up his keys.

'When will you be back from Clonmer?'

'Clonmel. Tomorrow sometime.'

'Call us here from a pay phone. I'll meet you somewhere. After that you will use this number in London.' He handed Scott a second slip of buff-coloured paper. 'Once we go on to orange you will go underground. If you say the word *meal* it will be in Waterford's bookshop at noon.

If you use the word *tea* it will be the GPO at nine-thirty in the morning. You now have a drop point. There is a pipe and tobacco shop on Nassau Street.'

'Petersons,' Scott said.

'Ask for Mr Hobday,' Tilby said nodding. 'He will take anything you have off your hands.'

'So after today, what?'

'Persse has told you. We may want you to sneak into the PM's place and have a little heart to heart with the fellow. After that you will have orders from your own people.'

He arrived at Clonmel just before eight that evening and kept driving through the village until the turning the bus driver had described loomed up on the left. From there it was two miles down the road. There were a handful of farms off either side and he planned on leaving his car somewhere quiet and walking the last mile or so.

A few minutes later he found what he was looking for. There on the right in the headlights were a cluster of outbuildings and a barn. Lights winked through trees up on the hill. The house, he thought. He drove past the buildings, rounded the bend and came to a halt. Then he turned his headlights off, reversed back up the road and slid the car in behind one of the sheds. He got out, pulled a small rucksack from the boot. From it he took out a light-weight dark balaclava and pulled it over his head. He then took a pistol from the pack, inserted a magazine and cocked the action before easing the hammer forward to the half-cock position. He put it into the pack's side pocket and set off at a fast pace.

It was a hour later when he almost walked into the fence. It was high, twelve feet and well constructed. He looked along the fence line in the moonlight. Small nodules interrupted the symmetry of the pattern. Interesting he thought. He dropped his pack and listened for a minute, then, satisfied that nothing was moving nearby, he pulled a small instrument from the pack and touched it to the fence. The light glowed. Naughty naughty he thought with a grin. Two-forty volts of naughty naughty. The electric line was high, too high for a cow to rub against it. Cows only needed twelve volts to get the message. This was intended for people. He ran the tester up the fence and found a second electrified cable at ten feet. No tremble sensors.

He took a pair of insulated gloves from the pack, pulled them on and finally slung the pack over his shoulders and began to carefully climb the fence. On the airfield side there were vehicle tracks, deep ruts in the soft ground.

Fifteen minutes later he was approaching the first of a series of buildings along the western side of the runway and the edge of the apron. The taxiways spread out towards the runway, dark and smooth in the soft moonlight.

Scott stopped and pulling a tiny torch from his pocket he moved up to a window at the first building.

Tilby sat back in the chair, his waistcoat undone, a glass of scotch in his hand and reviewed the day so far. Kevin Hargadon had been recruited and had agreed to begin supplying intelligence from whatever sources he had, both professional, from the newspaper, and personal. His first job was to look into the editors of Dublin's two biggest newspapers. One was new and the other had a family. Both were targets for the as yet unidentified invaders. One or both may already be bought and paid for Tilby thought. The department already had someone looking at senior people in RTE, the broadcasting service. He sipped the drink, the ice cubes clinking against the side of the glass, relishing the dry peaty taste.

There were three lists. The Blue list was people the Service wanted out of Ireland. They were too influential to be allowed to stay and risk arrest when the silence ruptured. They were broadcasters, scholars, celebrities whose faces were recognized, whose voices were familiar in living rooms across the country.

The Red list were potential collaborators, people who stood to gain. Until they understood the nature of the invaders they would not be able to prepare that listing.

The next visitor was crucial. He was at the head of the last list, the White list. The list of people who the service thought would be best placed to form the central command of a resistance network. The planners, the thinkers, the strategists, the high command.

He looked at his watch. Dr Peter Morris was late.

Scott moved down the line of buildings, checking each as he went. Some were low structures, office-type accommodation with stores areas, and others were higher, hangars big enough to store three or four single-engine aeroplanes.

He had passed a picket, seen the glow of the guard's cigarette in the dark and heard the low rumble of conversation with his friend.

He moved on. One of the low buildings seemed to have been laid out as classrooms and he let himself into the darkened corridor and checked three of the small rooms. They were furnished with students' chairs, each with a small writing surface along the right armrest, blackboards and notice-boards, but they had a deserted feel to them. No residual tobacco smells, no chalk dust hanging in the air, no filled waste paper bins, no litter. He moved on.

At the first of the hangars he dropped to one knee and, shielding the red beam of his torch, carefully scrutinized the rear door. There were the tell-tale wires and contact points of a reasonably sophisticated alarm system.

He could work through it, but it would take time. He stepped back and looked left along the wall. It was surprising how often doors were alarmed but windows were simply left locked. Nothing to the left, but a few metres along to the right was a big window. He moved down and looked at it. No problem. He looked at his watch and then moved on to the next building. Get the basic recce over with, he thought, and go in on the way back.

The next building was the first of four two-storey structures each with a balcony running round the upper floor and fire escape-type exposed stairs at each corner. Muted music and laughter came from the upper level of the second building, but nearer Scott a door opened and light flooded out on to the landing and he settled back into the shadows.

The man began to move down the steps towards him.

Tilby stood, his back to the mantelpiece, his hands in his pockets, his head cocked forward and peered over the tops of his half-lens glasses. Dr Peter Morris sat in the armchair leafing through a special file put together by Century House. It contained enough material to present their case powerfully, either standing alone or in support of other devices. Morris was an academic and would appreciate and value the varied sources and the research, all of it self-validating, so Tilby had opted to let the file do the talking. Morris looked up at him, his finger keeping his place between the pages of the file. The look was mixed — disbelief, anger and suspicion.

'Take as long as you like,' Tilby said.

'I don't need to finish it to take the inference,' Morris said, thinking, Jesus they have done it, I was right all along. Something is dreadfully wrong here, and has been for months, maybe years.

'Why don't you finish it, anyway?' Tilby said soothingly. Morris continued reading, this time pulling a pencil from his pocket and making marginal notes.

Tilby smiled and walked to the table, poured himself another drink. It had been a little difficult getting Morris to come to the house and Tilby had to use his connections with his old college at Oxford. That had been his previous life, before he had discovered that he actually liked intelligence and was rather good at the backroom end of what was a thankless, nasty job. Simply, he liked the challenge to his intellect. It was a game with huge stakes and far more challenging than a group of hungover undergraduates grappling with European history in the Napoleonic period.

Twenty minutes later Morris was finished.

'Well?' he said.

'Well? . . . No. Things are far from well. Would you like a drink now?'

'What do you want of me?' Morris asked.

'I want – we want,' he corrected himself, 'we want you to digest what you have read and act on it. Want is the wrong word for it. Suggest. We suggest that we are correct in our assumptions. We also suggest you are in a position, if you believe us to be correct, to do something about it. To do Ireland and your people a service.'

'Look, I suspected something like this. Shit, a year ago, but I'm trying to take all this in. Don't pressgang me into anything.'

'God forbid,' Tilby replied. 'No. You must think about it. But rest assured you are one of a few. A very few.'

'Why me?' Morris asked.

'You have been away. They, whoever they are, won't have you marked yet. You are still young and you have ready access to groups of people who will also help. Universities are marvellous places. They are full of people ready to defend an ideal. You are respected. Not only within the confines of the university, but within the community. Thinking men and women know your name. And to do what needs doing you will need the support of thinking people. This will not be the masses in the streets. Not unless you want masses of bodies.'

'Will it come to that?'

'We think upwards of thirty billion dollars have been spent. No one, no individual, no nation would allow that kind of investment to be compromised. They will have plans in place for the day they are caught with their hands in the cookie jar. They will rationalize that they have paid for everything. They will not accept that there are some things you can't buy. Nations fall into that list along with love, everlasting life and a decent Cornish pasty.' Tilby sat down opposite Morris, holding his drink, his legs crossed. 'Make no mistake. They will have contingency plans.'

'Who are they?'

'Not sure. But whoever they are they're here, and they are here in strength. Some will have blended in, bona fide reasons for being here, others will be underground. The planners? The strategists? Somewhere far away. We have followed the financial slick upwind as far as Liechtenstein and Zurich. '

'You have used the word "invasion" in several places in this document,' Morris said, holding it up.

'We have.'

'Is that word used in its correct definition?'

'We believe so. This is an invasion. It's a subtle start, but no more or less so than the Trojan horse. This gift is jobs and money and an instant appeal that will keep the eye off the trap door as the soldiers drop out.'

'Assuming you are correct . . .' Morris began.

'Of course,' Tilby said smoothly.

'What is the role you see me playing?'

Tilby looked at him. Morris had taken off his glasses and was cleaning them with his tie. He seemed impossibly young for what they were asking him to do, more like a schoolboy.

'We think you should help establish and lead a resistance effort.'

The man had reached the bottom of the steps and was on

the concrete ground-level walkway heading towards him. Scott, his back to the wall in the recess had nowhere to go. Soundlessly he slipped his gloves off. If it came to it he would use his hands, but even as he pocketed the gloves he prayed that the man would walk past and not look into the dark recess. If he did he would have to be dealt with and that would mean the whole covert nature of the reconnaissance would be destroyed. The man stopped six feet away by a door and pulled some keys from his pocket. As he did so a slip of paper fell to the ground.

He opened the door and stepped inside. A light came on as the door swung back on its hinges and Scott moved forward, scooping up the paper the fellow had dropped and kept moving round the building into the welcoming darkness.

The last of the four two-storey structures was quiet and, suspecting he knew its purpose, he paced its length and width.

Finally he looked down the road that ran parallel to the runway.

At the far end he could see the silhouette of the old tower against the night sky and beyond it a radio mast, its red anti-collision light clear in the dark.

He looked at his watch. Time to be moving on. But the hangar first.

He had the window, old and wooden-framed, up on its sash inside a minute and dropped silently down on the inside. The area was an office of sorts, and he settled into a chair at one of the three desks and holding his small red-beamed torch in his mouth began to read what he could find on the desk top. He photographed some of it with a tiny automatic camera as he went, screening the flash with his body. There were invoices from local suppliers, inventory forms and a list of some kind. He scrabbled through the waste-bin and kept three scraps of paper, one of them being another list of sorts, the other two containing phone numbers. Finally he let himself through a steel door into the hangar proper. Tarpaulined mounds covered the floor from one end to the other and he moved forward absolutely silently. There was a picket outside the main doors at the other end. He could hear his feet scrape on the concrete of the apron. He lifted the first of the tarpaulin covers and slid underneath. Five minutes later he was out and moving back towards the fence.

Morris was appalled. 'All this investment. The product they manufacture and are sending out. Where is it going? This stuff suggests that the investment is real.'

'Oh, it's real,' Tilby said. 'These people are very shrewd businessmen. Ireland has a highly educated, comparatively inexpensive workforce. It's close to major markets. We traced some of the shipments leaving Cork. They were bound for the Gulf. Circuit boards and compact discs. Genuine exports into markets rigged, but very happy to buy the merchandise. That's the Trojan horse, the carrot, and they will leverage it when the time comes. The real threat lies underneath. The stick. The military that will reinforce the issue. That's what you people must address.'

'I'm no more qualified to lead a resistance than I am to fly to the moon,' Morris said, aghast.

'You won't be alone,' said Tilby reassuringly. 'This is not going to be a campaign of personalities. This is patriotism pure and simple. There will be a handful of you, a steering group, co-ordinators if you like. If the campaign goes on for extended periods then a natural leader will emerge. It may be you, or one of the committee, it may not. It doesn't really matter. What matters is that we help you people get something going.'

'But I wouldn't know where to start!' Morris protested.

'That's okay,' Tilby said with a grin. 'We do!'

'Predictably,' Morris countered.

'Look. All we suggest now is that you come to a planning meeting we are hosting for you. Meet some of the people you will have on your side. You will have input at every stage, as will the others we have identified. Each of you will bring particular skills and understanding.'

'Who are they?' Morris asked, looking up.

Tilby ignored the question.

'Look, if you are asking me to get involved . . .'

'You talk as if we were asking you to *get involved* with a British effort,' Tilby interrupted. 'That is not the case. We are suggesting that it might be a good idea if you people formed a resistance network. The problem is here in Ireland. We will help, but it's your problem.' He let that sink in for a few seconds before continuing, 'Others are in now. If you are in then you will meet them there and they will be the only contact you have with any other groups. From then on you will have your own people. It has to be that way. If one group is compromised then the others are safe. That philosophy extends downward with each team.'

'Ironic, isn't it?' Morris said softly. 'The British, for so long the enemy of Irish republicanism, now want to help us protect it.'

'Not so strange,' Tilby replied. 'Time has moved on. We are now neighbours and friends.'

'I want to think about it.'

'Of course,' Tilby responded. 'But tell no one. No one anything. Do I make myself understood?'

'With crystal clarity,' Morris replied drily.

Scott was back in Dublin just after three o'clock the following morning and he went straight to a call box he had seen near the small hotel he intended staying in. He fed in a coin and dialled the number.

The call was answered on the second ring.

'Yes.' He recognized the voice. It was Tilby.

'It's me.'

'Go ahead.'

Scott read the number off the phone face. 'Call me back.'

Thirty seconds later it rang.

'You are either very early or very late,' Tilby began nonchalantly.

'We need to meet. Soon,' Scott said.

'Oh. I see. Something for mother?'

Scott chuckled. 'Yeah. You could say that.'

'Why don't we meet where we met earlier. Do you remember the place?'

'I'll be twenty minutes.'

He parked his car five hundred yards from the house and walked the rest of the way. The street was in darkness and as he lifted a hand to knock at the door it opened.

'Come in,' Persse said.

'I thought you didn't want me coming here,' Scott began.

'Doesn't matter any more. We are moving tomorrow. Tilby's in the kitchen. Come through.'

Tilby sat in one of the kitchen chairs, a pot of coffee on the table in front of him and a cup in his hand. He was still dressed in the same suit and tie he had been wearing when Scott had seen him before driving down to Clonmel.

He held up the pot. 'Coffee?'

'Thanks,' Scott answered, taking one of the spare chairs and putting his small pack on another.

'So what have you got?' Tilby asked passing him a cup.

'I had a shufti round the airfield we spoke about. I think we know who the villains are. Some of them at least.'

Tilby's thick eyebrows lifted as he peered at Scott over his glasses.

'Do go on, dear boy,' he said.

Scott produced the tiny camera from the pack.

'There's a roll of film for the analysts here. I found some vehicles. Carefully hidden under tarps in an old hangar. BMTs and BTRs. The markings have been painted over. A fresh coat of drab olive. But the papers and internal stencils are Arabic. And I found a flag on the inside. Syrian.'

'B whats?' Tilby asked holding up a hand.

'BMTs and BTRs. Infantry Fighting Vehicles. Soviet built. All the Warsaw Pact have used them, and a good deal of the rest of the world with them. There were twenty-two of them.'

'Maybe they were . . .'

'Fuelled and ready to go. Maintenance records indicate servicing as recent as yesterday. Ordnance in the racks.'

'Ah. What does this mean? To you as a soldier?' Tilby asked.

'It's not my place to judge. You have your . . .'

'Amuse me,' Tilby cut in.

'Okay. IFVs are never used in isolation. They are used to move troops. Rapidly. Into and out of action. They are invariably used in support of heavy armour.'

'Good God! You mean tanks?'

'Yes. Tanks are very good as long as they are in open country and can keep moving. As soon as they slow or stop they must be supported and defended by men on the ground. Those men are moved in IFVs.'

'Never alone?'

'Some countries use them for riot control. They can be used to get troops quickly to trouble spots, but generally they are up where the serious action is taking place. The newer ones are equipped for service in an NBC environment.' Scott paused and took a good mouthful of his coffee. 'Twenty-two? That's more than a company in our terms. It's most of a battalion for the Sov style. If it's a battalion it's quite possible that their role is support. Support of something bigger. Combined ops. Modern battles move so fast that if infantry are to keep up, and they are essential because you can't hold ground without them, they must be able to move as fast as the tanks. On that basis I would say there are ten or twelve MBTs not far

73

away, and there are certainly other vehicles.'

'Like what?' Persse asked blowing smoke out as he spoke.

'Recovery vehicles, command vehicles, maintenance trucks, flatbeds, tankers. There is unbelievable paraphernalia in keeping even light armour in the field. There may also be an air defence variant somewhere. An IFV fitted with radar and a SAM battery or a light AA cupola. All armour is vulnerable to attack from above. Their crews are shit scared of aircraft.'

'Could whoever — we'll get to that in a minute — have twenty-two of these things here to use as a show of force? Red Army style?' Tilby asked.

'What? Like in Prague?'

Tilby nodded.

'I guess so, but tanks are even better for that. To most they are very big, very noisy, and very scary. Even sitting parked somewhere.'

'What about people?'

'Found four buildings big enough for barracks, but only one seemed occupied. It was big enough for about two hundred men. Pickets at two points that I saw. Vehicle patrols cover the fence line at some time. I didn't see any, but the tyre tracks are deep and fresh.'

'Right. You say a Syrian flag.'

'Yeah.'

'You would know . . . ?' Tilby probed gingerly.

Scott's look said I know it's your job to ask and it's mine to answer, but I do know what the hell I am doing. 'Red along the top, white centre, black base, two green stars on the white panel.'

'Jolly good,' Tilby said. 'Well, get it written up for the gnomes at Century House. Persse is going back in the morning. He can take it for you.'

'It's time to get some more people on the ground here. We now know what we're looking for . . .' Scott began.

'Lots of men with good suntans and moustaches,' Persse finished drily. Syrians? he thought. Third World country at best. They don't have the money to mount a thing like this, he thought. Both he and Tilby were sceptical. In their business layers were the norm. One layer concealed the next and so on. It would be almost inconceivable to have discovered the nature of the enemy from a stencil on a door. Too easy.

'The armour,' Scott said. 'We need to find the armour. If they have MBTs here it will tell us what type of action they are planning. If the biggest bit of kit is a BTR that's another story.'

'How many would you advise?' Tilby asked.

'Twenty or so. A couple of weeks. That would allow us to cover a lot of ground. My people. They know where to look.'

'I'll get on to Century House tomorrow. In the meantime the PM has moved down to his constituency. Limerick. The ambassador's meeting was a lemon, the PM was very cagey, very tense, but he did hand the recognition device over. We'd like you to get in and have a chat with him. Tomorrow night. Then if the back-room boys want you back for a debrief on the Clonmel thing we'll let you know. You have been cleared to go in on your own.'

You must have some record, young man, Tilby thought, as Scott took the envelope. He had never seen or heard of Whitehall ever giving a junior officer carte blanche to hold a conversation with a head of state. It was all a bit Riley Ace of Spies for him.

'Essentially you are to do what you have to do to get him alone and hit him with the issues. Persse will be down that way. He will organize transport and get you as close to the area as he can.' Tilby pushed a sheet of paper across. 'This is a narrative. The latest we have on him and the family and a few suggested questions or angles. Read it now and then I will answer any questions you have.'

Scott read the four typed pages quickly. The summary was succinct and complete.

'This is enough.'

'Record the conversation if you can. The lab people will want to stress test his voice.'

'If I can,' Scott replied warningly. They all knew the residence would be wired.

'This,' Tilby said, passing a second envelope, 'is as much as we can muster on the layout of the house. Most of it's from a women's magazine who liked the way it was decorated.'

Scott shook the contents clear. It was a series of clippings and photocopies.

Persse grinned. 'The pictures are a tribute to Laura Ashley bedrooms and the Provençal Mexican-look kitchen. I guess that's what you rely on when you have budgets like we do. The Americans would have computer aided walk-through diagrams in full colour, and would have used a satellite for something.'

'I'll have a look at these later. What's the alarm?'

'Something fitted by the local Chubb people in the mid-eighties and upgraded by the police two years ago. Pressure pads in the drawing-room and dining-room doorways, laser alarms in both those rooms and the sun room at the back. Nothing in the kitchen that we know of. Lastly, this is the recognition device.' He passed a carefully torn photograph across the table. This half was a young boy astride a bicycle, with a hand and wrist from someone larger off to the right, in the missing half, holding the handlebars.

'Who's this?' Scott asked.

'The son . . . the one no one has seen for some time.'

Before Scott had left young O'Connell and his friends for Birr he had set up a few procedures. One of those was that there would be no regular meeting. If they needed to get

76

word to him then they would advise one of their group who would be the contact point. Scott left that to them and they had chosen Aisling, so it was the pretty dark-haired girl whom Scott telephoned when he arrived back in Limerick.

'Have you somewhere to stay?' she asked.

'No. I'll get a B and B somewhere'

'There's a room here. We can talk,' she finished pointedly.

An hour later he was sitting in their flat.

'The other two are away. Touring vineyards in Spain. I haven't told David you phoned. You said not to.'

'Good,' he said. 'What have you got?'

'Well, it wasn't my idea and I haven't met him, but there is someone David thinks we should approach.'

'Go on,' Scott replied, rubbing his eyes. He was tired. No sleep the night before and very little the night before that.

'He is a farmer. Down in Kerry. He is a solid local type. Wife, family, successful dairy operation. He is also a man with a reputation. Apparently he simply will not put up with injustice. The type to solidly, in his own time, take on city hall and win.'

'Who found him?'

'David had a friend. Graduated last year and now works for this chap. Apparently he is about to start creating a fuss about a compulsory purchase. We think it's the same people who have bought the rest and that makes him on our side.'

'Could be,' Scott said carefully. 'What's the fuss about?'

'A compulsory purchase of his wife's land. Some little stone cottage and a few acres of rocks left by her mum. Apparently some big aerials appeared there. O'Sullivan reckons they will never last the first winter storm, and so if that was the reason his wife had to give up her little house then it's bullshit. He is going to start giving out about it.'

'Aerials. I'd like to see those. Can we get him to sit still till we can do some checking? If he is going to be any good to us then we don't want him drawing attention to himself.'

'Not sure about that,' Aisling replied. 'We can try.'

'Give me his name and address. I'll get my people looking at him.' She went into the kitchen to find her handbag and when she returned she handed him the slip of paper. He read it and then screwed it up and threw it into the ashtray.

'Forget the name. If he's in he's in. If he's not then you don't need to remember it.'

Aisling nodded. 'Do you want something to eat?'

'Only if you are. I can get something up the road,' he responded.

She smiled. 'It's no problem. Look. I know you don't tell people your name, but we can't go on with nothing. How about I make up a name for you?'

'And what might that be?' he asked.

'Oh, I don't know,' she smiled again. 'How about Conor? You look like a Conor. Dark and mysterious.'

She prepared food for them both. Minestrone soup heated while she broke chunks of fresh bread from the loaf and peeled fruit into a bowl. They ate in silence and when she stood to make coffee he looked at her, his blue eyes softening for a second.

'My name is Aiden.'

When she returned he was asleep in the chair, so she took a blanket from the hall cupboard and covered him. She then sat opposite drinking her coffee and watched him sleep, angry at herself for being prepared to guard him, guard his rest like a broody chicken simply because he had told her his name, but not wanting to leave him there on his own, the familiar tingly feeling in her tummy. Resisting the urge to tuck him in, she settled back into the old armchair with a book.

In Hereford, England, twenty-two men from the Special Air Service regiment made preparations to leave for Ireland. The group, comprising seven three-man teams and

78

an intelligence officer, would arrive in ones and twos over the course of the following day. Until the arrival of their 'boss', Major Busby Grogan, who was in London attending a detailed briefing, they would settle in, organize transport, find somewhere to stay and get the feel of the place.

In London the senior CIA man at the American Embassy had been in the meeting most of the afternoon. Quickly and succinctly briefed on what the British Intelligence people were working on, and having seen the bulk of the evidence himself, he shelved his disbelief and asked for the meeting to be suspended until he could get more senior people involved from their headquarters in Langley, Virginia. The following day seven people arrived, three from CIA Langley and four from the State Department, including a personal emissary from the US Secretary of State Edwin Marsteller.

Sir Huw Tristan-Carter, Great Britain's ambassador to the United Nations, received a telephone call asking him to return to London for a briefing at the same time as the American emissary's arrival in London. Sir Huw was not the usual career diplomat. He had joined the Foreign Office late after an exemplary early career as a strategist and negotiator with Jardine Matheson in Hong Kong. He had been offered the governorship of the colony, had accepted, done a brilliant job and three years later had returned to Britain heavily tipped to be the next man in the British chair on the Security Council.

Sir Huw was a hard-liner, a gifted if plain speaker, a negotiator, a man who pulled favours, drove deals, made things happen. He was also a keen collector of jade and he received the recall with pleasure. He would take his wife with him and make sure they had time to look in at Sotheby's, where the new oriental collection was gathering for the winter auction. He mused over the call after putting down the receiver, trying to fathom what was going on. Usually it was all utterly predictable, the media exposing the issues hours or even days before they became a subject of conversation in the halls and corridors of the UN, and that was well before he was usually briefed to make a British position known. But this time nothing. Not a clue.

At London's Heathrow airport Andre Hyland, the Irish army officer and centre on Ireland's national rugby side, sat in civilian kit awaiting the dawn and his flight home. He had just spent two months with the Irish contingent on the UN peacekeeping mission in Macedonia and was going back to Ireland to rejoin his unit.

He was rather pleased. His promotion had come through, and while he wasn't the youngest commandant in the Irish Defence Force, the rapid promotion said much about his future. He was now very much on the fast track and being groomed for bigger things. Watching the crowds move through Terminal One he saw a familiar face and smiled. Robby Dugan, the young Scots Black Watch captain and his nemesis on the rugby field was walking quickly towards the baggage carousel with a pretty girl at his side. He thought about wandering over to have a chat, but thought better of it. He would lose his seat and Dugan and the girl looked to be in a hurry. At one point Dugan looked his way. Their eyes met and Hyland grinned and made a flicking motion with his wrist, his fingers curled round to touch his thumb. Dugan, recognition dawning, grinned back and gave the Irishman two fingers. They waved and went their separate ways. The next time they met recognition would be neither so swift nor so pleasurable.

In Dublin four men broke into a flat in a South Side house and subdued the occupant with simple threat and a blow that broke his cheekbone. They taped his mouth shut and bundled him, terrified, into the back of a waiting car. Kevin Hargadon was never seen again.

## 3

Persse drove like a professional, with economy of movement, clear judgement and never exceeding the speed
limit. Beside him Scott, a small bag at his feet, sat in
silence. It was coming up to that time of the morning well
before the dawn, when the senses are at their lowest ebb,
that burglars and attacking armies favour.

'There's a place down in Dingle that we should see.
Aerials. Big transmitter towers too, by the sound of it.
There's also a man down there that might interest us.
His wife owned the land they built on. He is very pissed off.
He's older than the kids here, a farmer. Sounds the right
type.'

'Who is he?' Persse asked.

'Patrick O'Sullivan. His farm is off the Castleisland road
towards a place called Scartaglen.' Scott fished round in
the bag at his feet. 'Do you want a sandwich?'

Persse looked across at him, one eyebrow raised, surprised that the soldier had thought about bringing food.
'Yes please.'

Scott passed him two wrapped in greaseproof paper.

The job on the PM's place had been put back by a day, so
he spent the time covering areas nearby and returned to
the flat at nine that night. Aisling was out, but he left a
note and went straight to sleep.

She had woken him just before one o'clock. Some time
while he had slept she had cut sandwiches, thick, sensible
ones filled with egg mayonnaise and cold ham, and she
had made thermos flasks of coffee. There was also a towel
in the bathroom and the water was plentiful and hot when

he stepped under the shower. Once in clean clothes he felt like a new man and when he had laid out his kit on her living-room floor, the lights on and the curtains drawn, he had not asked her to leave while he checked it. There was a set of grand master keys that would open any door with standard locks. There were picking tools, a roll of insulating tape, pliers, sixty feet of nylon line and the ultimate burglar's tool, a jemmy bar. This particular bar was ultra lightweight and made of advanced polymers. There was also a small black electronic device with a meter. It was a bug finder, an audio counter-measure device for finding hidden microphones, and finally a small tape recorder of the kind used by executives for dictation, but twice the weight and seventeen times the price. This tiny Aiwa machine could record conversations fifty feet away. The entire pack only weighed five pounds and if anyone was caught in possession of the array by a policeman it was deemed proof of intent to break and enter and sufficient cause for arrest.

'I spoke to London last night. Your suggestion has been met. Some of your mates are arriving tomorrow. The officer who briefed you when you came in?'

'Yes.'

'He's coming too.'

Scott nodded. That meant he had a senior officer in country, but command in the SAS was a fluid concept. They would often defer command down the line because a man of more junior rank might have skills or experience that made him more suitable to command that particular phase of the operation. He would wait and see. Grogan could leave him alone or call him in to work with the squadron element. He could even leave him in command, but that decision would have been made back at Hereford by the colonel.

Colin Mahoney, the Taoiseach of the Republic of Ireland,

kept a residence in his constituency. The house, originally a farm dwelling, was at the end of a long gravel driveway that left the road and meandered up a hill. The drive was lined with trees and there was a newer gatehouse built by the police where it met the road. As the two men drove past they saw the police vehicle parked behind the gatehouse.

'We want the next left,' Persse said. 'After the trees.'

'How close can you get me?' Scott asked.

'According to the map it's a mile or so from the second bend in the road. That's a mile across farmland. Anything closer and we'll be rumbled. That way in will bring you up to the house's northern aspect.' A few minutes later Persse pulled the car to a halt in a lay-by.

Scott got out and walked round to the boot as Persse pulled the opening catch from inside and then got out himself.

'I'll move off and wait somewhere. Make a couple of calls,' he said. 'If I'm not here when you get back then return in an hour and then each hour after that for two more hours. If I'm still not here then I'm fucked. Make your own way in.'

'I'll be three hours at most,' Scott replied. 'There's coffee in the flask. Save me some.'

Persse held up a smaller flask, metal and shiny in the moonlight, grinning. 'This beats the shit out of plain coffee on a dark morning. Laced with a touch of the navy.' He took a swig and offered it to Scott.

The SAS man shook his head.

The Gardai in the grounds had fallen into a routine, the trap of bored men on patrol. Even the dog with the big handler seemed bored. Scott timed them past his point behind the kitchen four times and each was exactly the same. Six minutes. He let them go past him and moved up to the house, a fleeting shadow over the dark grass.

The kitchen door was every thief's dream. A tired Union two-lever stood under a Chubb snub lock, and both moved silently under the turn of the grand master keys. He stood for a second in the kitchen, sweeping his hooded red torch-beam round the floor looking for a dog's bowl. There had been no mention of a pet in the article or briefing notes but better to be sure. There was nothing. He moved into the hall and took the stairs two at a time, silently and light on his feet like a cat, his balaclava down over his face.

The master bedroom was the door to the right at the head of the stairs and he went straight to it. It was slightly ajar, left the way parents leave a door to hear a child's cry in the night.

He eased it back a bit further and crossed to the bed, pulling the half picture from his pocket, and raising the balaclava as he got closer.

Mahoney slept on the right, his larger form obvious in the dark. Scott moved back to the windows and as quietly as he could drew the curtains all the way.

He then moved back to the bed, switched on the bedside light and slipped a hand over the sleeping man's mouth.

He woke suddenly, frightened and strong and Scott's other hand moved like a striking viper holding his half of the picture up close to Mahoney's eyes. The man settled back as Scott dropped the photo and put his finger to his lips indicating he wanted silence. Mahoney nodded and Scott slowly raised his hand from the prime minister's mouth. He then moved back from the bed and dropped his pack silently to the floor. He pulled out the ACM box and began to move round the room, watching the sensitive needle swing. It shifted to the right suddenly. Scott moved forward and peered around the rim of the dressing-table mirror. A small beige button-sized device was stuck to the edge of the decorative frame. He kept moving and when the needle swung again he found a second device in the telephone by the bed.

The woman slept on.

He looked back to Mahoney and pointed to the bug in the phone and put his finger back to his lips. The prime minister's expression of shock gave in to one of resignation and exhaustion, like a man close to giving up.

He didn't know, Scott thought. He hadn't realized they had done the house. He pulled a pad and pen from his pocket and scribbled, 'We need to talk'. Mahoney shook his head, his eyes pleading, saying leave us alone please.

Scott wrote 'NOW!' in capital letters, his own expression firm, holding up the photo of the missing son to drive his point home.

Mahoney finally nodded. He pointed upwards and made stair-climbing motions with his fingers. Scott nodded and held out a hand for Mahoney to lead the way.

The stairs to the attic dropped from the ceiling in the third bedroom and were down. Boxes that someone had been moving earlier were on the floor and Mahoney stepped over them and began to climb the steep steps as quietly as he could. Scott followed and as they reached the top he brushed past Mahoney and levelled the ACM meter and began to sweep the walls and beams. It was clear.

He turned to Mahoney.

'My name is Scott,' he whispered. 'I am here to help.'

'I don't know what you people are talking about,' Mahoney whispered back. 'Just leave us alone.'

'Bullshit,' Scott hissed. 'You give in to these pricks and you will never see your son again. Neither will any of the others. And you will have betrayed Ireland.'

Mahoney's eyes widened briefly and his shoulders slumped. 'You know?'

'We know,' Scott replied, this time in Irish, 'and we want to help.'

'You are Irish?'

'My mother's from County Offaly.' Scott smiled. 'I'm Irish enough to know when things aren't right. London can see it too.'

Mahoney stood his ground. 'Just go. Leave us.'

'You can't deal with this on your own or you would have. Your hands are tied and there is a gun to your head. Only a fool says no to a friend's offer of help and you are no fool, Colin Mahoney.'

He was weakening. Scott could see it in his eyes.

'So do you want to help your son come home?'

'What . . . what are you offering? They have our children. Not just my son. Many others. We . . .'

'We will get the hostages back. And we will help you. But we must know who we are dealing with.'

'You are sure of this? The British government's position?'

'Absolutely. Furthermore,' Scott said, not knowing if it was true but understanding America's importance in Ireland, 'the White House are aware that something is amiss and we are briefing them constantly.'

'I don't even know where to start,' Mahoney said, rubbing his eyes and sitting down on an old cabin trunk.

'We must set up somewhere my people can talk to you in private. That means understanding who is watching you. How many, where, who is in charge.'

'I wish I knew,' he muttered. 'They have a man in my office now, and several in the building. There was the man who told me they had taken Tom. I haven't seen him for three or four months. He was a one,' he finished bitterly.

'How do you mean?' Scott asked.

'Smart. Smooth. Confident. Definitely had authority. You learn to recognize that even when they try to play it down. He was no simple messenger.'

'What was his name?'

'Didn't say and no indications.'

'What did he look like? Describe him.'

'Dark, swarthy, good-looking once, but now getting heavy like all of us. Mediterranean. Spanish. Cypriot maybe.'

'Arab?' Scott asked.

'Could be. But Lebanese or Egyptian Arab. Looked like a banker rather than a thin hawkish desert type. Does that sound silly?'

'Not at all. It all helps,' Scott replied.

'Had a fellow with him. Younger, slimmer. Hard eyes. Hard like granite. Stood like a soldier. You know, chest out, arms behind his back.'

'Not a bodyguard?' Scott probed.

'No. I have them. You can pick them. They move constantly, their eyes are everywhere, jackets are unbuttoned. This man was calm. Icy calm. He was almost there to observe. That was the feeling I got. An observer watching for his own reasons.'

'The one in the office. Is he always there?'

'Yes. He brings me a letter from Tom once a fortnight or so.'

'What about the car?'

'Still have my driver and the escort of course. I'm not sure if we are followed.'

'Difficult. Your detail would tag them,' Scott said. 'They may well rely on the fact they have your son to keep you honest for a few minutes in the car each day.'

'They didn't tag you,' Mahoney said drily.

'I hope not. Anyway. This house is wired like a sound studio. They won't be far away. I want one of the letters from Tom. For paper analysis.'

'Got them downstairs.'

'Good. Now then, this is important. When did they take him? What happened that spooked them?'

Mahoney smiled. It was a tired, weakened version of the smile that had won many an election.

'We caught the buggers red-handed. Young chap called

McCaffrey in the Finance Department. He was doing a study on foreign ownership. Specifically the Germans and their holiday homes and cottages. They now spend significant DMs here. Enough to warrant a separate category in planning terms. Well, he stumbled on too many transactions that ended nowhere. Corporations buying not only companies but private properties. Odd tracts of land, that sort of thing. That raised the whole issue of foreign investment in industry. He put two and two together.'

'And cried alarm,' Scott murmured.

'No. Got killed,' Mahoney said flatly.

'Say again.'

'Dead. They showed me a picture of his body. A little lesson for anyone who thought they weren't serious about the hostages. I don't know who they are. But they are extremely ruthless. Clever too. They have thought this through. There is a whole batch of passports missing from the printer. Twenty thousand or so I am told. They have them. They now control the issuing of those documents. God knows how many of them are now walking round with Irish passports. With those, and the correct procedures followed, you understand, they can claim this is an internal Irish problem.'

Scott looked at his watch. It would be light soon. He needed to be well away by dawn.

'Then give them an Irish solution,' he said, his eyes flat and hard and his voice laced with menace, 'Are you prepared to meet with my people again?'

'Providing we don't risk harm to the hostages. Yes.'

Scott was pleased. The meeting had gone well. Now it was time to get things on a more formal footing. Make it easy for Whitehall to allow further meetings and a stepped-up intelligence-gathering programme.

'Can I tell my people that you are asking for help? Officially, in your capacity as Taoiseach?'

Mahoney paused and looked away, thinking of his son and the threat of death hanging over him.

'Sir,' Scott said, feeling Irish and wanting to help, but knowing that it had to be asked for. 'Ireland is an independent nation. If the British . . . if we are to help we must be asked to do so. By you or by a majority of the Senate or the President. There is no time for niceties. Do you think that if it comes down to it any of you will be allowed to act? People will be disappearing in the night. Frightened to speak out. There may be camps. Detention centres. By the time you can run due process according to the constitution they will have stepped up whatever they have planned.'

'I know that, young man. I was studying European history before you were born,' Mahoney replied frostily.

'Well?'

'Well what?'

'Sir, I am a serving officer in Her Majesty's armed forces, and authorized by the Secretary of State for Foreign Affairs to bring a message back from you. Do you have a message?'

Mahoney's shoulders slumped, the statement he was about to make at last admission that things were out of his control for ever.

'I do,' he said, his tone the exhausted delivery of a man almost beaten as Scott lifted the microphone and checked the tape was turning.

'For the record, for historical reasons, for my personal political beliefs in Irish republicanism and the sentiments of the overwhelming majority of the people of Ireland, there is no government that I would wish to appeal to less than the British government. However, given the extraordinary situation we find ourselves in, the Government of Ireland will be pleased to accept any help offered from friendly nations to help her . . .' he paused, thinking about the words, the emphasis heavy when he continued '. . . restore Irish constitutional law and order and the independent freedom of her people should it become necessary.'

'I will pass the message on,' Scott said, putting the tiny tape recorder into one of the voluminous pockets of his zip-up jacket. 'The next time we get in touch will be in your car. Check down between the seats,' he said, thinking fast, 'and if you want to talk to us wear a yellow tie.'

'Here's the tape. He's willing to talk again.'

'Good. I spoke to the office earlier,' Persse said. 'We're to drop this off and head down and see this farmer type tonight. They've also identified a phone number off one of the papers you nicked at the airfield. It's in Limerick.'

'That was quick.'

'I was back there by nine A M. Anyway, as we're here they want me to have a look. You can come along for the ride if you like.'

He looked across at Scott. It was getting hairy now. People who could deploy armoured fighting vehicles, kill a ministry employee, kidnap the children of half the country's elected officials and bug the prime minister's home with impunity would kill again without compunction and they knew it. This was bread and butter for Scott. He was a professional soldier, an officer in arguably the world's finest special forces unit. A man who expected to have to kill in the line of his work and equally expected that people would try to kill him. Someone he had never met. Not to be taken personally. That's what war is all about. A peacetime deployment of an SAS squadron was open acknowledgement that it was time for direct action.

But for Persse it was a step across a narrow line. Intelligence officers don't kill each other. The 'wet' work is never discussed, carried out by others from another building and only when the situation is desperate and where no other alternative exists. He had only ever heard of one occasion. It was in Cyprus in '71, when a particularly brutal multiple killing had shocked the intelligence community. They had a rogue and a chap was flown in from England to deal with him. A small, thin man in a cheap grey suit and with a tuned Walther 9mm, he had been taken to the house where they suspected the culprit to be hiding. He had walked out three minutes later, the job done.

But never by real intelligence people. It was the unwritten rule. It was counter-productive. Assets walked. Networks dried up. And Persse didn't like violence. He was never much good at it. They were always stronger than him, or faster, or whatever. The courses were always tough and he just scraped through the test sessions by using a mixture of cunning and nastiness. The last time he had been in the Cotswolds house where the sessions were conducted he had nearly electrocuted his opponent. He could never have handled him with the martial arts or unarmed combat they were taught, so he disconnected the two-bar heater and gave him the direct current as he touched the door handle. He passed, just, because it was him that walked out and that was all that mattered in the long run. The next grade would take him out of the field, but for the moment he was exposed to the opposition's heavies and without a couple of the minders, the forward pack, from the basement at Century House he wanted someone riding shotgun if it got nasty.

'Want to come?' he asked casually.

'Sure,' said Scott, yawning.


They found Pat O'Sullivan in his barn. The old stone building had been converted and there was now a service bay for the farm vehicles and work benches. Shelves of spares and small oil-stained cardboard boxes covered one wall and on the floor an old compressor chugged away.

O'Sullivan stood, the air line in his hand, blowing compressed air down a fuel line that obviously came off the large piece of equipment that lay disassembled on the bench.

'Pat O'Sullivan?' Persse asked.

He looked up and then back down at the fragments of muck and oil being blown from the line on to a piece of newspaper spread on the floor. Finally he stepped across and shut down the compressor, wiping his hands on a rag.

'Who might you be?' he asked.

'My name is not important,' Persse said cheerfully.

'Well you can fuck off, then. I'm busy.'

Scott forced back a laugh and stepped forward. This was where his Irish half would be useful. 'We need a minute of your time, Patrick,' he said in Irish, 'to talk about a cottage down on the Dingle and the masts the buggers have put up. Then we will be out of your way and you can have that generator running before the evening milking.'

O'Sullivan's eyes narrowed and he walked closer, his size menacing. 'Who are you and what would you be knowing about that?'

'Friends,' Scott said, then switching to English, 'and we will be needing friends soon, all of us. There's more than just the stuff at the cottage, Pat. There's shit everywhere and you know it. They are saying you are going to do something about it. Well so are we. Yer man here is from London. So let's have a cup of tea and a chat.'

'What's London got to do with it?' O'Sullivan asked.

'We are in it,' Persse said, regaining control, 'because they are in Dublin. Where do you think all the jobs are coming from? They have invested huge sums of money. They have bought businesses, houses, land. They have bought people and they have blackmailed others. They are controlling the government. They are everywhere. The Taoiseach's son? The one no one has seen for a few months? They have him somewhere. Along with the children of half the members of the Dáil.' Persse stepped forward till he was inches away from the big farmer. 'You have children. I saw their bikes at the house. Think about it. You. Your family. Others like you. You have the most to lose.' He paused then to let his words sink in. 'Now they say that you are going to have a go. You can't do this one on your own, Pat. We have to do this together.'

There was silence then while Scott and Persse stood and watched the man's face. Finally he spoke.

'How do I know you are not with them?'

'If we were,' said Persse, 'you would be dead. Others are.'

'And how do you know I'm not with them? You wander in here. You tell me your business. You don't know me from Adam.'

'I don't think you are with them. They, whoever they are, are beginning to get a look about them.' Persse stopped and lit a cigarette, inhaling deeply before looking the farmer square in the eyes. 'If you are? Well it's all very well sneaking into a small neutral European country like Ireland and being a clever bastard. It's a bit different taking on the other part of these Isles or their people. It's been tried a lot over the years, so we are rather better organized. If you are one of them? Well, we would go and one of his mates,' Persse jerked a thumb at Scott, 'would come back one dark night. It wouldn't be to explain treason. It wouldn't be to tell you how you have betrayed Ireland and your people. It would be to take care of things. Make sure you didn't finger anyone else. It would probably be to kill you. But then,' Persse smiled, a flat, almost apologetic sort of smile, 'that's conjecture, because I don't get involved in that sort of thing.'

O'Sullivan grinned. 'You better come down to the house. There will be tea about now.'

An hour later they were still there. They had moved from the kitchen into the study when the children came home from school for their lunch. Scott was pleasantly surprised. The room was old and crammed with books. The Yeatses, obligatory in any Irish home, were well thumbed and stood alongside Homer and Aristotle. Popular classics were wedged between reference works and heavy hardback editions of modern novels. A small computer stood incongruously on the flat surface of an antique roll-top desk, and a modem link ran down to the telephone socket on the wall. A fax machine sat on a side cabinet alongside cut crystal decanters, and in the corner two old and much loved fly rods stood awaiting a day on the river. Two large chairs dominated the area either side of the open fireplace and between them on the carpet was a half-finished child's jigsaw puzzle. O'Sullivan stepped over the small cardboard pieces and chose to sit on a log seat at the edge of the hearth, its surface polished by many hours of pressured corduroy, puffing on a briar pipe.

Scott looked up over the fire. There was no Virgin Mary in this room, no crucified Christ on a cross. This man was a pragmatist.

'So that's the situation as we see it,' Persse finished.

'And no one has any idea who they are?' O'Sullivan asked.

'No. We don't know yet. We do know they aren't Irish and we do know they are not western European.'

'What now?'

'Tell us about the cottage and what you saw there,' Scott said.

'Transmitter masts, some big receiving aerials, a couple of satellite dishes. The last bit I didn't recognize. Could have been a microwave link.'

Scott was impressed. 'A microwave link?'

'I hadn't seen one before,' O'Sullivan grinned. 'A mate of mine had a look. He gets *Popular Mechanics*, the ham radio magazines and things. He knows his stuff.'

'Can you show me on a map?'

O'Sullivan got up and left the room. A moment or two later he was back with a road map. 'Here,' he said, pointing. 'There's a turning before the bend. Not marked, but it's there to be sure. Katriona's father put it in himself.'

'Thanks,' Scott said.

'Your friend,' Persse said carefully. 'He can be trusted to be discreet, can he?'

O'Sullivan smiled. 'I know the people hereabouts. He's a Kerry man and he can be trusted. But there's some that would need watching, so you be careful who you go talking to, now.'

'Might be easier if you were to find good solid men. Men who can be relied on when the time comes.'

'It might,' he answered cautiously.

'Think about it,' Persse said. 'I will talk to my people. They have a man from Dublin already.'

'One man? That's bugger all use to anyone. Especially down here,' O'Sullivan muttered.

'Why?'

'It's different as chalk and cheese is Dublin and Kerry. One man? This thing isn't going to be sorted out with fiery speeches from a soap box. Pearse or bloody De Valera all over again. They won't last five minutes. This will be different.'

Good, Scott thought, very good. I like this one. I could work with this one.

'Put it this way,' O'Sullivan said. 'There's local boys who would have an attitude about this.'

'Your "boys",' Persse said. 'Nothing yet. We're not ready. If they catch on to us too soon it will make it twice as difficult to get rid of them.'

O'Sullivan gave a sheepish grin. 'It's a bit late to be saying that now.'

'Why?'

'Well I went back down to the cottage last week. You could say I got tired of waiting for the winter weather.'

'What did you do?'

'A bit of elbow grease with a hacksaw and, as my old father would say, a judicious application. Anything more than a breeze and the whole bloody lot will come crashing down.'

'Did you cover your way?' Scott asked quickly.

'I'm not daft, boy. Glazier's putty in the cuts. Looked just like the cable,' he replied, adding, 'Buggers hadn't even given it a coat of primer.'

'Did you cut direct through? Ninety degrees?'

'No,' the farmer answered. 'Nine cuts, one through each top strand of the cable along about sixteen inches. Windward side only. When it comes down it will be frayed for a couple of feet. Look natural enough.'

This laddie is good, Scott thought. Just how I would have done it.

'Well try and curtail your enthusiasm for the moment.'

'I couldn't have left it, you see. It wouldn't have been right.'

'That's important to you, is it?' Persse asked rather sarcastically and was surprised by O'Sullivan's utterly genuine response.

'It's got to be right. If it isn't, make it so,' he replied seriously, standing up.

As Scott and Persse got into the car a few moments later the farmer leaned in the window. 'If you decide to send one of your mates back on a dark night, tell him he might need some friends. I'll leave out a bottle of whiskey for them.' His tone saying he hadn't forgotten the threat and he didn't give a damn.

'Yeah,' Scott replied drily, 'booby-trapped, no doubt.' O'Sullivan roared with laughter and waved as they drove away.

As they drove northwards on the N21 towards Abbeyfeale, the soft, moist Glanaruddery mountains off to the left, Persse looked across at Scott who was dozing beside him. 'What did you think?'

'Me?' Scott opened his eyes and sat up. 'I liked him. Smart, canny, seems to cover his tracks well enough. I think he is probably quite powerfully motivated. This "got to be right" thing . . . and the country yokel bit is a façade.

He's smart like a fox, extremely well read and I'd reckon formidable at anything he put his mind to.'

'A natural leader, would you say?'

'Definitely.'

'I agree. I think Tilby should meet him somewhere neutral. I think this boyo might just be what we're looking for down this way.'

In Dublin, Peter Morris, already aware of security, walked down to the nearest phone box to the flat they were living in and dialled the London number Tilby had given him.

'Count me in,' he said. Even over public phone lines there would be no mention of anything.

'Good.'

'I want to bring someone over with me,' he continued.

The planning meeting was scheduled for the following Bank Holiday weekend, the first get-together of the new Irish elements with the back-room people.

'Oh?'

'I think he will be invaluable. Take my word for it.'

'Very well. If you think he will fit in our little group, but please consider what you can do if he would rather be elsewhere.'

'He likes us already. It had occurred to him that someone might be putting things on an agenda some weeks ago, but wasn't sure if there was a club of like-minded fellows. If you get my drift.'

'Perfectly,' Tilby replied.

Later that day Kevin Hargadon, the journalist, failed to make his third call in to his controller and Century House reverted to the Dublin embassy asking them to tip off the police that something might be amiss. One of four recently arrived Secret Intelligence Service controllers at the embassy made a note to have assets check his place of work and his home. Standard procedures then said roll up any network immediately. Set the rabbits free. But there was no network, not yet, so they would wait twenty-four hours for news. If no word was forthcoming the person would be posted missing and the stakes would have been raised.

MI6 now had a large presence in Ireland. This was an operation without precedent. Even in the tense, dirty days of the Cold War they only ever ran locals with a handful of staffers in the biggest Soviet bloc countries. But here, without a network of locals at hand and with urgent needs, proxy for the true government, they had done the unthinkable, the dream of every service chief since the war. Possible only because it was Ireland, with common language and customs, they were throwing their own people in at every level.

There were now forty-six SIS staff en route, and thirty-one technical specialists from their sister service MI5 – electronics and telephone engineers, communications experts and the surveillance teams, the watchers. Once the insidious enemy had been found they would mount the counter-watch, following, tapping phones, gathering information to feed back to the planning team and Century House.

The old animosity was largely dead, but at times the relationship between the two services was uneasy and with a clear mandate from Downing Street a senior civil servant had been drafted in to oversee co-operation. The prime minister had made it clear. Any petty territorial disputes or bickering and he would fire everyone concerned. The operation was simply too important.

Persse pulled the car to a halt.

'That's it,' he said, 'the office services place on the ground or the estate agent above.'

They both knew that with more time they could have drafted in the technical resources to do it properly from the start. With a wired building they could monitor conversations, telephone calls and meetings. This really was doing it the hard way.

'Okay. How do you want to play this?' Scott asked.

'Go in and ask about a flat, I suppose. Wait here. If I'm not back in twenty minutes . . .'

'When you get back I'll do the photocopy place,' Scott said.

Persse took a packet of chewing gum from his pocket and popped a couple of pieces into his mouth. Finally he stepped from the car and pulling his coat around him walked up the street to the small two-storey red brick building on the corner.

He was back two minutes later.

'That's a front if ever I saw one. Definitely someone there. I heard them. Wouldn't answer the door and it's not closing time. The sign matches the one in the window, but the phone number is different.'

'How did it feel?' Scott asked driving the car away. To anyone else it would have been an odd question, but intelligence operators often rely on the intangibles, the atmosphere, smells, the feel of a place or a person to support other more obvious indicators.

'Wrong,' Persse answered. 'Didn't feel as though there was a regular presence there, not like a business should, but there was something . . . like I was being watched. I want to come back. What do you think? Tonight?'

'Save it for the techies,' Scott suggested. 'If they were watching you and they were suspicious they'll be half expecting something. That means things getting nasty. I'd keep an eye on it for twenty-four hours.'

Persse nodded.

'It's four now,' Scott said. 'Go home. Get some kip. Relieve me at midnight.'

'Ten,' Persse said. 'I'll be back at ten. But let's change the car first.'

Scott waited in different places. Sometimes in the vehicle,

sometimes out, in a shop nearby or in the window of the pub across the street. In that time he changed his shirt twice and by the time it was truly dark he was wearing a blue jumper. It wouldn't fool a professional, but it would help if the person being watched didn't suspect anything. At eight that evening a man left the building zipping up a windbreaker as he crossed the street. In the dull yellow glow of the streetlights Scott couldn't see much, but tagged him as under thirty, heavy-set, with reddish hair and of average height. He returned twenty minutes later, a wrapped package of what looked like takeaway food under his arm and entered the building. The lights were on in the back half of the upper floor. Finally at nine, bored and tired of waiting he got out of the new car, a Ford estate, and walked down the street. Ten minutes later he was in the small yard-like parking area at the back of the building. Above him like an invitation against the wall stood the main sewerage down pipe. He looked around, made sure no one was looking and quickly scrambled upwards, his treadless tacky-soled climbing shoes noiseless on the brick wall either side of the pipe.

The window looked into what estate agents and brochure copy writers called a studio kitchen. A sink sat beneath the window and on the small ageing Formica draining board stood a two-ring electric cooker. Three dirty cups and some plates were lying in the sink.

The paper wrappers from the meal brought back stood on a small table, but what interested Scott was the wiring that ran into the junction board. They had beefed up the supply for some reason. Scott looked back at the food wrappers. Three cups. Were there three men? He had already discounted women from his thinking: the room was too bare and too functional. And these men were not line soldiers. No soldier would leave dirty kit lying around. They eat and wash their gear immediately.

He looked back over his shoulder. There was a block of

flats a few hundred metres back. Five or six of them would have a view into the other windows, and certainly some-one on the roof could observe much. He dropped to the ground and made his way back to the car.

When Persse arrived back he briefed him.

'One showed himself at eight. Went out for fish and chips or something. Five ten, reddish hair, stocky with a paunch. I had a shufti in the back window.'

Persse flicked a look at him. 'I thought we agreed to wait for the techies?'

'We did. We will need them. I think there are three of them in there. They've upgraded the wiring to heavy three-phase supply from something a lot more basic. I think that means they're running heavy gear in there.'

'Like what?'

'Dunno. Air-conditioning perhaps. Big radios perhaps. They suck up a load of juice,' Scott replied. 'Anyway, there's a block of flats a few hundred yards back behind the building. If the security there is like the rest of Ireland you could walk up on to the roof. A grandstand view of the back of our building.'

'Right. Piss off and get some sleep.'

'I'll be back at four.'

'Negative. They have someone else coming in to baby-sit these arseholes. You're to hook up with Grogan.' Persse handed Scott a slip of paper. 'Here's the meet point. You're booked on a mid-morning flight.'

Just before eleven that night he arrived back at Aisling's flat.

'Don't you ever sleep?' she asked. She was wrapped in an old terry towelling dressing-gown, her crossed arms holding it closed over her nightie. Her hair was loose, falling down over her shoulders in soft dark waves.

'I'm going to now if you will let me have a piece of floor somewhere,' he grinned.

She returned his smile, pleased to see him again. 'Did

you talk to your people about O'Sullivan?'

Scott ignored the question. She knew why. 'Hungry?' she asked.

'Yeah.'

'Serious food or are we into munchability?'

'Munch-a-what?'

'Munchability. Let's see. Hot toast, smeared with thick peanut butter that sticks to the roof of your mouth, or anchovy paste, or boiled egg and soldiers?'

'Ah yes. Understand,' he replied. 'Peanut butter on toast sounds great,' but she knew he was hungry and decided on more.

'Tea?' she asked over her shoulder as she walked to the kitchen.

'Please. Can I have a bath?'

'Of course. Use Fiona's room. It's the one on the left. The bed's a bit lumpy but it's better than the floor. She's away with her parents for a few days.'

Later they sat at the table, Scott, clean with his hair still wet from the shower, dressed in a light tracksuit that was as near as he owned to a dressing-gown, a pot of tea and a plate before him. On the plate was half a French loaf and between its layers were sliced onion, tomato, lettuce and a rump steak cooked rare. Alongside the huge sandwich was a pile of oven chips that had been liberally sprinkled in vinegar. He suddenly realized how hungry he was and began eating.

'David popped round today,' Aisling said.

Scott looked up.

'I didn't tell him you were in town,' she said.

'Good,' he mumbled through a mouthful.

'You don't trust him do you?'

'I trust very few people, but David less than most.'

'Why?' she asked

'He is too chatty by half,' he replied, lifting the sandwich again.

'He can keep a secret when he has to,' she responded pouring tea into her cup then his.

'I doubt it.'

'Oh yes he can,' Aisling said, softly but firmly. 'He lives a secret.'

'What kind of secret?'

'He is homosexual,' she replied.

Scott looked up. Ireland, Catholic in the extreme, was notoriously strait-laced.

'Technically, you can go to jail for it here.'

'I know,' Scott said, feeling marginally better. It also means you can be blackmailed, he thought. But no one who ever worked with a gay could doubt their courage. Far from all being the simpering waif-like things of comedy, two of the bravest men he had ever worked with had been gay. 'I thought you and he were . . . you know.'

'That's what people are supposed to think,' she said.

'Tell him we know and we don't give a stuff.'

'Why? I shouldn't have told you at all.'

'It will take a load off his shoulders. It will build a bond and it will make any attempt to blackmail him harder.'

Aisling nodded. 'Oh well,' she said, stealing a chip from his plate and changing the subject, 'then you might want to use him for your local contact soon. I'm moving.'

'Oh?' he looked up.

'Dublin.' She grinned happily. 'I just got a great job. It's the best law firm in the country.'

'How soon will you be moving? I am too, but the guy who comes in after me will need a contact and a place to stay. David lives with his folks,' he reminded her.

'Next week. I don't start till the first but I need to find a flat or something.'

'Fox Rock?' he asked, naming one of the more exclusive residential areas of Dublin, a grin spreading across his face.

'I wish,' she replied. 'No, something in town. Can't afford much.'

Scott thought quickly. 'You in for the ride all the way?'

'Yes,' she said firmly.

'Sure?'

'Absolutely.'

'If you'll put up a few people every now and then, get something bigger than you need. A couple of spare bedrooms and preferably with an attic. Easy to get to with several ways out. I'll get the funding cleared with my people. In fact, go for the country somewhere south of the city. Beyond Bray or down on the Nass road or near the racecourse or something.'

'North okay?'

'Could be.'

'I know a farmhouse on the Dublin side of Trim. County Meath. It's perfect. Half a mile off the road. Fields and lanes all round. Outbuildings and everything. The land is leased to another farmer.'

'Can you get it?'

'Oh . . . I think so . . .' she said with a grin, teasing it out. 'It's my father's.'

Grogan was sitting in a pick-up truck, a flat cap on his head and a twinkle in his eye.

'Well if it's not the wild fucking Irish rover himself. How are you doing, son?'

'Fine, thanks. You look a cunt in that cap,' Scott replied, getting into the front beside him.

'I'm Welsh. That's the trouble with us. We look like cunts in anything other than a miner's helmet.' Grogan started the engine and pulled into the traffic, paint tins and other things rattling in the back as they hit a bump.

'Central props did well with this,' Scott said, looking round the litter-strewn cab. Sweet wrappers, old papers and cigarette butts were everywhere.

'Good innit? The lads have found a place not far from here. It will do for a couple of weeks as an RV point. Have a bit of lunch and you can tell 'em what you want 'em to do.'

Scott flicked him a look. 'You staying on?'

'Afraid not, sunshine. I'm just here to brief you. You are OC till further notice. I'm going back to play Cluedo with the Whitehall warriors.'

Scott smiled. Grogan had the wonderful ability to downplay everything. Helping the senior government planners and people at Century House put the take-over pieces together was hardly playing. Scott looked across at him. The short stocky man was an outstanding soldier, a brilliant tactician and a fine leader. He was due to return to his unit soon and Scott had no doubt that it would not be long before he was made up to lieutenant colonel. In the Royal Green Jackets that was no mean feat, he thought.

'So. You have what you asked for. One score-odd nicely kitted out in jeans and Nikes. The spooks have got a few rugby teams here, too. A fellow called Persse, ah yes you know him, well Persse will be running 'em. Give whatever you get to Persse. His comms back to his people are all set up.'

'I know,' Scott said. 'He's well briefed.'

'You have the lads for two weeks. Enough?'

'Should be.'

'Just in case things hot up a little we have some kit. Get it bedded down somewhere. A second load will be coming in tomorrow across the border. Hennesey will be driving it down with Scaglen. It's a forty-foot container. There's three more to get stored before the week's out.'

'Jesus. That's a lot of kit. Do you know something I don't?'

'Nary fear, my little cherub. The truckloads are for the friendlies.'

Weapons caches. Things were moving now, he thought. Three containers, one hundred and twenty tons of weapons, mines, ammunition, supplies that could basically equip a regiment.

Grogan pulled into a small warehouse complex and stopped the truck beside another just like it.

Once inside the briefing began.

Mary Kelly lay back in the tangled sheets and rumpled blankets of her small bed and watched Sam getting dressed by the light of the candle that stood in its heavy recycled glass bottle on the bedside table. Its light was soft and as he pulled his jeans on, she snuggled down into the bed and watched the long line of his muscular back, the olive complexion of his skin in sharp contrast to his white boxer shorts. She was pleased. The lovemaking had been gentle and full of touch and caress, his strong fingers tracing the curve of her breast before running down her side, slow and sensuous. He had bought food, hummus from a new deli that he had found and arab bread. After they had finished, he couldn't wait and she found his passion for her, saddlebags and all, irresistible; they sat naked on the bed and dipped bits of the bread into the hummus, sharing it and feeding each other.

Later he smeared some on her breasts and as she giggled and shrieked he held her down and licked it all off and they did it again. He seemed to understand her, her need to return to Ireland whenever she went away, her need to spend time with her family, her love of her people and the city where she was born. A previous boyfriend, an English musician, kept trying to get her to stay in London with him and never understood her passion for Dublin. He had no time for his parents and although they only lived thirty miles away, he only saw them every couple of months. Sam understood family and home and the bonds they created and any man in her life would have to accept that.

They had talked about it one day and Sam had smiled and said, 'I know. I love my homeland and my family too. I would die for them.'

'I would die for mine, too,' she said simply, meaning every word. 'Could you ever be happy here, Sam, here in Ireland?' she had asked. 'Maybe you could learn to love it like I do.'

He said he was sure he could and changed the subject to tell her of a time he was in New York and had worked in a pub with an Irish guy. She listened, smiling, loving the way he spoke and moved his hands gesticulating to emphasize the points. She knew herself. She knew she was falling in love. It felt wonderful.


Although the government maintained permanent standing committees whose sole function was the handling of situations that threatened Britain, because this was essentially the problem of a neighbouring country the job would be divided. While the professionals would have direct input, most of the ancillary planners, a mix of Irish and British, would be based outside London.

The planning team had taken over a country house in South Wales. Massive grey Victorian walls and a uniformed guard kept the curious at bay, while behind lay the real security. Military police patrolled the grounds and their own intelligence people controlled the access past the second gates halfway up the long rhododendron-lined driveway.

In what was once the drawing room the first meeting convened. Petra Wallis and Sally Richards were seated along the west side of the huge table. Tilby and a junior staffer sat beside them. Opposite were members appointed by the Cabinet Committee, a representative from 10 Downing Street, and six senior people ostensibly from the Ministry of Defence, but it was obvious from their appearance and demeanour that they were senior serving officers in the three armed forces. The MoD group and the man from Downing Street would come and go as required, but the two Americans at the table, Lyle Clayburg and Robert

Boyle, represented the CIA and would be on permanent attachment as liaison officers. An empty chair at the head of the table was reserved for Sir James Marshall who would head up the group.

At the far end sat Peter Morris, Pat O'Sullivan and the man brought along by Morris, Professor Kiernan.

Someone passed a note to Petra Wallis.

'Sir James will be late. We are to start and he will join us in a few minutes.'

The meeting began with a briefing on the latest developments, the discovery of the armoured vehicles and Scott's recorded conversation with the Taoiseach. A general discussion followed over what the passports issue would mean, the whole area of nationality taken by subterfuge. They also discussed the short-term effects of the massive investment and the fact that unemployment was the lowest in recorded times and finally the talk moved on to the implication of civil unrest, not powerful fighting resistance working to its own agenda, but street riots and mobs.

There was agreement around the table that this was to be avoided. If the arrivals had killed to hide the facts they would certainly kill to protect their plan and the money they had spent in working towards their goal. The untrained, however zealous, would be killed like so many sheep.

Sir James Marshall strode into the room. A career civil servant and a brilliant planner, he had worked with every major emergency or contingency committee in the last fifteen years. He knew the way the machine worked, knew who to talk to, who to see to get things done, which tape to cut. His chairmanship had been anticipated by most of the people gathered round the table and unlike most very senior civil servants he was known for his plain speaking. He had arrived from London the night before and after dinner he had taken the new arrivals aside and spoken at length with each, a full two hours with Professor

Kiernan. He went straight to the head of the table. 'Thank you all for coming, especially our friends from across the water.' He looked round the faces. 'Let's establish why. Our objective is to assist in an operation. An operation to return constitutional law to the people of Ireland. You are here to assist in interpreting and developing the policy and strategy that will direct the working teams that are moving into this building as we speak. You have heard the latest int, so let's get straight to it. Shall we start with you, Professor? How do we do it? Help three and a half million modern neutral Europeans take their country back with a minimum of risk?'

Sally Richards sat back, pleased. Marshall had done his homework and was correct in his deference to the man Morris had brought along.

Kiernan, well into his seventies, was the grand old man of Trinity College and one of the most respected historians in Europe. When he spoke he delivered his words with the confidence of an expert and of fifty years of experience.

Marshall thought about the conversation they had had the night before. Kiernan had explained the way he thought they should move forward and he had just sat back and listened.

'Whatever we do, we risk long discussion on the rights and wrongs. Whatever path we take will have its followers and its opponents. These are people long used to being militarily neutral, but reserving the right to comment ad nauseam, while their cousins abroad have provided the backbone of armies and police forces for three hundred years.' He smiled ruefully. 'Initially they will be either passionately for or passionately against. There are perceived benefits in the minds of many. Don't forget there are jobs now, where there was seventeen per cent unemployment. Food on the table. There are a few that will say they deserved it, other will say it's bought and paid for, it's not our problem. But the vast majority I am sure

109

will feel it is wrong. We don't need divided camps. I suggest we go for a more basic emotion. De Dannan, the mother, Ireland, Rosaleen under threat, and below that, remove all doubt and make it Celtic.'

'Celtic?' someone asked.

'I had the same thought last night,' Marshall said. 'Professor, perhaps you can explain the Celtic thing for us all.'

Professor Kiernan smiled, his old eyes twinkling in a face like creased pink parchment.

'Certainly. The Irish are a small surviving niche of a much larger group. They are the purest strain of what is now a much diluted culture. There are scattered small groups of very pure Celtic blood in the Scottish outer islands, but in essence the only remaining substantial population of Celts remains in Ireland. Incidentally, the name Scot comes from Scotti, which is Irish Gaelic, and was the name given to the Irish Celtic invaders who colonized northern Britain. They held back the Romans there, where Hadrian built his wall. But the Romans for all their influence in later centuries never reached Ireland or the Isle of Man. In fact when Caesar came ashore in Britain, he was met by Celtic warriors in four-wheeled chariots. They had a system of roads. Much of the credit given to the Roman road builders is due to the Celts. Three hundred years before Christ there were hospitals in Ireland. They had stone buildings and forts that stand to this day. This was a strong culture that produced filigree art, enamelled cups, gold chalices and engravings.

'Later, at the time of the Viking invasions in the tenth century, they still escaped large-scale cultural dilution. Later still the Norman invasion similarly failed to substantially alter the bloodlines. Outside the east coast, an area already populated by the remnants of the Vikings, most of them were largely unaffected. The culture grew and the enlightenment continued. While Britain and Europe fell into the dark ages Ireland remained apart and in time sent missionaries back, to preach the word and take writing, medicine and learning back into the void the barbarian invaders had left.'

He removed his glasses and polished them with a hand-kerchief.

'It is thought by historians that it was Ireland that kept learning and Greek and Roman literacy alive until the Renaissance. But for all this it was still a Celtic culture. Its resilience is unbelievable. For instance, English dialect has been spoken in Ireland since the third century and yet to-day in the west and in particular the Aran Islands there are places where only Irish is spoken.'

Professor Kiernan paused to put his glasses back on his long, bony nose and lifted his tea cup, his other hand carefully holding the saucer under his chin in case he spilt any.

'They are a paradox. They represent the best and the worst traits of the Celts and the culture remains strong, but to find true cohesion in a people that has traditionally bickered among themselves you must find a basis, a com-monalty that levels all other issues.'

One of the people, the man from Downing Street was fascinated. 'Go on, Professor. Take your time,' he said.

'There was much movement back and forth between the islands. They did their share of invading,' he said with a smile. 'They invaded England several times in the fourth century. So much movement back and forth and not all the invasions were unwelcome. A young missionary called Patrick left these shores sometime in the sixth century and brought Christianity to the Irish. He is now our patron saint. It is that man's arrival in what was a pagan land, a land of druids, that helps make them what they are today. The move from druidism and stone worship was significant, but the elements are still there. The expression "Land of Saints and Scholars" helps to illustrate what I mean. Their acceptance of Christendom was easy because druidism also was a basic belief in an afterlife. The *tuatha*, the extended families, small chiefdoms if you will, were the basis of Irish Celtic culture. In the time of the druids, each *tuatha* had its druids and bards. In time each had its own bishop. Above this level there was constant feuding between the chieftains and the kings, some allied to one High King or another. Tara was the place of the High Kings. At Tara there was a stone upon which the High Kings of Ireland were crowned. The legend said that if the stone trembled then the king was genuine. The Stone of Destiny. Our Excalibur, if you will. This stone was lent to a Scottish cousin for his own coronation in Caledonia. The Irish King asked for it back. It was never returned. It finally turned up in London and is now the Coronation stone in Westminster Abbey. But I digress. We were talking about family, yes?'

Marshall nodded and he continued.

'These elements of family, the *tuatha*, and strong religious convictions are enshrined in the modern constitution. It holds the family unit sacred, family units where it is still common for a mother to want one of her sons to go into the priesthood. Beneath that papal fervour lies the emotive literacy, the passion of the Celtic Irish for poetry and writing, for the thoughts of men. And this passion is pre-Christian. Throughout Irish history the bardic poets wielded enormous power. The druids could write. They used Greek. But they also believed that writing things down allowed the disciplines of learning to soften. Their bardic poets were expected to remember well over two hundred poems word perfect, and in that ability was the survival of Celtic legend and myth. The reverence of the people for a well-turned phrase, for prose and rhyme, gave power to those who could construct the poetry. So this is a modern society that still holds that reverence for writers and thinkers. Look at the numbers of great writers Ireland has produced, and it is a small nation we are talking about.

A nation so different to the Germanic peoples with their Teutonic virtues of strength and blind obedience.

'The Celts have their soul exposed and their art forms display this. They are preoccupied with death and legend, superstition and myth. They are historically fierce warriors who would die to defend an ideal. They are also freethinkers who love to argue everything, talk it to death around the firesides, write about it, and all the while the Sacred Heart peers down from the mantel . . . Saints and Scholars.'

'How do we . . .' Marshall asked, finally wanting to come to the point.

'Call them to arms?'

'Yes.'

Kiernan looked up at Marshall as it if were obvious.

'Appeal to the Celt in them. Use the legends, the poetry, the history. If there are fewer than fifty million people of Irish descent out there in the world, then I will be the Pope. Each will have to make his own decision, but they will come. The sons of Ireland will come home. And the others.'

'Others?'

'If you go for the Celt, you will get the Celt. Wales, Scotland, even areas of England . . . they are essentially Celtic.'

'I would have thought the last thing the Irish wanted was another British army on Irish soil,' Marshall said.

'Yes and no,' the Professor replied. 'The historian Robert Kee expressed it well. He said that the two populations, British and Irish, had for so long been not only partially racially connected, but also connected politically and ad-ministratively that for all their many differences in characteristics they could not easily be thought of as be-longing to separate countries. In truth the animosity that exists is an example of that bickering we were talking about. Bickering within a family. If help comes from

Britain it will be welcome. Family always is . . . and it is one family. Having said that, you need not worry about that. Not if the returning force is Celtic and positioned as such . . . would the British help?'

'Early signs are positive, but hesitant. This will appear as an Irish problem. We can't be seen to interfere,' Marshall said, stating as carefully as he could Whitehall's confusion over the issue, and the growing opposition to any overt effort from some influential back benchers who had been brought into the loop. 'This may have to be a civil insurrection. If as you suggest we can expect the Irish to return home, then supported by other "Celts" they would need no other flag other than that of Ireland itself. A gathering of the clans? Am I right?'

'Indeed you are,' he said firmly, then wistfully: 'The homecoming. Many of us have often thought about it.'

'Can you write a scenario for us. How we bring them home?'

'Oh yes,' Kiernan said with a smile, 'that we can do. They will hear the call of the drum. The problem will be in keeping the numbers manageable.'

Sandy Marshall looked up at him, his pencil poised over a pad.

'You said Rosaleen or something earlier?'

'I did.'

'What is that a reference to?'

"'O my Dark Rosaleen, do not sigh, do not weep . . .'" Kiernan quoted, 'It's from a poem translated by James Clarence Mangan. It's full of powerful imagery, and every Irish person knows it. Mangan describes Ireland like many other writers, as a woman, Rosaleen. In this case she is in trouble, hence "my Dark Rosaleen".'

Marshall smiled. 'Dark Rose,' he said softly.

# 4

It was a French intelligence officer who picked it up. He was leafing through a batch of surveillance photos from the day before and selected three that were interesting. Not for the Sûreté but for the British, who had asked them for anything unusual they came across on particular Arab groups. Not the run-of-the-mill extremists but the movers and shakers, the money men, and anyone with a Mediterranean Arab link. This sequence of shots had been taken in Zurich.

He laid them out on the table and swung the light over. The standard format was twenty-five by thirty centimetre high-definition prints and the new processor down on the third floor could turn out work with the kind of detail that only time and a magnifying glass could improve on.

The officer leaned forward, picking up his glass. His brother was in print design and had given him a printer's glass. If you set it on its tripod over a page you could count the dots on magazine pages, see the different colours that made up the hues and tints. A very clear magnifying glass indeed. He swept his eyes across the group of faces at the rear of the delivery van.

In the foreground three men, well known to the intelligence services, walked from a building. They were Jalal Abdullah Husseini, Karim Nabeel and Salim Nunu. All three were connected to the Palestinian Liberation Organization, not the paramilitary or direct action factions, but the intellectual end. They had been previously seen with the thinkers, the spokespeople and the negotiators at the peace tables. But it was the pair at the back that made it interesting.

Obaid Kassabian was the new fix-it man for the Saudis. After Adnan Kashoggi had hit problems with the Americans he had risen from nowhere, taking over Kashoggi's role as middleman and procurer for the seamier side of the huge weapons and defence contracts. The word was that he had unlimited direct contact with King Fahd and was a familiar figure in the private *majlis*. There had also been reports in recent weeks of brief late-night visits to Libya, Syria, Kuwait, the United Arab Emirates, and fleeting encounters with diplomats from Oman, Qatar and Bahrain.

It took the officer three hours to identify the second figure in the background with Kassabian. He finally used a scanner to feed the image into a computer which enhanced the size and then searched thousands of records for a match of the face. Seven minutes later he had a name and began to read the file.

Henry Haddad was a Lebanese businessman, one of the many who had commuted between Beirut and the USA during the Lebanese civil war and twice he had come under FBI surveillance. The Federal Bureau of Investigation were increasingly uncomfortable with intelligence that indicated that Haddad was spending too much time in the Bekaa valley and beyond it, in Syria. In the Bekaa were the training camps of the fundamentalist groups like Hezbollah, the party of God, and once the extreme wings of the PLO.

Nothing was ever proved and the surveillance was suspended after Haddad's behaviour in the USA proved to be exemplary. He had however been linked again with the Palestinians and the Syrians since the surveillance had ended.

He batched up the photographs, printed the display from the screen and sent the file up to his section head. That evening the section head met the MI6 resident in Paris. They had worked side by side for many years and settled comfortably with their drinks in front of them. The Frenchman pushed a buff envelope across the table.

'You owe us now, Charlie,' he said. 'We have found something you have been looking for.' He sipped his pastis. 'Another thing, mon ami.'

The MI6 man looked up.

'The Lebanese. He came into France on an EU passport. It was issued a year ago.'

'What country?'

'Ireland.'

'As long as it wasn't one of ours,' he said casually.

Twelve hours later the Swiss police agreed to a request from the British and began a major surveillance operation on each of the men who had attended the meeting in Zurich. The Palestinians would have been followed and monitored routinely, but Henry Haddad and Obaid Kassabian were new to the Swiss authorities and they had to walk a fine line between a European nation's strongly couched request and the interests of their own bankers who prided themselves on their country's ability to maintain the privacy of those doing business with them.

The operation under way, the Swiss handed it back to the British when the two men flew on to Grand Bahama and then separated. Kassabian returned to the Gulf and Haddad flew back to Switzerland to a meeting with a lawyer in Gstaad.

A Century House driver left to collect a man who had reluctantly agreed to travel to Wales and remain out of touch till further notice. On arrival at the country house that accommodated the planning team he would be asked to sign the Official Secrets Act.

Peter Maynouth was an Arabist. Classically trained at Cambridge, he had promptly dropped all the teachings and immersed himself in the souks and bazaars of the Arab world. He had spend most of his working life in the Middle

East and had advised the Foreign Office on three previous occasions, the last being just before Iraq's invasion of Kuwait. Now living in London, he was paid as an analyst by the publishers of the *Economist* magazine.

Arnold Cleaves looked up as Sally Richards walked into his office.

'Morning, cherub,' she said brightly. Cleaves raised an eyebrow at her. His tiny team were still working long hours trying to trace the financial movements that concealed the mass buy-outs and takeovers in Ireland and he was tired.

'The name Obaid Kassabian mean anything to you?'

'Yes,' he replied, leaning back in his chair. 'He has the Saudis' cheque book. The bankers love him. Falling all over themselves to get at him.'

'Henry Haddad?'

'Know him. Wouldn't be in the same room as Kassabian. Haddad is a little less salubrious, to say the least. We picked up a scam involving the World Bank that he was behind in '88.'

She dropped the photograph on the desk. 'There they are together. Thick as thieves. The bunch in front are villains too.'

'Oh dear me, yes.' He peered through his glasses. 'Yes. This is very significant. When was this taken?'

'Three days ago. We have them watched.'

'Oh yes . . . yes, this is good. If these two are involved then I know where to start looking for things that are smelly. But odd. Very odd indeed.'

'What?' Sally asked, delighted with his enthusiasm.

'Obaid Kassabian is big league. Moves at government levels. What on earth is he doing in the same group as Henry Haddad? Haddad is strictly a trader, a middleman.'

'Joining forces, perhaps?'

'Perish the thought. With Obaid's power base and

Haddad's connections it would be like — well, they could pull just about anything off. We have files on Haddad, not extensive, but enough to start pulling.'

'Obaid?' Richards asked.

'The Shadow,' Cleaves muttered. 'That's what the fraud arm of the World Bank called him. Could never pin anything on him. But too many deals went off without a hitch. We don't have anything hard on Obaid Kassabian, not a dickie bird.'

'What's his function?'

Cleaves thought for a second or two, taking his glasses off and rubbing the lenses with a clean hanky he plucked from his breast pocket.

'You could best liken him to a managing director. He has a seat on the board and makes the day-to-day decisions, but somewhere is the board chairman who has the real power. Obaid, for all his Harvard Business School and billion-dollar-deal background, is still a hired man and he is on the market for anyone who can meet his fees. He doesn't have the money to mount something like this. We have to find his backers. The policy men.'

At that moment a smile crossed his face.

'What?' she asked.

'Something occurred to me a few days ago. It's way out, almost implausible, but now that we have the Shadow involved, and a hard-nosed dealer like Haddad, then it becomes more plausible.'

'Explain.'

'Obaid Kassabian is big league. The big league is fairly carefully tracked by the major banks and investment houses. Who is moving money. Who is re-investing. People like Crédit Suisse and Deutsche Bank, the big boys, have staff based in the Gulf watching and talking to the movers down there, as they do in Monte Carlo, London, anywhere that major private investors live and work. These people won't really seriously talk to anyone with under a million dollars to invest. Private banking at its very best. Well, there is a deal that went wrong in Spain. An investment ostensibly by the Kuwaitis. Gruppo Torres. It's gone pear-shaped and there is still a very quiet witch hunt on.'

'How pear-shaped?' Sally asked, suddenly interested.

'No one knows. I'd say somewhere between twenty-three and thirty-five billion dollars' worth. The Kuwaitis admit to twenty-three.'

'Twenty-three billion dollars!'

Cleaves laughed. It was a bitter sound that rasped off his tongue. 'The original fund was more like thirty-five.'

'My God. I didn't know that that sort of money was anywhere but in government budgets.'

'It's a sizeable amount,' he said drily, 'about two years of their stated GDP, but the interesting thing is that a few people in the business always suspected that it was more than just Kuwaiti money. They are shrewd investors. They wouldn't sink that much into any single fund or project. It has also been suspected that the fund goes back pre-eighties, to the big boom days of the high oil prices. Even so there had to be others, spread the load a little. Now imagine a man like Obaid Kassabian, with a huge resource like that. Imagine, just for a minute, if that thirty-odd billion dollars wasn't lost on lousy investing. Imagine if it had been carefully channelled out over the last three or four years or so. The numbers relate. It's about two-thirds of what it will have cost.'

'Is it possible?'

'Oh yes. Raise the rest like any other loan. With the calibre of people employed on accounts like this, and a public relations campaign feeding the business press little titbits on how the fund is losing money, by the time there was a public accounting to anyone it would be common knowledge that the fund had taken a hammering. The principals who normally are the only people pushing for an inquiry, in this case the Kuwait Investment office – well, after a thing like this they don't push at all and the whole thing just fades away. Then there is a fund awaiting use, or funds already working that were considered lost. It has effectively disappeared from the system. The money boys are not tracing it any longer.'

'Why would the Kuwaitis do this?' she pondered aloud.

'It may not be just them. Have you ever visited that part of the world?'

'No.'

'I did once. Went down when I was with the World Bank. Had a few weeks in Riyadh. They, the Gulf Arabs, are fascinated by wet, cold, snow, forest, all the things we Europeans take for granted. On holidays we go to the beach and lie in the sun. They think we are crazy. They come to Europe to see rainfall, grass in fields, snow and lakes. They just love it. Maybe they want to buy a chunk of it.'

'But they already do. Shit, half of Mayfair and Belgravia is Arab-owned.'

'Not the same as owning a country, is it? The last thing left to try and buy when you have everything else?'

'No. Too simple,' Richards retorted. She stood up. 'I want you to go down to the planning group. Meet and brief Maynouth. He is about the best modern Arabist we can get our hands on for the duration. Offer him your idea. See what he thinks.'

'I could, but I'm better here. Running this trace,' Cleaves replied. 'Anyone can do it. You. It's easy enough.'

'Okay,' she conceded, 'give me the notes, but I still think it's too simple. If the Kuwaitis wanted to buy a massive chunk of Europe they would just make an offer. Not kill. Not bring in heavy weapons. It's just not their style.'

That evening Maynouth sat down in one of the recently equipped meeting rooms with Sally Richards. She was tired after the long drive and wanted nothing more than a hot bath, but chose to bring the Arabist up to date on the Gruppo Torres issue. She sat in one of the armchairs, her legs tucked under her and a notepad across her knees.

'Does that help?' she asked as she finished, reaching for a cigarette. She had just started smoking again.

'Everything helps. I knew about Torres,' Maynouth said. He was a tall, rangy man with big hands and long blond hair brushed back from his forehead. His face was tanned a deep mahogany colour and that combination with his green eyes made him look like an ageing surfer.

'The problem is the people you are dealing with. The Kuwaitis have enough problems right now, without biting into an issue like this. They are private people, proud, and believe it or not they don't covet anyone else's territory. As long as their land produces the oil it does and they have a historic legal and moral right to it, why would they want someone else's country?'

'What about the rain and cold and snow thing then?'

'They can buy that every summer. These people are incredibly wealthy. They can go anywhere anytime they choose. Why take on the wrath of the world with an act like this?'

'You're saying it's a lemon, then?'

'Kuwaitis, yes, it's a lemon. But like your man Jeeves . . .'

'Cleaves.'

'. . . Cleaves, I don't believe that the Torres fund was all Kuwaiti cash. It's . . . was too big.'

'So they could be in cahoots?'

'Possible, but more likely they put up some cash and let someone else manage the fund. What do our American friends think?'

'I'm going to tell them now. The States is awake. They can pass the information back to their own people.'

'I've never found them much good,' Maynouth muttered. 'However, the Kuwaitis may have agreed to allow the other party to use the KIO name. That would bring instant credibility. If someone walked in with a few billion dollars you might want to know where it came from. If he says he is representing the Kuwait Investment Office, you grin and invite him to sit down.'

'So a group of people or countries pool a fund for a single task. The money is carefully "lost" so there can be no comebacks. An operational group then begins using the money for their devious pursuit.'

'Yes. It fits. Whoever produced these funds, either for outright use or as a loan, would be big enough to want to wash their hands of it if it went wrong. Governments do it all the time.'

'Iran–Contra?' Richards said.

'Precisely,' Maynouth replied. 'And the other thing to consider is that most Arab governments are not accountable to their people as those in the west are. You have a clutch of emirates who are notoriously secretive, little more than benign dictatorships. In actual fact they work very well. Their people are well fed and well looked after. I have never been a believer in democracy for democracy's sake. You have the kingdom. The Saudi machine is just a bit bigger than the other Gulf emirates, but essentially the same. They have no common law. Their law is *sharia*, the law of the Koran. Allah determines all things. All these Gulf states have an internal problem. An odd mix of religious tension between Shi'ites and Sunnis, those people who want a democracy and the fundamentalists. The Kuwaitis are under enormous pressure to hold broader-based elections and the house of Saud gets weaker by the year as the opposition grows.

'Then you have the Baathists further north, in Syria and Iraq. Secular as opposed to the Islamic administrations. And you have a clutch of others, some where it is almost anarchy like the Lebanon and Algeria and some that function quite well in the western sense like Egypt. Egyptians don't consider themselves Arab in that context. In spite of

Hosni Mubarak's vaunted role as an "Arab" leader, the average man on the street considers himself Egyptian, quite different from Arabs. Egypt is the only country in the region that has any kind of accountability to its people because they do have an election every now and then. Any of these administrations could be in this, because all of them are largely unaccountable to anyone.'

'But who? I heard it once said that the only thing the Arabs agree on is to disagree.'

Maynouth laughed. 'You are right.' He swung one long corduroy leg over the other. 'But they do have things in common.'

'Like?'

'Everything from their language to *shwarmas* – what you call doner kebab – to Islam. And anyone who thinks that Arab solidarity is a myth is a fool. They have a developed sense of nation. Anyway, let me think on it.'

'Right,' Sally said, standing up. 'I'll leave you to get on with it. Here's a copy of the report and photos of the two men.'

She spent the next two hours briefing Sir James Marshall and Petra Wallis.

Maynouth paced round his room. He had been in there most of the day. Three trays with used coffee pots, cups, saucers and debris lay on the table by the door. The catering staff supplied by Century House would bring another tray of coffee in an hour. A flip chart stood in the corner and jottings covered its surfaces. Further notes were piled up on the desk, and a set of reference books and files from his office were laid out across the bed. A pink folder, its yellow band denoting its minimum security status sat atop the pile on the desk. It was a précis of the Interpol movement reports on suspected individuals, and he had chosen nine names from the list of six hundred regularly tracked and requested further information.

He had scribbled out three scenarios and over the morning he had been fleshing them out. Now he needed to substantiate where he could, put meat on the bones of the plot and see which were too thin to bear flavour. He turned back to the photos he had been given the night before by Sally Richards. They were the computer enhancements, but tucked in behind them in the same envelope were the originals. He pulled the images clear and looked at them, a smile creasing his tanned face. 'You son of a bitch!' he shouted in delight. An hour later he had abandoned one of the scenarios.

That evening at eight o'clock they were gathered in the main conference room, a Royal Marine guard at the door and patrols in the grounds. Petra Wallis, Peter Tilby, Sally Richards, Lyle Clayburg, Robert Boyle and Sir James Marshall sat round the table as Maynouth set out his papers.

'I have two scenarios to offer you. The evidence supports only two and that's the way I am leaning. So let's cover those. It was the photo that tipped it. The one of the two men in Switzerland.' He held it up. 'Wood for the trees, I'm afraid. Everyone immediately noticed Kassabian and Haddad, but these three in the front are just as interesting. They were mainstream PLO once upon a time. Now they are the active end of a new group called Al-Husseini. Husseini is an old Palestinian name. From what I have seen the Husseini are typical of the modern Palestinian activists. They are clever, articulate and well motivated.'

'So are the Israelis,' Clayburg said smugly.

'Ah see!' Maynouth rounded on him, looking very like a young Richard Harris, his coat-flaps swinging. 'That's just the point. You said Israelis. You didn't say Jews.'

'So?'

'Most confuse the two. It's a bit complex because the Palestinians have no problem with Judaism as such. It's Zionism they detest, and Zionism, in their view, is nationalism pure and simple. The Palestinian Muslims have no complaint with Palestinian Jews or with sharing the Holy Land with them. The problem they have is when a bunch of Russian or Polish Jews arrive. For Palestinians it is Arabness that is the issue. They feel they, as Arabs, have been forced out of their homeland to make way for Europeans, Africans and so on. It is not a case of who is Jewish or who is Muslim or who is Christian, for that matter. It is a case of who is Arab, or more correctly Semitic in a Semitic homeland.'

'Sorry,' Clayburg said. 'Run that one by me again.'

Others nodded in agreement.

'Ah,' Maynouth muttered, then he smiled. 'Backtrack, I think. Do you want a three-minute history of why this situation exists?'

'I think that would be useful,' Marshall said. He was very close to the issues, but he knew that others weren't.

'Right.' Maynouth reached into his pile of papers and pulled clear a map which he clipped to one of the flip chart stands, pulling it round so those gathered in the room could see it.

'The Western Med. Forget the names of places now. We are talking from the birth of Christ. Then you had communities, peoples, but no borders as we understand them. This place was called Palestine. It is the established home of a genetically Semitic people and has been since way before recorded history. One group of those people, separated only by a religious faith, the Jews, consider it their home, their land promised by God. The others? A handful of Christians but the rest pagan. Remember Mohammed will not be born for another four hundred years yet. But irrespective of that, it remains a land inhabited by Semitic people. Arabs. The years pass. It is still a Semitic land. Be they Jews, Christians, or followers of the new prophet Mohammed, they are Semitic.

'The crusaders roll through, kill and plunder, and later

the Ottomans do the same. The people of this land are used to invaders. They are the crossroads of the old world. They are a village people, pastoralists, farmers, growers of whatever the land will sustain. They have very tight communal identities, a strong sense of family, of decency and hospitality to strangers or travellers. The Ottomans administer the land, but the people, be they Muslim, Jew or Christian, are largely left alone. It's bearable. In some villages and remote areas outside the ancient walled cities they would not see an Ottoman official from one year to the next. Life goes on and suddenly,' Maynouth raised his hands and paused, 'we are in the twentieth century and the Great War, when the Ottomans, now better known as the Turks, side with Germany and their empire collapses. The Great War ends with Palestine in Britain's hands. Another administrator. Life goes on. But things are changing. Britain, now reluctantly administering much of the Near East and Arabian peninsula, starts defining borders and encouraging these new places to formalize their identities, with the true arrogance of the empire. Remember, Britain is at the height of her colonial power. What was just an ancient land called Palestine now has defined borders, and new neighbours. TransJordan. Syria. Lebanon. Egypt. But the frontiers are on the new maps only and the traders cross the mountains and river valleys as they always did. But something is happening out in the world. Something that will affect the villagers and people of the land, something that has nothing to do with them, is unforeseen, and that they cannot either predict or prevent.

'Pogroms against other Jews have been taking place for centuries in North Africa and Europe, but in the last hundred years it's accelerating. Now these are not necessarily Semitic Jews. They could be Caucasian or African, but that sense of Jewishness is overpowering. Their religion spoke of the promised land. They could be lithe and black and have lived in Ethiopia for a thousand years, or blond and Polish or Russian, but they are Jews and this, this promise, was what held them to their faith under centuries of persecution be it just a taunt or the sword itself. Next year in Jerusalem. The phrase on every Jew's lips. The dream of coming home to the promised land. Zion.

'So the critical mass is gathering and its momentum is finally provided by Adolf Hitler. With his Final Solution he galvanized the remaining Jews into action. Never again would they be at the mercy of another in another nation. It was time for the promised land. If you were a Jew then you supported that ideal, with money, your contacts, yourself. It had ceased to be a religious issue and was now one of nationalism. These people called themselves Zionists.

'Into Palestine they come, the trickle that has been there for years becomes a steady flow and they clash with the local population and British administrators. As early as December 1945, with Europe still smouldering, there is a terrorist strike. In April of '46 the Jewish extremists plant a bomb that kills seven people in a British army camp. By May what was later to be called the Exodus is under way, with 1500 Jews a month entering Palestine, legally or otherwise. As far as the world, consumed with guilt over the Nazi treatment, is concerned they need somewhere to go. Poor old local villager watches this with growing dismay. Picture the conversation between typical Palestinian and young fresh-faced UN fellow already depressed with the Anglo-American mandate. The old villager? They may need somewhere to go, he might reason if he was at all interested in what was happening outside his valley, but why here? Why must Poles and Russians be allowed to come into my homeland? They are not Palestinian. They are not even Arab. He says this to the Englishman with the mandate from the UN.

'But they are Jews, he replies. The old boy knows some Jews. The chap who comes through from Jerusalem with trade goods and paraffin is a Jew. Good man. So is the knife grinder in the neighbouring village and their physician is also a Jew. So what? our villager replies.

'Well, the UN man says. They need somewhere to go. What's wrong with wherever they come from? the villager asks. It's not that, it's well, it's the Holy Land. I know, says the villager. I live here. My people have lived here for thousands of years. It's holy for all, Muslim, Christian and Jew, but it's an Arab land. These people are not Arab. Well, the UN man says, it's really just that God promised this place to them. Says who? the villager replies. Well, them. It's in their book. Oh, the villager says, it's in their book, that they can have this place any time they want?

'Well no, replies the UN man, it's not that simple. No it's not, says the villager, thinking this guy is gaga, and I have crops to bring in, and thinking why don't you piss off to where you came from. If they need somewhere to go then give 'em your place, but don't give them mine.'

There were a few chuckles round the room. Good, thought Maynouth. They are beginning to understand one of the most complex issues of modern times.

'Right. So the new mandate is under pressure, both from the people of Palestine and from within. The Americans, with half of the mandate, are under pressure from the new Jewish lobby. They are arguing with Britain. The mandate says the British will remain in Palestine until the Jewish–Arab animosity settles down, but news leaks of an increase to immigration quotas to allow a total of one hundred thousand Jews into Palestine. The Arabs react and stone British troops. The Jews are still hitting back and now it's getting organized. They have formed the Haganah and Irgun Zvai Leumi and modern terrorism is born. Attacks increase and the Americans, still singing to a different song sheet from the Brits, suggest, from no lesser a personage than Truman himself, that an adequate area be set aside for a Jewish homeland. Partition. The Jewish attacks continue with eight British soldiers killed. The assassins retreated behind a mob of stone-throwing youths. The kids of the intifada learnt their tactics here. David Ben-Gurion and Golda Meir appeal for the violence to stop, but it doesn't and in March of '47 big bits of Palestine come under martial law. The British have decided to go anyway. It's a no-win situation for them and they are heartily sick of it. Virtually overnight, they do it. The Palestinian Arabs with no administrative culture — remember, they have been ruled by the Ottomans and the British for the last four hundred-odd years — have no well organized group or solid political or administrative machine to take over, and they are caught short. On 15 May the Mandate ends and within hours the Jews, the Zionists, preparing for this day, have taken the country and renamed it Israel. The Palestinians are fighting back, but it's too little too late and over the next few years they are forced out of more and more of their areas. Whole villages moved at gunpoint. Refusal was met with extreme violence. It was ethnic cleansing. The Jews were good at it. They had been the subject of pogroms, ethnic cleansing in Russia and Poland and Germany and they had learnt how to do it. So there it is. For one of the world's great religions it is the promise come true. The Promised Land is real. Zion. For the displaced Palestinians, sitting on their pathetic bundle of possessions, all they could carry, in Jordan, Lebanon and Syria, the end result was a Arab people forcibly removed from their Arab homeland after thousands of years to make way for Europeans and Africans. They want it back. They want to go home to their villages. It is a huge problem, with merit on both sides but for the Palestinians it has nothing to do with religion. It's a land grab. Okay?'

Everyone nodded.

'Good. Then scenario one.' He went to the overhead projector and began quickly writing on a sheet of acetate. 'A group of Arabs put together a fund to buy a country. A new homeland for the Palestinians. Add the Gruppo Torres fund to the money the PLO control already and you have a lot of power.'

'How much do they have?' Sally asked.

'Arafat does their investing. My sources say he currently controls almost twelve and a half billion dollars of PLO money. Now then, for all the real support they have, the Gulf Arabs and the Jordanians find the Palestinians a pain in the arse. Millions of literate, clever, ambitious people cannot be left itinerant for ever. They become a security problem. Witness Kuwait after the invasion. Even an investment this size would be worth it in the long run. Just to get them settled down somewhere. Give the Palestinians somewhere and remove a possible long-term security threat from their own countries.'

'The Kuwaitis would seem to be involved here somewhere, right?' Marshall said. 'We all agree that much?'

Everyone nodded. Maynouth let him talk on.

'Well, I just can't see the Kuwaitis doing anything for the Palestinians after the way they behaved during the Iraqi invasion. They fed them, gave them jobs, a future, security and then Saddam walks in and the Palestinians crossed over and supported the Iraqis. They hate them now.'

'We concur,' said Clayburg.

'True,' Maynouth said, 'but the Arabs have a view to the long term. Far more than we do in the west. A betrayal is forgotten as new alliances are formed in a few short years. Betrayal is a fact of life in that part of the world. There are constant palace intrigues and power games. An example is Saudi. One prince is the Minister of Defence with the army and air force reporting to him, while the next in line is in charge of the National Guard, a force of equal size. They cancel each other out. One couldn't stage a coup without the other. It's similar thinking throughout the region. Why? Because no Middle Eastern king or emir actually

131

trusts anyone. The Sultan of Oman turfed out his own father and there have been uprisings in most of the states in the last forty years. Betrayal is nothing shocking there. It's the national sport. Having said that, yes, the Kuwaitis are pissed off at the Palestinians, but that won't make the problem go away. The Gruppo Torres fund was set up well before the invasion, some people believe some years before. The Kuwaitis may have wanted to pull out. They certainly have other things to spend the money on now. But the others, whoever they are, let's say the Syrians, the Saudis, the UAE, the Qataris, the Omanis and just for the hell of it the Bahrainis, let's say they have pressured Kuwait to leave their money in. The Arabs have a saying, "The enemy of my enemy is my friend and the friend of my enemy is also my enemy." That kind of thinking actually exists. It's strong enough for pettiness to be left aside to address the main issue. The Palestinians are a thorn in everyone's foot, but they share an enemy and that makes them friends. So how to get the Palestinian thing sorted out once and for all? Buy 'em a small nice country. Long term there could be cute trade relationships, swapping oil for butter, milk, meat, all the primary produce Ireland is famous for producing. Even if this thing is moving ahead at max speed, when will they be ready to stand up and say "It's ours"?'

'Early in the new year, perhaps,' Wallis said.

'The timing would be about right. In January, Syria gets its turn on the Security Council. That gives them a voice in the chamber. Even the sessions held in camera have their voice and ears present. That's important. Remember when Iraq invaded Kuwait? They waited till Yemen, a friendly country, was on the Council.'

'They can't hope to win in the long run,' Marshall said. 'And strategically that's nothing short of stupid. And anyway, according to you and other Arabists they don't want another country. They want Palestine.'

'Which brings us to scenario two,' Maynouth said, 'the above' – he was scribbling again across the acetate – 'but with a difference.' He stood back, jabbing at the screen with his pen. 'All of the above but, remembering that the Palestinians regard Zionism as nationalism and they say it has snatched an Arab land from the Arabs and filled it with Europeans, they take a European land and fill it with Arabs. The bargaining chip. The Irish lobby in the States is as strong as the Jewish. They say, you give us back ours and we will give you back yours. They would hope that federal funding for Israel would stop overnight. They would see the pressure on the Israelis as immense. They would feel justified. They would cite precedence. Remember the friend of my enemy thing. They would say, we are just doing to you what you did to us.'

'You're right about the Irish lobby,' Clayburg said. 'They wouldn't take this lying down.'

'But the Irish didn't create Israel,' Sally Richards said sensibly.

'No,' Maynouth said, 'for the Palestinians that was us. The British and the Americans. Don't you see. Ireland is part of the British Isles and for many inextricably linked. If they did it to Iceland or Portugal it would have a few perception problems. But here, so close? It's better than just a European country. It's perfect.'

'My God,' Wallis said. 'Could the PLO manage a venture this size?'

'Five years ago, no,' Maynouth answered, 'but lately yes. Fatah, the mainstream group, is just one of thirteen organizations that the PLO forms the umbrella for. The other big one is the PFLP under George Habash. Habash is a Christian, powerful. He split the PFLP away from Fatah because he didn't like the conciliatory tone that Arafat was taking.'

'Sorry, that was?' Sally asked.

'Being happy to settle for the West Bank and Gaza.

Habash wanted everything or nothing. A liberated Palestine. He called Arafat a wimp and headed for Libya. Well, in '92 a growing movement called Hamas began to scare both of them. Hamas is best described as a group of Sunni fundamentalists. I don't need to tell you how extreme they are.' People round the table nodded. They knew about Hamas. Two bombs had gone off in London in the summer, one outside the Israeli Embassy. They believed Hamas to have been responsible.

Maynouth continued. 'Most of the fundamentalists are Shi'ite. Hamas was growing. It worried them both and with a common enemy they again joined forces. Right throughout the end of '92 and all of '93; right through the peace talks, and to date Fatah and the PFLP have been working alongside each other. Together they made the PLO very powerful, powerful enough to pull this off. *And*,' he repeated it, jabbing a finger, '*and* be organizing it while the peace talks were going on, what's more. I never thought they would be happy with just Gaza and the West Bank.

'And then, when the Hamas supporters clashed with the Palestinian police in Gaza the writing was on the wall. As we now know, the breakdown in the peace process was only weeks away. Once it went Arafat and the Fatah mainstream were left with one last-ditch effort: Plan B. Under way for some time, there is no subtle pull-out now, no quietly selling up and easing back out again. It's on. It's big. It's audacious – but they are desperate.'

Marshall, a man used to dealing with democratic governments, got to the nitty gritty. 'What mandate do they have?' he asked.

'There are three million Palestinians world-wide. They have been supporting a variety of groups for years and have been largely disappointed. Now they will give support in any manner to any group who will deliver the goods. Palestine. If someone could meet that objective the

Palestinians would sanction anything. Murder. Acts of terrorism. Blackmail. They feel all these acts have been perpetrated on them often enough. Add to that the fact that over one hundred countries consider the PLO the legitimate government of Palestine, and offer them diplomatic status. In fact more countries recognize the PLO than recognize Israel. They have the mandate. Both from their people, who vote in a congress set-up, and the world.'

The next day his theory was thrown to the wolves as several senior Foreign Office experts were drafted in. Also drafted in to view the scenario was Sir Huw Tristan-Carter, British Ambassador to the UN. They tossed the idea around, tore it to pieces, rebuilt it and at the end of two days they agreed with him. The CIA at Langley also agreed the scenario was not only possible but likely.

Later, after the Foreign Office team had gone, the executive team met.

'Now we just have to prove it,' Sally Richards began.

'Enough messing about,' Petra Wallis said. 'Let's snatch someone.'

That was music to Sally ears. 'Who? Haddad?'

'No, let's get a line on the lawyer he visited in Gstaad. He will do nicely.'

'I'm not hearing this,' Marshall said.

'Good,' Wallis responded.

'Look, you can't just kidnap someone,' he said.

'Oh no? Just watch.'

'I forbid it,' he snapped.

'Sir James,' Petra Wallis gathered herself up to her full height and gave him the stare that was known to intimidate cabinet ministers. 'I'm not some pimply graduate you can forbid to do anything. Don't tell me how to gather intelligence. Taking one of the opposition for a little ride and a chat is accepted practice. Your job is to co-ordinate Dark Rose. You can't do that until we know exactly what it is. These people are nasty. They have proved it. They set the rules. They started it. Well . . . we can also be nasty.'

'We can take him if you like,' Boyle said. 'We have assets in Switzerland.'

'Thanks for the offer,' Wallis said sweetly, 'but you know what your fellows are like. All helicopters and over-kill. We will do this. One of our chaps in an old Volvo. You can send someone to watch if you like.'

Later that night when Sally Richards had returned to London to organize the kidnapping of the lawyer, Tilby phoned Petra Wallis on the secure line.

'Morris phoned today. He wants to bring in a new man. Not on the ground, but at your end. Says he has skills and resources we can use.'

'Who is it?' Wallis asked. The creative people were moving in in three days' time, the types who would put together the supporting material. There were already forty-three assorted specialists and staff in the main build-ing. Everyone from designers to editors to copywriters, procurement and production people. She wondered what resources this new individual could bring.

'His name is Tony O'Malley.'

'The businessman?' Wallis asked.

O'Malley was Ireland's wealthiest expatriate. Managing director and major shareholder of one of the world's biggest conglomerates, he was a figure frequently quoted in the press.

'Yes.'

'What's he got?'

'Morris thinks, and I agree, that we need someone to pull together the frilly bits. Kiernan's stuff and all the work that goes into it. O'Malley is a dynamic, successful man. Used to getting things done with tight deadlines. Morris thinks we should ask him to head up the production teams doing the public face and the psy-ops stuff.'

Wallis looked out of the window. Across the field in the darkness she could see the lights of Wilden Hall, the second big house on the estate. The building had been earmarked to accommodate the creative teams who would bring Professor Kiernan's Celtic call to arms to life. It would need someone over there. Someone respected. Someone who could get things done.

'Good idea,' she replied. 'Get on a plane. Go and see him.'

By two the following afternoon Tilby was in the Philadelphia headquarters of the giant food conglomerate where Tony O'Malley was king. He had been driven to the shiny five-storey glass building housing the executive offices by a CIA man who had flown in from Langley.

'I'll come up with you, son,' he drawled. 'I have a letter from the boss. It just might get us past the flunkeys quicker than your smile.'

Tilby smiled his thanks and together they walked in. He hadn't brought a coat and for August it was getting cold. They ignored the various desks and signs asking visitors to report and just followed their noses.

O'Malley's office was on the fifth floor and the lift doors slid soundlessly back on an expanse of spotless carpet running all the way to the floor to ceiling windows. In the middle, like an island in a sea of cream was an antique oak desk. Behind it sat a very efficient-looking woman in her early fifties.

'Can I help you?' she asked.

'Yes,' Tilby answered. 'I'd like to see Mr O'Malley, please.'

The woman looked nonplussed. She knew her employer's appointments better than she knew her own. He had none this afternoon.

'I am sorry,' she said, 'but if you call in advance and advise the nature of your business I can try and fit you in sometime.'

'Please ask him. I have come all the way from London.'

'I am sorry,' she said firmly. 'Now if you would like to phone . . .'

'Come with me,' the CIA man said. Tilby followed him pushing past the side of her desk.

'You can't go . . .'

They were in.

O'Malley sat in shirtsleeves behind a desk. He was a lean man of medium height, with sandy brown hair and a wide, intelligent forehead. The woman fussed past them.

'I'm sorry, Mr O'Malley, they just barged past me. Shall I call security?'

'That won't be necessary,' Tilby said. 'We won't hold up the important wheels of industry any longer than we have to. After all making tomato sauce is earth-shattering stuff.'

O'Malley stood up. 'I'll stop peeling tomatoes for a minute,' he said drily, 'and you be brief. What do you want?'

'Ask not what your country can do for you, but what you can do for your country. Said, I believe, by a president of this, your adopted homeland.'

'Get to the point.'

'That is the point. What you can do for your country. Can we speak alone?'

'Mrs Ellingworth has been looking after me for ten years. There isn't much about me she doesn't know. I trust her implicitly.'

Tilby wanted to protest against her presence, but he knew that if O'Malley trusted her and he came on board then he would probably bring her in with him. He nodded.

'You are a citizen of Ireland.'

'I am. That is a matter of public record,' O'Malley answered.

'Are you a patriot, Mr O'Malley?'

138

'That's an odd question these days.'

'If you heard the drum calling, Mr O'Malley. If Ireland was under threat.'

'Yes. I am a patriot. Of course I am.'

'Mr O'Malley, I usually tell people I am employed by the Foreign Office. I won't insult your intelligence. I work for the British Secret Intelligence Service. MI6 if you like. We believe, Mr O'Malley, that Ireland is the subject of what you would call a buy-out. Not hostile yet, but any minute. Ireland has to all intents and purposes been invaded. Not with tanks or soldiers, although they will follow, but with money. Lots of money and secrecy and ill intent. The new owners are going to protect their investment with force. The Irish people, once they find out, are going to take a dim view of it. We thought you might want to help.'

O'Malley swept his glasses off his face and leaned forward. 'Is this some kind of a joke?'

Tilby walked closer and handed him a small white card. 'This is the private number for Her Majesty's Secretary of State for Foreign Affairs. Call him. He will verify who I am.'

'I'll go one better. I'll call Colin Mahoney. I know the Taoiseach.'

'Do that and his son will suffer. You know young Tom. Mahoney's lines are all bugged. Tom is a hostage, along with many others,' Tilby replied.

O'Malley stared in disbelief.

'Sir,' the CIA man said, holding up a card identifying himself, 'if it will help, I am authorized to give you my director's number. He is most concerned that you understand the gravity of the situation.'

O'Malley looked quickly at Mrs Ellingworth. 'Cancel everything today and tomorrow and get some coffee in here if you will.' He turned back to the two visitors. 'Take a seat, gentlemen. I remain to be convinced. This kind of thing simply does not happen unnoticed. I have a few questions and you'd better have good answers.'

Two hours later he asked his last. 'You know what I do. You haven't flown here for nothing. What is my role as you see it?'

'We have a group of people in an annexe to the main building. They will be delivering the creative end of things. We need someone in there moving them along. Not some civil servant. Some one who gets things done for a living.'

The following day they met again and by mid-morning O'Malley was committed.

'This broadcast production team you mentioned. That's all so far?'

Tilby nodded.

'I'll go one better. Production teams just produce what they are told to produce. I'll bring in my own creatives and campaign people.'

'Is that necessary?'

O'Malley grinned. 'There's more to selling tomato sauce than putting it in bottles. I have the best marketing management team in the business. Those same skills can design, create and sell your Celtic dream very effectively. Then there's the back-up. Sourcing, procurement, logistics. I'll round up a few of them from our London operation who can keep their mouths shut.'

'That is an absolute prerequisite,' Tilby said firmly.

'We can funnel a lot of the work back through the company's UK operations,' he said thinking aloud. 'That will mean we can tap into existing buying relationships, use the company muscle to get things done without anyone ever knowing the end user till we are ready for them to know.'

Tilby nodded. The same idea had occurred to him, but he hadn't yet suggested it because he thought O'Malley would draw a line between his personal involvement and that of his company.

Professor Kiernan had arrived back in Wales and while a

steward carried his bag up to his room he ambled around the ground floor looking for Sally Richards. He preferred her to Petra Wallis. At his age he found overly ambitious people tiring and besides he mused, justifying it to himself, Sally was rather like his daughter.

He found her in the library. The gracious room was now over-furnished with grey MoD desks and trestle tables and people. Analysts, researchers and specialists worked on all the available surfaces.

'Hello, Professor,' she smiled, 'welcome back to Butlin's. Fancy a cup of tea?'

'Yes, thank you.' He was pleased to see a friendly face.

'Ready to razzle dazzle us?' she asked, walking with him towards the tea trolley that had taken up permanent station in the great hall.

'Yes I think so, but there is something I want to start straight away. If you could see it under way I'd be most appreciative.'

'Sure. Reports from Pat and Peter are good. They have already expanded their little groups.'

'Yes,' he said, 'I spoke to Peter this morning.' And as they filled their cups from the urn he told her about the little job that needed doing.

That evening Marshall returned from London in an ebullient mood. As the executive team settled at chairs around the table and Professor Kiernan fussed about with his notes Marshall spoke addressing them all.

'We have the Cabinet Committee meeting tomorrow.'

'What does that mean?' Petra asked.

'There has been a suggestion.' His phrasing meant it had come from one of the contingency committees in London. 'A suggestion strongly reinforced by colleagues at the MoD, the minister and our American partners. There is considerable resistance, but hopefully the cabinet may authorize the use of British forces in some manner. The Americans will also be considering how best they can bring their military machine to bear, without the perception of an American invasion. There will be caveats, obviously . . .'

'Our lads?' Sally interjected.

'Yes. Our lads,' he said. 'I haven't discussed it with you people because it is a purely tactical issue, but the prospect of thousands of well-intentioned people turning up to liberate Ireland is appalling. The people, qualified people in the MoD and three services agree. What this needs is a modern, highly professional, well-trained fighting force, not a bunch of gung-ho volunteers.'

'There's nothing wrong with volunteers *per se* is there?' Wallis asked.

'No,' Sir James answered, 'but what we are talking about here is the prospect of many dead and many injured. Combat. Body bags. Massive traumas. Blood. Guts. Amputees. Burns.

'The best way to minimize that is the use of trained people. What has been suggested is that elements of the British armed forces, the elements that meet the Celtic description, do the job. They can be reinforced by Irish, but only professional soldiers, airmen or seamen. No one will be trained from scratch. We just won't have time.'

Petra Wallis looked up, about to speak, but Marshall held up his hand. 'I'm in full support of that suggestion.'

'I know that. Isn't this a case of a rose by any other name?'

'It may be. It will not be a force fighting under a British flag as such. We are working on the details, but there are ways of . . . presenting things, shall we say. Shall we proceed? I believe the professor has a few ideas.'

Kiernan, fussing with his spectacles, began to talk.

'I thought it worth while to cover what it means to be Irish. Not in the sense of living and working there today, but to be a first- or second- or even third-generation American or Australian or British person whose people came from Ireland. Can I have the lights down, please?'

Someone got up and drew the curtains and the professor switched on a slide projector.

'The bond is nothing short of extraordinary. Compare it to the feelings manifested in the Polish, the Germans, the Ukrainians, or any of the other large nationality groupings that migrated away from their homelands and it stands out as stronger. You only have to walk the streets of New York, Boston or Liverpool to see them, and the next time you see those faces it will be in Dublin, in Cork, in Galway. The fundamental difference with the Irish is they keep coming back. They may not like it enough to want to stay, it may frustrate them, but they keep returning. Someone once said it was because the Irish have soul. This soul, this Irishness, this Celt runs deep through these people and the location doesn't seem to affect it, other than to often make the Irish abroad seem more ambitious and more successful than his brother or cousin at home.' The professor stopped and blew his nose noisily before continuing. 'Perhaps it's because the opportunity is there, perhaps it's because at home anyone different or achieving more than the other people in the street is resented, is likely to be pulled down by the mob. It doesn't matter. The bond does.'

Kiernan pressed the advance button on the slide projector and an image flicked up on to the wall. It was more than just a large ornate headstone, but less than a true monument. Twelve feet high, two figures flanked a central engraved block that supported a Celtic cross. The sculpted figure on the left was of a girl. The simple cape covering her shoulders was held together over her heart by a Celtic brooch and her right hand supported a sword that rested against her thighs, its point resting on the ground between her feet. Her left hand reached up holding a spear and a faithful wolfhound sat beside her gazing adoringly up at her. Below the girl in bas relief on the huge plinth was a harp, the ancient symbol of Ireland. The figure on the right was similarly dressed, but wearing a bonnet and holding a scroll. Below her was a shield of stars and stripes and an eagle, its wings spread, perched on the top. Between the figures of the girls, words were carved in the stone. Below the ornate Celtic cross was a bust of the man who was buried there.

'This grave is in a run-down graveyard beside the ruins of an old church. The site is almost in the shadows of the Neolithic mound at Dowth in County Meath. The words inscribed are not important. What is important is the sentiment. This man left Ireland for America and returned late in his life to try and do the right thing by his birthplace, the old country. The symbolism is rich. The girl on the left, the faithful Irish wolfhound at her feet, is the perfect image of Irish womanhood, strong, supportive, humble, beautiful but natural. On the right she has changed into a daughter of the revolution, presumably with the declaration of independence or some such in her hand, American, and proud to have a place in such a great country; but the girl is the same, the cloak, the Celtic brooch, the virtue; and she remains undeniably Irish, undeniably Celtic. This imagery is common in Ireland. It reflects the mood and the emotions of families uprooted and torn apart by famine, poverty, hopelessness and simple bad government. But it also demonstrates the bond that exists between Ireland and her sons and daughters. The velvet chain.

'This grave is in the middle of nowhere. It's not uncommon. Its sentiments are so fundamental that they no longer merit mention by the observer. It is that sentiment that we must use, but . . .' he paused and looked at the group, 'in the light of Admiral Marshall's comments, now use in a focused manner. We shall need to remind the sons of Ireland of that velvet chain, but only the sons of Ireland we want. The trained soldiers that Ireland needs. The second part of the effort will be aimed at the people of Ireland, to justify, endorse, give credence and authority to a modern-day Celtic rising. It must be a new rebellion with powerful links to the past, to the roots of Irishness. We will need to give them back their past and to do that we will need to re-create it. This is what I propose we do.'

Professor Kiernan began to elaborate on his thoughts.

The following morning a man in his early sixties walked into the offices of Debrett. He claimed he was co-ordinating the research work for a firm of city lawyers and gave them a detailed brief of his requirement.

'You understand,' the manager said, 'that birth and death records in the Republic of Ireland only date back to the early years of the last century and in some areas there is nothing until 1870, well after the famine.'

'I do,' the man replied. 'We just need a plausible line and a series of choices for realism's sake. It will never have to be proved in a court. There is no will or property involved. Our client wishes to remain anonymous and the search is for personal interest's sake only. However it must be completed in two weeks. Your fee may be structured to accommodate that urgency and any, how shall we say, redeployment of resources.' A very handsome advance ensured that the work was commenced immediately and that same day the Debrett researchers began tracing the family tree of the O'Donnells of County Donegal.

At the same time a sleek corporate jet touched down at Luton airport. As it taxied in towards the terminal and the waiting limousine, Tony O'Malley and the three people with him stood up and stretched their legs, gathering up coats and briefcases. He bent down and looked out at the grey English sky and thought for the hundredth time that day about the four people he wanted from the London end. This was the creative team, the people that would transfer the brief into words, images, film, pictures and hopefully emotional responses in the right people.

It would be then handed over to the production team that was in place and the three managers that had travelled with him. They were, he thought, the best executives in their disciplines in corporate America. One was a procurement wizard, another a logistics specialist and the third was what the juniors on the second floor called a shitfighter. In Cairn Foods Corporation if you had a problem you sorted it out. If you couldn't you called in a shitfighter, one of the handful of 'Project Managers' and using contacts, motivational skills, experience and sheer bloody-mindedness they bulldozed their way to the objective. That team of seven supported by a handful of absolutely trustworthy personal assistants were capable of producing award-winning successful campaigns delivered on schedule time and time again.

By nightfall O'Malley and his team totalling fourteen people were ensconced in Wilden Hall and he walked immediately to the main house to meet the people he would be working with.

Wallis, the two Americans, Marshall and Kiernan were waiting.

'Mr O'Malley,' Marshall began, 'thank you for coming.'

'Mr Tilby was eloquent and persuasive,' O'Malley responded. 'I have conditions.'

'Oh,' Petra Wallis said, 'and what might they be?'

'Fairly simple. My team are not hampered by your civil service thinking. We will keep you updated on progress, but content, design, media and delivery will be our responsibility. Once my people have the brief and the critical path is established we get left alone.'

Marshall bridled at the remark but Petra Wallis raised an eyebrow. 'And what are you prepared to give in return?' she asked.

'What this endeavour needs,' he replied firmly. 'You will get a complete campaign, delivered where you need it, on time.'

'Fair enough,' she said, warming to his directness. 'What do you need to get started?'

The briefing from Kiernan and Marshall took all day. While the professor spoke O'Malley's team listened, some smoking, some taking notes, others firing questions across the room.

O'Malley's first request arrived just as the briefing was finishing. A large box containing a series of video tapes and two dozen books was dumped on the table. It was everything that the best four bookshops in London could offer on Ireland and the Celts, and everything that the BBC could offer from their library.

At eight that night they sat down to eat at the huge refectory tables in the main dining room with the creatives, television production team and technical support people. The atmosphere was a little formal so O'Malley called the head waiter over.

'There a booze cabinet in this place?'

'Yes, sir, but it's locked over in the closed part of the house.'

'Open it. I'll take the rap,' he replied.

'Sorry, sir.'

'How about you and your buddies take the evening off and just leave the keys?'

The man smiled. 'Sorry, sir,' then leaned forward, 'but if you were to look in the pantry table drawer you might just find the keys to the cellars.'

O'Malley stood up a few minutes later and disappeared. When he returned he was pushing a food trolley laden with four cases of wine. An hour later the two groups had meshed and were one big party and he knew that by the morning when they started work in earnest they would do so as a single group. All he needed to do then was give them purpose.

Across at the french windows the security detail had settled in for what they knew would be a long night and someone had gone down for more wine. Someone else had phoned the main house and issued an invitation to the executive committee to come down and slum it.

He tapped a spoon on the table.

'Ladies and gentlemen . . .' Bit by bit the chatter and laughing stopped.

'Before you all get inebriated I have a few words.' O'Malley paused and took a sip from his glass. 'You all know why you are here, what we have to do. Some of you I know and I have worked with, others I know by reputation. We have got a hell of a job to do. We are going to have to produce a campaign that will reach into people's hearts, show them their past and their history and hold up the richness. I am here because I am Irish. Most of you are not, but you are Celts, you are family.'

They were watching him now, their interest teased by the emotive words and O'Malley worked the pause before carrying on. 'This time business has been employed by politics for something truly beneficial and an opportunity to use your skills for something truly decent has arrived. We all knew there was more to life than a thirty-second slot selling toothpaste or yet another documentary about the Labour Party conference. You are going to have the chance to use your skills to free a people, to right a wrong. We are short of time, but if each of you do your part we will get there.

'We are going to be cooped up here for the next three months or so. Tomorrow I will make arrangements for a few comforts and as from now you are all on my company executive payroll in addition to whatever compensation you draw from your regular employers. At the end of the project, your performance having produced the campaign on time, there will be a substantial bonus for each of you . . . So on behalf of my countrymen I thank you in advance for your efforts and,' O'Malley held up his glass, *'Go n'eirigh an bothar leat.'*

Behind him Petra Wallis and Sir James Marshall, who had received the telephoned invitation, had heard the address. Marshall, with his long experience in motivating others, recognized a master at work and smiled.

'What was that?' Wallis asked.

'It's Irish,' Marshall replied. 'It means "may the road rise up to meet you".'

The smaller of the two men was immaculately dressed in a three-piece suit and expensive shoes. His thinning hair was swept back and as he looked down at the man in the chair he spoke.

'So we know the big picture. I just want you to tell me the details.'

The lawyer looked up at him. He had been taken from the small car-park at the building which housed his office. No fuss, no drama, just a hand under his elbow and a searing pain up his arm as he was led to the waiting camper van and driven a short distance with the other man, the American, at the wheel.

'You can't do this. This is kidnapping!'

'Yes, it is,' the Englishman replied, 'and I can. I can do what I like. You see I have the moral high ground and you are nothing but a parasite, a criminal scumbag. So I can and will do exactly what I please.'

'NO! You can't. Your government never sanctions behaviour like this.'

'We have covered that. What a naïve fellow you are. Of course they haven't, because they don't know. They don't want to know how we get our information. They just want it. Now, we can do it the nice way or the nasty way. That's up to you.'

The man paled, his fingers gripping the seat arms and tugged experimentally at the duct tape that secured him.

'Oh no, no blood, no hose-pipe beatings, no pulled fingernails,' the Englishman said, with a little smile.

149

'Makes a mess and I have to return this to Avis this afternoon. No, I'll use a nice little designer drug. You have heard of pentothal? Yes? Read a few spy books? Well this is son of pentothal. Pentothal two, the mutant returns. Sounds like a movie title,' he said cheerfully, pausing and pulling a small case from his pocket. He opened it and extracted a hypodermic syringe and one of the three ampoules that lay snug in the cut foam interior.

'Mutant is right. The trouble is it has side effects. I don't care. I mean,' he smiled flat and hard, 'it's not my mind. Not my memory.' He plunged the needle through the ampoule's soft cover, held it up to the light and drew some of the clear fluid down into the barrel of the syringe. 'Had a fellow once thought he was Napoleon afterwards. He is still a bit odd. The dosage, you see. It can differ for each individual so afterwards, well, you might just be a bit fucked up for life.' He smiled again and squirted a small fountain into the air. 'Your choice, sport. Hard or easy?'

'Do as he says, son,' the American said. He was tall, a lean leathery sun-tanned man with a down home country manner. 'You know what the boys call him? Hannibal. Hannibal the Cannibal. Now me, I'm just a dumb good old boy red-necked shit kicker from the Deep South. I'd just kick the fuck out of you. At least you would walk after a week or two, remember your momma's face, that kind of thing. But Hannibal? Well. Just agree to co-operate.'

The lawyer was terrified. This Englishman obviously enjoyed this sort of thing.

'I'll talk. But you have to protect me afterwards,' he said to the American.

'No. But I won't tell them you said anything. You will be back at your desk later. Just like a long lunch. I'll be back again, you see. There will be more. We are going to become firm friends.'

'All right,' the lawyer said. 'Just keep him away from me.'

The Englishman stood up and turned away to the fitted sink. As he put the syringe down on the draining board alongside the ampoule of distilled water, he smiled. This was the way it should be. Neither of them wanted to wait for the doctor to come in from Century House, the man with the real truth drugs. Then it would take days and it did have its dangers, but most of all the Swiss lawyer would be out of the picture long enough to be noticed.

# 5

The man sat back in a garden lounger. He wore slacks, an open shirt and a panama hat. His face was lean and the tan gained on the boat was now fading to barely darker than his sandy blond hair.

On the table was a tea tray. In the shadow of the teapot, now growing cold, an ant laboured away with a large crumb that had fallen from the plate of biscuits and a bumble bee hovered uncertainly over the nearest flower beds.

He opened one eye lazily and watched as his wife moved among the last of the roses. Considering the rainy cold August they were looking good for September. God had done it again he mused, lying back and relishing the warmth of the sun. An Indian summer.

Edward Montague Montgomery Stewart was forty-four that year. He was a father, a keen fisherman, a yachtsman, a military historian, a fine tactician, a soldier and considered by the junior officers as something of an eccentric. But then they mused that most brilliant soldiers had something of the unusual in them and they were in fact quite proud of their divisional commander. His trademark tartan tam o'shanter was an affectation his men loved, as was the curly walking stick and his occasionally wearing a kilt.

Educated at Eton, he had entered Sandhurst in 1966 and had learned that when you were as abrasive and unforgiving of fools as he was, to survive you needed luck and a mentor. To reach high rank you also had to be an excellent all-rounder, a man who could command by sheer force of personality, charisma, oustanding intellect and ability. You needed to stand head and shoulders above the pack, be proven again and again in command situations. He had all the requirements. 'Monty', in the Irish Guards, had been the youngest major in a peace-time British army and when appointed had been the youngest colonel on the staff list. As a captain he had done two years with the SAS, and fought and won the Military Cross in the follow-up operations after the Dhofari uprising in the Sultanate of Oman. Shortly after rejoining his parent regiment he was made second in command. After two tours as a staff officer, broken by a command in Northern Ireland, he was promoted to officer commanding the Irish Guards. In 1991 he was promoted to brigadier and given the 5th Airborne Brigade, renamed from the 5th Infantry Brigade a few years earlier.

An army career could stall any time after the rank of captain. Officers were judged on their ability to command and those who rose above major were watched very closely indeed. One day the development, grooming and promotions would stop. They had either risen to their level of competence as deemed by those mightier than they in the Ministry of Defence, or they had finally made one powerful enemy too many. Although he was a classic fast-track career officer, 'Monty' Stewart had been expecting to hit the wall since he was a lieutenant colonel and if his command of the 5th Brigade was the culmination of his career, so be it. For him there was no finer mixed unit in the British army.

Two years later, again to his surprise, in 1993 he was promoted major general and made General Officer Commanding 3rd UK Division. From his headquarters at Bulford he commanded his old unit the 5th Airborne Brigade, the 3rd Commando Brigade and a heavy brigade that would take on a new designation, but was currently going through the pains of defence cuts.

But now thoughts of things martial were eased out by

the warmth of the day and he dozed in the sun, the politics and Whitehall warriors forgotten, enjoying the last few days of his leave. The first two weeks had been spent aboard a friend's boat, either lazing in a secluded bay or sailing the Swan 65 through the warm blue waters surrounding the Balearic islands.

Helen enjoyed it, too. When he had first taken her sailing she had been frightened when the boat heeled over, but now she could take the wheel and hold a course with two reefs in the sails while lesser mortals lay green in the bunks below. The four of them sailed whenever they could and it was one of those easy relationships that the years had rounded and smoothed like a stone on a river bottom.

A substantial sum left by an aunt in her will made him independently wealthy. As GOC 3rd UK Division the MoD would have supplied a residence, but he chose to make his own arrangements. On the salary paid by the army he could never have afforded the house with its four and a half acres of paddock and garden near Salisbury. It was under half an hour from his headquarters and yet with its thatched roof and Tudor beams it could have been three hundred years away or anywhere in England.

There was a happy burst of barking from the house and a pair of labradors bustled out of the door escorting and playing with a man. He was in his thirties, neatly dressed in slacks, an open shirt and a hacking jacket. He was James Dalby, an intelligence officer attached to the division.

'Hello, James,' Helen called, putting her basket down. 'Lovely surprise. Tea? I can heat the pot. Edward will have more.'

'Thank you, Mrs Stewart, I will,' he replied, rubbing one of the dogs under its ear as it rolled blissfully on the grass.

Stewart opened his eyes and squinted lazily from under the brim of his hat.

'Ah! Jimmy,' he said. 'How are you?' Stewart's delivery was staccato, a clipped bark that echoed images of empire.

'Fine, General. Thank you. How was the holiday?'

'Excellent, Jimmy. Excellent. Wore a pair of shorts and not much else for days at a time. Weather's so good, no wonder the Dons get nothing done. Pull up a chair.'

Dalby reached into a pocket, pulled a buff envelope clear and handed it to Stewart before sitting at the table.

'Good God! Reduced to runner are you?' Stewart said, taking the envelope and opening it.

'Came through this morning, sir.'

There was silence for a few seconds as Stewart read the typed note. A signature was scrawled along the bottom.

'Everything all right, sir?' Dalby asked.

'I should say so, Jimmy. I'm up to London tomorrow. Another bloody sub-committee in Whitehall wanting to reduce the army, no doubt.'

Dalby wasn't fooled. He had known General Stewart not only as his divisional commander and as commander of Five Brigade, but also when he was a very junior liaison officer in the Falklands campaign. Stewart, then a fire-brand of a colonel, was attached to General Moore's staff and one thing was for sure. When his jaw clenched as he read or thought there was something on.


'We need to meet right away,' Petra Wallis said into the phone. 'There will be others at the meeting, the usual types with vested interests.'

'I understand,' Marshall replied. That meant MoD and the Americans.

'Two o'clock today in London. Come to my office and I will drive you over. Can you bring the other two?'

'We'll be there,' he said. He looked at his watch. Six in the morning. He buzzed for the steward and when the man knocked he didn't bother pulling on his dressing-gown, instead just opening the door dressed in his shorts. 'Get Miss Richards and the professor up, please. Tell them we leave for London in twenty minutes.'

They arrived just after one and as they drove across to the MoD meeting room Petra brought them up to date.

'The snatch worked. We now have the asset on our books.' She sighed, wondering where to begin. 'Maynouth was right. The objective is definitely to pressure the world over Palestine. Secondly, they think they just may be able to hang on to it if they look as though they are prepared to fight. Planned with the assistance of the Lebanese in return for a massive interest-free loan in the rebuilding of Beirut, it will be enforced by, wait for it, the Libyans. Standing army, air force, the works. Other Arab states have put in token bits of support like equipment, but the wild card will be the one group who have promised massive support when the time comes.'

'Who?' Marshall asked.

'Iraq. Saddam bloody Hussein has promised men and equipment to support the Palestinian brothers in this new phase of the struggle. Etcetera etcetera. They have refused, apparently. Too much bad press. They are unhappy about using the Libyans, but acknowledge they can't do it on their own.'

'So the resistance will face Libyan regulars and Palestinian fighters,' Professor Kiernan said.

'Correct,' Wallis said. 'Obviously the Libyan involvement will be couched as answering an appeal for help from legitimate authorities.'

There was silence then as the big car eased through the streets towards Whitehall, each of the occupants thinking about the implications. Finally Kiernan spoke. 'Well if they want a fight,' the old professor said firmly, 'they have got one.'

Patrick O'Sullivan looked round the small group gathered in the cottage. All wore balaclavas and all had chosen a name.

'You are all wondering who the others are. Don't ask

and don't volunteer your identity. Most of you do know each other but you will never discuss this with anyone outside the group. These people are the only ones you will ever meet. There are others, to be sure, but you won't know them. All you will know is your own cell, the boys you have found.'

'But what if one of us is arrested and, you know . . . beaten up.'

'If any of you are ever picked up you must hold on for as long as you can. Give the others in your group time to get clear. We will cover the drills for that,' O'Sullivan replied. As he spoke a man moved through the shadows behind him unwrapping something on the old table.

'Let's get on with it. You are here tonight to learn the first of a few lessons.'

The man at the table moved forward. In the dim light they could barely see his eyes through the holes in his balaclava and when he flicked on the goose-neck desk lamp that illuminated the table surface even his accent was indistinct.

'You can call me John. It's not my real name, but it will do. You people have made a decision. A decision to fight when the time comes. The style of fight you take to the enemy makes you an irregular. You can be the scourge of an army a hundred times your size because they never know where or when you will hit next. You will never get involved in pitched battles. You will hit and run. But you have one thing in common with a regular soldier. You will learn to use the tools of war, and like him you will learn it and learn it and learn it. You will then teach your own teams. More like me will be coming to help but you will begin on your own.' He held up a short stubby weapon with a curved magazine. 'Tonight I am going to show you how to strip, clean and reassemble the weapon you will be using. So listen carefully. You life will depend on what you take away from here tonight.' The man held the rifle down in the light.

'This is a Kalashnikov Model 47. You have seen them in the movies and on TV. Some of you will have the folding stock models of the 47, the AKM, others the more modern 74, but they are essentially the same weapon. This is the most commonly found assault weapon in the world. You will be using it for two reasons. It is very rugged and absolutely dependable and it is the weapon of choice of your enemy. That means you can steal and use his ammunition. This rifle is a German design refined by old man Kalashnikov and manufactured in most of the old Soviet bloc countries. It is accurate and lightweight and it will kill at distance, although you will probably have trouble hitting anything over three hundred yards due to the short barrel. The magazine holds thirty rounds and although the weapon will fire on full automatic, you will never do that. Anyone tell me why?'

'Because the last half of the magazine will be going up into the sky?' someone asked. The SAS man nodded.

'Correct. It is wasteful and dangerous. Murphy's law says that the time you need a new magazine is the same time as your opponent finds you in his sights.'

He felt better about the group as they began to interact. All had owned shotguns and understood the basics of cleaning and care, of leading a target and range, of ballistics and trajectory. In the coming weeks they would learn to use the rifle in daylight, in the dark, until they could hit what they aimed at and strip it and rebuild it blindfolded. Then they would move on to the other weapons, the easily concealed H&K MP5 that the Americans would be providing and grenades. Two of each cell would be trained to use the Carl Gustav anti-tank weapon and they would also learn the basics of what could be achieved with a length of cortex, C4, detonators, timers and a power source.

The moment personal strengths began to emerge, so would the specialities. A second pair would be taught how to use the micro satellite communications gear, another given basic medical training, enough to keep someone alive after a fire-fight.

The most important lesson of all was the psychology of the irregular. The thinking, motivation and rationale that wears down and finally defeats the opponent. They had to believe it could be done and they would be given a series of lectures on the stages of an armed struggle, the Maoist theory, with numerous examples of where the irregulars had won.

Finally the best pair of each group would be singled out and taken away for three weeks of intensive training in a camp in the bleak heather moors outside Elgin in Scotland.

O'Sullivan was pleased. This core group of nine men would each go back and recruit his own cell. Once the time came they could create havoc across the entire south-west of Ireland.


A woman in her forties, heavy and with a slight limp, lugged a shopping bag up the street and finally sat down on a bench by the park gate, the bag held across her lap, both hands clasping the worn handles. Her coat was old and dirty and as people passed her she held out her hand.

Across the road a big car slowed down and pulled into the underground parking area as a bus pulled to a halt and people clambered off hurrying away to wherever they were going. A young man, mingling with the passengers, crossed the street.

As he passed the woman he reached into his pocket and dropped a coin into her hand. 'Have a cup of tea,' he said.

'Generous little shit aren't you?' she said looking at the ten pence coin.

The man chuckled. 'He's all yours darling.'

'Thanks,' she said sarcastically as he walked away.

She pocketed the coin, the same one he had given her

yesterday when he had been dressed as a tourist complete with camera. Up the street a taxi was parked, its driver in the tea-shop.

In Dublin the MI5 surveillance teams, the watchers, had isolated four people they believed to be bad guys within the structure of the Taoiseach's office. They along with others were followed until routines were established and all contacts were photographed and identified. Every day they isolated more of the organization, its residences and operational areas.

Captain Scott had deployed his men around the counties and they were following up the leads that were coming through from the sifters and the fledgling resistance. The SAS men had been given one county each, twenty men searching for further arms stores and base camps, and two men now dedicated to training the first resistance cells. The SAS men provided training where required, but were pleased to be told that they would be relieved of that role in the next few days. Four American Special Forces A-teams were on their way in. The Green Berets, specialists in training for armed resistance, would relieve the SAS men for intelligence gathering. A system of responsibilities was drawn up, and operational areas were divided between Patrick O'Sullivan's group in the south-west, Peter Morris's eastern cells and Rory McMahon, Scott's boyhood friend, who had a fast-growing, very professional group in Birr who would cover the central area. From there they would launch their campaigns as far as Kildare, Longford and Roscommon.

All that was now needed was a small group in County Wexford and a larger active unit in the north-west. Both came within days.

An SAS sergeant, David Kenny, who had spent the last three days sniffing around in County Wexford, was sitting in his car watching a building when he noticed something odd. The building was a new barn and utility shed the size of a small warehouse. Recently constructed, it didn't gel with its surroundings, an ugly green metal-cladded monster in among the smaller stone sheds and walls that were rural Ireland.

There had been comings and goings. A group of men had moved in and yesterday a woman had arrived, a short raven-haired individual in her twenties. The men fitted the profile, but only loosely. They were an odd mix, not the short-haired look-alikes that he had found in New Ross and Carrick-on-Suir. They were, he felt, the local detachment, the enforcers that would be there when the time came. But these were different. These were individuals in every sense, all wearing jeans and casual western clothing and the woman seemed to be giving the orders.

He had taken a set of pictures of her from the hill over the old farmhouse the day before and had spent the morning watching the farm and was about to drive away when it happened. A car pulled into the farm's driveway and came to an angry halt on the mossy damp gravel of the courtyard.

A girl climbed out, blonde and angry.

He turned the engine off and, knowing the car couldn't be seen beneath the trees, he climbed clear and settled down at the end of the hedge with a pair of binoculars in time to see the two women arguing, the blonde and the dark-haired one. The dark girl's hand flashed and too far away to hear the slap hit he knew it had hurt as it knocked the blonde's head back. She was dragged into the cottage by two of the men and Sergeant Kenny, who had decided that she was a friendly, sat back to observe.

Half an hour later a vehicle pulled into the drive and three men got out. Short hair. One in charge gesturing with his thumb to the other two. A few moments later they returned, pulling the blonde girl with them.

He decided to follow them and when they turned on to the road to New Ross he decided to stop them. Covert is one thing, he rationalized, but watching a friendly civilian getting slotted was another. He overtook the car and drove fast for two or three miles before pulling the car to a halt at an angle, so that it not only blocked half the road but concealed the narrow farm entrance ahead.

As the car came round the bend he flagged it down, standing in the way as if there had been an accident. The car drew to a halt and he walked forward and was at the driver's window before he pulled his gun out of his pocket and pointed it into the car.

'Out.'

The driver's annoyance turned to amazement. Sergeant Kenny cocked the action, and pushed the barrel into the man's neck. 'Out. Now. All of you or I'll fucking well shoot,' he snarled, his voice taking on the thick accent of the north, of Ulster, where the ability to sound like a local was essential if you were to survive living in the heartland of the IRA. He flicked a look into the back seat where the third man sat with the girl. Her hands were tied and she had been beaten. Her lip was split and blood was congealing in a cut over her eye.

The men were moving, but in the wary way that men do when they are unsure. The one in the back was looking at the man in the front passenger seat awaiting a signal or orders. The boss. Not an officer. A sergeant perhaps, Kenny acknowledged to himself. 'Wallets, money on the deck. Move it.' He knew they were armed, but he didn't want them to know that he knew. Watching from the corner of his eye he turned to the girl. 'Jesus! They do this to you?'

She nodded. 'Please help me,' she said.

The man on the end went for his gun and Kenny's hand flicked back slamming the barrel of his heavy Browning across the man's temple. He dropped like a stone and Kenny reached down and took his wallet from his jacket pocket and the Tokarev pistol from his belt. He looked at the next man pointing his weapon at his head.

'You got a gun?'

The man nodded.

'On the deck. Butt first.'

He took both men's guns and spoke again. 'Your turn, shitheads. Your money or join your friend.'

The pair handed their money over. Their boss out of action they had capitulated and any thought of resistance was gone.

'You come with me. At least I'm not going to beat you up,' he said to the girl. She nodded. Kenny pulled the keys from the ignition and threw them into the grass on the roadside. A minute later they were driving away, Kenny driving the car fast, wanting distance between them and the incident.

'Who are you?' the girl asked. She had started crying, soft tears rolling down her face.

'Just someone who doesn't like seeing women getting slapped around.'

One hand reaching up gingerly to feel the cut on her lip.

'Well. Thanks,' she said.

'Why did they do it?' he asked.

'It's a long story. I was just being silly. Briget told me not to,' she sniffed, feeling her lip again.

'Who's Briget?'

'My sister.'

Kenny drove for a few minutes thinking it through. They knew her. They might know where she lives. They could be there soon. Now possibly, certainly today.

'Where do you live?'

'Near Waterford.'

'Do they know that?' he asked

'I'm not sure.'

'I'll take you back there now. Pack a bag. Have you got somewhere else to go?'

She looked at him. 'Why are you doing this? You don't know me. Anyway, I don't want to move. I like my flat.'

'They had something nasty planned for you. They know you know that. They will come looking for you.'

She thought for a few seconds. 'You know who they are, don't you?' She paused before adding, 'I could go to my sister's for a few days.'

Kenny drove her home, evading her questions, and when they arrived he walked her to her door.

'Be quick,' he said, his eyes scanning the street.

Briget was identical. The moment Kenny saw her he realized they must be twins and without the cuts and bruises her sister sported she was very attractive indeed. The blonde hair framed a clear-skinned fresh face. Her jaw was square, too square for the look to ever be considered classical, but her ice-blue eyes made up for it. They were piercing and flecked with something hard and suspicious as she stood in the living-room doorway.

'It seems I have to thank you. Sue gets indignant and always wants to take on the world. I'm sure we have taken enough of your time,' she said formally, ushering him towards the door.

'What set her going?' Kenny asked.

Briget opened the door to the street. 'Thank you again.'

'I think you should move. They may know where you are.'

'I'm sure they do,' she replied acidly.

Kenny moved his car round the corner, where he could watch the road that the house fronted on to but be largely concealed by the hedges and fences. An hour later there had been no movement at the house. Silly bitch, he thought. He looked at his watch. The incident on the road had happened three hours before. If the hostiles had good intelligence they would know that this girl had a sister, particularly a twin. He thought about it. They could try Sue's flat and then come here, or maybe another family member's house. No, he decided. If they knew the girls then they knew that they would stick together. They would come here. He decided to stay. The time it took them to arrive and the manner of their arrival would say much to an observer. He wouldn't interfere this time. The girls had had their warning. He couldn't make it any plainer than he had. When they came he would just take pictures and observe. He had done his bit. Almost compromised himself in the process. If he had been, the boss would be very pissed off indeed.

He was still justifying his waiting around when they came.

A blue Transit van pulled up to the kerb and a small four-door saloon with two men pulled in behind it. This is good, he thought. Classical Third World snatched pickup. No back-up, no closed streets, but even as he was thinking it, he was dropping his camera to the car floor and reaching for his bag. Fuck it! Fuck it! Fuck it! In it was a balaclava mask, a silencer and magazines for his handgun, nine millimetre like the first but these loaded with soft-nosed Glaser safety 'stopper' rounds. The Glaser rounds, specially developed for special forces, were considered safe because they stopped in the body and didn't travel through into innocents or through walls. They were also called stoppers because the nine millimetre hitting the body and stopping, expended all its energy on surrounding tissue. Someone shot with a Glaser round stopped. Dead.

He screwed the silencer on to the barrel and with the mask in his pocket crossed the back fence gate at a run. But if he had to use the gun then he had failed. He would have bodies to clear up, and they would be missed by their own command within hours.

The back door was unlocked and he moved into the kitchen fast. The two girls were sitting at the table. Startled they reacted, Sue in some instinctive gesture raising her arm to cover her injured face, but Briget rising, a bread knife in her hand, her eyes flashing with defiance.

'They're at the front. Quickly! Come with me!' he hissed.

'And you brought them, you bastard!' she responded. 'Touch us and I'll cut you!'

'I'm a friend! Stay here and you will die,' he replied. 'You have a few seconds and they'll be knocking on the door pretending to be the fucking gas board. Now move it.'

Briget thought quickly, weighing the alternatives, and finally she took Sue by the hand.

They were out of the door when they heard footsteps on the path. To cross to the back gate they would be in line of sight of whoever was walking round the house. Briget tugged his sleeve and gestured and seconds later they were in the garage; the door swung silently shut behind them as the first of the men moved round to the kitchen door.

As Kenny pulled his gun clear from his waistband, its ugly silencer unmistakable, he waved them back behind the tea-chests and boxes at the end of the garage behind an old Ford Sierra that was on blocks.

He pulled the spare magazine containing the Glaser rounds from the bag and ejecting the original magazine from the gun into his hand, he inserted the man-stoppers and cocked the action.

He began willing the men to leave, willing them to go. If you want to live, then don't come this way. Just wander round the house and go. Don't look properly. Don't see the tea cups on the table, don't come looking or I will fucking slot you and everything will go pear-shaped.

He stood frozen against the wall, his eye to a crack in the door frame and watched as a minute later the kitchen door was pulled open and two of the men walked into the back garden, looking around them as they moved back towards the path. Both were armed. Kenny recognized the jutting shapes under their long coats as automatic weapons of one kind or another.

He gave them two minutes and then led the girls over the back fence and down through the gardens to the end of the street where they collected his car and were soon driving towards his rented farm cottage.

Sue had taken two analgesics that Kenny had found in his kit and, secure in his awesome competence and the adrenalin gone from her bloodstream, she now slept in the back seat.

'It's time you came clean,' he said softly to Briget. 'Why are they after you?'

'I'm saying nothing,' she hissed.

'Oh,' Kenny said, dropping the northern accent and falling back into his soft native Inverness lilt, 'little madam is a tough guy.'

She looked at him. 'Who are you? You're no provo.'

'Why would a provo be in bed with them?'

'They give them guns, training. Why not?'

She knew they were Arabs, he realized. 'Why don't you start with what happened to Sue at the farm?'

'You saw it?' she replied, the realization dawning. 'You were watching . . . you stopped the car deliberately.'

'Why did she get thumped?'

'Who are you?'

'Fuck who I am,' he snapped. 'They were going to slot her. She has really pissed them off. Those three men were a clean-up squad. And the four this afternoon were serious. They want her out of the way. So I'll ask again, what has she done? What has she done or said or threatened that would make them react like that?'

'You know about them,' she said flatly. It was a statement not a question.

'Yes.'

'Who are you? British?'

He nodded.

'Why?'

'Because it's about to go from bad to worse and your

167

people are in no way able to deal with it,' he replied honestly.

'Gutless bastards.'

'They have their reasons,' he replied.

She looked at him, proud and strong, her eyes flashing defiance. 'Maybe, but I'm not taking this lying down and believe it or not we don't need the bloody British to sort out our problems.'

'No one says you have to, but we need to know what's happening. Where they are. What they are up to. It's not just us, either.'

'Who?'

Kenny said nothing, just watched the road.

'The Americans?' she asked.

'What's it to you?' he replied. 'You aren't prepared to help. Like they say, you are either part of the solution or you are part of the problem. I don't have any more time to waste on wankers. I'll drop you in the village.'

She sat beside him silently for a few seconds and finally she spoke. Her voice was soft, almost as if she was thinking aloud.

'My brother is a farmer,' she began. 'He's not really our brother. Sue and I were orphans. Our parents died in an accident when we were small. We were taken in and John had arrived the year before, another lost waif. We grew up together. He is twenty-four now, four years older than us. He bought that farm. The place you found Sue.' She looked at him then and smiled. 'She loved it there.' Kenny noticed the past tense.

'John borrowed the money for the farm. He was meeting payments okay until two months ago and they jacked up the interest and foreclosed. Overnight. No warning. No letters, no nothing. John was furious as you can imagine. He went to the people, created a fuss and we haven't seen him since. That was a month ago. Yesterday we heard that new folk had moved on to the farm.'

'Are there others?'

'Two at least that I know of. That's how I made the connection. Same finance house. Same people. Something nasty is going on. It's not like the Germans with their cottages. This is sinister.'

'And you want to stop them?' Kenny said.

'Oh yes,' she said, 'and I will.' She dropped her voice in case Sue was awake to hear her, 'You see, I think John is dead. Sue and John. They are . . . were very close. Adored each other. They are not going to get away with that. No way.' Her voice was laced with a quiet conviction. Kenny knew she should be recruited.

Next day she was interviewed by Peter Morris and Gordon Persse and two days later she was advised that if she formed a resistance cell, people could be found to train and equip them. She told them she wanted her boyfriend in. He could be useful and they listened with growing interest.

It was Rory McMahon, the Birr veterinary surgeon, who found the last leader. His wife's sister had been 'walking out' with a man for some years and since there was no talk of marriage they were often the talk of Ballina. Joseph Connor O'Reilly was a thin, untidy intense man whom women temporarily wanted to feed and mother. Temporarily because there was a hunted, haunted madness about him sometimes and a depth and an intensity in his eyes that made other men uneasy. His poetry was beautiful and wild like the sea against the cliffs and when he recited it, his voice a rich timbre like poured treacle, people stopped to listen and women forgot the torment in his eyes and saw into his heart, and while he spoke they loved him. People would ask to hear a piece, politely to be sure and the bar would go quiet, the Uillean pipes squeezed into silence and Joseph O'Reilly would drink from his glass and begin, the windswept hair and patched jacket as much part of him as the words he spoke.

Rory drove up the next weekend and he and Joseph took a glass or two together while Rory felt the way. He was in no doubt of the outcome. Joseph, who loved Ireland as only an Irish poet could do, would die for her if asked. It was the sort of cause that would drag him from his dreams and give reason to everything.

The following Tuesday the five of them gathered in a Dublin safe house, the lecturer, the farmer, the poet, the vet and the student. The intention was to clarify communications and lines of command and to preserve security each was given a code name that would remain theirs for the duration.

Kiernan had chosen the names. The recipients thought they had been simply plucked from history, a random meander though the pages of a book. But Kiernan had chosen them carefully, names for latter-day bards to weave into stories, names that tugged at an Irish heart, names that lent historical credence to the cause.

Pat O'Sullivan became Fergus, Rory McMahon became Conan, and Briget Villiers took on Cuchulain. Peter Morris took the name Murtagh, from Murtagh mac Erc, a High King in ancient times. Joseph O'Reilly was delighted with his code. He became Finn mac Cumhal, a warrior from deep in Celtic legend. Collectively they would be called Tuatha de Dannan, the folk of the god whose mother is Danna, but already they had a far more basic name and one that was to be in common usage. Down in the southwest where Pat O'Sullivan's groups had already settled in they were calling each other simply, and without any disrespect to the women in the cells, the *Buachailli*, Irish Celtic for the 'boys'.

Aisling watched the man strip back the last of the wires and finish the connection. The conduit ran away from them, inside the lining of the attic insulation to the sealed room at the end. Boxes and old trunks layered in cobwebs covered the floor. Ingeniously, a set of thin steel cables lowered a four by four beam from the high attic roof. Once dropped to its lowest setting one could walk the length of the beam over the top of the cobwebs and dust to the sliding panel in the false end wall. On the other side a state of the art multiband transmitter receiver sat on a small table, back-ups nearby. A satellite receiver dish was built into the roof and a skylight could be slid back at the precise time to receive signals, facsimiles or coded computer data. The cable ran away down the conduit and through a buried pipe up to the stand of trees on the hill above the house where the antennae were concealed. In the last week the house and outbuildings had been transformed. Once Scott had approved the site things had happened very quickly.

The Vietcong had used underground facilities and tunnels. Everyone thought it highly unlikely that anyone would do that in modern Europe, which was precisely why they chose to do it. A small but expert detachment from the Royal Engineers had arrived and using a mixture of their own equipment, re-painted yellow and driven across the border, and locally rented plant, they had begun work at a feverish pace, resistance personnel helping by chatting to the locals who noticed and spreading a story about new sewage pipes.

For every man operating a machine at surface level there were ten below ground. There was now a tunnel between the basement and the barn and a second that ran to a bolthole on the far side of the woodshed. Both were wide enough for people to sleep in the passages. From both the house and barn smaller emergency exit tunnels ran down toward the river. Resistance fighters could exit from rat-holes at a dozen points along its length.

Work had transformed the old basement of the ruin down by the river, too. There beneath the rubble and stark remnants of the fire that had destroyed the house in the thirties was a tunnel that would lead to an air-conditioned bunker where medical supplies and basic equipment would allow treatment of wounded resistance fighters. There were fourteen weapons caches within twelve miles of the house.

The farm would be the command centre of the resistance and in the attic data coming in could be analysed, decisions made and instructions and orders sent out. Everything would be backed up in Wales and if anything happened to the farm's occupants or equipment then Wales could assume command in seconds.

Local area commanders would take their orders on strategic issues from their high command, at this time comprising the five regional commanders and Kiernan. Localized tactical strikes were up to them. What they hit and when they hit it would be a regional commander's decision. All Kiernan asked was that they consider the big picture and be prepared to divert resources to strategic targets if requested. There were already differing philosophies. Pat O'Sullivan, the leader in the south-west, was hugely aggressive. He wanted to hit out at every opportunity, in direct contrast with Rory McMahon who was applying a more considered approach, mindful of the risk of terrible reprisals.

The MI5 engineer finished the work on the cables and began putting away his tools. Ten minutes later he was on his way back to Dublin. The house was quiet for the first time in days, the work completed except for the finishing touches that they would do themselves over the coming days.

Aisling found Scott in the kitchen, filling the kettle. He looked tired, his eyes rimmed with red and his movements slow like one conserving what he had left.

'You look dreadful,' she said. 'When was the last time you slept for more than an hour?'

'Dunno,' he answered. It didn't matter. Sleep was the

last thing he had time for. He had spent the last weeks criss-crossing the countryside, linking up with his scattered force to debrief them and issue new orders. There were now more than twenty cells reporting to the five area commanders. When O'Reilly and Villiers had their areas up to strength there would be somewhere between twenty-five and thirty six-person active service teams, each supported by local people who would feed them, hide them, treat their wounds and pass them information. It was hoped that once it all began those cells would form the basis for larger formations, the recruits coming from a people at last forced to the realization that they had an enemy in their midst. Scott himself had supervised the caching of arms in a hundred locations, each cache only known to him and one other local area resistance member.

'I'll sleep tonight,' he added. I'd better, he thought. Tomorrow's job would be unforgiving of error. 'London think it's time we began the lists. We have to look at each of the people concerned. Home, office, families. Establish how we get them out, routes, times, numbers.'

'I can help with that,' she replied.

'I know,' he smiled. 'That's why I'm telling you.'

They sat at the table and Scott began to brief her on the first half-dozen people that London wanted extraction plans for. She tried to concentrate on what he was saying as he spoke, but sitting close as she was the old feeling was there, the churning tummy, the desire to reach across and just touch him mixed with the need to mother him, feed him and put him to bed like the second night they had met. When he had finished she stood up to freshen the pot.

'Have you got a girlfriend, Aiden?' she asked matter-of-factly.

'Sorry?'

'A girlfriend. Anyone special?' She was facing the wall, her heart pounding. She couldn't have asked facing him.

She was modern and clever and well educated, but she was still Irish and Irish girls don't go asking that sort of thing.

'Not any more,' he said with a short laugh.

'Oh?' She hoped she didn't sound pleased. 'Why not?'

He smiled, rubbing his eyes, the memories flooding back. It was always the same. At first they liked the officer and gentlemen bit, the thought of dashing uniforms and the season's balls exciting. But there wasn't enough of that and he was away too often. The fact that he never spoke about his work was exciting in its own way, but the time they thought they would have together didn't exist. The last two leaves he had tried to spend with someone had been interrupted and soon the very mystery they had initially found exciting was an issue. The last had been the daughter of a army man. Lucy. He thought she would understand if anyone would, but even she tired of the absences and the insidious flow of negative remarks began. Eventually Lucy, at first so welcoming in her little flat in Windsor, became like the others, resentful of the cancelled dates and infrequency of it all. The final time he had arrived unannounced after driving down from Hereford. It was to be a surprise. It was. Using the key she had given him he let himself into the flat and found her in the throes of an orgasm being administered by a youthful guards officer. She had been seeing him for some time and he was eminently acceptable to the family. He heard they later got married. For the last two years he had spent so much time deployed or in training that he had never sustained a relationship for more than a weekend. It just wasn't worth it.

'I dunno,' he said. 'It doesn't work.'

'Why not?' she asked, turning back to him, her voice sounding small and querulous.

'They want to be part of your life, I think. You know, be involved in it, its decisions and options. They want open, honest relationships, plans and fun and consistency and I could never give them that. They want to be able to plan a dinner party and know you will be there and say, "How was your day at the office dear?" '

'And you say, "I could tell you but I'd have to kill you?" ' she said, repeating the old joke she had overheard when with the men in the barn one night.

'Yeah.' He laughed. 'They don't like that.'

'I can't see why,' she said drily, with a hint of sarcasm, and smiling immediately to ease the truth.

'I can,' he replied.

'That's half the problem fixed then,' she said. 'Look, ah . . .' She retreated back to the sink, pushing her hands into her jeans pockets, her hair swinging, nervous and stammering. Jesus, what am I doing she thought. No. I have to ask. He never will. God, I wish I was American. They do this all the time. She looked him directly in the eye. 'If you get a night off sometime, want to see a movie or something . . .' Please don't laugh, please don't say no or I shall die, I will anyway. 'God I'm so embarrassed,' she added, grinning. 'Anyway, I know already so you don't have to kill me.'

He looked at her, the smile beginning around his deep blue eyes and dropping down to his mouth.

'I'd love to,' he said.

Later that evening he stood behind her as she brushed her hair and slipped his arm around her waist. She melted back into him and closed her eyes. Then she turned round and faced him, holding his arm in place in case he stole it back.

'Do you fancy me?' she asked.

'Mmmmm,' he murmured.

'Really?'

'Yes, really.'

'Then why did you make me ask you out!' she blurted.

He ran his hand through the hair that lay against her cheek.

'Really?' She nodded. 'Because I thought there was no way a girl as beautiful as you would not be engaged or something, because I had given up creating these kinds of problems, because if this thing blows there will be no time for it and because I was afraid you would say no, because it could be a whole can of worms . . .'

'Well,' she lifted her finger to his lips to stop him talking and then folded her arms across her front like the first night they met, 'that's honest enough and I'm very flattered. Now you are going to bed and if I see you up before o six hundred hours you will be in trouble. Understand, soldier?'

'Yes, ma'am.'

'Kiss me goodnight, then,' she said, moving closer, wanting to feel his hard body against hers.


The next morning Scott met a man who had flown in from London. He was a very talented thief who specialized in fine art and those who knew said there were few alarms in Europe that he couldn't break through. That had been his downfall. His *modus operandi* was well known and his vanity couldn't resist proving his professional skills every so often. A year before he had been arrested by London's Metropolitan Police and was serving the first of six years at Her Majesty's pleasure.

Under a long-standing arrangement with the Home Office, certain prisoners with particular skills could earn credits for sentence reductions. This was however the first time breaking and entering would be temporarily included on the approved list of community services.

Jack 'Pliers' Parsons was delivered to Scott by a hard-nosed detective sergeant. 'He's all yours. I want him back this time tomorrow.'

'Fine,' Scott replied.

'And son,' the detective finished, 'don't lose him or my guv will have bloody kittens, all right?'

'Yeah.'

They watched the detective drive away before the man, a thin-faced slim fellow in his fifties, turned to Scott.

'What's the job, then?'

'I'll take you to have a look at it now. We go in tonight.'

'No. I work alone,' Parsons said.

'You do as you are told,' Scott said with a smile.

Half an hour later Scott pointed over the road from their car.

'The Museum.'

'Ah. Historical bric-à-brac,' Parsons said. 'Not my forte, but I do know a thing or two about it.'

'You ever been in there?' Scott asked.

He nodded. 'Had a look a few years ago. Ancient bronze and gold is difficult to shift. A few collectors will take it, but it's not easy, my son, not easy at all. What are we after, some of the gold?'

'The Ardagh chalice, the Tara brooch and the Cong cross,' Scott replied casually.

Parsons, smoking, almost choked on his cigarette, and coughed loudly.

'The Ardagh chalice? You must be fucking mad!'

'Why?'

'There's not a kid in this country who doesn't recognize it. Christ! The Tara brooch? It's Ireland's bloody crown jewels.'

'Getting breezy are you? Can't manage it?' Scott taunted gently.

'No. Nicking a painting is one thing, but I won't lift a nation's treasures. Too emotive. Too big.'

Scott grinned. 'Let's go and have a look, shall we?'

'We'll have every rozzer in Ireland after us,' Parsons replied miserably.

They walked separately into the high domed entrance hall, Scott stopping to buy the guide book at the souvenir counter as Parsons expertly scanned the windows and door for the tell-tale alarm wiring that would be the first level. Further in there would be laser beams. Scott meandered his way through to the room where the Cong cross, the Tara brooch and the famous Ardagh chalice sat inside glass cases. Each was a unique specimen, each an example of the finest workmanship of its kind and each absolutely priceless.

Schoolchildren moved in a noisy swirling gaggle and through them he watched Parsons as the master thief familiarized himself with the layout and security systems.

Eventually he sidled up to Scott. 'Pathetic, really. They deserve to lose the lot. I know heavy-handed yobs who could turn this place over and not get rumbled.'

They left and Parsons had Scott drive him to a hardware store where he bought a few basic tools. They visited another three stores before the thief was satisfied and the purchases filled a small duffel bag.

That night he demonstrated the skills he was so proud of and exactly four minutes after slipping the lock on the staff access door they were in front of the first glass case. The cross, its fine filigree work rough to the touch, had been found in Cong and was thought to have been made in the eleventh century. It stood over eighteen inches high, the size of a large processional piece, and Parsons wrapped it carefully in bubble plastic before sliding it into the duffel bag. Next came the Tara brooch. Metal with inset gems, it was a cloak clasp similar to a penannular brooch. Scott slipped it into his pocket. He looked again, shrugged and lifted a gold torc and a pair of earrings out of a neighbouring case, and finally they approached the case containing the Ardagh chalice.

Parsons waved a finger at him, then squeezed his palms together raising an eyebrow. Scott nodded. A pressure plate. If the chalice was lifted with the circuit intact the alarms would go off. Parsons dropped to his knees and peeled back the linoleum floor exposing the wiring. He created a second circuit with a piece of wire and two crocodile clips below the cabinet and as Scott watched, his heartbeat increasing, he cut the wires above his new clipped circuit. Two minutes later they were letting themselves out of the building.

'Those earrings you lifted,' Parsons said casually as they took the road northwards. 'They on the list?'

'Mind your own business,' Scott replied.

'They are priceless. You know that, don't you? They were made about eight hundred years before Christ.'

His tone was not of avarice but rather one of concern. Scott realized that his reluctance to steal national treasures was not because they were difficult to sell, but because he had his own peculiar brand of ethics.

'They'll be safe enough,' Scott said.

At that moment a scientist working late at the government forensic laboratory at Aldermaston finally made a match. The letter written by the Irish prime minister's son was on paper widely available throughout the world. The pad, commonly used in offices, was made in Manchester and sold in seventy countries under nine different trade names. The envelope was a little more useful. A cheap acid-based dye led them to a Greek manufacturer, which limited sales to the eastern Mediterranean. There the search had stopped, until someone tried to lift the smudge off the reverse of the letter. Using delicate chemicals the compound was lifted clear and separated into its constituent parts. The make-up was a mixture of sweat, some skin cells, and a particular soil containing fine traces of iron ore.

An item of the young man's clothing was procured from his parents and hair and skin samples were lifted from the jersey. A DNA analysis matched. Saliva taken from the adhesive flap matched. The thumbprint smudge was definitely that of the writer. Then began the exhausting search for the origin of the soil. Geologists pointed them towards north Africa and MI6 requested their men on the ground in Algeria, Morocco, Libya and Tunis to begin providing samples of whatever ochre-coloured sand they could find. Matches were found along the north African coast, but sandstorms could lift sand from one location and deposit it a thousand miles away.

There was however only one location along that coast with iron ore deposits.

Wadi Shati.

Six hours later the Pentagon received a request from the British intelligence services channelled through the CIA.

The Deputy Director telephoned his counterpart. After some small talk, the Pentagon man, a three-star general, asked what he could do for the CIA.

'We would like a good hard look at a place called Wadi Shati.'

'Where's that?' the general asked.

'Libya.'

## 6

CIA staffer Paul Stowitz was at the wheel of the car as they passed through the gates into the rear car-park area of the Pentagon. As he parked the car he mulled over what he knew about the people they were meeting and their capabilities.

The National Reconnaissance Office, a highly secret department of the Pentagon, was charged with one mission: satellite spying. Employing a series of space vehicles they could monitor everything from a given nation's agriculture, the crops they would have to feed their people in the coming winter, to the traffic on a road at a given time.

The latest satellite series, the KH-11, were the size of a bus and able to photograph or transmit images in real time. High-resolution cameras could allow an observer in the US to watch a vehicle a continent away, establish its make and model. Efforts to design a camera that could actually read the number plate had, he thought, so far failed, but people and animals could be counted and watched. The KH-11s were backed up by Lacrosse radar imaging satellites that lacked the fine resolution of the KH-11 but could see at night and through cloud or fog.

By changing the planes of their orbits, satellites could be drawn together or moved apart to scan new areas and, with each track lasting ninety minutes giving sixteen full orbits every twenty-four hours, each target area could be viewed and photographed three times a day.

The CIA team walked to the Pentagon itself and after the usual security checks and issuance of badges were shown to a low classification meeting room deep inside the complex. There they waited for their counterparts from the NRO. They were standing and talking when a note was delivered.

The senior man smiled. A third party was expressing interest in the meeting. Robert Conroy was the National Security Adviser to the White House. He was wanting a report.

The door swung back and two uniformed men entered followed by a civilian.

'Ha,' one of them, a major, barked. 'Cloak meets dagger. Welcome to the fun factory! I am Jack Makdad. This is Colonel Travis and the civvy is Andy.'

The men shook hands and finally they sat down round the table, the CIA men one side, the NRO men the other.

'What can we do for you?' Major Makdad asked. 'You want a look at Libya, right? No problem. Tell us what are you looking for and we will give you the images.'

Stowitz smiled. Two years before the Pentagon had denied the NRO even existed. For them to be this co-operative the word had obviously come from on high.

'Wadi Shati. Somewhere nearby there is a camp. Hostages. Those people plus guards, tents, support areas.'

'Wadi who?'

'South of Tripoli, about halfway to the border,' Stowitz said.

'Ah,' the colonel said. 'We only run the beasts over the big airbases and known military camps. That far in? I don't think we have much.'

'Can you get it?' Stowitz asked.

'Re-task the elevens . . . mmm . . . everyone wants that,' he said almost to himself.

Stowitz passed the note from the National Security Adviser over. 'Conroy is waiting for the director to tell him how I got along. What shall I tell him?'

Makdad read the note, one eyebrow rising for a second.

'Tell him you got along real well,' he said resignedly. 'We will have to clear this, but we should be able to start sweeping tomorrow night.'

The civilian leaned forward. 'Sir, what are we looking for?'

'A camp,' Stowitz answered. 'As I said.'

'Sir, boy scouts make camps, and the marines make camps. A camp can be a handful of hidden lean-tos or half a million refugees under acres of canvas. Now what am I looking for?'

Stowitz began to describe what they thought the camp should comprise.

Morris sat at his dining-room table, a sheaf of notes, papers and reference books spread out before him. The last few days' newspapers were piled up – he was pleased to see the reports that the police were no nearer any firm leads on the thefts from the Museum. Dealers had commented that the pieces were so rare and so instantly recognizable that they were bound to turn up soon. Morris smiled at the thought and pressed on with his work. Hidden among his notes in the same hand-written script and in a code he had devised was the latest report from O'Sullivan. He had taken the details over the phone barely an hour ago and the next call would come in to the public phone box down on O'Connell Street at exactly seven that evening, in fifty minutes' time. There was a complicated switching system in the junction box that would re-direct the call through a series of computer codes to a telephone installed at his home.

Millie's youngest brother was a computer engineer at Telecom Eireann and he was working magic for the boys. Morris looked up at her as she pottered about the kitchen. It was her turn to cook tonight and on her way home from her job at University College she had picked up minced beef and tomatoes. She made the best hamburgers he had ever eaten and the thought of them made his stomach rumble.

She would be out later, visiting her family, when his own meeting was due at the church. In spite of her early reluctance she had proved to be a remarkable selector of potential recruits. Because of her relationship with the local resistance leader she had been forbidden direct contact with any group or candidate where they knew she was involved, so rather like the recruiting for the British intelligence services at the Oxbridge universities before the war, she had passed names to Morris who channelled them back for screening and recruitment. UCD now had four active groups among the faculty and students and the sure knowledge that when the time came the groundswell of support would be there. He was delighted with the contribution so far. His own discipline, political science, was not something you could apply pragmatically to everyday problems, but the applied sciences people from UCD were a totally different proposition. Chemists, computer, electronic and civil engineers, physicists, physiologists and medical students mixing together produced a group that could tap phones, hack into computers, analyse drawings, and treat or create illness.

There had been resistance and discussion about the involvement of the British. Many of the students raised on Irish history and republican pride, and too young to know what they were facing, questioned why they needed help at all and why if anyone it had to be the British. Older, wiser people explained it patiently, but the suspicions were not easily allayed. In spite of that recruiting continued.

Recognizing that the best results often lay in the most dangerous tactics, the County Dublin resistance, frustrated with the slow, methodical, pedantic recruiting style of MI6, had broken the rules. To recruit the people they needed they ignored Century House's warnings of the dangers of recruiting relatives.

Morris had argued that it was not a spy network they were building, not a handful of deep cover agents that needed a family as cover, a family that knew nothing of their double lives. He argued that the essence of Ireland was the family and the blood bond could overcome the risks. Immediate family members had been warned and then allowed to bring another into the group. He was also delighted with the make-up. Historically, resistance had been provided by active people, doers rather than thinkers, but in Ireland for every active person prepared to pull a trigger there were two prepared to bring other skills, contacts and abilities. This was the best educated resistance force in history and now he was brushing up his own education. The books laid out before him were all Waterstone's could provide on the Palestinian question. As an academic he knew that to defeat them they would have to understand what motivated them, how they thought, how they worked, how they structured their actions. Know your enemy. He finished reading the paragraph.

'Did you say something about Spanish students the other day?' he asked Millie.

She stepped into the doorway, wiping her hands on a tea towel and looked at him. With her long legs encased in jeans and boots she looked slimmer than her curves usually allowed. She seemed in a good mood tonight. It had not been easy lately, the hours he was working putting a strain on their relationship he had not expected.

'Sorry?'

'Spanish students. Did you mention something about them the other day?'

'Umm yeah.' She nodded. 'Dickie, he's on the faculty. His sister teaches English at some place down near Bray. Well her contract has been paid up but they let her go. The students, all Spanish speakers, are there, but what they are doing is the thing. Not learning English. All sixteen of the staff were let go.'

'Spanish Spanish, or Latin American?' Morris asked.

'Spanish, I would think,' Millie responded. 'Why would Latin Americans fly all the way here when they could go to the States for half the price?'

'Can you find out where this place is?'

'Yes I suppose so, but why?'

'Just something I read here. Did you know there are four hundred thousand Palestinians in Chile?'

'No.'

'Well, we have been looking for Arabs. Ethnic Semites, if you like. How many of us could tell the difference between a Spaniard, a Lebanese, a Greek, an Armenian, or,' he said, 'a Palestinian?'

'My God,' she said, 'the students. They could be Chilean Palestinians?'

'Yes. And how many other "students" here this year were the same?'

'But the summer is over. They have gone,' she said.

'Or have they just gone to ground? This Dickie guy,' he added, 'how well do you know him?'

'Wouldn't trust him. Drinks too much and talks too much,' she said firmly.

'We need to start sniffing about,' he said, 'see if the male/female split of students this year was the same as usual.'

He helped her finish the meal and they both left the house a little before eight, Millie going to see her parents and Morris to his rendezvous.

The willingness to recruit family had paid immediate dividends. One of the Rathmines people said he had an aunt who was highly placed to help. Morris couldn't believe their luck when she turned out to be a senior secretary in the Taoiseach's office.

He immediately contacted Tilby and together they considered what would be the best approach. The woman was conservative, steady, pedestrian even. A middle-aged lady, a civil servant. Because she was fiercely Irish and very old-fashioned it was Kiernan who brought her over. The old professor wandered with her through the ordered lawns and waddling ducks at St Stephen's Green, and over the course of an hour convinced her that taking secret messages to her Taoiseach was no betrayal. When she arrived home that evening the priest from the church was waiting for her and if she had any doubts then his firm endorsement of Kiernan may as well have come from the Pope himself. She had known the priest for fifteen years and if he was with Kiernan then so was she.

She delivered her first message two days later, the Taoiseach's eyes barely registering as he opened the morning's work. There among the papers, minutes and bound documents was a simple folded page and from her desk in his administration office, the mirror on the filing cabinet carefully shifted a few inches, she could watch his face. She was still not convinced and she waited. The note said simply that all was well and to adjust his tie in acknowledgement. A few seconds later he reached up and shifted the knot of his tie and she breathed for the first time in what seemed like minutes. She then began to watch the three new people, the ones that Kiernan had warned her about, now fiercely protective of her prime minister, angry that anyone could do such a thing. She sat there at her word processor thinking, you are not alone any more, Mr Mahoney, we are here, a rising pride in her heart that she had never felt before.

The next day she slipped past his personal secretary and put a document on his desk, something she had never done before. The man stood up, his eyes rebuking her for the breach of protocol, but Mahoney also looked up and for the first time in her life she did something that her mother had warned her would send her to the gates of hell. It was something done by tinkers and harlots. She winked at him.

He caught on immediately and that evening gave instructions that she was to transfer to the inner sanctum, the private office, her new work station only fifteen feet from his.

Morris silently sat behind her in the church. They had ceased leaving messages for Mahoney in his car the moment they had this alternative.

'Don't turn around,' he said. She jumped, startled by the voice.

'Jesus, Mary and Joseph! You keep doing that and I'll die of fright, young man,' she said *sotto voce* when she recovered her composure. They had explained the dangers to her, explained that she could drop messages in the dark corner at the back of the confessional, but she chose to have the contact, chose to feel the camaraderie and until tension rose Morris had agreed to meet her in one of four rotating locations. Until then he would play down the danger.

Morris smiled. 'Nerves of steel, eh?'

'Don't be cheeky,' she replied. She was secretly enjoying all this. For forty-five years she had done her mother's bidding, joined the civil service, gone to church, all the things that nice people did. But for forty-five years she seemed to have lived without reason, and now she had one. It was a good feeling.

'One of them was in most of the day. Number three,' she began. They had numbered the individual minders until they could pin names to them. 'There is to be a meeting next week.'

'Oh,' Morris said.

'Three said that there would be a letter soon. He joked that it would be coming from the sun to the cold. He thought that very funny, I suppose.' She chatted the way that older people do, but Morris let her talk knowing every detail would come out, every nuance. 'The meeting will be in Malta,' she said.

'How do you know?'

'He said "after Bubaqra" to the Taoiseach.'

'Bu-what?' Morris leaned forward.

'Bubaqra. Malta. This one is an arrogant little so-and-so. Thinks he is so well travelled. I was in Bubaqra before he was born. My father had a passion for the Middle Ages. In particular the Order of St John. As children we got dragged round Grand Harbour and Valletta while he explained where the Turks attacked and where the Knights met them and who did what to who.' She smiled at the memories. 'Bubaqra is a tiny place on the other side of the island not far from the Blue Grotto. We rented a small house there. Used to drive across to Valletta. The traffic is terrifying in Malta,' she added.

'How is the Taoiseach?' Morris asked as he wrote the details down in a form of shorthand he used.

'Good,' she replied drily. 'Oh he's looking old, drawn, exhausted half the time, but considering all, he is bearing up well. I think the fact that we are there in the office with him gives him support. He slips the notes to me like one to the manner born.'

The SAS in conjunction with the resistance had identified sixty sites where there was activity. Scott had debriefed each team in turn, building the profile of each location, numbers of men seen, numbers possible and the equipment they had discovered. Communications were given away by aerials and antenna and vehicle tracks and the amount of rubbish hauled away told observers much, as did the actual locations.

This information was fed back to Persse's group who in turn passed it back to Britain and the planning teams in Whitehall and Wales.

Scott was pleased. His small team had achieved their objectives and Grogan was due in the following week. He had also managed to persuade his mother to move back to

England for the next few weeks, into the Cheshire house that his father had left them. He didn't want to be worrying about her if it went off.

He had buried the stolen artefacts on the farm. A consultant had driven down from the north, from Belfast, and prepared the items for a few weeks of musty damp storage. He had arrived equipped with sachets of moisture absorbent silica the size of children's bean bags and after wrapping the precious objects in bubble plastic the sachets were added and the whole lot was sealed in lightweight spun aluminium camera cases. That night Scott buried them beneath a tree down near the stream. There they would be safe until they were needed.

His relationship with Aisling had moved from the awkward probes where adults once again become unsure adolescents, feeling the ground and seeking reassurance before moving ahead, to something more comfortable. He spent most of his time with his command, travelling from county to county and the fleeting visits to the farm became blissful retreats where rest, good food and Aisling's warm curves against his back as he slept helped him recharge his batteries. He had now been technically in the field since July, almost two months with never more than a few hours off at a time.

For most of Ireland life continued as normal. The long warm days of summer had drawn into autumn. The days were cooler, crisper, shorter and as people hurried to work or home, they noticed that leaves were beginning to fall from the trees and they pulled their coats close against the wind. Moira Kelly, stalwart of the church group, stood at her favourite table in the hall, her cakes out before her on a gingham cloth that had seen service for a decade or more. There were a dozen women with their wares on sale for the church. Jars of preserves, jams and chutneys were stacked alongside the summer's sweet honey and at the table opposite Moira's a woman sold home-made fudge and offered her husband's early pumpkins. People milled about looking at the produce and a slight, pretty, dark-haired girl stopped at Moira's table eyeing the variety of freshly baked cakes. Moira looked at her and smiled. This child was not happy she thought. Student. Homesick perhaps.

'Excuse me,' the girl said, 'that one. Is it ahhh . . .' she was looking for the word.

'It's a banana cake,' Moira replied. 'Delicious!'

She girl nodded and smiled quickly, her attention drawn to a rich dark cake one row further back.

'Oooh, chocolate! Ahh, how much please?'

Moira told her and her face fell. God love her she thought. Can't even afford a cake.

'You are a long way from home, aren't you pet?'

The girl nodded.

'What's your name?' Moira asked.

'Raishma,' she replied, quickly adding, 'I am from Madrid.'

'You are missing your home, aren't you?'

The girl nodded shyly.

'Well, Raishma, it's late and business is slow.' Moira picked up the chocolate cake, careful to keep the clingfilm wrapping intact. 'Here. Take this now and enjoy it.'

'No. I could not accept such . . .' Raishma replied, but Moira thrust the cake forward and would not take no for an answer. 'Ah go on now, take it. It won't last. Best to be eaten.'

The girl's expression was one of amazement and confusion. Moira thrust the cake forward again with a firm smile. 'Ah go on now . . .'

Raishma smiled. 'Thank you. Thank you very much.'

'You're welcome, pet. Now cheer up. God knows, you'll be home soon enough.'

\* \* \*

General Stewart climbed from the car and stretched his legs. The drive down from Bulford was long. Wearing a civilian suit, he could have been an executive from the city, from Lloyd's perhaps, or a very senior civil servant, but it was the way he moved that gave it away. His back was ramrod straight and as he preceded his brigade major up the steps he looked very fit indeed. Marshall and Sally Richards were there to meet him.

He thrust his hand out to meet Sally's, a buccaneer's grin across his face.

'Edward Stewart,' he said.

'Sally Richards,' she replied smiling. His grin was infectious. 'This is . . .' she began to introduce Marshall, but he cut in.

'Hello, Monty.'

'Good God. Sandy Marshall in the flesh!'

'A course,' Marshall explained to Sally. 'This fellow took seven hundred matches off me playing pontoon one night. Nerves of steel.'

She raised an eyebrow and led them inside. Two hours later they walked down to the small house where O'Malley was working his team eighteen hours a day. Stewart was introduced around the group and he had a few words for each as he passed.

One of the artists, caught by his aquiline looks and fair features imagined him in uniform and watched him move about. His eyes seemed to miss nothing as he reviewed the work in progress.

'My God,' she said, almost to herself, 'he is magnificent.'

'It's called command presence, darling,' her colleague said drily. 'It's dead sexy and he is oozing it.'

'He's perfect. The Celtic warrior. The War Lord. The Chieftain. Even his name is right. He is probably related way back in time.'

'Bollocks,' the other replied. Five minutes later she looked over to the other girl's drawing board. A sketch was taking shape. 'What's that? The hat they wear?'

'Sort of.'

'They all wear berets, right?'

'Yeah. They will need a badge. A symbol. All regiments have cap badges. Ours will, too. But ours will be different. Ours will have . . . a cockade. Like this,' her hand flicked across the page, 'three feathers, one orange, one white, one green mounted on to the back of the Celtic badge. Like a fleur de whatever.'

'Yeah,' said the other artist, excited now, 'but smaller, two inches high, so it doesn't rise above the top line of the beret.'

The girl finished the sketch with felt-tip pens and held it up.

'Nice. Very nice. It's what we have been looking for. What did you call it?'

'A cockade.'

A voice behind them spoke. 'It's called a hackle.'

It was Stewart. He had crossed the room and had been watching over their shoulders. 'Many regiments have them, or their variant.'

'Oh. Does that mean we can't use it?' the artist asked. She was nervous this close to the chieftain.

'Not at all. But you will have to work out a way to leave their original kit intact.'

'I don't understand.'

Stewart smiled. Civilians rarely did.

'The army is broken into regiments. It's almost tribal,' he replied, his delivery short, informative rather than lecturer-like. 'Most have old illustrious traditions and battle honours that go back hundreds of years. Their uniforms have taken that time to develop. Not the green battle dress, but the other bits that make up the picture.'

'The accessories?' the other artist offered.

Stewart laughed softly, images of matching handbags and gloves coming to mind. 'Yes. You could call them that.

But it's the right to wear them that is important. Everything from the cap badge, the type of headgear, the belt, the buttons, to the colour of their mess kit; everything is designed to be different to the others. Each difference was earned in some way and is now jealously guarded. It is encouraged because at the end of the day men don't fight for Queen or country. They fight for the regiment and their mates. Any device that will help foster that kinship, that tribalism, is valued. So if you want to dress 'em up, and they will love that, you have to make sure they can keep the other bits, the bits that make them an Irish Guardsman, or one of the Glosters, or one of the Black Watch.'

'Glosters?'

'The Gloucestershire Regiment. They wear a cap badge back and front. They won the right to do that in 1801 when they fought back to back against the French in Alexandria. The Glosters were amalgamated last year, but they kept the right to wear badges back and front, even in their new regiment.' He smiled. 'Now they don't wear a hackle, but for those that do . . .' he leaned over, taking a pencil from her hand and sketched an upright feathery flower-like shape over a beret. 'Most of them look like that. Perhaps they would wear it on its side or behind yours or something. Anyway, in action we wear steel helmets and try to avoid anything too colourful for obvious reasons, so this sort of thing would need to be able to take being stuffed into a pocket.' He stepped back, his demeanour now very relaxed. 'I have an encyclopaedia of the regiments. If you like I shall send it over to you.'

Half an hour later he was on the road back to his command, pleased with what he had seen. Orders were due any day now. Orders that would see him throw his men into a new training exercise for a new mission. The war gamers had worked this scenario several times and the plans were now being dusted off and revamped. If the hawks could overcome the doves in Westminster he would take his division into the first Western European campaign since the Second World War. Under no existing national flag, it would be the largest free force in history. If they couldn't then it was all a huge waste of time, and the word coming back was there was considerable resistance to any overt military assistance.

The men sat in the car, Kiernan in the front with the parish priest and Tilby and the local resistance commander, Joseph O'Reilly, in the back. They waited. O'Reilly, the poet, softly tapped the seat back as he hummed an old tune, the others sitting in silence.

'She won't be long now,' he said.

Debrett had done their job well. They had given MI6 a list of five names, all of the same branch of the O'Donnells, all born since 1970. Of those, three lived in Donegal. They had seen two of them that morning. Both were young men and sparse files studied over the previous days had not managed to give the real feel of a live person, the presence, the personality and the character that made them what they were. So they were watched and Kiernan had found reason to talk to both in the course of the morning. One was an estate agent and the other helped his father on his farm.

Neither had inspired the old professor and so now they waited for the last of the O'Donnells. They had no picture of this one. She was young, nineteen and a student nurse. They had seen her school record and she had done well, passed her leaving certificate with good grades and important-ly spoke fluent Irish. She would need the intelligence, the ability to learn quickly, she would need the Irish language, but above all she would need presence. Some-thing to make people notice her, something fiery or serene, tranquil or mesmerizing.

'There she is,' O'Reilly said.

Up the road past the stone wall and the crossing was a figure on a bicycle. She pedalled firmly, a smile across her face as she called to the big rangy dog that ran at her side. Every now and then she turned her face to the wind, smelling the sea, and the gusts gently lifted her long chestnut-coloured hair. Her face was clear, her skin creamy and her eyes, they could now see, were a soft green colour under high curved brows.

'Good grief,' Tilby said, 'she'll do me.'

'She is magnificent,' O'Reilly said softly, his eyes never leaving her as she stepped through the gate to her parents' house. 'Perfect.'

'I want to talk to her,' Kiernan said. 'She looks right, but I will need to talk to her.' Thinking, she is familiar for some reason, but unable to place the memory.

'Christ on a crutch,' O'Reilly exploded. 'The choice is this little darling or yer man in the house place or the other lad milking his da's bloody cows! What shite is this? She is a nineteen-year-old Irish virgin, a rare beauty in a land that produces them like so many pounds of bloody butter.'

'She must have it. She must or we won't have time to give it to her,' Kiernan replied frostily. 'This person isn't some piece of verse from your drunken ramblings.'

'Not yet.' O'Reilly grinned. 'But by the time she returns she will be.'

Kiernan looked at the priest who had remained silent this far.

'You meant what you said. About the family. No skeletons in the cupboard?'

'They are good people. Her father is the most honest man I know. There was a son. He was killed in a hit and run several years ago. The Provos running from something, the locals said. I was there when Maeve was born. She is strong. Honest. Intelligent. Decent. She is all they have. If you people do anything to harm her I will . . .'

'Relax now, Father,' O'Reilly said, his eyes taking on the deep intensity that worried people. 'No one will harm her. You have my word.'

The priest had been recruited only the week before and then only after several other senior church figures around the country had given their tacit blessing to the venture.

'Can we go in?' Kiernan asked.

Behind them in a second car fifty yards down the road three of Scott's men watched. They were the minders, there to make sure that nothing happened to Kiernan and his party and in particular the girl.

The girl's mother opened the door to their knock. She was a slim woman in her late forties, wiping her hands on her apron and taking them in with wide intelligent eyes, one knee holding the dog back.

'Father! This is a surprise,' she said.

'Hello, Mrs O'Donnell,' said the priest. 'I have a visitor for you. He has travelled up from Dublin.'

'Dublin, you say,' she replied, looking Kiernan over. 'It was you out in the car, then?'

Kiernan nodded.

She regarded him suspiciously for a few moments and then her natural respect for the church surfaced. 'Well, you'd better be coming in then. I'll stick the kettle on.'

They were shown into the front room and waited in awkward silence, the sounds of cups and saucers being arranged coming through from the kitchen. Kiernan's old eyes swept the room. It was like a thousand others up and down the country. An open fireplace dominated one wall. Above the white painted mantel that was crowded with family photos and small spotless china figurines was a picture of the Virgin Mary. Two ageing armchairs flanked a big, comfortable-looking sofa and a bookshelf and dresser unit gave the back wall a heavy safe countenance. A carved wooden crucifix hung over the door.

'Well,' she said, appearing with the tea tray laden with a

cake and all the crockery to make a major event of a cup of tea the way only the Irish can, 'here we are, then. Oh, Maeve,' she called, threading her way towards the coffee table, 'I have forgotten the biscuits.'

Kiernan reversed out of her way and at that moment Maeve O'Donnell entered the room. She moved with a dancer's grace. Poised without being obvious, she smiled at him, her smile shy without being timid, simply he thought because they hadn't been introduced.

'Maeve, this is Mr Kiernan,' the priest said.

Kiernan stepped forward and as she offered her hand he took it. The shake was firm and dry. He looked her in the eyes. They were what his mother would have called knowing.

Mrs O'Donnell began passing cups of tea out and they all got themselves seated.

'Will Mr O'Donnell be joining us?' Kiernan asked.

'He might be back in time,' she replied. 'He has driven down to Sligo. Who would like a piece of cake?'

'Will that be your home-made, Mrs O'Donnell?'

'Of course, Father,' she said, smiling.

'Then I shall,' the priest answered smiling back and holding up two fingers an inch apart. 'Just a small morsel, mind.'

She cut a substantial wedge and slid it on to a plate with a smile. The Father did like a nice cake. All knew it.

'Mr Kiernan?'

'Just a small piece, thanks,' Kiernan replied. He knew the ritual as well as any. So did Maeve. He was aware that she was observing the proceedings with an amused smile, an expression of the pleasure that close family felt in each other's company, observing their idiosyncrasies and loving them all the more for them.

'So what can we do for you, Mr Kiernan?' Mrs O'Donnell asked, handing him a plate burdened down with chocolate cake, the slice larger if possible than the priest's.

'Well, Mrs O'Donnell, I am really here to see Maeve. I think we may wish to offer her a position.'

'Maeve has a job,' she replied quickly, flicking a look at her daughter. 'A good job. She is a student nurse. Not that we aren't grateful, mind you.'

Maeve gave her mother a look and then turned to Kiernan.

'What sort of position, Mr Kiernan?' she asked. Her voice was clear, the accent softened by an education somewhere in the south. Kiernan smiled. She was Irish enough to want to explore every avenue. He had no doubt why. Donegal had limited opportunities for a young person.

'It's a public relations type of role,' he said, waving a hand. 'You would be thoroughly trained, of course. Some travel. Decent salary. Doing something worth while.'

'Nursing is worth while,' Mrs O'Donnell said quickly.

'Mother,' Maeve said, her voice softly reproving, then looking back at Kiernan. 'I was offered a job like that last year. It turned out to be offering people perfume in a supermarket. What I would like to know is how you found me. I haven't been looking for a job.' Her voice had taken on a firmness that he liked. Where in another nineteen-year-old there would have been uncertainty, here there was strength.

The bleeper in his pocket went off. Three shorts. Someone was coming. He got up and looked out of the window. A car was pulling to a halt in the driveway.

'Who is this arriving?' he asked quickly.

'I'm sorry . . .' the mother began.

'Just answer my question, please,' Kiernan replied.

'It's my husband. He's early,' she said, her tone showing she didn't like the way the conversation was going.

He took the bleeper from his pocket and pressed a button before slipping it back.

'Good,' he said with a smile. 'Maeve, I can understand

your suspicion. Let's just say we had to find you. It's taken us some weeks.'

There was the sound of the key in the lock and a man's voice.

'. . . men in a car down the road. Wonder who they might . . .' his voice trailed off as he saw the visitors in his front room.

'They are with me, Mr O'Donnell,' Kiernan said. 'I am . . .'

'There's only one kind that has men sitting in cars around here. State your business,' he snapped.

'He's all right, Ray,' the priest said soothingly, standing, his cake plate in his hand. 'He's no provo. He is from Trinity College in Dublin.'

'He wants to offer me a job, Dad,' Maeve said.

'Oh . . . I'm sorry. Go off half-cocked sometimes. Mr . . .?'

'Kiernan.'

'Welcome. A job now, is it? Well it's a fine thing to be offered a job, but you have been told no doubt that my daughter is training to be a nurse.' He gave a look filled with pride.

'We have. The role I have in mind is a little larger and – how shall I put this? – will be infinitely more influential on the world we live in.'

Mr O'Donnell studied him with eyes that had seen horse traders and tinkers come and go over the years. He settled on the sofa beside his wife and took a proffered cup from her hand.

'Lots of big fancy words there, Mr Kiernan. What is it you are asking my daughter to consider?'

Time, Kiernan thought.

He dug into his pocket and pulled a slip of paper out.

'You know the good Father here. His boss is a man by the name of Madigan. Bishop Madigan.'

'I know of him,' O'Donnell said.

'This is his phone number. He is expecting you to tele-phone him. Tell him I am here. Ask him what you will. Then we can proceed, but I warn you, I will not be able to tell you anything. All you need to know is that Maeve,' he looked at her and smiled, 'if she decides to join us, will be safe and will do something of value, something that will make you proud of her.'

'I have no great love for the church,' O'Donnell said. His wife shot a look at him. 'But I have known the Father for twenty-five years. If he vouches for you, then I accept that.'

'There are also these,' Kiernan said offering two folded pieces of paper from his jacket pocket.

O'Donnell took them and began to read. The first was hand-written by the Taoiseach, Colin Mahoney, and mentioned Maeve's name and that what Kiernan was asking was important for Ireland. The second letter was on headed notepaper from 10 Downing Street. It simply mentioned that Maeve would be temporarily visiting Britain as a distinguished guest of Her Majesty's Govern-ment.

He finished reading and passed them to his wife. As she bent her head, Maeve slid closer to read over her shoulder.

'Can you tell us what she will be doing?' he asked.

'Representing Ireland, in a way.'

'That's all you can say?'

Kiernan nodded.

'In England?'

'Initially.'

'When does she start?'

Kiernan looked at Maeve. She had just finished reading the two notes. Disbelief across her face, she began to read again.

'We will want her to leave with us now,' Kiernan replied.

201

'Hang on,' Maeve said firmly, her voice gathering strength. 'Just hang on. You're talking about me like I'm a child, or not here, and I am neither. What is it that you want me to do that takes a letter from Mahoney and one from the prime minister of Britain?'

That's better, Kiernan thought, delighted. Show some fire, girl. You will need it.

'I can't tell you yet. Let's just say it's a matter of national security, and you will be doing Ireland a service. A great service,' Kiernan replied, adding, 'I have students at Trinity who would do it without question.'

'Do it without question? Sounds like the Waffen SS,' she replied. Her mother gave her one of her looks – well-brought-up Irish girls didn't speak like that to their elders – but she stared back at the professor, eye to eye.

Kiernan chuckled. He was clearly enjoying the banter. 'But not you, Maeve O'Donnell?'

'No. Not me.'

'Tell me,' he asked, 'about your philosophies, your politics.'

'My philosophies are eclectic,' she replied. 'But rest assured I have read Machiavelli,' she finished smiling.

'And?' he asked, through a grin.

'And I believe in altruism, fair play and justice. My politics are right of centre, but only because the left has consistently shown itself ineffective. People left to get on with it usually do quite well. Is this an interview?'

'In a manner of speaking,' Kiernan replied, 'although I'm more interested in the way you deliver your position than its substance.'

'You sound like my tutor,' she replied.

'You were at university?' he asked quickly.

'UCD. I left after six months,' she laughed, brushing a lock of her shining hair from her face. It was a bright cheerful sound. 'I wanted to do something real. My course was full of marvellous but absolutely useless information.'

'One last question,' he said.

'The answer is yes,' she replied.

'You don't know what I am going to ask.'

'Oh yes I do. You will ask me if I accept the job.'

He smiled. 'You trust us, then?'

'I saw you once in Dublin,' she replied. 'You were walking along a path at Trinity. You wore an old shapeless jacket and your socks didn't match and you didn't care a bit. I liked that. I think you are honest and if it's you I am working for, then it's all right.'

He looked at her mother, smiling, the memory of her now bright, the girl with her two friends walking the path and later singing in the street. 'Mrs O'Donnell, if you don't mind I will ask two colleagues to join us while Maeve packs a few things.' He looked at the girl. 'Just enough for a long weekend. We will provide everything else.'

Tilby and O'Reilly joined them and sitting with the parents explained the security issues, that they could not phone Maeve, but she would call them regularly. He also gave them a post office box number to which they could write letters.

'Don't tell people. Just say she has gone to a new job in England,' he finished.

Finally, as they prepared to leave, Mrs O'Donnell wiping a tear from her eye, O'Reilly stepped forward.

'Now then, Mrs O'Donnell,' he said in Irish, 'don't be fretting now. She's going across the water for a couple of months is all. And when she returns, as God is my witness, you will never be so proud again.'

He didn't tell them that just before she returned they would have to leave themselves. Head for the border or go into hiding. They couldn't stay here. Not when she returned.

The woman was excited. The liaison that had begun almost accidentally two months ago was now the highlight of her week and as she turned off the engine she opened her bag and checked her make-up. She was forty-four years old with two children at university and her lover was barely older than either of them.

She looked at herself, checking her lipstick, noticing that the crow's feet round her eyes weren't that bad, and the highlights in her blonde hair were really rather good, justifying what she was about to do, telling herself she was still attractive, not simply still needing to feel wanted and desirable, but desiring. Feeling desire, feeling herself go gooey and moist when they kissed, feeling the hunter, loving the conquest just as she thought men must. They had met in a gallery. Bored, her husband sleeping up in London during the week, she had looked for interests. She had moved among the guests at the new gallery's opening, bored with them and the intense bitchiness of the conversations, but dreading going home to the big, empty house. They had talked and finally escaped together to a wine bar down the street.

She finished her scrutiny and almost ran up the steps like a teenager.

Her lover met her at the door and whisked her in and the woman stood back to take her in, wondering yet again how she could be so lucky. Mona de Cruz was a dark-haired, flashing-eyed beauty with ripe firm breasts, slender thighs and legs that went on for ever. When the thighs wrapped themselves round her face she wished it would never end. They started as usual with a bottle of wine and talked about the day, Mona parading herself in a short loose skirt and halter top, her skin golden and smooth, knowing that the older woman liked to watch her move around, bending to pour wine into the glass on the floor, feeling her eyes on her breasts and the warm cleft between her thighs.

They had made love for the first time, Mona making the woman beg to taste her, teasing her and finally allowing her, standing in high heels with the riding crop, her pelvis thrust forward so the probing tongue could reach. The woman would do anything for her.

Then they talked, sitting in bed like lovers of old, the sheets scrunched up and the wine bottle on the bedside table.

'Bloody Charlie hasn't been home for a week,' the woman said.

'He's busy,' Mona said, 'affairs of state. Gives us time to be good to each other, doesn't it?'

'Mmmm.'

'Anyway what's so important as to keep him away from a woman like you?' Mona asked, trailing her fingers over her stomach. 'I couldn't bear to not have you.'

'Some damned thing. Yet another cabinet meeting. So we can't go on holiday again. This is the second year we haven't gone skiing. I complained and you know what?'

'What, baby?'

'He told me that there were people that were going to have a really shitty Christmas and winter and to stop complaining. He said people would be dying while I wanted to drink mulled wine. He called me a spoilt bitch,' she finished indignantly.

'Do you want to spoil me?' Mona said, spreading her thighs.

Later they talked some more and just before five, the woman, the wife of the Permanent Under Secretary in the Ministry of Defence, climbed back into her Volvo and drove home.

Mona de Cruz, née Sayigh, who was French but born of Palestinian parents, waited an hour and then walked up to the phone box on the corner and phoned her uncle. Six months of work was about to pay off.

Peter Morris's Dublin resistance network was now in place and recruiting had almost stopped. He had developed two distinct wings. The first were academics and specialists and included people as varied as Telecom Eireann engineers, municipal workers manning pumping stations and people who controlled the country's electrical supply. There were doctors, engineers, technicians and scientists, drivers, mechanics, electricians and tradesmen of every kind, all who had something to offer. The second group were the fighting arm. With intelligence and technical support from the support wing they would be able to target, get in and do their job. With ages varying from eighteen to fifty, and of both sexes, the only common denominator was their love of Ireland and their willingness to bear arms and take risks.

The American Special Forces and British SAS had done the rest and nineteen groups of six had crossed the Irish Sea to a training camp that had been established on the edge of the Brecon Beacons. There were now just over a hundred and fifty trained fighters in greater Dublin and Morris's problem was one of command. He had finally selected three deputies. Two now controlled units of forty-odd people in frozen areas on the South Side, one taking the entire affluent urban and suburban areas of the south and east, the other the badlands of Tallaght, a natural hotbed of republican sentiment. The third took the entire sprawling toughness of the North Side of the Liffey, including the depressed areas of Ballyfermot and Ballymun with their bleak tower blocks and constant violence. The northern commander had seventy-six fighters and an equal number of support personnel. Communication systems were in place and discipline was extremely tight. Morris was ready.

Major Jack Makdad, the National Reconnaissance Office staffer, sat back and looked across at the CIA team as they worked the images on the bank of screens before them. The KH-11s had been delivering images for thirty-seven hours now and the first full sets of pictures were available.

The tapes that had been locked away were retrieved and analysed second by second, with image enhancement by computer by the analysis team.

Four hours ago Makdad had taken three sets of stills across to Stowitz at Langley.

The CIA man had poured over the pictures, his team each side of him at the table doing the same. The blow-ups were black and white, the images grainy, but in each picture there was evidence of habitation, vehicles and tents casting shadows, tracks and paths, and in half a dozen of the prints figures. From the angle it was difficult to tell if they were men or women, but the tapes would offer more.

'You got the tapes for these?' Stowitz asked.

'We have,' Makdad answered. 'You will need special clearance.'

'Not for me. I wouldn't know what I'm looking for. I will get clearance for three people. One of them will be a Brit and two will be mine. They will, if they find what they are looking for, ask for more passes over the areas they are interested in. They will then want blow-ups of the prints.'

'Good enough to plan something? You want in very close, yes?'

Stowitz had nodded and somehow he had gained the clearances in forty hours – unheard-of since the Gulf War. The analysts had been at it for six hours now and had identified three camps that held possibilities. Each image on the screen could be printed as hard copies and they were moving through the tapes, selecting images, zooming in, enhancing and finally printing and the process was slow.

It was the middle of the evening when one of the CIA men saw something on the tape.

'Whoa. Back up.'

'What?' asked the Englishman.

'An arm maybe. An upper arm. Short-sleeved shirt, maybe. Very white.'

'There?' the Englishman asked. He was shuffling the tape back, the hardware facilities rather like those in an television edit suite, except these were hooked into computers and other hardware that television producers only dreamed they could afford.

'Okay. Move forward slowly.'

On the screen three figures moved, their long shadows distorting against a surface.

'Stop. Now you see the shadow. That's a tent wall or something. Where the bulge there crosses the shadow.'

'Okay. Let's come in on that and get a print.'

'What's the place?'

Someone looked up the log and read off the preliminary report.

'It's down as an army camp.'

'Why?'

'Hang on. There's a cross reference here. Tape nine, F2 1567.'

He walked to the wall rack and pulled the tape down. A technician stepped forward to load it on to a second machine.

A few minutes later the technician stopped the fast forward at 1560 and punched the signal up on one of the monitors in front of the team.

It was a high shot, the lens cranked back so the area covered by the image was perhaps a kilometre across rather than the twenty metres of the previous images.

'Stop.'

'Fuck me,' the Englishman said.

'Yo. Those are triple A units. There's what, one, two, three revetments in that one shot. That's a . . .' he pointed with a pen at the screen, 'light gun of some kind in there. That cover could conceal anything. Even an MBT.'

'Where's our tents, then?'

'That could be them starting there.' The pen had dropped to the bottom right corner of the screen.

'So the question is, what are the heavies defending?'

'Could be their own.'

'No. I agree with you. The arm looked white to me. No suntan. I want another look. We want every pass to cover this site till otherwise advised. Differing times, commencing soon as possible.'

Makdad wandered over to them, his briefcase in his hand. 'Found something, gentlemen?'

'Enough to want to see more.'

He put his briefcase down and leaned over the console. They showed him the arm and then the high sequence showing the defensive perimeter.

'We can pass this plot again,' he said casually.

'Can we get closer?' one of the CIA men asked.

Makdad didn't answer the question.

'Major,' the CIA man began, 'do you have kids?'

'Yes, sir. Three. Two girls and a boy.'

'Well, Major, what we are looking for here is kids. Someone's kids. About a hundred and thirty of them we think. Hostages. Now can you imagine if it were your kids? What if someone had taken your girls? Ever thought about one of them in trouble and you not able to help, not able to do anything?'

'I have. Just tell the duty supervisor which plots you want overflown,' was all he would say. He collected his briefcase from the top of the filing cabinet. 'I'm off duty in ten minutes. Usually have a drink down at Red's Bar. Anyone interested?'

They all declined, but three or four minutes later one of the CIA men got up from his seat.

'Where you going?' the Englishman asked.

'For a drink.'

'For a drink?'

209

'I pulled the major's file last night. He usually goes straight home.'

Red's was a working men's bar complete with a television over the counter and faded flyspecked wallpaper. Makdad was nursing a small beer and a bowl of nuts when the CIA man joined him at the table.

'Thought I would join you, after all. Nice place,' he said.

'It's a shithole,' Makdad replied.

'So why come here?'

'How deep you in with the Adviser?'

'I'm not. Stowitz is. But, he has a genuine interest in this.'

'You will need him,' Makdad said.

'I'm listening.'

'We put up a new eleven last month. This mother is mucho secret. It looks like any other eleven but word is it has a new lens. Big one. High resolution. The boys call it "Hawkeye". This lens will get you close enough to recognize faces, read letters six inches high, maybe more. To most of the NRO and certainly to anyone outside, other than a handful of people it does not fucking exist. Are you with me?'

'I am.'

'The defence adviser to the White House will be one of those handful. Nothing short of a full request from the President will get that mother tasked before testing is complete. Over to you.'

The following morning the Director of the CIA had a meeting with the White House defence adviser and at three o'clock in the afternoon a written order from President James S. Davis arrived at the Pentagon and was whisked into the NRO.

The new satellite, termed by those who knew the KH-11S and called 'Hawkeye', was tasked for the first time that night. Her orbit would be altered to bring her over the target plots and she would provide three passes a day, each day slipping back by a few minutes.

Kiernan sat in the big old armchair, Sally Richards to his right with Maeve O'Donnell opposite. They were in what was once the upstairs parlour, but in more recent years it had been used as a library, sewing room and was now what the Americans, Sally was sure, would call an interview suite. She was there so Maeve wouldn't feel intimidated by the men and had insisted on that. Three men with strong personalities like Kiernan, Morris and O'Malley could intimidate almost anyone and that wasn't the intent.

While they waited for O'Malley and Morris to make their way across from the small house they busied themselves with trivia and coffee served hot from a Cona machine that someone had purloined. The cups were, however, MoD, heavy, chipped and no doubt taken from some store somewhere.

Sally studied the girl as she spoke with Kiernan. In jeans and a jumper she looked superficially like everyone her age, but she sat with a straight back and her manners among her elders and betters were impeccable.

Morris and O'Malley breezed in apologizing to all and, coffee in hand, sat in the last two chairs, Morris in a hard-backed number against the window.

'Right,' Kiernan said. 'Introductions, I think. This is Peter Morris. He is the founder of our little effort. He holds a chair at Trinity. This other gentlemen is Mr O'Malley. He is a businessman. Gentlemen, this is Maeve O'Donnell.'

'Thanks for coming, Maeve,' Morris began. 'How much do you know about Irish history?'

'Not much,' she replied. 'The same as any other person who went to school there, I suppose.'

'Well let's start from square one. Then we can cover the history that is relevant, and finally,' he smiled, 'you will understand what it is we would like your help with.'

She nodded.

'Good. It's perhaps best if Sally picks it up here. It was her people that alerted us.'

Sally smiled across at the girl. 'Maeve, I work for the Foreign Office. A few months ago our Dublin embassy was approached by a rather brave young man who had stumbled across something.' She told the story of David O'Connell and the subsequent intelligence operation by the British in conjunction with the infant Irish resistance. She held back nothing, telling of the hostages, the disappearances, the identification of key enemy staff, troop concentrations and the preparations that were under way.

Maeve listened with growing concern, her indignation mixed with disbelief. By the time Sally Richards was finished her eyes blazed with a righteous fury.

'The bastards,' she said. Her voice was like ice, frozen with conviction.

'So we are going to take it back,' Kiernan said. 'To do it we are going to return to our Celtic roots. How much do you know about old Celtic Ireland?'

'Not much,' Maeve replied.

'Peter will take you into the detail over the next days, but in basic form Ireland was composed of a series of Tuatha, chiefdoms, clans, call them what you will. Each Tuatha or family owed allegiance to a higher authority, a local king and they in turn usually, although not always, swore allegiance to the High King.' He took his glasses off, put them in his coat pocket. 'The High Kings varied over the years and sometimes legend and myth have confused the facts, but they existed. They based themselves at Tara. As you know there hasn't been a High King for hundreds of years and in the last few years we have seen the development of a constitution and a modern republic.'

He stood and walked to the window and looked out over the lawns and gardens that Capability Brown had designed. The silence was almost absolute and all that could be heard was the big grandfather clock.

'But the constitution will be suspended by the Libyans and the PLO. They will, we are sure, declare martial law and that will be that. No constitutional rights. No common law.' He turned back and faced the room, his old eyes taking her in. 'We will need a pivot point, a new visible leader, something for people to hold on to in the dark days ahead, something old Irish, something Celtic. So . . .' he looked at her and smiled. 'We are going to reinstate the monarchy.'

'Oh,' she said.

Across the room Sally Richards smiled and looked at O'Malley. His eyes were misting over.

'The O'Donnells were the last of the High Kings,' Kiernan continued. 'You, Maeve, are the last in your line of O'Donnells. You wondered what we wanted you to do? We want you to be Queen. You are going to be crowned at Tara.'

'I'm sorry,' she replied, shaking her head, 'I thought you said . . .'

'I did.'

'You mean . . .'

He nodded. 'You will be crowned at Tara. You will be our Queen. You will be Maeve, High Queen of Ireland and Queen of the Celts.'

# 7

'You can't be serious!' Maeve retorted.

'We are.'

'But there must be others. Someone else better? There are millions of O'Donnells!'

'Not like you,' Kiernan responded. 'You are perfect.'

'But . . . but I know nothing about it!' she protested.

'May I?' O'Malley asked.

Kiernan nodded.

'Maeve, the professor knows about history. My forte is creating the right perception, finding a demand, even creating one and then meeting it. Can I explain why it must be you?'

She nodded.

'Right. One, if we had a man, and there were two we looked at, we would enter the age-old competitive bit: why him and not me? Ireland has traditionally had kings. But every now and then a woman ruled, and what extraordinary women they were. The most famous was your namesake, Maeve. She ruled in Connaught. Two, whoever takes on the role, the crown, will need to amass popular support very quickly. The person must be inherently appealing for all reasons. In your case it's easy. You will be every mother's daughter, beautiful, proud, intelligent, dutiful, loyal and there when others need you. For men you will be a figure they can love and honour, much as most British men will instantly choose Princess Diana over any other member of the royal household here. Debrett's did their job well. We can't prove you are the only heir, but you have as much right

214

to the throne of Ireland as any and none of the others can even come close to the kind of king or queen Ireland will need.

'A people under a jackboot need something to cling to, something to strive for, something clean and decent and righteous. A monarchy also provides a legitimate form of government to the nation and the world.

'You want to help. The best help you can be is to accept the crown. Ireland needs you.

'There will be a new house of O'Donnell. Don't worry about not knowing anything about it.' He grinned. 'You will have the best teachers available. You will be trained, tutored, dressed, supported and backed up like an actress on a movie set. You will never move without your advisers and your staff. By the time you need to behave like a queen you will be one. You will be a fairy-tale princess that came in their time of need and Maeve, they will fight and die for you as they will for Ireland herself. Why? Because you will be Ireland. Everything she stands for, everything she hopes for.'

She gave a small nervous laugh. 'Dear God, you are serious!'

'Very,' O'Malley replied.

'Well?' from Kiernan.

'Of course,' she replied, lifting her head and looking him in the eye. 'I'll do what needs to be done.'

## 1 October

At the 3rd UK Division Headquarters in Bulford, General Stewart awaited the arrival of his visitor. Normally on a visit like this he would also have his staff present, but the visitor from the Defence Operations Executive had opted for a private meeting. The group could have included the Deputy Chief of Defence Staff (Commitments) and members of the General Staff, but Stewart knew the real reason for the single visitor and he knew there would be no buggering about.

Lieutenant General Sir Robert Cooke, the Deputy Chief of Defence Staff, was a three-star general but to Stewart's surprise he arrived in his own car and wearing a civilian suit.

They settled immediately into Stewart's office and a subtle but effective security detail was deployed in the anteroom.

'I always disliked this room,' Cooke said, settling back into one of the two leather chairs.

'Was yours once, was it sir?' Stewart asked with a grin. He knew it had been but he played the game. He disliked it too. In fact he found the whole of Bulford a dreary place.

'It was. Seems like only yesterday.' Cooke pulled a sheaf of papers from his attaché case. 'Update time, Monty. Whitehall reckons that we have another two possibly three months, but when it happens it will go quickly. First course will be the UN. But they also say the UN will bottle out. It took them almost a year to approve the blockade of Croatia. There's no reason to assume they will move any quicker in this instance.'

'Right,' Stewart muttered.

'The resistance is in place. What will happen when the balloon goes up is anyone's guess.'

'As long as they don't start it,' Stewart said. 'I will need every day I can get.'

'We will request they exercise patience. I think it safe to say it will depend on just what happens. It may be civilized. If so then all well and good. If they screw up and get brutal then there's no way we can stop the resistance. They will attack.'

'That will alter priorities for my command.'

'If it's very bad then every day it goes on people will be dying. There will be incredible moral pressure to do something. At least that will pressure the doves. Bloody

216

liberals.' He snorted. 'Anyway, the Foreign Office has got some senior people piling the pressure on wherever they can, and the PM leaves for Moscow tonight.'

'Moscow?' Stewart asked.

Cooke quickly explained Maynouth's theory and let slip that the intelligence services had confirmed it. The Russians, broke, with a huge standing army, were critical in the plan. If they could be convinced it would not be in their interests to support the Palestinian position, then the UK and USA could apply more pressure. Cooke left it open for Stewart to interpret. 'You are to assume you will move. Your force will be altered. You are Joint Commander with Air Marshal Williams at High Wycombe.' Stewart nodded. He knew his opposite number on the mainland would be either Williams or the four-star admiral at Northwood. He had met and liked Williams. The air force man was good, very good and his role would be to serve as the link between Stewart on the ground in the theatre of operations and the government, both Ministry of Defence and Downing Street.

'Orders will be through tomorrow. We can run over that in a minute.' Cooke put his papers down and looked at Stewart. He smiled. 'Right, Monty. You are to treat this as training for a secondment. With your command. You will train and equip here in Britain. You will not fight under a Union flag. If we get the go every man, and Monty, I mean every man you take, must be a volunteer. For the duration of the seconded deployment you and all your men will be technically on leave.'

'Seconded to whom exactly?'

'We aren't sure. It may be a government in exile, but the creative lads have another angle. One that will carry its own momentum. Details on that when available.'

'What about support?' Stewart asked.

'The planning chaps see it as LandAir for the first fifteen hours. During that time the Free Irish Forces will include ten strike squadrons from the RAF. They will be painted in

Irish colours. After that you will have to survive with your own force which will include air corps elements and two squadrons of ground strike aircraft based north of the border. The other issue is that the Americans came through last night. If it happens they will support from the sea, same deal, Free Irish Forces, but no personnel fighting actually on Irish soil. There will be two exceptions.'

The DCDS reached for his tea and took a sip. Stewart knew one of them. There were Special Forces elements from Fort Bragg in Ireland already.

'They will have specialists on the ground and if absolutely necessary they will allow, and I quote, "forward deployment of their rotary wing air assets". Presumably they mean we can stick their helicopters somewhere useful. Why they just can't say it in English, God only knows . . . Anyway, forward air controllers and liaison are here?'

'Yes,' Stewart replied.

'Defence Operations Executive has agreed the order of battle. Your division will supply the main elements, but you will have support.' He passed Stewart a portfolio of papers. 'You will need a force that size to draw on because of the volunteer issue. Details in here.'

Stewart took the buff MoD manila folder. 'Tell them I need every day I can get,' he said.

'I will, but Monty, I have a feeling we aren't going to start it. They are.'

The questions began, the DCDS answering what he could and referring others. Two hours later they were finished, the first of many meetings.

'Get your top people together. Head over to Wilton when you are ready. There has been a planning team there for two weeks. Have a look at the int. We will expect to see some updated scenarios in a week or so.' They stood up and began to move towards the door, but Cooke stopped and turned to face Stewart. 'One last job I have today,' he said. 'With big chunks of the other services in on the act and the Americans you'll need a third star, for the time being at least.' The Deputy Chief of Defence Staff grinned, and shoved his hand out. 'It is with great pleasure, Monty, I advise that effective today you are acting lieutenant general.'

Edward Montague Montgomery Stewart, the man who never expected to be promoted past lieutenant colonel, was stunned for a second. 'Good God,' he retorted finally, a smile spreading across his face. 'You must all be mad.'

He telephoned his wife and told her to book a table somewhere for dinner that evening and then, with his brigade major in the outer office keeping the world at bay, he opened the buff folder to see what he was being given to fight a campaign with.

Fifty minutes later he closed the folder and, his cap and baton in hand, he left the office to look for his driver.

Lance Corporal Anders was by the car and as Stewart approached he swung up a snappier salute than usual as he opened the door.

'And what's got into you?' Stewart asked. He liked the man, but salutes weren't his forte.

'Rumours, sir. They say I'm driving a lieutenant general. Not transferring me are you, sir?' he asked with a grin.

'What? And inflict you on someone else?' Stewart retorted. Obviously Anders had been chatting with General Cooke's driver. The British army's unofficial intelligence net. It was, everyone had to agree, often better than the official channels.

'The lads will be delighted, sir. Congratulations.'

'Thank you. Now take me home, if you will. Got to walk the damned dogs.'

An hour later, dressed in twill slacks and a jumper, his wife at his side, he called the labradors and they stepped out of the back gate. She waited for him to begin, knowing that when he suggested a walk with the dogs it was their talk time. He had something to say.

He waited until they were under the spread of the big oaks, the trees that had somehow survived the '87 hurricane, at the edge of the common land. The dogs, happy and panting as they sniffed the ground, loped on ahead. Stewart took his wife's hand. 'I'm going away for a while, Helen.'

She looked away for a second before lifting her head, blinking away the rising dampness in her eyes. The last time he had said that it was the Falklands.

'How long?' she asked.

'Don't know yet. I'm taking my chaps off for some training first. Once we are away there will be no leave for them.'

She expected nothing else. If his men could not get home to see their families then he would deny himself the right. He was that kind of commander and that kind of man.

'When?' she asked taking his hand in both of hers.

'October fifteenth.'

'That gives us a week or so,' she said brightly. 'Will you be home for Christmas?'

'Hope so,' he said. 'They have given me a job to do.' The understatement was typical. His voice quivered then. He was normally one who controlled his emotions carefully and she understood immediately that this was something that meant a great deal.

'Bumped me up a notch. Acting. Given me the finest tri-service command assembled since the Gulf,' he said almost disbelievingly.

She stopped and turned to him, her face expectant.

'Yes,' he said, 'tonight, if you would be so kind, a lieutenant general would like you to join him for dinner.'

She put her hands to her face, her surprise and delight complete. 'Oh Edward, I am so proud of you. A third star! Well done, my darling!'

'Acting only.'

'No. You'll get to keep it. I just know it.'

They kissed in the dying light and she held him tightly. 'Be careful,' she whispered, 'and bring your boys home safely.'

Maeve O'Donnell's 'finishing' was moving ahead at a frantic pace. O'Malley's public relations people had structured a series of events between the more formal sessions, events that they called 'teasers'. Early in the planning process the palace had agreed to help wherever possible and the first set had been a carefully engineered series of photographs of Maeve with members of the British royal family. Four of the royal watchers attached to the big dailies had been advised that they would be able to photograph the Princess of Wales, temporarily out of her retirement from the public eye, lunching at a favourite restaurant, but that her friend would not be identified for the time being. They were told that to wait for the identity to be revealed would be in their interests. There were also pictures of the Queen walking her dogs at Sandringham, Maeve's lithe figure photographed between the Queen and the Duke of Edinburgh. The more formal programme included time with palace officials, historians, speech tutors, grooming experts and the planning team. The speech and grooming people again provided by O'Malley pronounced her a natural. A thousand years of breeding counted, they said. Statements and viewpoints were rehearsed over and over, Maeve put under stress by a battery of cameras and people role-playing as reporters.

She was taken through the West End of London to equip her with an appropriate wardrobe, a name designer whose clothes were worn by the Princess of Wales driving her round and helping her put together her workaday wardrobe. Costume designers had begun work on the ceremonial attire, reaching back into Celtic history and imagery

221

for the style they would need when, with the cameras in attendance and the world watching, they would make history.

When she posed for the 'official portraits' the society photographer famous for his pictures of royalty dressed her in a classic Hartnell suit. A string of perfect pearls set off a brooch made by and on loan from Asprey's, a copy of the three-feathered hackle that the Celtic force would wear. Queen Maeve's own emblem. Fifty tiny but perfect emeralds were mounted alongside a cluster of white diamonds and the third feather was made up of diamonds of equal size, but yellow. The deep gold backing gave the yellow cluster an orange tint. The gemstone feathers were fixed into a solid gold Tara brooch.

Behind her the draped backdrop was the colour of her eyes and the lighting had taken the photographer and his two assistants hours to set up.

'My God,' said Kiernan. 'She is perfect.'

'She is almost too beautiful,' O'Malley said.

'No,' Sally Richards retorted. 'She is strong enough to overcome that. The moment she speaks or moves it's there.'

Sally was becoming very fond of the girl. Their rooms up on the bedroom floor were side by side and Maeve had taken to dropping in for a chat before bed. Sally understood immediately that she needed to play the big sister role and most nights they talked and drank cocoa until late. The night after the photos were taken Maeve sat in the easy chair, legs gathered under her. Casual, her wavy hair down and dressed in jeans and a jumper, her homework was scattered around her on the floor. At the desk Sally finished some work.

'What is the brooch worth?' she asked.

'About a hundred and fifty,' Sally answered.

'God, I just can't believe I was wearing a hundred and fifty thousand pounds' worth of jewellery this afternoon.'

'Sod the bloody jewellery,' Sally said. 'I'd do anything to be photographed by that man. He is brilliant.'

'Do you think I can carry this off, Sally? Really?'

Sally put down her work and looked over at the girl. 'Yes I do.'

'Ireland is so, so new to its political identity,' Maeve said. 'We have only been a republic since 1922. I can't see anyone wanting a monarchy, even for a short while. Let alone me.'

'If the time comes that you have to strut your stuff, sweetie, you will be everything they need,' Sally said firmly. 'All you have to do is hold up the flag and they will rally to it. It shouldn't matter who holds it, but it does. The team across the way are building a legend, a romantic tale to stir the hearts. It's a whole lot easier with you than with your prime minister or Professor Kiernan or Peter Morris or any of them.'

'But I mean . . . me? For Christ's sake. The biggest group I have ever stood up in front of was in Grafton Street.'

'Talking?' Sally asked.

'No. Singing. We shook the tin,' she replied with a grin.

'Don't worry. As your mum would say, you'll be grand. How did you find the Princess of Wales?'

In Moscow, the British prime minister, his visit a well-kept secret, was shown into a meeting room with the Russian president.

'Hello, Vitaly,' he said.

'Peter. Welcome to Moscow.' He spoke through his interpreter.

'Can we begin?'

'Please do. Prime Minister, you are always welcome here officially, so forgive me if I was wondering what brings you under the cloak of secrecy.'

'You know, Vitaly,' the prime minister replied, noting the formality in his counterpart's words. They had been on first-name terms for two years at least. 'You know as well as I do. The same agenda as last time.'

'Prime Minister, I told you last time. We have legitimate interests in the Middle East and like any nation with a growing energy requirement, we wish to, shall we say, consolidate those interests for the future . . .'

Two hours later he showed his visitor to the door where the discreet escort waited for the return journey back to the airport. It had not been a good meeting.

Stewart looked through the one-way glass observation panel into the lecture room. He had elected not to use the staff college but instead had opted for his own facilities at Bulford.

The room was full of officers, colonels, lieutenant colonels, majors and the odd intelligence captain. The cap badges represented the elements that would make up his command. There were many faces he recognized from his own division. Maroon-bereted para officers stood mingling together. His own marine commandos stood alongside the other big grouping, the officers from the three battalions of the Guards Division.

The Scots Guards, the Welsh Guards and the Irish Guards were equally well represented, as were the officers of the Royal Regiment of Wales, the Royal Irish Regiment, the Black Watch and the Gordon Highlanders, and round the main group were the support elements, officers from Artillery, Logistics, Engineering, Air Corps, Medical and Signals. The handful of liaison officers from the sister services stood out in their blue uniforms.

These men would be the commanders of his forces. Much would depend on them, on the respect they had from their troops, because when the training was over and volunteers were called for it would be the bond with their mates, the respect for their officers and the pride in their regiments that would determine how many crossed the line. Esprit de corps. The fighting spirit.

It would be from these regiments that Stewart would call for volunteers. A few dour souls in Whitehall had said to expect as low as forty per cent in some regiments and as high as ninety in others. There would be those with babies due, family pressures, those who given the choice just would not fight. The holes in the ranks would be filled by others that Kiernan had promised, professional soldiers that could be dropped into existing units.

There had been unhappy people already, not because they didn't want to get involved, but because there was the smell of something going on and they were going to be left out. The commanding officer of the Duke of Edinburgh's Own 7th Gurkhas, who had a battalion rotated off the 5th Airborne Brigade, was absolutely furious and had stormed into Stewart's office the day before.

'Now see here, Monty,' he had bristled, 'my chaps have been part of the Brigade for two years. Training all that time. Now something's on and we are out? Bugger that!'

'Not their fight, Bob,' Stewart had responded reasonably. 'You will understand, I'm sure.'

'There is no such thing as a fight that my boys aren't on for,' he had retaliated.

'No,' Stewart said.

The Gurkha officer made a hurumphing noise. 'Well . . . just wanted to make me point . . .'

'You have. If it's any consolation, there's no unit I'd rather have at my side than your seventh, but not this time.'

The Gurkhas were not Celtic, not in anyone's wildest dreams, and this was not only arguably the cream of Britain's armed forces, but a very Celtic force indeed.

His adjutant stepped up. 'Your officers are assembled, General.'

'Thank you.' Stewart turned to the other men in the room. One, the officer commanding the 3rd Commando Brigade, had been designated second in command and

Stewart was delighted. Brigadier David Forbes, a Royal Marines officer, had been his classmate on many courses and they thought alike on most things. Forbes was the archetypal marine, right down to the angle of his beret.

The second was the Minister of Defence. Just arrived from a marathon session in the cabinet, his tie loosened, he was there to make the government's position plain, so the men could make balanced decisions. The third was Peter Tilby, the fourth Professor Kiernan and the last was Aiden Scott. He had been recalled to brief the officers in person.

The group moved through to the main lecture theatre, where those gathered were getting themselves seated. Aiden Scott, who had arrived straight from the airport, was wearing jeans and a working man's coat and felt conspicuous among the rows of senior uniformed figures. He stood behind and to the left of Stewart as the Minister of Defence stepped forward.

'Good morning, gentlemen. Thank you all for coming today. I'm going to get straight to the point. I am here to assure you that what you will discover this morning is the genuine state of affairs. It is highly classified. You all deal routinely with classified material and I will not insult your intelligence by suggesting otherwise, but at the end of my address you will be asked to make a choice. Quite simple. You are either willing to become involved and carry out your chosen profession in this instance or you are not. If you are not, then you are simply to stand and leave the room. The briefing will then commence. For security reasons, once in gentlemen, you are in.

'You will notice that there are no officers from the Defence Council, Executive Committees or the Chiefs of Staff. That is because what brings us here today is not a matter of Britain's national defence. Rather it is one of the defence of a neighbour and a friend.' The minister had taken his jacket off and now stood in shirtsleeves, his hands moving as he spoke. 'I am here to assure you all, bullshit and campaign speeches aside, that this endeavour has a good deal of cabinet support and that I might add of the palace. As you might expect there are people who are not keen to see British military involvement in anything, but for the time being you will assume we will take some sort of active role in the events you are about to be introduced to.

'Your commands have already been earmarked for a job. This force is to, or should I say may be required to, carry out an operation tagged as "Dark Rose". If so, you will be under the command of General Stewart,' he indicated Stewart who stood to his right, 'equipped, supplied and paid by the MoD. You will, however, not be operating under a Union flag.'

He paused to let that message sink in.

'You will be temporarily seconded to a friendly country's armed forces for one specific operation. That in itself means this is an all-volunteer force. No one has to go. That's all you will be told by me. You must now decide if you want to be included. Those of you who decline for whatever reasons will be replaced by officers who are willing, for the campaign only. I will leave you with General Stewart.'

The minister was escorted to the door by Brigadier Forbes as Stewart stepped forward and placed his cap and baton on the desk. The room was charged with expectancy. He wasn't surprised. Career soldiers chose the profession for various reasons, but at the end of the day they were just that, soldiers. They trained all their working lives for what most of them called 'the next fixture', the next major war. Most of them believed they were part of the finest standing army in the world and deep down they wanted to carry out their task, for real at least once. Even so this group was different. Many of them had seen action, in the Falklands, in Northern Ireland and in the Gulf War. For this group there was no romance in a fire-fight, no

227

glory in death. Of all the men in the army they were the one group that could fairly be asked to decide, then and there, if they were willing to fight someone else's war.

These men were.

No one had moved.

The atmosphere was electric. Stewart waited for a full minute until finally a voice from the back said drily, 'I think we are all in, boss.'

There was a ripple of laughter around the room. Scott recognized the voice. It was his colleague Busby Grogan, the SAS intelligence officer.

Stewart grinned. 'Good,' he said. 'I know you are all dying to know just what the devil has been going on that drags you all in here.' He paused for a second or two.

'Eire. The Irish Republic. It has been invaded.'

The surprise was almost total. They were too well disciplined to gasp or talk, but they sat up in their seats, leaned forward, their eyes full of questions already.

'We will commence with a bit of the background from the Foreign Office. We will then come up to date with the latest int. Save your questions for afterwards.'

The Foreign Office man was in fact Peter Tilby, but the men in the room were not to be told he was an MI6 intelligence officer. He covered the background and then handed over to Kiernan who told them of the resistance and the preparations made to date and finally Scott moved up to an overhead projector. The secretaries in the support function had allowed him use of a photocopier and Tilby had handed him a carousel of slides, a collection of the recent material he had supplied to Century House. No one introduced Scott, but his clothing and casual confidence identified his regiment.

'Right,' he began. 'Sitrep as of 1800 hours October 14. Land forces. We have identified heavy armour, some artillery, mobile air defence systems, BTRs. Deployed as follows.' He put up an overhead chart, a layout of Counties

228

Louth, Monaghan and Cavan. Small symbols represented main battle tanks, infantry positions where they had concealed their fighting vehicles, and air defence units. 'The MBTs are mostly T-62s, but we have confirmed at least a dozen 72s. They are currently concealed in sheds, barns and the like. We did find some prepared revetments. Can I have the slide projector please?' The lights dimmed and the projector fired a beam of light at the screen. Scott pressed the advance button and an image appeared on the wall. 'This was taken four days ago. Revetments for, as you can see, four tanks, and yes, they are close to each other. The angle doesn't show it here, but a line of trees conceals the position quite well. There are another four of these positions. We also found this.'

The image changed and through the gloom of a tractor shed with hay bales in the background was the unmistakable silhouette of a track-mounted radar guided anti-aircraft gun.

'A ZSU-23 triple A unit. This one is definitely Libyan. Still has its unit markings. Two others like it that we know of so far. Oh . . . there's a couple of crates of SAM sevens down on the right-hand side of the picture. We opened that up. The gear is old. Half of it was corroded.' He turned to face the room. 'The deployment is even across the three counties, and much heavier to the south where we have, so far, found the following.' The slide changed on the screen and Scott continued. He showed photographs of armour, trucks, air defence units and other associated equipment and he showed the locations of known elements of troops.

'Maintenance equipment that we have found suggests that only part of the force has arrived. We found a mobile comms and command unit in Kilkenny. Big enough for a multi-brigade action.

'Some heavy gear is in,' he concluded, 'with a small garrison force. We estimate that we have found thirty per cent of them. The rest will follow.'

All the officers in the room knew that the Libyans used Soviet doctrine and that meant they were up against at least two divisions. Armour and mechanized with support elements.

'Any questions?' Scott asked.

A hundred hands were raised in the air.

## 23 October

Deep in the NRO facility in the Pentagon the analysts were spending their seventeenth day poring over images that had come in from the KH-11 satellites. Most of their time was spent working on the material that had come in from the 'Hawkeye' and the files were building. They could now recognize faces of guards and knew what time their shifts changed. Yesterday they had struck gold. Just as the Hawkeye passed overhead a group of nine people were walked across the quadrangle between tents accompanied by guards. This was the first time they had managed to get in close to anyone other than camp staff since the upper arm image.

While one of the Americans looked through the basic material the other two began the scanning process. The software was new, illegally copied by a whizz kid at Scotland Yard, a state-of-the-art photo match system, a space age identikit, that could scan a photograph into its memory. Then the software would re-draw the shape of the head and features with a series of three-dimensional images. Once this was complete the system could then scan every image from the satellite data seeking a match. Like fingerprinting it established points of similarity and finally they were assured would overlay its images over the match it considered 'fixed'.

MI6 had managed to provide photographs of thirty-two people who they believed were hostages. The photographs came from newspaper files, school records, the families, and some were stolen.

All of these had been scanned into the system in London. Now it was time to let the computer do its work and with the big gigabyte mainframe's beefed-up processors it would take no time at all.

'Ready?' the Englishman asked.

The computer operator nodded.

'Let's do it then,' he said.

Behind him one of the CIA men lit a cigarette, the tension building.

At that moment in the south of England an Irish naval officer had arrived to take delivery of his command after a major refit. His Peacock class patrol boat returned to the yards every three years for hull inspection and routine but heavy repairs. She was a fast coastal defence craft, 180-odd feet long, with torpedo tubes and capable of 33 knots, and at thirty-three years of age her commander, Lieutenant Eamon Kavanagh, was as proud of her as any captain of any ship. She may not have been as big as the Irish navy's one bigger ship and her tubes had never held live torpedoes, but she was his and as he walked the catwalks alongside her now gleaming hull he was as pleased as punch, a broad smile across his face, his black curly hair peeping from under his cap.

'Nice job they've done, Eamon.'

He turned. There was a tall fellow making his way down the catwalk towards him.

'Yes,' Kavanagh responded, trying to see through the gloom; finally the approaching figure moved into the light. 'Well, well, well. Toby Markham, *Dia dhuit*!'

'Hello, Paddy.' Markham, smiling, took the proffered hand. They had done three exercises together, all involving fishing boats in the Irish Sea and had become friends, taking time together when circumstances permitted. They exchanged pleasantries for a few minutes before Markham asked, 'Time for a beer later?'

'Not tonight. My boss is coming in. Tomorrow maybe?'

'Tomorrow then. Confirmed, yeah?'

Kavanagh looked at his friend. They had never confirmed a date to do anything, just taking things as they happened.

'It's important, Paddy,' Markham said softly. 'Eight at the Three Bells?'

'I'll be there,' the Irishman said.


The software took each satellite image in turn and matched it to the three-dimensional diagrams it had created from the photographs, 93 possible match points on each image, each stage happening on the screen as they watched. The CIA man was on his third cigarette. Most of the images had not got past the third or fourth attempt at a match point before the machine moved on, but finally the little flashing light kept moving across the screen, figures flicking over down in the bottom corner.

'It's on to something,' the machine operator said casually. 'The bottom figure is its count.'

The counter had settled on 63.

'How many do we need?'

'Not sure. Doesn't it say somewhere?'

'No. Better phone London.'

'It's three AM there,' the CIA man said.

'Tough,' the Englishman answered.

He walked away to find a phone and was back twenty minutes later. He had a big grin on his face.

'Well?'

'They reckon anything over thirty would be enough for a warrant. Sixty and they would go to court.'

The CIA man punched the sky with his fist. 'YES!'

'What number was that one?' the Englishman asked, sitting at the screen again.

'Ahh, eighteen,' the operator answered.

'Eighteen is . . .' his finger moved down the list ' . . .

Vicki Slaney. Daughter of a senior police officer.' He looked up at the other two. 'Good enough for me. I'd like copies of all the material for my people. In particular the layout, roads, terrain, defence systems, tents, bogs, the infrared tapes. The lot.'

'You got it.'

The material was in London the following day and by nightfall a small group of Pentagon operations planners had been invited to London.

Lieutenant Kavanagh was five minutes late, but found Markham wedged in at the crowded bar. He accepted the pint of ale thrust towards him over the heads of other drinkers and followed Markham's pointed finger towards a quieter corner table. Its surface was sticky, crowded with dirty glasses and crisp wrappers and as they sat, one of the barmen leaned over them scooping up the glassware and wiping a damp cloth over the surface.

Markham waited until the man moved away before holding up his glass. 'Cheers.'

The Irishman lifted his glass and drank deeply. 'It's good to see you, Toby,' he said gently.

'And you. Family well?'

'Grand,' he replied, then continued with a smile, 'Get on with it, boy.'

'What?'

'This place, Toby. You hate bars like this. No soul. You haven't smiled all night. So whatever's on your mind, get it out and let's go somewhere nice and settle in for the evening.'

Markham looked down at his glass for a second or two. He didn't like intelligence work and he didn't like using his friendships for things he didn't understand. He had just been told. Get your friend somewhere quiet.

'There's trouble, Paddy,' Markham said gently looking up at his friend.

233

'Well if I can help, I will.'

'Not for me. For you. For your people.'

Kavanagh's smile dropped. 'What kind of trouble?' he asked.

'Serious trouble. There are people waiting to talk to you.'

'What people?' Kavanagh asked defensively.

'Mine and some of yours.'

Kavanagh sat back, his eyes sweeping the crowded bar, thinking fast.

'The only reason I'm still sitting here is we are friends. If you are trying to involve me in something unethical or something that conflicts with . . .' Markham held up his hand to silence him.

'Just hear them out. This is classified. I'm not in at that level, but I have been told to tell you that either way, this will affect you. It will affect your command. Your family. Paddy, these are the good guys. Just hear them out.'

'Where are they?'

'Upstairs.'

'My people?' Kavanagh confirmed.

'They are there.'

'Navy?'

'I don't know.'

'I'm not going. This is in direct . . .'

'Eamon,' his friend said, 'Briget is there too. She's here to talk with you. She suggested you.'

Three hours later Lieutenant Kavanagh was in and the resistance and the Century House planners knew a great deal more about the other handful of Irish navy commanders and the actual scheduling of patrols. The objective was to attempt to manipulate events and have the navy's only true warship, their Eithne class vessel with her Dauphin helicopter, and as many of the six light patrol craft as possible, at sea when things got nasty.

Century House felt that the Irish air force would have

been deeply penetrated, with their senior officers blackmailed already. Combat aircraft were not something anyone wanting to control a country allowed to take off.

A significant portion of the Irish army was attached to the United Nations for peacekeeping duties and would be out of Ireland anyway. Whatever light armour, their Scorpions, was left would be neutralized very quickly, within minutes. That left only one command, junior enough to have possibly escaped the blackmail process, that could be useful. The suggestion was made to recruit the officer commanding the Ranger company. The Rangers were as near as Ireland came to a élite light infantry force. When it happened they could hopefully slip into the night, if necessary on foot, to a prearranged rendezvous. They could then be broken into a series of fast-moving, hard-hitting elements working with the resistance force.

Mona de Cruz paced the area by the bay windows nervously watching the street. The woman had cancelled their last meeting, something about a child's accident, and her uncle was most insistent on more information. She wasn't sure why. She had just been passing everything as usual, but this time he had wanted a meeting at once, wanting to understand exactly what the woman had said, the tone, the inference. She was angry. They were putting the pressure on her to provide more information without telling her why. He had just said that the wife of the man from the Ministry of Defence was now the single most important intelligence target they had. They wanted to know which people were going to have the shitty Christmas. They had wired the flat the following day, a man coming from an electronics shop in Shepherd's Bush. He put a tape recorder into the hat cupboard in the bedroom. There were microphones under the sofa and under the bed. It was all rather amateur, she thought. They had left a cable sticking out and she had to kick it under the bed and cover a section of it by moving the mat. She had to switch it on as the woman arrived.

To an extent she liked the sex. Having it done to her was nice and it was getting better. She looked forward to it now and having it done to her didn't mean she was a lesbian. You were only a lesbian if you liked doing it to another woman, she rationalized.

She saw the car reversing into a parking space. She smiled and went to the bathroom to freshen herself. She stopped, remembering the tape recorder and pulled the stool over so she could reach the high cupboard.

An hour later as they lay temporarily sated on sweaty wrinkled sheets Mona began to gently probe her lover.

'Winter is here,' she said, pulling the blankets over them. 'Look, it's dark outside already. Such a shame about your skiing, darling, or has your poor husband changed his mind?'

'Poor?' the wife retorted. 'I'm the one who is being hard done by.'

'I'll make it up to you,' Mona said breathlessly leaning over her. She smiled quickly, enjoying her deceit. It hadn't been this good since school and moreover she hadn't a clue.

'How?' the other woman asked in a little-girl voice.

'Why don't we go away for the weekend sometime? We can, you know, do it all night then. Wouldn't that be wonderful? To have all night. I hate these hurried afternoons.'

'Yes . . . but . . .' she began, thinking quickly. 'I suppose I could get away.'

'I know a place. A place in Spain. Huge beds. They have a bowl of fruit in the rooms, big bananas and things,' she said, running her finger down the other's leg. 'It's only an hour away on the plane.'

'Sounds fabulous,' the under secretary's wife said.

'But I'm a little . . . little scared. Well no, not scared. Concerned.'

236

'Why, darling?' the wife sat up. 'About what?'

'Well, your husband. He is an important man. He knows things we don't. Remember he said some people were going to have a really shitty Christmas. Well, maybe we'd better stay in London. After all, if things are going to get nasty somewhere . . . well, it's such an uncertain world. Maybe we should stay closer to home. I know! How about Ireland! There's a new exhibition at a gallery in Dublin. We could go over, see the pictures and then spend the rest of the time in bed. But . . .' she slumped forward, her voice dejected again, 'maybe it's not safe there either.'

'I'll find out,' the under secretary's wife said soothingly. 'I'll just tell him I want to go to the exhibition opening. If it's not safe then he won't let me go.'

'And we will have to stay here,' Mona said.

'There are bananas in London,' the under secretary's wife said, her voice husky as she reached across beneath the sheet.

'Promise you'll find out,' Mona asked.

'Promise.'

'Then come here. You'll like this.'


Scott's teams of Special Air Service continued their surveillance and intelligence-gathering operations ceaselessly. The planning teams now hard at work at High Wycombe, Bulford and Wilton required daily updates and were now asking for fine details.

The only halt in recent weeks had been for the arrival of their beloved special operations vehicles. In a cross-border smuggling operation of audacious proportions, sixteen of the specially produced Land Rovers had been transported across into the Irish Republic, and had been hidden in pairs across the length of the country. The vehicles, with 20mm cannon, Milan anti-tank missiles, mortars and light machine guns, were formidable indeed. The firepower in the hands of five-man SAS teams would be used to supplement resistance actions and harass the enemy in his exposed rear.

Scott's twenty-two-man force would remain on the ground for the time being, but many other SAS troops had been recalled to Bradbury lines and were en route from their deployments all over the world.

The prime minister's approval granted, the planning to rescue the Irish hostages in Libya had begun, and American liaison teams from the US Marines and the US Navy had arrived in Britain.

This would be the biggest deployment of the Special Air Service regiment since the Gulf War and early scenarios demanded that the camp containing the hostages and the airstrip nearby be taken and held for up to two hours. This would mean the complete neutralization of opposing forces. The first plan called for 88 SAS troopers, supported by air, to 'neutralize' or contain the approximately 700 Libyan troops guarding the remote site.

At the headquarters of United Kingdom Land Forces, in Wilton, preparations were feverish. Staff in the unprepossessing low brick buildings were planning a series of training exercises in Wales, Scotland and the Isle of Skye. This time, however, the public relations teams who would ordinarily be planning press visits and conducting meetings with local authorities were told to keep the operations under wraps until further notice; when news was released, it would be a low-key announcement of routine training. In the regiments all leave and courses were quietly postponed and junior officers told to grin and bear it. Such was the management that each of the men who had an event cancelled thought he was the only one affected. Places on courses were rapidly filled by other names, so no one outside Wilton or the task force was aware that a portion of the British army was on increased readiness.

Deep within the facility in the operations branch, G3

OPS, a full lieutenant general had taken over planning for the support elements of Dark Rose, the thousands of details for getting Stewart's force on to the battlefield, supported, fed, refuelled, rearmed. Other detailed administrative functions would be completed at Stewart's headquarters at Bulford Camp.

On 27 October the last British army elements of 'Celt Force' arrived in the exercise area and live firing and laser combat commenced in earnest. The last two battalions in were Warrior equipped, part of the 3rd UK Division Heavy Brigade, and refresher training began.

It was now that the inevitable happened. A journalist employed by the *Daily Telegraph* as their defence correspondent and supplier of freelance articles to, among other publications, *Jane's*, put two and two together. He noticed the early departures of battalions for training, the unscheduled movements of others. He began to try his usual sources and two line officers, normally happy to see him, were suddenly unavailable for lunch. Three separate sources within the MoD were equally elusive and his fourth, delighted to have one of their irregular chats, was no use. The journalist gently squeezed the pips. 'Come on. Something's going on. You mean to say you don't know? I thought you were onward and upward. Seems you've been left out of this one, sport.'

The man grimaced and looked back down at his coronation chicken. 'I'll see what I can find out.'

He already knew. What the journalist didn't know was that his lunch guest was in fact a military intelligence officer. He reported the conversation on his arrival back in the office and a hasty meeting was convened for early that evening, to be chaired by none other than the Secretary of State for Defence himself. He was a veteran politician and a genuinely popular man, even among the opposition, who had to agree that he was very good at his job.

He now sat in his favourite old wing chair, one leg swung over the arm, other ministers in the department around him and a clutch of the department's senior civil servants on the hard-backed chairs that had been pulled over from the long conference table.

'I think we have to accept that we have been lucky thus far,' he pulled his glasses off and swung them in his hand as one of the junior ministers spoke.

'It's my view that if one journalist is on to it then others won't be far behind.'

'Mmm,' from the Secretary of State. 'Well, let's appeal to their better natures. I think . . .' he paused as an aide passed him a note and he read it silently before slipping it into his pocket. It was confirmation from the Security Service, MI5, that they were able to advise if and when any of the major publications were going to turn their attention on the story. So far it only seemed to be the *Telegraph*'s defence correspondent. ' . . . let's get the editors together tomorrow morning if we can. Find somewhere nice and neutral.'

'And if they don't have better natures?' one minister asked. A few people grinned. The man who had just spoken had been the target of a tabloid attack on his sex life only six months before. Single, he had got away with it, but he was now tagged 'Randy' by all.

'Then they will have to abide by the constraints of a D notice. I shall warn them tomorrow that if we have to move to a D, then we will put censors into the building for as long as is necessary. I think we'd better get a D under way anyway and if someone gets silly then we have the machinery in place.' The minister looked across at his number two. 'The usual, please, John,' he finished. 'I think we are well justified to consider this is a matter of national security.'

The *Telegraph* journalist was taken off the story the following lunchtime by his editor.

'I can't believe I'm hearing this,' he said incredulously. 'Something humungous is breaking and you are telling me to do a story on bloody Vospers again? This is most of the bloody 3rd UK. Ten thousand men, count 'em, ten, on manoeuvres, shit! That's more grunts than took the Falklands back.'

'Relax, Herbie,' his editor soothed. 'When the time comes we are in. Front row seats. That's from the top. Until then you stay off the story and you keep bloody schtumm.'

The journalist, respected in his profession, a man who had reported from the Falklands, the Gulf and Bosnia, stood up.

'Sorry. It's big. There is a right to know issue here. If you won't publish, then . . .'

'Just sit down, Herbie. Do I have to spell it out to you? There is a D notice pending and a government censor waiting to sit at a desk alongside yours, and don't give me this right to know claptrap. Now you are a good journalist. You got on to this and you will be the first allowed back. But if it breaks early then people will die. That's all I can say. If you don't like it then see travel. We need someone covering Ethiopia.'

'Bugger Ethiopia,' the reporter said. 'Look, why don't I just work up the background? I know who is moving. Then when it breaks, we are ready.'

'I'm not sure that . . .'

'Look, did you promise not to publish or not to do anything?'

'Publish,' the editor said thinking quickly. 'You're right. I only agreed not to publish, as did the others. Okay, get on to it.'

The under secretary's wife saw her lover on the 29th and said, in the course of their lovemaking, that her husband had forbidden her to go to Ireland.

The moment she left Mona telephoned her uncle and arranged an immediate meeting. In her opinion, and the opinion of the others who heard the tapes, the under secretary had a solid reason for preventing his wife from going to Ireland – they knew or suspected something. The appraisal was flashed to Amman.

# 8

## 30 October

The man had stepped up beside Morris on the pavement and walked beside him long enough to say, 'One hour. The Green.'

He was one of the section heads and Morris cancelled the meeting he had arranged to be there.

'One of my fellows. He is into birds. He was out looking for something last night. Spent the night a couple of miles from the airport. Says there was an awful lot of planes coming in. Too many. He worked his way across. Saw one off-loading people just before five this morning. Just a small thing that was different.'

'What?' Morris asked.

'They were off-loading the other side. Not at the passenger terminal. Down towards the end. Straight into buses. No customs, and they were all men.'

Morris stopped and looked at him. 'Sure?'

'He's a good man.'

'How many in total?'

'Full plane, I guess.'

'No. How many planes?'

'Five in three hours. All big ones. You know. Jumbos.'

People walked round them on the path towards the bridge over the pond. Morris looked up at the sky. It was leaden and soon it would be dark.

'Shit . . . All right. I'll take it from here.'

'If you are going to have a look, he knows a place at the wire where you can get through.'

Morris agreed and told him where they should meet and then went to find a phone.

Three hours later Scott phoned him at home through the linked circuits and Morris asked if they could meet that night.

'It's important.'

Just before midnight Morris parked his car at the meeting point. Behind him somewhere in the dark Scott and one of his men waited. Another sat in the front seat beside him, a nine millimetre pistol in a bag on his lap. A few minutes later a car stopped beside him. A man got out. He was in his forties, wearing a heavy tweed coat with an old flat cap on his head and rubber boots on his feet. The SAS man watched him approach, his hand on the gun.

'You Morris?' he asked.

Morris nodded.

The man leaned down, his arms on the window.

'Buggers are scaring my birds. Found a pair of corncrakes. Must be the only ones this side of the Shannon.'

'What time did they start coming in?' Morris asked.

'Been here since the spring, probably.'

'No,' Morris countered patiently. 'The aircraft.'

'Oh. Just after one.'

'Think it will happen again tonight?'

'Well, if it doesn't you have wasted the night,' he said with a chuckle. 'They should be coming. The vehicles are back.'

'What vehicles?' Morris asked.

'They were there last night, too. Big pick-up types. Like in the American movies. Driving round the perimeter every now and then.'

Morris looked at the SAS man, who nodded and lifted a small microphone to his lips and began to speak softly to the vehicle behind them.

'Can you show us where the hole in the fence is?' Morris asked. The man nodded.

'Jump in.'

An hour later the trooper beside Scott lifted the camera and checked it. He looked across at Scott and raised a thumb. The powerful night vision lens was coupled to a surveillance camera and in turn linked to a backpack battery and recording unit. It was bulky, but the quality of the images it was capable of producing made the weight worth while.

They were dressed in black, balaclavas pulled down to prevent skin glare in a sweeping light, lying down well inside the wire. The grass was fifteen inches high and they were lucky that the big tractor-driven rotary mowers hadn't been round this end of the airport for a while.

It was cold but they lay still. This was one of the things they accepted about their role. The waiting. Tonight it would only be hours. Scott had once spent eleven days watching a path in Armagh, eleven days in a hole in the ground, waiting for a man to collect from a cache. He had finally come, a man with seven killings on his record, sniffing the wind, canny like an old fox, slowly circling the place until he felt sure he was safe. He had dug down beneath the bracken, lifting the oilskin-wrapped rifle from the buried fertilizer drum and as he stood, the evidence in his hands, Scott had shot him. Six hundred yards in the dying light of an autumn day, the heavy bullet passing through both legs just above the knees.

He had gone down, no fight left, and Scott called the support in, the helicopters arriving putting fresh men on the ground, RUC Special Branch men supported by fusiliers.

Waiting was a discipline like any other.

Three jets landed in the first hour they were there and it was the last that taxied past the taxiways that led to the terminal, moving ponderously towards the darkness of the maintenance areas that were now closed.

'Start recording,' Scott said. Their suspicions were

confirmed when one of the two pick-up trucks that had been parked off the runway started its engine and turned on to the perimeter road.

The trooper ignored it, and focusing the lens he softened the image intensifier and looked through the viewfinder. The big lens allowed him to watch the wheels turning on the main bogies, the scene harshly backlit by the aircraft's landing lights. Suddenly they dimmed.

The trooper increased the light intake, booting the intensifier and looked back through the viewfinder. There were three cars lined up and a line of buses and the giant aircraft lumbered to a halt.

'I have coaches,' he said.

'It's them, all right,' Scott said. He was looking through a thirty-power night sight. 'I want to count them down the stairs. If you see anyone giving orders, try and get close-ups.'

'It won't be the Eighteen Thirty holidays rep,' the trooper said.

Scott smiled. He looked for the truck. It wouldn't be far away now, and they were only fifteen metres back from the road. He swung the sight, finding the vehicle moving out past the terminal.

'Vehicle ten o'clock half a mile.'

As it came past both men remained absolutely still, the trooper covering the lens with a black woollen-gloved hand so it wouldn't reflect light. As it moved past he again focused on the aircraft, men now pouring down the rear stairs.

Beside him Scott watched, hoping that Morris and the bird man had remained behind the fence as he had asked. On the airfield the men were obviously coming down the stairs in arranged groups, sections and platoons, because they boarded buses together, others effectively marshalling them towards their designated transport. Each man carried a duffel bag. There was no doubt that these were troops, in spite of the civilian clothing they wore.

There were four other aircraft that night, each a 747 jumbo with its livery painted out, each one full. As the two men gathered their equipment and began to move back towards the fence, Scott wondered how others had done. He had three men watching Shannon airport, the other major facility that had runways long enough to take a wide-bodied long-haul jet, but had had no time to get anyone to Knock.

The logistics were staggering. Each aircraft needed eight coaches to move the arrivals. Eight at fifty each was four hundred off each flight. Five flights into Dublin, five the night before that they knew of, maybe another ten at Shannon over the two nights. Even without Knock it meant a possible additional eight thousand men on the ground and not a shot had been fired. They would be, he thought, deployed before dawn, linked up with their equipment, weapons, vehicles and command structure, only to disappear from sight in God knows how many warehouses on a hundred farms.

Scott was over the border in Ulster by eight AM and stopped at the first telephone box he came to. There was no time to mess about with drop points and meetings trying to get someone at the embassy in Dublin.

He called the number he had for Century House and a few seconds later was put through to Peter Tilby.

'It's Scott.'

'Ah,' Tilby said, knowing instantly that something was amiss.

'I'm in Newry. Get someone to pick me up. I have a message for mother.'

'Why not come for lunch?'

'No. I have plans for later today. Can't be changed.'

'I see.' Tilby was thinking fast. 'Head for the PO. I'll have a friend in a white Granada come by in about fifteen minutes.' He paused. 'Anything mother should know now?'

'I think the fixture has been moved forward,' Scott replied casually. 'The extra players are arriving. I've got some holiday snaps too.'

'Sure?'

'Affirmative. Maybe more tonight.'

'I see,' Tilby said. His mind was racing. Jesus, it's only November, we aren't ready yet. Something has happened.

'Okay. Meet my friend and we can talk some more from his place.'

Scott replaced the receiver and left the booth, walking towards the small post office. He was back in Britain, but he didn't relax. Although there was supposed to be a cease-fire, this was Ulster and he was a Brit soldier in a place where the local Provisional IRA were everywhere. And old habits died hard.

Tilby swung his office door open. His secretary, a woman whose skills he shared with two others, was sitting at her desk. 'Get me Sally Richards. Now. Is the DDG in?'

'Yes. Meeting till noon,' she replied.

'Interrupt it. Tell her I'm coming up. Put Sally through, and there will be a call coming through on the secure system. Put that through as well. Then get on to ops. I want a courier to collect a package in Ulster. Get the details from Don Barry in Warrenpoint.'

She was writing swiftly on a pad and as he headed for the staircase she picked up the phone.

Petra Wallis was putting down the phone as he entered her outer office, three others filing out past him.

'Go,' she said.

'Scott's been on. He's our Hereford asset in County Dublin and officer commanding. He's calling back on a secure line in a few minutes. It looks like there are troops arriving in Ireland. He has photos or video or something. He says it's on.'

'What did he say? Exactly?'

'He said the players are arriving and the fixture has been moved forward. That's what they call the next major war. A fixture. I have a courier collecting the material he has.'

'How do you rate him?' she asked.

'Scott? Outstanding,' Tilby replied.

She nodded, more to herself than to Tilby. Human intelligence was the best. Better than satellites and any number of analysts.

'What time is he calling?'

'As soon as they are back at the house. Ten minutes maybe.'

'Let's wait and talk to him. Where is he going?'

'Our place in Warrenpoint.'

'Right. Assume his assessment is accurate,' the Deputy Director General replied. 'I will grab the DG to listen in. You get on to Wales and gather them together in the comms room.'

She looked at her watch. 'There is a cabinet committee meeting at five. I want the material here by four, and checked. Four copies. One for us, one for the planning team, one for MoD and one for the cabinet meeting. How did they arrive?'

'No idea. Aircraft probably.'

'Get it checked. Then make sure we are watching on radar tonight. Ports and airports in case there are more. God! They are landing aircraft right under our noses?'

'It's easy enough. They've kidnapped enough senior people, and Irish domestic radar would simply be told to expect traffic by the operations people.'

'Get on with it.'

'Right.'

'Then let's find out what the hell has happened. All the indicators said January sometime. They don't have a friendly in the Security Council until then.'

'For the Palestinians the bulk of the UN is bloody friendly.'

'We need to know,' she said firmly.

'You think they may know we are on to them?'

'Yes. I'd be surprised if they didn't. Anyone who can mount a job like this has got an intelligence structure and this has got to be the worst kept secret in the world. How many people here know about it? In this building, the cabinet, the MoD, and the Wales team, a hundred? Two? The resistance have God knows how many people running round. One of them may have said something to their wife or son. Anything may have happened.' She turned to face him. 'Are these "players" Palestinians or Libyans?'

'The pictures will tell us that,' Tilby replied. He lifted the phone on her desk and dialled the big house in Wales, speaking clearly over the secure line.

He had barely put the phone down when it rang again.

'Yes? Put it through.'

He pressed the speaker button and replaced the handset.

'Aiden?'

'Yeah.'

'I've got you on the squawk box. I'm with the DDG.'

'Okay. Began night before last, we think. I didn't get out till last night, but we have the following going down certainly at two major airports, namely Dublin and Shannon, last night. Wide-body jets, nine 747s and one DC10, offloading all male passengers. They landed technically after the airport had closed down for the night. Not much happening and bugger all traffic around. Taxied down into the dark away from the terminals and began off-loading. Buses there waiting. The men came down in squads and were loaded into buses in squads. People with clipboards moving among them. They were dressed in civvies, but the haircuts and the baggage were military. They were humping green kitbags, you know the round American-type duffel bag . . .'

'Any identifying features? We need to know if they were Libyans or Palestinians.'

'They were army. Could be either, but as Palestine doesn't have a standing army and these were definitely currently serving, I'd say Libyan.'

Petra Wallis leant forward. 'Can you elaborate?'

'They look like soldiers. Act like soldiers. Badly motivated and a bit sloppy, but soldiers nevertheless.'

'Did you get a count?' Tilby asked.

'Haven't see the tape yet, but the planes were full. I'd say we could have had between six and ten thousand over the two nights. I'm going back tonight and I've got a couple of people going up to the third airport big enough. A place called Knock.'

'Good.'

'The video is ready here, with an audio report on tape.'

'A courier is on his way,' Tilby said. 'Well done.'

'I'd better go. I want to be back there tonight.'

'Captain Scott,' Wallis said, 'what is your appraisal of this development?'

There was a pause, a few crackly seconds before Scott answered. He was uncomfortable with the question. The Deputy Director General of one of the country's intelligence services did not normally ask junior army officers for their assessment of anything.

'I think that these people, wherever they are going to be billeted, or deployed, cannot be hidden for long. I think their timetable has changed.' He paused again. 'I think it's on.'

'Thank you,' she replied.

Scott hung up.

'Get a team together,' she said to Tilby, 'to see this tape when it gets here. I want some military types as well.'

'Sure,' he said. 'You don't think he is right, do you?'

'I don't accept everything people say. I am an intelligence officer,' she responded defensively. 'I want to check and double check. I want different opinions and viewpoints of anything that is subjective or open to interpretation.'

251

'I accept that. But I have met Aiden Scott. He is competent and absolutely unflappable. I would rate his analysis very highly indeed, better than some warrior from Whitehall.'

'What is your point, Peter?' Wallis asked.

'I think we should assume he is right and get moving regardless. If the boffins agree, all very well, but there are things that we should get under way right this minute.'

She studied him. Peter Tilby was in her experience very easy-going and rarely got excited about anything. If he felt this strongly then it was because some ancient instincts were working.

'Agreed,' she replied. 'What do you want to do?'

'Ask comms to get on to GCHQ. From now on all traffic, every squeak, ex-Ireland to be decoded and transcribed. They will have to beef up their resources immediately. Let's get on to Wales. Kiernan must call his dogs in. They mustn't start this. If they do we lose the advantage. Get on to the MoD. Their people should see this tape as soon as we do. And I think we should suggest that Scott's command is topped up. We need to have more of our people on their way in there tonight, enough to find these others and pinpoint their exact locations.'

Four hours later a lean uniformed man in his fifties, one of the senior officers from the MoD, concurred with Scott. He had viewed the tape seven times.

'He is right. No doubt about it. Soldiers move in a particular manner. Even dressed in civvies, they still move in groups, answer to orders, find themselves moving into lines and rows, they follow their non-coms. It's a different feel and appearance to a group of civilians or, I suppose, fighters. I've seen fighters. They move with a studied nonchalance, they see themselves as individuals.'

Tilby came into the room and handed Wallis a typed sheet. It was a printout of a sector traffic log from the

Government Communications Headquarters in Cheltenham. Transmissions out of Ireland had increased tenfold overnight. They advised they had tripled the shifts simply to handle the volume of traffic.

On the third and fourth floors of Century House teams of people were viewing the tape, some to establish who owned the aircraft and trace the flight origins, others to start photographing the enhanced close-ups. The files on Libyan officers were sparse, but they hoped for a match.

At the house in Wales, Kiernan was putting together a careful statement. He was by now if not the acknowledged leader of the resistance, certainly its guiding hand, firm and measured. Downstairs the planning team had gone into emergency session, establishing what they could move forward and when.

Morris looked in the fridge. It was empty, with only a couple of carrots and half a container of yoghurt sitting sparsely on the shelves. In the last days the schedule had been such that all routines had broken down.

He shrugged. He wasn't hungry anyway and it seemed days since he had seen Millie for more than few minutes at a time; then all they seemed to do was argue. He was tired now. The full-time job during the day and the nights spent in meetings, travelling or, like the night before, spent getting to know his enemy were taking their toll. He was tense, too. The pressure was building and he was carrying much of it, unable to confide in anyone or voice his concerns. He had to be the rock. Steadfast and calm. He didn't feel it.

There was a knock at the back door. He walked down the hall and opened it.

'Don't you ever do that again,' Scott said. 'You check who it is first.'

'What are you doing here?' Morris asked.

Scott pushed his way past him into the house. 'When was the last time you slept?' he asked.

'I got some last night.'

'Bullshit,' Scott said. 'You were with me last night. A catnap in a car seat doesn't count.'

'What's this about?' Morris said tiredly, then the realization dawning. 'Millie. Millie said something.'

'It's about you,' Scott replied. 'You are no good to anyone if you haven't rested. If you think the pressure is on now, you're wrong. It hasn't even started yet. But it's about to. So tonight you stay in. Millie will be home with some hot food. Eat it. Then go to bed.'

'I'm not a fifteen-year-old.'

'So stop acting like one. Peter. Listen to me. It's about to break. Tomorrow, the next day, soon. There are people who say that the next major war will only last fifty hours. You know why? Because with modern night fighting equipment, the battle will run twenty-four hours a day. The fittest army will win, because their men are still awake.

'You have to be fit and rested. The lives of your people depend on it. You are in command. You fuck up and people die . . . When Millie gets home, you eat together and then you sleep. Both of you.'

Morris nodded. He was too tired to argue and besides, he knew Scott was right.

'I have a man across the street,' Scott said with a smile. 'If you move he will take a dim view of it.'

'It's really on, isn't it?'

Scott nodded. 'I believe it is,' he replied softly.

'Till last night,' Morris said, 'till last night I was hoping we were wrong, that it was all some huge mistake. Now I'm scared. I'm scared because it's real and people are going to die. My people, and somehow I ended up in charge of this area and I'm not qualified for it. I'm a political scientist. I'm not a soldier. Eight thousand of the bastards in two days. Christ, what are we up against?'

254

'You're not alone,' Scott said.

'All your people, and don't get me wrong they have been great to date, but all they have said is that they will help.'

Scott thought quickly. The last thing they needed was a despondent commander, a man who had been kept out of the loop.

'They will come,' he said. 'I'm just the first.'

Morris smiled. ' Yes. You are here. With your men. But how many are there of you? Twenty? Twenty-five? What can twenty-five of you do?'

'You'd be surprised,' Scott said drily.

'I learned something watching the Gulf War on television,' Morris said. 'I learned just what trained professional people can do. Us? Half of us have had a week in one of your battle camps and that's about it. I'm shit-scared, Aiden. I'm shit-scared of seeing bodies in the streets. Women, kids, old people, just ordinary people, trying to fight a professional army.'

'Firstly,' Scott replied, 'calling these Libyans a professional army is a joke. They are a fucking rabble. Badly trained, badly led and badly motivated. Now let me tell you who is coming. The Celts. Just like Kiernan asked for. Only these are modern Celts, elements of the finest standing army in the world. I was there, Peter, I helped in the briefing. A division is coming, probably the best-trained, best-motivated division that has ever gone into action. Look at me,' he said. 'They will roll through these wankers like they weren't even there.'

'Volunteers, right?'

'Yes.'

'And what if they don't volunteer?' Morris asked.

'These people are soldiers. They have trained for years for just such an occasion as this. They are itching to use their skills. They are extremely aggressive. It's my guess there are regiments who will be pissed off they're being left out.'

'But what if they don't volunteer? What if they say this isn't our fight? Will they be forced into it?'

Scott didn't answer.

'I thought so. That's what scares me, Aiden. That all our years of neutrality and declared independence — it's a funny thing about independence. The nations that constantly harp on about it rarely are. Those that are, rarely mention it. All our years of harping will have finally left us standing alone.'

'Stop thinking like a political scientist, and think like an Irishman. They will come. Now get some rest tonight.'

Morris let him out of the back door and Scott disappeared into the dark like a cat. Millie had not been talking to him but to Aisling, and Aisling had seen fit to tell him.

By nine-thirty that night Kiernan's message had arrived with the area commanders. It simply urged restraint, and requested that they did not initiate hostilities.

In the *Dublin Evening Press*, an organ that invariably supported Fianna Fáil, the governing party, a small item on page seven described increased security at the country's major airports as part of an ongoing and long-planned anti-terrorist exercise.

At dawn the following morning MI6 officers supported by members of the resistance began visiting the people marked for evacuation. The list of thirty-four people included radio and television personalities and other people known in the media, musicians, writers, commentators and shapers of opinion. Each would not only provide a valuable face for the invaders, but could be used by the resistance in the same way. Their faces, their voices and their sheer credibility could shine like a beacon in the coming dark of night. Nearly all disbelieved what they were hearing, but others admitted that something seemed afoot. Those that agreed to move north across the border for a few days were to call in sick and await transport within the hour. Immediate families were included in the evacuation plans. With others the resistance could only ask that they keep silent and think it over. They were confident that the events of the next week would change many minds. Others refused to leave for the best reason: if things were going to be bad then their place was with their communities. Radio One's best-known presenter, who also fronted a late-night television show, expressed those sentiments and eventually, after an hour of failed efforts, they telephoned Kiernan who asked an old friend living in Britain to call him. He was finally convinced that he could do more across the border than in Ireland. By lunchtime twenty of the thirty-four were en route to Ulster or London. Eight of those that refused to go were given a phone number to call if they changed their minds. The final six were left alone for the time being because they were already being watched by the invaders. They would be 'taken' by armed members of the resistance in the coming days.

Expatriate Irish people who fitted a similar profile and were already in the USA, the UK or elsewhere in the world were advised not to return to Ireland without first telephoning a number in London.

Two men, resistance members and men of the cloth, made a visit to their Cardinal, the head of the Catholic Church in Ireland. It was not to ask him to leave, rather to brief him and ask him to stay come what may, and explain his role in the coming days.

'This is preposterous,' the Cardinal said as they walked together through the gardens. 'It's unbelievable! Modern Europe?'

'Your Eminence, we are here to support you in the days ahead. Please speak to your secretary. Have us transferred to your staff here,' the first representative said. He was a bishop.

'I'll need to consult the Holy Father.'

'We'd rather you didn't contact the Vatican, Your Eminence. Your phone lines will be tapped. We don't want to give them any reason to arrest you. You have a vital role. Besides, the only support from Rome will be spiritual.' The speaker was Father O'Leary whose parish covered suburbs on the southern side of Dublin. 'We are, however, not on our own. We have friends. Friends who will provide more . . . material support. Our role will be to visibly support the people and the effort. To be seen and to carry out the traditional role of the church in troubled times and conduct one or two special ceremonies.'

The Cardinal turned and faced Father O'Leary. 'Are you not forgetting, my son, who heads the church here? Are you, a parish priest, determining the role of the entire Irish church? Its policy?'

Father O'Leary looked his Cardinal square in the eye. 'With respect, I am not political, Your Eminence, otherwise I would be wandering these halls like those who are.'

'How dare you speak —'

'I dare nothing but to clear the air here,' he interrupted. 'There will be no place for posturing in this effort, no place for the weak or the indecisive. Our role is to support the resistance. Support the liberation, whatever way we can. If you will not do it then we will go round you. Some of the things we need to do should come from the office of a Cardinal of Rome, but if not then the true faith of the humblest priest will serve us. The choice is yours, Your Eminence. I pray that you see the path clearly ahead.'

Father O'Leary walked away, his strides long and angry.

'He means well, Your Eminence,' the bishop said, 'and he is as good a priest as we have.'

'He could learn respect,' the Cardinal snapped. 'I would no more desert my flock than he would. Now,' he said mellowing, 'what more do you know of these developments?'

*　　*　　*

Irish Embassy staff in Washington and London and other major cities were summoned by their hosts and in the presence of senior government officials the diplomats were briefed by intelligence officers. The briefings ended with strong suggestions that they did not contact Dublin as that would simply accelerate the clamp-down, but instead make preparations to deal with their nationals and the media. They were advised a resistance was in place and arrangements for an interim 'government-in-exile' had been established. The resistance and its leaders would form an executive committee and in consultation with senior Irish civil servants staffing embassies abroad, they would determine policy, issue media statements and organize the liberation.

## 4 November

The factory was one of the new investments in Cork. Sprawling over six acres under one roof, the production lines built computers under licence to a big American manufacturer and had opened the year before with a fanfare of publicity.

In the rear of the building was a series of loading docks and the device was placed against one of the supporting columns where it met huge roofing beams over the central store and clean rooms.

When the timing device reached the pre-set time at five AM it closed a circuit between the battery and the detonator. The detonator exploded the four kilograms of Semtex it was inserted into, blowing a massive area of the roof straight upward. The blast wave blew out walls, pulverizing the clean rooms and stores, ripping through prefabricated walls as if they were made of paper and throwing one 36-foot steel column 400 feet to land like a gigantic javelin in the field behind the factory.

There was no warning to the authorities. A security

guard, one of four on duty, died as he was plucked from the ground by the blast wave and impaled on one of the forks of a parked fork-lift truck.

The second part of the device, designed for incendiary action, exploded forty seconds later, as the dust was settling. Burning phosphorus arced through the air setting fire to other areas of the works. The sprinkler system never operated, the feeder pipes severed in the first explosion. By the time the gate guard had phoned for the fire brigade and they had arrived the building was an inferno.

Ten minutes later and across the country in County Galway another blast ripped through a rubberware factory and the adjoining light engineering works.

At five-thirty, twenty minutes later, a man telephoned the offices of the Press Association claiming responsibility. There was no one there at that time, but his message left on the answering machine and later analysed by the police, said his organization wanted Ireland for the Irish, and the foreigners could take their investments and 'fuck off'. More attacks would follow.

At the same time the resistance got word through to London, using their high technology signals equipment for the first time.

The attacks were not theirs.

Century House moved the operation on to Red Status. Staff in Ireland, theirs and those from MI5, were told their priority for repatriation.

Deep inside the building the MI6 analysts and strategists believed it had begun. At 8.45 the Director General drove himself across to Downing Street and took the rear entrance into Number 10, where senior members of the cabinet were gathering. The prime minister was already in session with senior men from the MoD.

By ten that morning a spokesman for the 'New Irish Businessmen's Association' said the attacks were despicable, the work of cowards, and they would not be frightened off by anti-Semitic violence. The statement was brief and did not detail what the 'New Irish Businessmen's Association' was, or whom their membership comprised.

While a government spokesman said that the perpetrators of the heinous crimes would not go unpunished, the Garda investigators immediately looked northwards. The only people in all Ireland with Semtex and the predilection to use it were the Provisional IRA over the border in Ulster.

They had sympathizers in the south, people who fed them, hid them when they were on the run, people who wanted a united Ireland. That afternoon nine known IRA sympathizers were rounded up, five of them in Tallaght and three in the bleak towers of Ballyfermot. All nine had hidden active members of the IRA in earlier years.

At dusk a further twelve SAS soldiers arrived in the Republic of Ireland. Dressed in civilian clothing, they crossed over in the course of an hour at three different points and began to make their way southwards towards a rendezvous with one of Scott's two sergeants.

That night another bomb exploded. The device, concealed in a rubbish bin, was targeted at a firm of investment managers and this time there were more fatalities. The blast ripped across the street, imploding windows and showering the street and pavements with window frames and shards of glass. Four people died instantly and six others within minutes, all of massive trauma.

Shortly afterwards a mob that seemingly came from nowhere stoned cars on a side road off O'Connell Street. A driver was dragged from his car and beaten senseless. The words 'Arselicker' and 'Foreigners out' were sprayed across the wall over his comatose body. Shocked police could find no one that could identify any of the assailants. All wore hats and masks of some kind.

All police leave was cancelled and off duty Gardai were called back in to work. By morning graffiti was scrawled on walls at a dozen points around the city. Similar incidents were reported in Cork, Limerick, Galway and Wexford.

The Dáil, Ireland's parliament, went into emergency session and when a bomb blew a foreign-funded meat processing plant apart at eleven that morning, killing seventeen workers, members of the country's defence forces were ordered to return to their units. A decision to deploy them on the street to reinforce the Gardai was expected any minute.

Many people who had never experienced violence on this scale stayed at home for the day, keeping their children off the streets and out of schools, watching the news on television for the latest developments, flicking between RTE 1, the Irish broadcasting service's prime television channel and the British BBC which many Irish homes could receive without satellite dishes.

At two PM a fire broke out in the maintenance shops of the city's bus company. It spread rapidly, destroying forty vehicles. Police suspected arson.


'That's it. It's on,' Scott said. Around him, lounging against walls and sitting on the floor, were the thirty-three men of his command. Some looked almost bored, some smoked, and others watched him with interest. They all listened. The briefing had been short. Fifty minutes.

'From here on out this is enemy territory. Treat it as such. You all know where you are going. Be there by tomorrow and go to ground. Get your gear together.'

As they stood to move out, already segregated into their teams, he looked at the new arrivals, pleased they were finally there, but disappointed that there were only half of what he needed.

He knew why. Busby Grogan hadn't said much, but the arrival of the Americans and the planning teams meant that the Libyan raid was imminent.

Scott had thirty-three of the 22nd SAS regiment's men in Ireland. The remaining members of the unit were all that was left to meet on-going commitments and conduct the rescue.

Until the raid was finished, these men were all that were available and the first major issue of weapons would take place here. Tonight they would split up and cover the country opening caches and issuing the contents to the resistance. The irregulars' biggest problem was always re-supply: pre-positioned secondary smaller caches containing ammunition, explosives and other ordnance meant they could fight without husbanding their resources.

In each resistance area an SAS team of four soldiers and an NCO would support their efforts, aid in planning, give training, provide advice and gather intelligence.

In London the Chief of the General Staff was waiting for General Stewart. The temptation to get involved beyond his mandate was enormous, but like most good commanders he understood that he had chosen his field commanders and must leave them to do their jobs.

There was a rap at the door and it was opened immediately by his aide who announced his visitor had arrived.

Stewart was dressed in field camouflage and his boots were splattered in mud.

'Apologies, sir. I was with my boys and your message said it was urgent.'

'No problem, Monty,' the CGS replied, indicating a seat. 'How's your training going?'

'It's coming together,' Stewart answered carefully, 'but my Warriors don't have spares. If you could put a rocket up someone, John, I'd appreciate it. Otherwise I'll take a drive down there myself.'

The CGS gave a short grunt-like laugh. 'I'll bet you would. Tea?'

'No thank you.'

'Want to get stuck straight in, eh?'

'If we may.'

'Good enough. When will your command be ready to move?'

'We are still planning for mid-January and we have work that can roll us into February if necessary. The navy people don't like the weather any more than us, but that can't be helped.'

'Earliest?' the CGS answered.

'January 1st, sir.'

'You saw video tapes from intelligence?'

'We did.'

'It's on, Monty. You don't have till January 1st. I want you ready to go in four weeks.'

'Are we cleared to go, sir?'

'Not yet.'

Stewart grunted. Politicians. 'Four's short, John. Can you give me six?'

'Sorry. Not likely. Things are moving rapidly now.'

'With due respect, General, this is not acceptable,' Stewart said. 'I have got people scattered over half of the country, and my planning people are working twenty hours a day as it is, planning something the wankers in Westminster can't even agree on. They know it may all be for nothing and I have a morale problem and bugger all support! Give me five weeks at least, and some spares for my equipment!'

The CGS, a four-star general, looked at him. No one had spoken like that to him, not since he was a green company commander. Stewart, a small fighting cock in comparison, glared back at him.

'Just remember who you are talking to,' the CGS said softly.

'Yes, sir. Sorry. Blowing off steam.'

The CGS sat back again. 'Right,' he said, somewhat mollified. 'If you are lucky you will get four weeks. Then you'd better be ready.'

'We'll be ready,' Stewart answered.

The CGS watched him leave and as the door shut his face split into a wide grin. He too had been outspoken and it had landed him in trouble. But true fighting commanders were rare. The army was full of well-meaning men in uniform, but only a few that were true fighting commanders, men really capable of leading a division into combat. Even fewer had the rare blend of experience, diplomacy, charisma and ability for tri-service command.

Across Whitehall the Chief of Defence Staff, his Vice Chief, and the Deputy Chief of Defence Staff (Commitments) walked the Chief of Naval Staff to the door, as they had done with the Chief of the General Staff an hour before.

The CNS proceeded immediately to the Admiralty where his CINC Fleet from Northwood was waiting with the Flag Officer Surface Flotilla and the Commander UK Task Group.

The Chief of Naval Staff was a four-star admiral as was the CINC Fleet. The other two men that sat waiting for him wore two stars, Rear Admirals.

He ushered them in as he removed his coat.

'I've got you all here at once to save me saying everything twice. Sit down.'

They found seats around the old polished oak table that the stories said had been with the Lords of the Admiralty for three hundred years. Some stories even said that it had belonged to Nelson.

'The Irish sitrep is very bad. It looks to have begun. You will have seen the reports.'

The three men nodded.

'Right. As it deteriorates further and the buggers show their colours the PM is going to seek a UN resolution and a mandate from the Security Council. He doesn't expect to get it. We, however, are to make plans to be able to blockade Ireland. The objective is to prevent further matériel or men arriving from Libya and points east. Let's define an exclusion zone and get a Notice to Mariners prepared. You've got four 42s, three 22s, and *Invincible* with a modest screen to begin with. I have promised the PM that we will be able to blockade the island within minutes of his orders, so the ships will be in place and patrolling. There will be Nimrods out of Gib using Searchwater as of 10.00 Zulu today, so we should have plenty of notice. I want your forces at sea as soon as possible.'

'Thirty hours, sir,' the CINC said.

'Good enough. Now then, this will present some conflict with Dark Rose, will it not?' The question was rhetorical. 'David, how's that all going?'

'Fine. Monty Stewart is a very able man. I can work with him.'

The Commander UK Task Group, Rear Admiral David Shoreham, was one of only three sea-going admirals on the Navy List. As such he was as senior a battle commander as the navy could provide and at fifty years of age youthful when compared to the grey-haired Lords above him. He had spent the last week with his staff in planning sessions with General Stewart and Air Marshal Williams, the Joint Commander at High Wycombe.

Unlike the Falklands campaign, where a long sea voyage and naval battles were inevitable, the overall command of Operation Dark Rose had been given to Stewart and Williams. This had rankled with a few senior navy officers but not Shoreham. Of the three joint or tri-service facilities, Wilton, High Wycombe and Northwood, only High Wycombe and Northwood, both NATO command bases, had the complex modern communications facilities they would require. With Stewart as three-star ground commander in the theatre, and in command of many aircraft, it made sense that joint command in Britain be the air force's facility at High Wycombe and the four-star commander who was based there with his staff. The navy's task would be to get Stewart's people safely ashore and support them with direct fire and helicopters.

The tri-service officers that made up the senior posts in the command were impressed with Stewart and his professionalism. He in turn had stated that he regarded them as professionals and he would not interfere with their commands once objectives had been set, unless of course events demanded changes in strategy.

The CINC Fleet spoke. 'Resources will be the issue. Plans thus far mean we will need some of the ships that you intend in the blockade line for the assault operations.'

That afternoon's five o'clock flight from London to Dublin was fully loaded as the BBC and the major wire services attempted to strengthen their presence on the ground. CNN had arrived that morning, with two complete four-man crews and equipment that allowed them to transmit direct to their satellite. The bombings and escalating violence were the big news story in Europe.

MI6 watched their arrival with interest. If they were allowed in then the Palestinians and Libyans intended to use the power of live media for their own ends. Once they ceased to be useful or started asking the wrong questions attitudes would change, they were sure. They didn't have long to wait. At eight PM there was a short press conference in the Conrad Hotel. A refined-looking man in his fifties read a statement from the 'New Irish Businessmen's Association'. The statement deplored the worsening violence against legitimate business interests in Ireland and the anti-Semitic nature of the attacks.

The association felt that they had no choice but to protect their investments and their workers. Some businesses would remain closed for 'a few days'. Others would regretfully have to lay off workers until things improved and since the government had appeared unable to offer them protection all would be employing private security consultants. These consultants would be fully authorized under the law to take whatever action was necessary to fulfil their roles.

The man who read the statement stood up and left the room without answering any questions.

The 'Today Tonight' show went to air too early to use the segment, but nevertheless gave the entire show over to the upsurge in violence, the savagery that modern Ireland had never seen, not even in her own brief birth-pains of revolution.

There was talk by one speaker of the disenfranchized, and another spoke of the growing anti-Semitism across Europe. But the one overriding feature of the report was how little anyone knew about the perpetrators or their real motives.

Moira Kelly was agitated. Sarah had phoned in tears. Her husband had just been told his factory was closed and to lay off his staff. His last salary cheque was modest, with no redundancy pay. She knew they were worried. They had just moved house and increased their mortgage substantially. She had a little money in the bank but not enough and she had a dreadful feeling that this was just the start. Simon also had a family. What if his job went also? He would know what to do. She had phoned him and he was due any minute as were Sarah and Alan her husband. David, Sue, Mary and of course Sinead would be there too. Baby Sinead, Simon called her. He loved her like a father would. The age difference was so great that he had walked her in her pram, explained why birds made nests, and put Band-aids on grazed knees as if he were her father. And she adored him. Thank God, she thought, that we are together. It was time to sit down as a family and discuss things. She wanted Mary and David to move home for a bit, but both of them had so far said she was being silly. Things were just a bit strained, but David had moved home anyway, his mother's feelings aside, considering that there should be a man around the home.

The talk started over the evening meal, Alan confused and angry, looking to apportion blame wherever he could.

'It's this rabble element,' he snarled, 'burning factories, businesses. No wonder people don't want to operate here. We had a good business!'

'There's more to it,' Simon said sensibly. 'You don't just stop manufacturing because you are at risk. You step up security. You keep going. You address it like any other issue. You don't lay off the workforce.'

'I did it under instructions from my board,' Alan snapped.

'The board you were so impressed with six months ago. The board that has just paid you off without so much as an agreed settlement?'

'What are you saying?' Alan threw his napkin on the table.

'That it smells,' Simon said. 'Simply that. I mean, shit! New Irish Businessmen's Association. For that read . . .'

'Look,' Alan retaliated, 'these people brought jobs, pay packets, futures. I wasn't aware that we were Arab-owned, but it should make no difference.'

'Oh, but it does!' Simon said. 'The Germans or the French wouldn't be locking gates at factories. Do you see the Americans closing up their operations here? No one should be closing up. It stinks. I reckon they are behind the trouble.'

'Don't be ridiculous!'

The others were quiet, Mary in particular. She seemed far away for some reason.

'It's all wrong,' Simon said, 'and if you support them you are disloyal.'

'I'm disloyal! Christ. You want the Brits in. You want to go running to those bastards.'

'We haven't had a problem with Britain for seventy years. Look outside, Alan. That's your bloody Arabs causing all the trouble.'

That night fires burned across the country. As the fire brigade arrived at one site, another was engulfed in flames. Stone-throwing mobs appeared from nowhere and an ambulance was attacked in Tipperary. There were also three more bombs and again the foreign investors were targeted.

When daylight arrived and exhausted firemen were still hosing down the blackened remains of buildings, many people arrived for work to find they were locked out, the gates shut.

Thousands of homes across the country received buff envelopes in the morning mail. Mortgages and loans were being recalled, with warnings that collateral would be seized in two days if payments were not met in full.

Military-type vehicles appeared on the streets near businesses owned by foreigners. Garda signs were painted on the doors, but the paint job had been rushed with cheap stencils and the men manning the vehicles were not wearing Garda uniforms. They wore fatigues.

A woman told them to get their truck off her grass or she would call the police. One of the men in the cab laughed at her and said they were the police. His accent was thick, she later said, like one of the language students.

The crew of a similar vehicle in Dublin waved an Irish flag from their truck and happily showed the reporters their Irish passports. The reporters noted that the weapons in the vehicle were loaded, and these 'Police' were like no police they had ever seen in a European country, more like armed militia. The pictures never made the morning papers or the local television, but those who had tuned into the BBC or those who had satellites saw the images of men with guns on the streets of Ireland, and were fearful.

A march was announced for the next day, with a well-known priest and peace activist as leader.

As the sun settled decent people locked their doors and awaited another night. In the public houses all the talk was of the fires and bombs and business was quiet. The night was a repeat of the previous night, fires and blasts, but this time opportunists took advantage of the overstretched fire and police resources. Gangs of youths who had crossed the Liffey looking for excitement got caught up in the mood and with a brick thrown through a shop window the looting began. Throughout the night the situation deteriorated and by first light thousands of pounds' worth of goods had been stolen and plate glass littered the streets.

At nine the following morning people began to gather for the march. It was to be a demonstration for peace and students, housewives, office workers, children and old people gathered in Pearse Street for the march down across the bridge and into O'Connell Street. Thousands turned out, dressed for the cold, young walking beside old, rich beside poor. They got as far as the General Post Office, the scene of so much of Ireland's recent history and symbolic of their nationhood, before it all went terribly wrong. Shots rang out from somewhere, a petrol bomb was thrown, exploding against a building, people running, scared, the old and the frail trampled underfoot, screams, as more shots were fired. Police trying to control the crowds were pushed over and one died as a Nissan pick-up reversing away from the panic ran over him.

Finally the street was empty, but for glass and debris and the bodies of the injured and the dead. There were six dead, two from gunshot wounds, one of whom was the priest who had led the marchers. Small groups of people hovered over the injured trying to help as the sound of arriving ambulances and police reinforcements filled the air.

Nearby other people huddled, some crying, others mute with the shock, their brains trying to take it all in, trying to understand what had happened.

As the news broke people gathered in churches, and families closed ranks, gathering in one home. Other people, expecting the worst was yet to come, began panic buying in supermarkets, stocking up their kitchen shelves. There was talk wherever people congregated, in the public houses, shops and churches.

The evening newspaper was entirely devoted to the crisis and although the pictures of the new Irish Garda vehicles and their crews were not to be seen there were plenty of pictures of youths smashing windows and carrying away televisions, stereos and other merchandise. The editorials were stern, labelling the government as weak and demanding swift action to protect the decent citizens and the foreign investors who had brought so much prosperity to the country.

'Jesus! Look at this!' Millie said. Morris looked over at her.

'This bloody paper has always been an unofficial organ of the party but this! The whole thing is a gross manipulation, I'll bet this editorial was written weeks ago in Tripoli or bloody Amman or somewhere.'

'Well,' Morris replied soothingly. 'At least it's no surprise. It's happening in almost the exact sequence we were told to expect.'

That night there was more spasmodic violence and the next morning the border crossing into Ulster was crowded as people, frightened by events, tried to get their families somewhere safe until things calmed down. With the familiar now under threat and no one able to explain why, or prevent it happening, the mood was one of fear, unease and uncertainty. People in the urban areas moved immediate family into the country to stay with friends and relatives. Many who had pleasure boats and small yachts were refuelling and making preparations to leave if it became necessary. Nothing was said, but the marinas and boatyards were busy for a weekday morning.

Sir Huw Tristan-Carter, the British Ambassador to the UN, had been given an almost unheard-of full mandate by his government and now he prepared to use it. Four requests to see the Secretary-General, to call an emergency meeting of the Security Council, had met with stalling and he stepped his efforts up a notch. He knew the man, from a huge north African state heavily Muslim in population, was under enormous pressure from his own government to stall. However impartial he tried to be, there were greater powers at work.

It was very late and with most of the staff already gone home he walked straight into the Secretary-General's offices, past his remaining aides, through the anterooms and straight into his private inner office.

'This is most irregular,' he said, looking up from his desk.

'If that's what it takes, then that's what it takes,' Sir Huw answered bluntly.

The Secretary-General knew that the ambassador wasn't going to be put off any longer.

'Please sit down.' He indicated a chair.

'No. This won't take long,' Sir Huw replied. 'I have made four requests for you to call an emergency meeting of the Security Council. You have chosen to ignore them. If you do not call a meeting first thing in the morning here is what I am going to do –'

'Firstly,' the Secretary-General countered, 'is this your personal statement or your government's official position?'

'My position is as official as yours – sir! I shall call a press conference in the morning. I shall announce an extraordinary emergency meeting of the Security Council. I shall then

273

explain why. I shall call into doubt your impartiality, your judgement and your integrity.' Sir Huw pointed to a small china figurine on the mahogany shelves that ran the length of one wall. 'For instance, I know what that cost. I also know it wasn't an official gift. I know where the money came from and that's not all and you know it.' The figurine had been a gift, but an illegal one, and paired up with a $200,000 sweetener for a certain individual's brother to bring influence to bear for the award of the contract for a dam project. Sir Huw had been calling in favours relentlessly for two days, using every contact he could muster to get the information he needed.

'I shall move that, in the light of this knowledge, your term of office be halted and new elections held. I shall also announce that in the light of our position Her Majesty's Government will cease any funding of any kind to this organization till such an election is held. I shall also announce the immediate withdrawal of my country's peacekeeping troops from every current deployment and any future obligations. Furthermore, let me tell you this, that if we go the Americans will follow. If you don't believe me, get on the phone.

'On a personal level, I shall use every influence I have in the world's press, and that is some let me tell you, to attack your country's tourism infrastructure and its safety record. You will see your revenues drop by forty per cent in six weeks. That I guarantee you.' Sir Huw stood back and sat down in the chair first offered. 'Now then, you are a reasonable man. I'm sure that, considering Her Majesty's Government's growing concern, you can call a meeting for nine tomorrow morning, with a full Assembly meeting in forty-eight hours.'

'Forty-eight hours! Impossible.'

'Ming Dynasty. Sotheby's. One hundred and seventeen thousand dollars. I have a copy of the sales slip.'

'All right.' The Secretary-General paled but surrendered.

'There will be protests, but forty-eight hours will be manageable.'

The Dáil, which had been in a series of marathon sessions since the crisis began, was unable to function. Old party animosities were further fractured as members argued the correct way forward, but those with the best intentions were thwarted by the members who knew the awful truth, and who had family members being held hostage. At three PM the president, who had been conferring with her advisers and the prime minister for the last thirty hours on the issue, suspended the Dáil and gave in to the calls for an emergency powers action. Those members whose children were under threat supported the step and at 4.27 PM on 9 November she announced that Ireland was in a state of emergency. Her declaration gave sweeping powers to the police, but she delayed her move to have the Irish Defence Force deployed to assist.

The following morning the skies were grey and a biting wind blew from the north, but people didn't notice. All they saw were the tracked and armoured vehicles that seemed to be on most street corners. Hastily painted in Irish army colours, they fooled many who never gave their own army a thought and wouldn't recognize their own equipment if they saw it. It worked for a few hours. That was all it took.

Each of the real Irish Defence Force's small bases had been surrounded and taken without a shot being fired. Groups of men wearing Garda uniforms took over the main police stations, port authorities, airports and border crossings. They moved quickly to predetermined plans, the presence of heavily armed men enough to deter anyone who tried to oppose them. Others wearing fine suits moved into the government buildings and by the evening of 10 November the invaders were in complete control across the country. The media were told that a statement would be issued the following day, but for the time being they were to act responsibly or suffer the consequences.

That night many people went to the border with the north, or tried to get themselves on to flights out of Ireland, offering huge sums for a seat to any destination. Boats slipped their moorings and headed out across the Irish Sea towards Wales, the smaller ones tucking in behind larger vessels and fishing boats.

At the United Nations, the British and American governments finally got their wish when the Security Council was called into emergency session. Arab diplomats, expecting the move for days, had been lobbying, offering cheap deals on oil and making vague threats to the French and the Russians. The Chinese remained noncommittal, making no statements until Beijing had instructed them on their position.

'This is an invasion of an independent European state,' Sir Huw Tristan-Carter said finishing his statement. 'The evidence before you proves it,' he added, pointing to the hundreds of photographs he had provided.

'Great Britain moves that this council must demand the immediate and unconditional withdrawal of all Libyan troops and Palestinian combatants from the Republic of Ireland forthwith, apply time frames and an ultimatum and in the interim must allow United Nations peacekeeping troops into the country to prevent any further bloodshed.'

The American Ambassador then spoke to the council, his address taking an equal twenty minutes and providing more irrefutable evidence.

'To conclude, the government of the United States of America seconds the motion put by Great Britain. There must be full and complete withdrawal.'

The Russian Ambassador intervened. He was a big heavy man, one of the new breed of hard-line right-wingers. 'It is the view of my government that this is a purely internal matter.'

That had been expected and the American Ambassador barely looked up from his notes. 'Let's get to the issues here,' he said, 'and ask the Palestinian representative and the Libyan Ambassador to appear before the council. Do you object to that?'

The Russian thought for a moment. There had been no instructions on this. There was, he knew, huge pressure being applied by the British and Americans in Moscow. He had been told to stand his ground, but not be obstructive. He shook his head.

The talks had begun.

At the lunch break Sir Huw sidled up alongside the Chinese Ambassador and spoke softly in Mandarin. He wanted a meeting with people he knew in China, very senior people indeed.

At 7.12 AM on 11 November on a small country road outside Listowel an old farmer was driving his tractor down to his fields. He had spent the night thinking about things in the cities, appalled by the news he had been hearing. Behind him a pair of green army trucks approached up the road. He looked at them over his shoulder and realized who they were. He didn't pull over to let them pass. He slowed down, pulling his trailer across the road so that nothing could pass and then sat there, his arms folded across his chest.

The resistance had begun.

# 9

The site had been copied exactly. Every tent, every path, every sentry point and picket had been re-created on the dry rocky plain. To the south a ridge rose to the same height and a flat area half a mile from the camp had been graded to make a landing strip. The Special Air Service officers had put their men into the camp under the cover of darkness no fewer than thirty times. The entry route for the vehicles took them over a carefully planned route for nine miles, a route that matched exactly the way they would have to go in.

'Let's do it again,' the colonel said. 'Blue team were seen again. That means dead soldiers and I won't have it.'

The site, found by the US Department of Defense, was in Arizona and was as near a perfect match to Wadi Shati as they were likely to find. Even the winter temperature was about right. The site was re-created after studying the satellite photos and observer reports, human intelligence, from a pair of SAS men hidden in a rat-hole a thousand metres from the real camp. From there they could, using the powerful spotting scope, look right into both the camp containing the hostages and the support area and bivouac. The bivouac area where some seven hundred troops were camped had now taken on a semi-permanent feel with generator powered lighting, rutted tracks, latrine and ablution areas.

Blue leader had to bring his troops across several hundred metres of broken but exposed ground, locating the guards and dealing with them silently as they moved forward. Blue team troops would take and hold the area where the hostages were held, Objective Alpha, while a second detachment suppressed support from the bivouacked garrison and held them long enough to be dealt with. A third group would take the airstrip. Without that there was no way out for the hostages. Blue leader's problem was compounded by the fact that the guards in the simulation were aware they were coming and looking for his men. In the desert they would have surprise on their side. The second restraint was in the weaponry. In the exercise it was made deliberately more difficult. Instead of using the silenced Heckler and Koch MP-5A3 within its normal effective range, they were only allowed to claim a silent kill if they got within ten feet of the guard they were stalking.

At this time, daylight in the Mediterranean, officers of the Irish army on attachment to the United Nations as peace-keepers were updated by the nearest senior Irish diplomat.

The largest group was deployed in the Lebanon, where trouble had flared again, and their officers were taken to one side by their commanding officer and the nearest ambassador, who had flown in from Athens. They were advised to begin making preparations to be lifted out with all their equipment within the week. They were to tell their men nothing but, as the news worsened, reassure them that all was being done that could be.

As they filed from the consul's office, the visiting ambassador spoke. 'There's more.' He held up an envelope. 'These are your orders. Came through last night.'

The colonel took the envelope and slit it open. Inside there were four duplicates of the familiar movement papers.

'I have been recalled,' he said.

'I know,' the ambassador replied. 'But I want you to ignore them.'

The colonel's face was a picture of uncertainty. He had

loyally followed orders all his life and now he was being asked to ignore a direct order from his command.

'You are now the senior Irish army officer outside the country. They want you back. But only so they can remove you as a threat.' The ambassador pointed to the window. Outside, a contingent of the 836 men that formed the Irish peacekeeping force were going about their daily duties. 'Without you and your officers these men are not really a threat to them.'

'What about the others? The lads in Somalia, Cambodia and Macedonia?'

The Lebanese team was the largest, with an infantry battalion supported by a recce squadron and a handful of combat engineers, but there were five hundred men in Somalia and another six hundred trying to keep the Greeks and locals apart in Macedonia.

'They got to the officers in Mogadishu before we did. Three of them flew out last night. We are hoping to get to them in transit somewhere. Regardless of that, you are the senior officer. I want you to ignore these orders. In fact I'm telling you to ignore them.'

'I'm not going to sit here on my arse and –' the colonel began.

'No, you will not,' the ambassador interrupted. 'You will do the right thing. It's incredible. They must have been laughing at us all this time. We were here, do-gooders, smiling in our cute little blue berets while they were planning to take our country from right under our noses. You won't be sitting on your arse, Colonel. Make no mistake. We will fight them. We will throw them back to whence they came. I want you to fly to London tonight. Meet our people. Sort out the logistics of moving your command. You will be part of a largely international operation, managed, we think, by the British. I hope you have no problem with that. This isn't the time for national pride or misplaced independence.'

'I will fight alongside anyone who is a friend,' he replied. 'It's too big for us to do alone.'

Further west a Royal Air Force Nimrod on patrol out of Gibraltar spotted a contact leaving Tripoli on its Searchwater radar. They tracked it for two hours before dropping down in the dying light to take photographs with surveillance cameras. As they turned for home they reported the ship as a 'contact of interest'; the aircraft that took over their patrol area would keep an eye on it.

Although most people stayed at home there were places where the violence that had begun as an orchestrated tactic to destabilize the Irish government and society was now returning upon its creators. All pretence that the invaders were legitimately assisting the civil authorities had collapsed under a wave of rage. In many towns people were on the streets taunting the Arab men in the armoured personnel carriers who were now dressed openly in military fatigues. People who co-operated with the invaders, or had made statements in support of the 'New Irish' were beaten up or tarred and feathered or worse. Four had been found dead, their heads wrapped in yellow plastic, 'Judas' written in red across their covered faces, each right hand holding a bag with thirty coins.

In Dublin's Ballyfermot youths gathered at street corners, yelling abuse as the APCs rolled past, throwing stones and half-bricks. A bottle arced through the air and smashed against the steel front of the leading vehicle and as it lurched to a stop and armed men appeared from the back doors, the youngsters heaved a volley of stones at them before running back into the concrete labyrinth of flats.

Behind them the resistance waited, observing techniques and drills, plotting the times of the patrols and watching.

In Cork a Libyan soldier was taken to hospital after a woman threw a scalding hot cup of tea in his face and in Limerick a petrol bomb was thrown from a rooftop. It missed its target, but even so, it raised the stakes and for the first time the Libyans shot live rounds at the nearest gathering of young people.

Others more level-headed, and hoping perhaps for some return to civilized behaviour, tried to organize effective protest meetings, but the turnouts were disappointing. Most people stayed away and the handful that arrived were the same at each, familiar faces at public gatherings, be they concerned with abortion rights or local community politics.

The government, suspended by the president when she declared a state of emergency, was inactive and although a few politicians had bravely stood up to be heard, three had disappeared. The vacuum deliberately left for two days by the planners was finally filled by a council, its make-up largely Palestinian, calling itself the 'New Irish Patriot Council'. They announced a press conference and when the international news crews arrived issued a statement. It announced that due to the increasing violence all journalists would be 'escorted' and would need passes to visit any area. Failure to comply would result in arrest and visas would be suspended. They were then told to leave.

Big jets continued to arrive. Resistance and SAS observers estimated that there were now over thirty thousand troops on the ground. The rest of their heavy equipment could not be far away and the RAF Nimrod patrol aircraft operating from Gibraltar flew twenty-four hours a day.

For the first time RAF Jaguars fitted with reconnaissance cameras in underbelly pods began overflying Ireland, filming troop movements and the equipment as it was deployed and redeployed in what everyone knew would be a constantly changing array.

The British Ambassador, Sir David Penny, who had been demanding to see both the president and Mahoney the prime minister to assure himself of their wellbeing, was refused access. Finally he stormed into the offices normally occupied by the Taoiseach demanding to see 'whoever was in charge'.

He was shown into an inner anteroom where he took a seat and settled back. He had been a diplomat a long time and seen these tactics before. Two hours later the door opened and three men entered. Two were young, in their late twenties or early thirties. The leader was a man in his late fifties, grey hair cut close to his skull, immaculately dressed in an Armani suit and wearing shiny patent leather shoes. His eyes were widely spaced and alert beneath a high, intelligent forehead.

The ambassador stood up, thinking, at least they haven't fobbed me off with some lightweight, as the smooth-looking Arab approached him, one hand extended.

'My dear ambassador. I do apologize for the delay. Would you care for a cup of coffee? Or tea perhaps. I know how you English like tea.'

Penny, a career diplomat, knew when to be nice and when to be firm.

'The delay was intentional. I know it and you know it. So let's forget the protocol and get to the point.'

The Arab stiffened momentarily. He had not expected such directness.

'As you like,' he replied. 'I am Khalil Ashrawi.'

'I want to see Colin Mahoney.'

'The Taoiseach is very busy,' Ashrawi replied evenly. 'Regretfully he is not receiving visitors. I am sorry you waited so long for nothing.'

'Why don't you ask him if he will see me? We have been friends for some years,' Penny tried.

'I am sorry.' Ashrawi turned to walk away but Penny, having got this far, wasn't going to give in so easily.

'You won't get away with this, you know,' he said softly.

'Get away with this?' The Palestinian turned back to face him, 'Get away with what? Get away with protecting what is ours?'

'It's not yours and you know it,' Penny challenged.

'Oh, but it is, Ambassador. It's ours, bought and paid for. I have been a citizen of this fine country for two and a half years now. Once I was content to be just that. A citizen. But troubled times call for new measures. Even your law, Mr Penny, your much-vaunted British law recognizes that possession is nine-tenths of ownership. Could we watch our investments, all our good work, go to waste?'

'You can't just take a country and expect to get away with it.'

'Don't be naïve. As I said, it's bought and paid for. Besides you, representing the British Government, are a fine one to talk. You have taken many countries. You took mine.' Ashrawi's eyes narrowed briefly, memories of his parents' home in their village vivid still. 'You gave it away.' He swung his arm indicating their surroundings. 'You even took this one once. At least,' he said with a wry smile, 'we paid for it.'

'There were wrongs,' Penny said, 'committed in ignorance a long time ago, and not just by the British, but by many, some of them your brothers.'

'I have no brothers,' Ashrawi replied. 'The last one was killed in '67. He was collecting water for his family. He never came back. We found his body a week later. He had been run over by an Israeli armoured car.'

'Look out there on the streets. There are armoured cars there. Yours. Would you see another family lose someone, because that's what will happen,' Penny urged.

Ashrawi shrugged. 'If people remain lawful they need fear nothing.'

'Lawful? Whose law? Yours? The law of the armoured car? The law of the gun? Why are you jeopardizing all the work you have done as a people? You have a representative in the UN. Pursue your cause –'

'Legitimately?' Ashrawi replied. 'This is legitimate. The problems here are those of an independent state. Internal problems. We will sort them out. The UN will not get involved here, as they did not in Palestine.'

'True. They have been somewhat impotent in dealing with Palestine,' Penny said, 'but that issue is between you and the government of Israel. There are no third party's armoured cars rolling through the streets there.'

'Everyone has their friends, Ambassador. Sometimes fate chooses them for you. The Libyans are here. Standing beside us. In a world of mealy-mouthed rhetoric that matters. And let me correct you. There is third country hardware in Palestine. American. It may be crewed by a Zionist, but likely enough he will speak English with an American accent. He may have gone to university there.'

'Do you think they will stand back and do nothing, the Americans?'

'Do nothing about what? The unrest here? Of course they will do nothing. They will not interfere in the politics of a third country, particularly a European country. Bush may have done. But this Democrat? I think not. There is no oil here and he won't aspire to a new world order that will only bring him body bags.'

'And you? Your people? What of your body bags?' Penny countered.

'There have been many. There will be many more. We will fight and die to protect what is ours.'

'And the Libyans. It's one thing to stand beside you. It's quite another to die for someone else's country, be it Ireland or Palestine. It's not their fight.'

'It will become theirs,' Ashrawi answered evenly. 'I must go. Thank you for your visit, Ambassador Penny. I shall pass your regards to Mr Mahoney.' He paused for a

285

second and his voice softened. 'He is quite well, I assure you. We are not barbarians.'

Penny nodded. He needed to keep the channels open now. The one diplomatic link they had.

'It has been said that all evil needs to succeed is that good men stand by and do nothing. I think you are a good man. I hope we can talk again. Maybe we can prevent bloodshed.'

'As you wish, Ambassador Penny,' Ashrawi answered formally.

As Ashrawi moved back to his office he was met by a younger man, tall, good-looking and wearing jeans and a sweatshirt under his windbreaker. Around his neck he wore a black and white checked *keffiyeh*, the bedouin headcloth that had become the symbol of the cause. Ali Jassem was thirty-six, fifteen years younger than Ashrawi who was his mentor and friend, and commanded the fighters in the south of Ireland, the three thousand Palestinians scattered across the farming and coastal towns from Dublin to Limerick.

'How did it go?' Ali asked. His accent was clear. Schooled in Beirut, England and California, his command of the English language was as good as Ashrawi's.

'As expected,' Ashrawi answered. 'He is a wily old one. Clever with his words. Lots of veiled threats one second and solid reason the next.'

'What do you think? Will they fight?' This was the question he had been trying to answer for three years now. No one could tell him. Not yes or no.

'They try the UN. That's started,' Ashrawi answered. 'But they won't get a mandate. This will be contained. A police action. Even with the slaughter in Bosnia they never sanctioned force. Once we start to negotiate even the few hawks will find themselves without support.'

Ali wasn't sure. They had discussed this a hundred times and his respect for Ashrawi was immense, ever since he had sat at his feet in the camps, eating *musakhkhen* and

286

*arakeesh* listening to the stories of the village in Palestine. It was there he had decided to become a *fida'i*, if necessary to sacrifice his life for the cause. But he had seen the mood on the streets and it made him uneasy. It reminded him of Nablus and Gaza. He had seen the look in people's eyes. It wasn't one of defeat or resignation. It was a look of cold rage, a hate that was waiting to break out from beneath the icy contempt that even old women had for them.

He walked down the hall with Ashrawi, his worry beads in his hand and thought about the news that had come through from Limerick. The Libyans had opened fire on a group of students. Thankfully no one had been hurt and a detail of his people had quickly stepped in to pacify the enraged Libyan officer.

Fucking idiot he thought. That's all we need. Trigger-happy soldiers out to prove a point.


The Security Council of the United Nations had gathered to work its way through a packed agenda and the Irish unrest was item one that day. The general mood on the floor of the reconvened assembly was that the problem was internal and not the business of the UN. Many countries had their own internal problems and the last thing they wanted was the UN even considering interfering in the internal processes of a member nation. The Arab nations had lobbied heavily in the last days, promising everything from low interest loans to cheap oil and drawn heavily on favours owed by Third World countries.

In the Security Council the British and American ambassadors were holding the agenda to point one as much as they could. Sir Huw Tristan-Carter and his delegation had been lobbying for two days now, supporting the enormous pressure that was being exerted by the prime minister. The Americans, caught in the cleft stick of their policy on Israel, were exerting quiet pressure themselves, but things were not looking good. Russia and France were both in the running for a huge series of weapons supply contracts in the Arabian Gulf, and both, the Americans suspected, had been promised cheap oil in some kind of offset programme. The Chinese were as pro-Palestinian and xenophobic as ever and the other members, the Americans and British knew, would be hard-pressed to see any reason why the situation in Ireland should be viewed as anything other than an internal problem. Most of them were silently gleeful at the thought of one of the precious EU countries in strife. After all the years of democracy talk, the power of the ballot box, it was poetic justice to see one of them crumble, however briefly.

The British and American delegations knew that they would get little more than a statement from the Security Council that night, a statement full of words like 'urges', 'peaceful negotiations' and 'calm'. There would be no mandate for the use of force. There hadn't been for Bosnia two years before.

The Arab administration in Ireland, the Emergency Council of the 'New Irish Patriots', called the moves at the UN provocative and announced that, to prevent subversive elements entering the country, the borders were now closed. In the next three hours large blocks of concrete were placed at crossing points to prevent vehicle traffic, and barbed wire was strung across the roads. Every known point was covered, leaving only a handful of walkways. Airports were closed and scheduled flights were cancelled. Anyone wanting to travel would have to make representation to the authorities. Journalists' visas were cancelled and all of them with the exception of a crew from CNN and a crew from ITN, the British independent news organization, and a handful of press men were put on the list for last aircraft leaving.

Further south people who had boats or private aircraft and were still in Ireland made their choices, crossing to

Fishguard, or flying low to Britain without filing flight plans.

In Dublin darkness had fallen as Sinead Kelly set out to walk the half-mile down to the shops to buy some milk. Her mother was caught up in town and she would want a cup of tea when she got home. She was a pretty child with black, wavy hair and long-legged in a gangly awkward way like many fourteen-year-olds, and as she stepped on to the street she looked around carefully as she buttoned up her coat. Her older brother Simon had warned her not to go out, but she would be careful and as she walked she watched the street ahead and listened for the sound of the truck that would signal that the Arabs were coming on one of their patrols.

Up at the crossroads where the shops and petrol station had served their customers for fifty years, a group of young men gathered. They had their pockets filled with stones and their hearts filled with indignation and they waited for the patrol that had come this way each evening for the last three days. One, older and wiser than the others, called them back from the roadside, telling them to wait in the shadows behind the pub, but they refused.

Twenty minutes later, as Sinead Kelly walked through the doorway into the shop, a man stepped from the pub, his cameras under the loose jacket he wore. The Libyan patrol, eight men in two green-painted Toyota Land Cruisers, approached from the north-west, coming from the city. As they slowed to take the bend the young men threw their stones, yelling taunts as they did so. One half-brick smashed through the windscreen and the leading vehicle slewed to a halt, armed men jumping from the doors. More rocks were thrown and when a second window shattered the officer in charge barked an order and two of his men opened fire, one spraying half a maga-zine in the air, but the other taking careful aim and shoot-ing one of the boys in the chest twice as he stood on the

289

edge of the road, his hands empty but his eyes full of defiance. He was thrown backwards to the ground by the impact of the bullets and as he fell the man with the cameras dropped to one knee behind a car and bracing his camera on the car boot, and hoping his film was fast enough, he began shooting the scene, the boy on the ground in the vehicle headlights, the spectators and a girl that seemed to run from nowhere.

She dropped to her knees and took the young man's head in her lap, trying to comfort him and cover the wounds in his chest as she did so. The officer walked forward, his pistol in his hand and said something to her, pointing the gun at her. She refused to do whatever he wanted, dropping her eyes back to the young man who lay dying. The officer shouted something and raised the pistol and Sinead Kelly, just fourteen years old, her eyes blazing at him, shielded the bloody body below her as best she could, the milk and her mother forgotten.

The officer fired. The first bullet took her in the face, the second full in the chest. As she lay in her final seconds of life he fired again, this time into the wounded young man she was trying to protect. The shot was aimed and careful and like the others in complete cold blood.

It became the turning-point. The man with the camera was from *Time* magazine and he headed straight for the airport. The magazine was going to bed in twenty-four hours and these pictures would, he felt, tell the story like no other.

News of the atrocity spread like wildfire. Two hours later a Libyan column of three trucks loaded with troops crossed a narrow patch in the road between Mallow and Killarney. The resistance were waiting. They set off a command detonated sequence of four land mines buried under the road surface. Twenty-eight of the forty-four troops were killed outright. The remainder were left propped by the roadside to wait whatever help might pass their way. As the six men in Pat O'Sullivan's own resistance band moved away into the night, he bent and put a placard round the neck of one of the wounded men. It said: 'Remember Sinead Kelly'. The soldier on whose neck it hung couldn't read English, but he wouldn't have bothered anyway. He was bleeding, terrified and just wanted to go home. He never did. He died before help arrived.

In Dublin's Tallaght the news of the death of Sinead fuelled emotions. People said it was murder and anyway you don't murder children, not little children. Ten minutes after O'Sullivan's attack down in Kerry, the *buachailli* in Tallaght went to work. A three-vehicle patrol skirting the edge of the development came under attack, but this time the stone-throwing boys were backed up by their older brothers and fathers. As the troops rushed from the APCs expecting another running skirmish, they were met with a hail of gunfire. Under a minute later they were all dead, their vehicles burning with plumes of black smoke billowing up into the night sky, the pyrotechnics spectacular as ammunition began to burn.

The reaction forces noticed that the bodies had been stripped of weapons and ammunition and the general purpose machine guns had been removed from the APCs' small cupolas. They were scared. From nothing to this. No survivors. No mercy. No quarter given.

The most spectacular attack came in the centre of Dublin. Planned for some time, its delivery could be executed in minutes. The two resistance men, the *buachailli*, who performed it were unusual in that they both had previous military experience and unlike the other two major attacks that night they were not assisted by the shadowy special forces men from Hereford.

Jamie Peters was the nephew of John Peters, the buccaneering innovative commander of a section of Mike Hoare's mercenaries in the Congo in the sixties. His uncle had been famous for a long dash in a handful of Land

Rovers across miles of the Congo bush to rescue a group of nuns being raped and systematically killed by the rebels. Jamie, himself just out of five years in the French Foreign Legion and a very skilful soldier, was there to protect the second younger man.

John La Touche had until three months before been a combat engineer in the Irish army. Trained on numerous courses in America, West Germany and Britain, he specialized in 'things that expand rapidly' as he once explained. He was an explosives expert. That skill coupled with his engineering degree made him a highly desirable resource in any military formation and when he finished his short service commission only six weeks before, Peter Morris had snapped him up.

The Libyan army officers were quartered all over the city and the country, but the highest concentrations were billeted in two old hotels on the South Side. The senior officers were all in the Shelbourne, but resistance leaders, mindful of the old building's historical importance, decided to only authorize an attack on the second location.

There were fifty-six middle-ranking officers in the building when La Touche and Peters crawled silently into the air space between the ground and first floors via the ventilation system. Twenty minutes later La Touche had added the detonators to the mounds of C4 explosives placed there the week before, and run the wiring back to the electronic trigger at the tiny battery that sat nestled above the lintel over the kitchen door. Staff in the building had been warned and the night porters due on to relieve the reception staff never reported for work. The duty receptionist who now just placed calls for the officers, routing them through a resistance recording cell, went home as usual, smiling at the guards at the front door.

Just before midnight La Touche nodded to Peters who sighted along the laser sight. He found the small light-sensitive disc-shaped cell in the optical telescopic sight and pressed the trigger. The laser beam came on, wavered for a second and as Peters swung slowly left the beam hit the centre of the cell. A microchip triggered an impulse to a microswitch at the battery and as the switch closed the small but crucially placed charges exploded in sequence. Just like a large structure being demolished with explosives, the five-storey building slowly began to collapse on itself, great clouds of dust rising from the scene, the tons of falling masonry making the ground rumble and shake. People heard it a long way away.

Nothing else was damaged. Even the two buildings that butted up to the old hotel still stood. Two men who were asleep in converted attic rooms were later pulled from the rubble alive. No one below that level survived.

At dawn while men shifted through the rubble for survivors, the Libyan command stepped up their security and standing orders were changed. Notices were issued that the perpetrators were criminals and would be shot. Furthermore, anyone assisting them would be shot.

The high command were in no doubt why these attacks had taken place. Letters six feet tall proclaimed the reason on the walls of the General Post Office. 'Remember Sinead Kelly' was on the lips of many that day, not least those of Ali Jassem.

He stood, almost white with contained fury, eye to eye with the Libyan army commander of the southern district.

'You know why! It's been public knowledge since the hour it was done! One of your people shot a child! Point blank fucking range! It was an act of complete brutality that will do nothing for the cause but damage.'

'They are armed bandits!' the Libyan general countered, drawing himself up to full height, uncomfortable with the way things were going. Yes, he had reasoned, it was regrettable, but the officer was his nephew, and besides it was only a couple of youths.

'With stones. Only stones!'

'There are almost a hundred brave soldiers dead!' The general snapped.

'Not until you shot one of their children,' Ali countered. 'Your troops started this! Your ill-disciplined troops!'

'Just remember why we are here,' the general replied threateningly, 'to assist you. We don't have to be here.'

'Now now, comrades,' Ashrawi soothed, stepping forward. 'I am sure we all regret what has happened. Let us go forward now together.'

The next act committed was not by the resistance but by the Irish Navy the following morning.

As the Royal Navy issued a Notice to Mariners, numbered 168–95, declaring a total exclusion zone surrounding Ireland, the Irish captain of the Eithne class ship *Deirdre* watched the last of his men go ashore with their armed escort. He had ignored the British warnings and now his ship had fallen into their hands. That was a disgrace in any navy in the world. Now he would put it right. If he couldn't get her to sea, as young Eamon Kavanagh had done with the *Kathleen*, he would do the next best thing. Sink her.

In the glimmers of the dawn light he now prepared to scuttle his own command.

He remained with the engineering officer and one more junior officer from the ship's company, the helicopter engineer. They all understood the risks. At best they would be interned like their comrades. At worst they might be shot.

They had convinced the Libyans that they had procedures to run through and had been there all night. A Palestinian had visited the ship, a man who knew his way round vessels, but he had gone and the junior officer with the guard detail had fallen for the story.

The senior warfare officer had spent a few hours the night before removing the charges from one of the few live rounds they had aboard for their deck gun. The rounds were old, but the charges were still good. Just before dawn the warfare officer and the captain had entered the magazine and loaded the remaining shells against the lower deck and against one bulkhead, only inches from the hull and five feet below the waterline.

Now, with his men ashore and the maintenance officer disabling the helicopter, they were ready. The engineering officer had rigged a crude arming device with a timer and five minutes later they reported to leave the ship, quickly because they weren't sure just how precise the timer would be. It was accurate to three minutes, but being an egg timer from the galley the twenty minutes they had agreed he should set it for could be either thirty or fifteen, or ten.

Seventeen minutes later as the truck they were loaded in was leaving the port gate there was a dull boom across the water. They couldn't see her but the *Deirdre* was settling in the water, her hull torn out in a hole six square feet in size. She would be going nowhere and fighting no one.

The camp their men were taken to was one of the early constructions that the engineering student David O'Connell had first found and photographed. A fence-laying truck had travelled the perimeter putting down six coils of razor wire in a triangular formation, the top coil twelve feet from the ground. The wire, supplied to anyone who wanted to buy it, was made in Nevada and came in three colours for captors concerned with aesthetics. The wire round this camp was haze green, muted beige and chocolate cream and inside its coils five hundred people of the Irish Navy were held. Tents lined the hard surface in rows and the prisoners wandered about inside at will during the daylight hours. Several had attempted escape and had been shot in front of the others as an example.

The captain, his engineering officer and the young aircraft engineer never got to the camp. They were returned to the port and executed, their bodies thrown into the water that now swilled round the superstructure of the ship they had scuttled.

Moira Kelly had been put to bed. Her grief was awful and she had cried throughout the night, deep gut-wrenching tears that tore at her soul. The neighbours had gathered round, brought cakes and food, and the family were all there to support each other. Simon was stunned, but had staved off the shock with sheer anger. A coldness he had never known filled him as he stood in the window looking out. Behind him in the gloom of the room Sue was weeping and held by Mary, but a silent Mary, strangely silent in her mourning. One of the neighbours, an old woman, said she had heard the cry of the banshee the night before, and she poured the tea knowingly, saying little Sinead has gone somewhere else, somewhere better, and only the good die young, and wasn't it troubled times they were having. Sue sobbed again and David's look silenced the old woman, who looked back at the teapot. Father O'Leary had been there all night, doing what he could. He had seen grief in many forms and when Mary, Mary who had said nothing for hours, picked up her coat he looked across at David.

'Go after her. Follow. Be there, but keep your distance.'

She walked down the road, her heart in turmoil, feeling loss. Her confusion was absolute and as she walked the tears came back, tears for little Sinead, for Simon, for her mum, for all of them. She felt used, felt betrayed, felt lost, felt something that was hers had been abused with deceit and cunning, and through the sorrow and shock the anger grew. Through her grief something was rising and her walk changed from the amble of the lost and lonely to something with purpose.

David followed.

Sam was there when she arrived, asleep in her bed,

where he had been waiting for her to return. She stood in the doorway to the tiny bedroom and looked down at him as he sat up and smiled at her.

'I was waiting for you,' he said, the smile there, but something else in his eyes. He was angry. He did not like waiting all night and although his bleeper had gone off several times he had ignored it. He held out his hand. 'Come to bed.'

She didn't move.

He looked closer through the early light and saw her red-rimmed eyes.

'What's the matter? Has something happened?'

'Persian,' she said softly, the tears coming again.

'What?'

'You said you were Persian.'

'Mary, Mary.' He got up, reaching for his underpants, the look on his face saying it all, 'I *am* Persian . . .'

'You are not,' she said, the anger now in her voice. 'You are one of them.'

'Mary, let's talk about this . . .' pulling up his underpants, grinning like a child caught out.

'Yes, let's,' she said, her voice flat, her eyes glittering. 'Let's talk about my little sister. My little Sinead.'

The realization sank in and Sam stopped. 'What's happened?'

'She's dead, you bastard. Your people. They killed her. She was fourteen and they shot her dead.'

His face dropped. It had gone off. The bleeper. He pushed the thoughts aside and stepped closer. 'Mary, it must have been a mistake. A terrible mistake.'

'You are one of them, aren't you? One of *them*.' She spat the last word.

'Remember you talked of your love for your home, your family, your Ireland?' he replied. 'Well, I too have a family, a home, a country. I love it like you love yours. But it's occupied. Yes, I am Palestinian,' he said with pride.

'You lied to me,' she whispered. 'You fucking bastard, you lied to me. You deceived me. And while you were in my bed, in me,' she said with revulsion, 'you were taking my home, taking everything I have, trampling on it, and now Sinead is dead.'

He knew it was coming and soon. He had been away for a week, supposedly in Limerick and this was the first time they had seen each other. He feared it would be today. The day Mary would find out, see him as an invader, an occupier in her homeland. Suddenly he remembered the day he had been at the wall, cementing the stones back in as the Israeli patrol approached, remembering the hate he felt, hoping he would be there when they detonated the pipe bomb. He understood the way she felt. 'Mary, I didn't kill her.'

'Yes you did, as surely as I did.'

'Mary, you didn't kill her,' he said gently reaching out to her.

'Don't touch me!' she hissed, moving back, revolted. 'You killed her. You and your, your . . .' She lunged at him.

He didn't strike back, he simply lifted an arm to defend himself and didn't see as she reached for the heavy recycled glass bottle on the bedside table, cheerful little wax drips down the sides. She swung it and hit him and he went down, but he came up and as he did her brother David burst through the door, taking it all in, and came across the floor, fast and lean like a panther, his eyes blazing. He took Sam at a run, slamming him back into the wall, and Mary, consumed by guilt and anger and grief, swung the glass again and again, hitting David in the process, her eyes now tinged with something insane. Sam was down, blood pouring from his head and David rolled up from the floor and pushed her back from them both, holding her till she stopped struggling.

'Stop now, whoa, whoa.'

'They killed her. He lied to me. He said he loved me, but he killed her and he took everything and . . .'

'Shssss.' He cuddled her for a few moments while she regained her composure.

'Is he dead?' she asked

On the floor Sam stirred and then began to stand, words coming from a smashed mouth. 'You don't underst . . .'

David turned, his eyes filled with rage, scooping up the glass bottle and it moaned as it swung through the air against the man's head, crushing bone as it shattered, bloody waxy shards of glass across the bloodstained bedspread.

'He is now,' David said, his voice cold and terrible.

He took over with a calmness she found unnerving. He wrapped the body in the bloody bedspread and cleaned the walls and furniture as best he could with Jif and a damp sponge from the tiny kitchen.

'The lease. Is it in your name?'

'No. I sublet. A friend. She is in Boston.'

'Good. We must go. Change out of that clothing. Dump it in the bin liner. I'll come back tonight and get rid of it all. Take a few things. You won't be coming back.'

'What?'

'You won't be back, Mary.' He knelt and took her hands in his. 'Not till it's over one way or another.'

It was Father O'Leary who knew what to do, Father O'Leary that took her away with him for a few days, who said he would find somewhere for her to stay in case they came looking. That night he said a prayer for them all, but especially for Mary and David who had committed a mortal sin. He sat them down and asked them to confess, knowing it would help them get over it. When they did he gave absolution and afterwards he prayed for the soul of the young man called Sam, at the same time as David was going back to the flat with two men that the priest had found to hide the body. By midnight he was preparing food for the five men, *buachailli* hiding in his crypt.

The Irish Defence Force were prisoners and detained in their original barracks. The fence-laying trucks had laid their concertina pyramids of chocolate-cream-coloured razor wire around the perimeter and had also sectioned the holding areas, separating officers, non-commissioned officers and enlisted men. The officers, most likely to be able to plan and attempt an escape, were in the centre ring. Their troops, without effective leadership, were considered a lesser threat and occupied the larger outer circle, while the sergeants and corporals occupied the space in the middle.

The young officer commanding the Ranger battalion had tried to escape with elements of his command but had been caught and was now in solitary confinement.

Rations were limited and in the first days people had been kept from the wire, but now on the third day, people who lived nearby were allowed to bring food that could be passed through to the men after the guards had inspected and taken whatever they liked the look of. Everything was wet, tents, clothing, and the limited bedding they had, but morale took a lift as the first rumours of the resistance began to circulate. Reports of hundreds of Libyan dead were welcomed, and although most thought them to be exaggerated, they were spread with glee. It was fresh material for the conversations which thus far had been limited to wondering how family were doing and what the UN would do about it and when would the Americans come. After all there was a new world order. You couldn't get away with this kind of thing.

All over the country as the first shock wore off a fierce pride began to emerge, a pride in Ireland, in their Irishness, and most of all in their resistance movement that had struck with such devastating effect in the last twenty-four hours, their *buachailli*.

Guinness sold in bars before the ten o'clock curfew drove people home was served with curious new marking drawn into the creamy foam on the top. The traditional shamrock design for the tourists had been replaced with a circle that had a bar drawn through it from two o'clock down to seven o'clock. It was a simple design, and clear to anyone Irish. It was the Tara brooch, and rumours now said that it was the resistance that had stolen it, that there was a tale to be told there one day, and people raised their glasses to *buachailli* and wished them well and said fair play to them, and may the saints protect them.

Bands and musicians playing in the bars and on the street corners found themselves inundated with requests for traditional music and songs. Words long forgotten were relearned, the lyrics of the songs that told of the uprising, of fighters for the cause, of men and women who fought the landlords and the English.

The resistance began feeding the tales, their latter-day bards moving among the drinkers in the pubs, family gatherings, church meetings. They told tales of Irish courage, of the fighting men of old, the Celtic legends, and they began to tell a new tale, one that appealed to all that gathered round them in the firelight.

'The legend says that when Ireland is in its darkest hour a queen shall come among us, a great queen, a powerful queen, but kind and wise, and she shall be crowned upon the Stone of Destiny, thus the true queen of the Celts, and she shall wear a cloak of green, the finest wool, held upon her breast by a gold brooch. You will know when she has arrived for the sky shall be bright with fires and the bells shall ring across the land. She shall gather a great army to throw back the hordes.'

A child looked up at the speaker, in this case an old man well known in the village. 'What's her name, then?'

The old man smiled. 'According to the legend she shall be called Maeve.'

'There was one of them once, right?' another older child asked. They had covered some Irish mythology in school, but he hadn't really been listening that day.

'There was,' the story-teller said, puffing on his pipe, 'and she shall return, for surely it is as dark as a man would let it get now.'

O'Malley's creative team had relocated from the house in Wales and were now set up in an old hotel in Enniskillen above the border in Ulster. The BBC had installed a pair of outside broadcast units in the car-park and converted an adjoining vacant shop into a studio. The OB units were hooked into the most powerful transmitters that the World Service could provide and for the last days people had been told by word of mouth what frequencies to listen on for news from the outside. With RTE, the Irish service, now a propaganda station and the normal BBC television and radio signals being jammed by the Libyans in most areas, they were desperate for the sound of a friendly voice from the outside. They would get it.

At 1800 hours GMT on the fourth day a carrier signal blasted out across seventeen frequencies and after a few seconds of silence the broadcast began with the three words that had so often made all the difference to a Europe at war.

'This is London . . . the following frequencies have been turned over to the Voice of Free Ireland and will be broadcasting twenty-four hours a day.' There followed a list of the frequencies. In the engineers' area outside the studio Kiernan and O'Malley waited for the British announcer to finish, watching as the engineer raised five fingers to the man who sat at the console. His was the most famous and most recognized voice in Ireland. Kiernan watched almost impassive while O'Malley, a more emotional man, felt a lump building in his throat. The engineer began to count down from five and finally pointed to the Irish announcer, fading him in as he did so.

'This is the Voice of Radio Free Ireland and I am Dave Burne coming to you live from somewhere in Ireland. There are others here, others who like me have had the privilege of serving you over the years. We shall continue to do so, as now it is more important than ever. Rest assured. We are not alone. The Celtic family is gathering. But till then, till the barbarian is driven from our shores, and he will be, we will be bringing you a mix of news, current affairs, music and things of interest, but the first thing we are going to do is let you know exactly what has happened and what is going on now and daily.

'To explain I shall hand you over to our chief correspondent, a man you all know, a man who used to be editor of "Today Tonight".'

The veteran journalist in the second studio settled himself at the microphone and began to speak.

In the great cities of America the people that had been watching the events unfold with mounting horror took to the streets. Like the intelligence people months before, the television and news gathering networks had put the pieces together. Britain's *Daily Telegraph* had scooped them all with a series of huge in-depth articles, the basis for much of the work the broadcast media networks moved into. The crisis was no more than an invasion. A pure and simple Palestinian invasion. The UN had declared the issue an internal Irish problem needing an internal Irish solution. That angered people.

America was in turmoil. Thousands converged on Washington representing the forty million Irish Americans. Banners proclaiming support from organizations as diverse as the Chicago Fire Department and the Catholic Church stood side by side. The call was for action and immediate action at that. Jewish and pro-Israeli groups stood up and shouted we told you so, marching from the other direction, while in the background their lobbyists piled pressure on the government to increase support for the Jewish state in the light of the new strength demonstrated by the Palestinians and their Arab backers. In the State Department senior policy makers were caught in the vice. Years of overt support for Israel and pacifying the Jewish lobby had been bad enough, but now a second group were demanding to be heard, a second group that they knew would have directly opposing views. The Irish, with their activity traditionally limited to fund-raising for a united Ireland, did not bring the sophisticated effort of the pro-Israel lobby, but they did bring muscle. Good, decent, hardworking Americans from all walks of life considered themselves Irish and they were on the streets raising money, collecting signatures and gathering support, while their senators and congressmen, men with names like Kennedy, O'Brien and Shaunessy, demanded action on the Hill.

In other meeting rooms in Congress and the Senate other lobbies had stepped up their activity. Lobbyists for the aerospace industry were pulling favours to get in to see their contacts. The heads of these industries had been told by their contacts in the Gulf that any drastic American reactions to the internal problems of Ireland would have equally drastic repercussions on defence equipment contracts and the purchase of high capital items throughout the Gulf States. The potential losses for Grumman, McDonnell Douglas, Boeing, Lockheed, Raytheon, Sikorsky, Bell, Honeywell, General Dynamics and General Electric were staggering, and the congressmen and representatives knew that behind the aerospace people would be the high technology and oilfield suppliers.

'Congressman,' one of them said, 'we understand how it is, but our people are concerned, real concerned,' he opened his hands wide and lifted his shoulders, the expression saying, what can I do, it's them that feel this way, 'that nothing too, how shall we say, too hasty is done.' The lobbyist was serious, his face perfectly shaved above the Hermès tie, altogether the young professional Washingtonian. 'In addition to this it might be worth while remembering just how many jobs the defence industry provides in your home state. Now if the industry loses major contracts in the next couple of years, well, layoffs, you understand? I mean, they just wouldn't have the work for all these people.'

'We have received no indication that there is any intent for punitive actions,' the congressman replied, 'so I wouldn't worry too much. Let's just see what happens . . .' He was a dry old campaigner, a Republican and a man whose down-home homilies, white suits and Colonel Sanders fried chicken looks had won him many elections.

'Congressman. You may not have the indications but my people have, from the top.' The lobbyist emphasized the last three words as if they might make a difference.

'From the top? Don't tell me . . .' The congressman responded drily. 'A fella in a dress with a tea towel on his head. Hell, boy! That dog just won't hunt.' He leaned back in his chair. 'Tell you what, son, when the government of these United States of America starts taking instructions from people like these I shall retire. Damn boy! They only got off their camels fifty years ago. Now I understand what your employers must be feeling, so you go back and you tell 'em you spoke to me and tell them that I shall consider their position. But tell them this. This country considers weapons deals, defence equipment contracts and suchlike as cream on the cake of an existing relationship. We don't look for cream where there is no supporting base relationship. It's just too sweet, too thick, makes everyone sick and regret it later. Furthermore, when someone we agree to sell high technology arms to jeopardizes the relationship that allows us to do that, it might just be us that says *hasta la vista*. So let's wait and see what official position they take, if and when they do, then we in the legislative bodies in conjunction with the executive bodies will decide what is to be done. I thank you for coming. You have a good day, now.'

On the East Coast people who had watched the Irish fans arrive for the World Cup the previous summer and who had been enchanted with the tens of thousands of good-natured people, 'Saint' Jack Charlton's green army, now thought of them behind wire, starving, under an oppressor's jackboot and rallied to the call. If New York City had ever adopted any group or nation above another it was the Irish and in the city that staged the famous St Patrick's Day parade every year, they turned out on to the streets in their hundreds of thousands, wearing the green football supporters' shirts, waving the Irish tricolour like it was their own. The mood was angry.

The Secretary of State, leaving a press conference where he been able to say little other than that his department was 'closely observing events', was advised by his staff that an Arab ambassador had telephoned and suggested it might be in America's interests for the Secretary to see a delegation the following day. No agenda was offered.

Two hundred miles off western Ireland Britain's Royal Navy patrolled the cold, blustery waters of the Atlantic. The screen of ships was ready to enforce a blockade the moment orders and their Rules of Engagement allowed. The Notice to Mariners had been issued forty-eight hours before and the navy had intercepted six ships so far. All merchantmen, none of the six had chosen to argue the point and had turned away to await owner's instructions and then proceed to Liverpool to allow inspection of their cargo. Only food and humanitarian supplies would be allowed through. Vessels cleared to enter Ireland would be allowed in through a narrow channel in the exclusion zone and all would have to unload in Dublin port.

The fishing boats had been most co-operative, and the only unpleasant scene had involved a French boat that accused the navy of all kinds of genetic deficiencies and some doubt over the legality of its parentage. The frigate captain had finally put a boarding party of five marines and an officer aboard her and they had explained the way things were going to be. One of the French crew had prodded a marine in the chest once too often. The marine later said his hand slipped, but the result was a rapidly moving gun butt that connected with the fisherman's face and three teeth spat through blood on to the wet deck. The point was made and a few minutes later the Frenchman turned eastwards threatening to report the incident to the European court.

At the northernmost point of her patrol, HMS *Dundee*, a Type 42 destroyer, began a long, gentle turn back towards the south, her Tyne cruise engines pushing her effortlessly through the water at fourteen knots, her big search radar with its long slow sweep looking out two hundred miles around her.

The latest in her class, she had been completed in 1986 and her 420-foot hull was narrow and built for speed. The Tyne engines were designed for cruising long distances at an economical speed, but her main power plant was a pair of Rolls-Royce Olympus gas turbines that could deliver 50,000 horsepower down the shafts to the controllable pitch propellers. When the Olympus engines, the same power units as used on Concorde, were pushed up to full power the noise from her funnel was that of a jet engine and racing forward towards her top speed well in excess of thirty knots the rooster tail of white churning water under her transom stood over twelve feet high.

She was the last of the third batch of Type 42s and although designed as an air defence warship she could engage not only aircraft or incoming missiles, but surface ships and, using her Lynx helicopter, submarines.

Her main armament was on the foredeck and comprised a self-loading 4.5 inch gun and a launcher for the Sea Dart guided missiles that nestled down in their magazines. The gun, made by Vickers, was radar controlled and could engage surface ships, incoming aircraft or fill its primary role, that of naval gunfire support for army or marine actions ashore. The missiles were equally versatile and could be used to take out missiles, aircraft or shipping.

Aft of the bridge were the ship's close-in weapons systems comprising a brace of twenty millimetre cannons either side of the ship and between them, standing alone like a white cylindrical dome-topped telephone box, was the Phalanx radar controlled multi-barrel gatling gun. The Phalanx in its 'goalkeeper' mode could track an incoming missile and when in range pour out thousands of rounds of solid steel that could literally blow a sea-skimming missile into fragments.

Now in the cold gathering dark of the north Atlantic the weapons systems were silent, the decks deserted. On the bridge the officer of the watch, Lieutenant Keys, stood with his legs spread to balance himself against the roll of the ship, watching her head come round. To his left a seaman sat at the wheel, a stainless steel butterfly-shaped object that the lieutenant thought would have looked more at home on a go-kart. He was from an old navy family and was one of the school that thought ships should have wheels; wooden with spokes wherever possible. The other new thing his family weren't too keen on was the other officer on the bridge. The recently promoted lieutenant was very good at the job, but his father always said a warship was no place for a woman. Lieutenant Penny Conway was one of the seven women aboard, but the only WREN officer.

He looked at his watch, then confirmed the time on the bridge chronometer. 'Steer one eight zero,' he said. The navigator had laid off the courses. 'Vasco', as all navigators are called, was now down in the wardroom getting a cup of coffee.

'One eight zero,' the seaman at the helm responded.

'Thirty-five both levers.'

'Thirty-five both,' the seaman responded. Earlier in the day they had been running on just one of the Tyne engines, but as the sea conditions deteriorated they had started the second engine to help smooth out the ride and prevent pitching and rolling as she moved down her course.

They were due to rendezvous with the Irish ship in two hours and both would proceed southwards toward the fleet oiler that would replenish them both with fuel, food and spares.

Lieutenant Keys looked out at the sea, the big rollers now breaking, the wind snatching the spume from the white tops. The *Kathleen* would be tossed round like a cork he thought. Tiny, displacing only 700 tons, her crew would wish they were aboard something a bit bigger. The Peacock class ships were designed for coastal patrols in the waters off Hong Kong, not long bruising passages in the north Atlantic. The word was that she had been given a patrol area adjacent to theirs, but lacking the air defence radars and weapons of bigger ships she was limited in what she could achieve and the patrol areas overlapped for this reason.

Sixty miles to the south HMS *York* was working a similar patrol and further south still was the aircraft carrier HMS *Hermes* with a modest battle group. Admiral Shoreham had made her his flagship, much to the relief of the other ships' commanders, who often found having to accommodate an admiral and his staff a strain on limited space.

To the *Dundee*'s north was HMS *Nottingham* and further north of the *Nottingham*'s patrol area was HMS *Brazen*, a Type 22 submarine-hunting frigate with a four-ring captain aboard.

They were ready.

In Ulster, the British part of Ireland, the Royal Ulster Constabulary put Operation 'Uncle' into effect. All known or suspected IRA leaders, with their intelligence officers, planners, quartermasters and policy makers were rounded up in a combined army and police operation. The IRA had remained shadowy since the cease-fire had been announced the previous year and they still held significant numbers of weapons. Sinn Fein were talking with the British, but everyone knew the IRA could be back in action within hours, if necessary, and everyone's worst nightmare was that they might become involved in the crisis in the Republic, however good their intentions. Sinn Fein assurances were one thing, but the Irish government-in-exile wanted the fighting arm to commit themselves. The last thing they needed was active service units digging up their arms and crossing the border to fight – it would be mayhem.

It only took six hours and fifty of the organization's most senior people were herded into an old drill hall at the bottom end of an airstrip occasionally used by the air force. Beneath the defiance and the swearing they were frightened, surprised and bewildered. Many of them had no idea that the RUC knew of their involvement and for others it was a humbling experience. The IRA protected its senior people well. They were distanced from operations by cut-outs and a command structure designed to keep them safe from arrest. As they entered the room they saw familiar faces and within an hour all pretence at innocence was gone. With armed soldiers at the doors they waited, talking among themselves, wondering what was going on. No arrest warrants had been seen yet.

Finally a very senior special branch officer stood before them on the stage. They all knew him. He had been the target of no fewer than six of their assassination attempts in the last five years.

'Well well well. What have we got here then?' he started. 'I don't think I have ever seen such a gathering of disreputable characters. Oh dear me no.'

A man seated towards the back lifted his head. 'Fuck you, Keegan.'

Keegan jumped from the stage and pushed his way through the men, his raincoat tails flapping, towards the speaker till he stood over him, using every inch of his six feet six inches to intimidate as he had done for twenty years.

'It's *Mister* Keegan, O'Hearn, you fucking provo scumbag.'

O'Hearn stood up and back, his fists balled. Keegan stepped forward again. 'You're not man enough, son. Bombing children is your style. Now sit down and shut up.' The man next to O'Hearn pulled him back into his seat. Keegan turned and paced back towards the stage, jumped up and faced the room, his eyes narrow and hard.

'Look around you. Anyone missing? Only two that I know of and you will get the word to them. Listen carefully.' He paused, letting it sink in. 'Things are getting bad over the border in the Republic. I am here to tell you that you people will not, I repeat, will not get involved. The people of the south are going to sort this out, with a little help from their friends. That doesn't include you. You are not welcome. If you do stick your noses in you will be nicked. No trial. No warrants. You will just disappear. Do I make myself understood? There will be no operations by your people either here or in the Republic.'

He paused again, sweeping his eyes over the faces before him. 'If you start it we will finish it. Once and for all. The Republic is a military zone and if you people start anything, military law will prevail.'

Professor Kiernan moved up from the shadows at the back of the stage. 'I represent the Irish Resistance. I am here to reiterate what Mr Keegan has told you. Although we accept your desire for a united Ireland we in the south have despised your methods for years. This is our fight. We don't need you. Not only do we not need you, but if you cross over and try to get involved you will be overlapping a very well planned and executed local effort with all the possible problems that brings. Please, don't confuse things even more. Stay out of this.' With that the old professor walked away, disappearing backstage.

'You the friends?' a grey-haired man seated at the front asked Keegan. His voice was quiet, level, the voice of a man used to being respected and obeyed.

'Maybe,' Keegan answered.

'Then *maybe* we will stand back.'

'Never you mind who the friends are. You will call it.' Again Keegan jumped down from the platform and walked the few feet to the Provisional IRA leader, finishing coldly in a whisper that could be barely heard. 'Or you will be the first to go, Eamon Burke, if I have to nick you myself.'

They faced each other, eye to eye. The man was the senior divisional commander and quite literally the head of the Provisional IRA. Their single fear other than the touts, the informers, was that one day the British would waive the rule of law, abandon due process and court procedures and just hit back. He knew Keegan was capable of taking him or any of them, and the RUC and army were full of men who would love the chance to even the scores. It had nearly happened before, after the Warrington bomb in '93. Besides, Burke reasoned, if the Brits were going to be helping over the border that made them friends of Ireland, all Ireland, for the time being anyway.

'The prod loyalists?' he asked.

'They are being told the same,' Keegan answered.

Burke nodded. 'You will know tonight.'

Across the Republic in Dublin, Limerick, Wexford, Waterford, Cork and a dozen smaller towns the occupation had taken on a dreary predictability broken only by the *buachailli* attacks and the increasingly solely Libyan reaction. While some said that every time the resistance attacked it made it worse for everyone else, most people tightened their belts and locked their doors at night, accepting that someone had to fight back, and supported their boys any way they could.

There were problems. Rory McMahon and Pat O'Sullivan had clashed after an operation O'Sullivan had conducted spilled over into McMahon's area, with dreadful consequences.

O'Sullivan's people had moved north-east after an attack, closely followed by a strong Libyan column. Every planner's worst case scenario had almost happened, blue on blue. O'Sullivan's *buachailli* cadre raced straight into a McMahon ambush zone. Luckily the observation team on the road, with seconds to spare, had seen they were not Libyan vehicles and signalled to the main party to abort the mission. Behind the fast-moving Volvo was the Libyan patrol and with nine vehicles it was a considerably different proposition to the small two-vehicle patrol they were expecting. McMahon's cadre leader, not prepared to leave the south-western team in trouble and against his better judgement, initiated a contact. One of his team was killed and the Libyan reprisal in McMahon's zone was brutal. He blamed O'Sullivan's recklessness and Kiernan was called in to arbitrate. Lines were drawn, procedures tightened, but the tension remained. Rory McMahon had already complained to Kiernan about O'Sullivan's ferocious attacks and the ensuing reprisals, but the big Kerryman had just shrugged. To Kiernan's surprise and pleasure it was Maeve who spoke to both men, using a woman's thinking and words to bring them both to heel. They knew well her growing influence in the British camp, their providers of supplies and ammunition, and they both found her impartial and fair.

The permits required for road transport operators had been withheld as a reprisal and shops had begun running out of supplies as trucks from warehouses failed to arrive with orders. Other shops now had shortages of even basic items after local Arab quartermasters arrived with transport and drove away with huge quantities of produce to feed their thousands of men, paying cash as they went from huge wads of notes. People had to queue for basics such as milk, bread, fruit and meat.

Some areas were experiencing power cuts, but for most the blackouts were a sign that the armed resistance was working. In many homes the lights going out meant a ragged cheer and hand-clapping, as someone reached for the candles: the boys had hit again. Passes were now required to enter industrial areas and some city centres. Road blocks with vehicle searches were commonplace, and as the prospect of running out of petrol became a reality there was talk of rationing. An Arab buyer turned up at a small farm and offered the farmer cash for his crop of vegetables. The farmer refused. The Arab insisted. The farmer finally agreed and then sprayed the entire purchase with a slightly toxic and certainly carcinogenic cocktail of banned chemicals. Another, rather than see his produce feed the invaders, ploughed it in.

Ali Jassem, the Palestinian commander of the southern district, was in a six-vehicle convoy that came under a shower of stones and bottles as it navigated round a pile of burning tyres on the North Side of Dublin. Up a street to the left a barricade had been fashioned from two wrecked cars, effectively cutting the street in two. He looked quickly at the scene. His mind had been elsewhere. Sam Abdul Jawad hadn't been seen for over a week. He felt guilty. He had forgotten to check out the girlfriend and now when he could have had her wheeled in and questioned he didn't even know who she was. We train our people to be secretive, to live double and triple lives and then we pay for it. A bottle hit the roof.

'We can snatch a few of them. Make an example,' his detachment commander said. She was young, in her mid-twenties, her people from Nablus. Ali shook his head. Examples would be what weakened their currently strong position in the UN. There must be no more atrocities, no expulsions, no internment of civilians, no outrage.

He wanted to keep moving through the bleak streets where litter and soggy newspaper piled up, where the sharp glass of broken bottles glinted in the headlights like the anger in people's eyes.

'What does it remind you of?' he asked.

'This place?' she asked.

'Everything,' he answered, reaching for the grab bar in front as the vehicle careered round a bend and another rock thumped on to the roof. 'It reminds me of us.'

'Us?' she queried.

'Yeah. Us. These kids out here. The rocks, the fires, the barricades. It's like the West Bank. Like Gaza. It's just the same. Except that this time we are the bastards in the jeeps. We are the patrols.' Ali swung an arm out into the gathering dark. 'This is their intifada,' he said.

Aiden Scott, still the senior SAS officer in Ireland, now moved under a variety of papers from one county to another, supervising operations, debriefing his soldiers, planning new attacks with the local resistance commanders and gathering intelligence. He was tired, but pleased. The SAS teams were functioning well and with only one exception his men had dropped into the local structure without causing problems. The only issue had been down in Cork where two of the local resistance had been unwilling to work with a stranger, particularly an English stranger. It was misplaced nationalism more than anything else and the resistance commander, the young blonde Briget Villiers, Lieutenant Kavanagh's girlfriend, that

Sergeant Kenny had found, sorted the problem out. Given her personal circumstances, the more Scott saw of her the more impressed he was. Her sister Sue, the girl Kenny had saved, had finally accepted that her brother was dead and her grief was absolute. She simply sat in a chair staring at the wall, crying. In normal times Briget would have sent her to a doctor for professional counselling, but that would have to wait. Now her behaviour moved between deep depression and a state almost catatonic, but Briget, electing to let time heal, continued her work regardless.

Rory McMahon, his boyhood friend, had been the last to go into a major action, but when he did so he acted with intelligence and panache, as if to prove to O'Sullivan how it should be done. He had, with his team, entered the local garrison under cover of darkness and destroyed their stores. He had aimed not only for the basic food supplies, but also for the precious specialities imported from home that he knew they would miss. Then he set delayed action incendiary devices that burnt out their accommodation and blankets. They would be cold and hungry for a taste of home. Morale would plummet. The following night, after twenty-four hours of rain, he had dropped mortar bombs into their lines and a sniper had shot three of their officers as they tried to reorganize.

He then waited to see what reprisals would be forthcoming and Scott had headed back towards Meath with just one task remaining.

The resistance had identified the Libyan officer who had murdered Sinead Kelly. He was quartered deep inside a facility, but watchers had plotted his routine. Although his patrol route varied each night he made the same twenty-pace walk to his vehicles every time.

An American 'specialist' based in the west of Ireland had been sent for. He was a Marine Corps gunnery sergeant, a man in his forties with close-cropped greying hair. He was a sniper, trained by the legendary Carlos Hathcock in

Vietnam, and on the rooftop beside Scott, 860 yards from the vehicles where their target would cross, he unwrapped his weapon. It was an M-40 A1, the marines' sniper weapon based on the Remington 700, but with a heavy barrel free-floating in a fibreglass stock. Mounted above the action was an Unertl 10-power scope. The marine could kill with one bullet consistently at ranges over a thousand yards.

They had measured the range with spotting scopes during daylight and now, with almost still air, he took up his position. Scott was there to spot for him, protect him and see him safely away after the hit. They didn't wait long, Scott refreshing his memory from the three photographs of the target the resistance had supplied.

'In the doorway,' he said. 'Your target. The man in front. Greatcoat and cap, lifting the cigarette.'

'Got him.' A second later he fired and Scott, watching through the spotting scope, saw the officer's head snap back as the heavy 7.62 hollow point bullet almost took his head from his shoulders.

'Confirmed,' Scott snapped. 'Let's go.'

Down on the street the resistance waited with three cars and they were away in under a minute, Scott heading northwards.

He had not been back to the farmhouse headquarters since the day the crisis had begun and now as he pulled his car into the bays behind the garage in the village he was looking forward to seeing the others, in particular Aisling. He hefted his bag over his shoulder and began to walk the dark lane towards the farm.

Peter Morris, now living there with his wife, was upstairs in the attic coding high-speed transmissions for the outside. The Libyans had come to the farm once only, wanting to know how many people lived there, their names and occupations. Morris had told them he commuted daily to the university and that he and Millie rented rooms from the owner who was Aisling. While this conversation was going on two of Scott's soldiers waited in the tunnel below, listening, in case someone upstairs pressed the panic button. One was a medic, there in case they had casualties, and the second was their electronics engineer, but both were fighting men first and foremost.

That had been three days ago and they hadn't been back since. Nevertheless the alarm system was in place and functioning.

Millie stood at the kitchen sink alongside Aisling drying the plates as they were passed to her.

'Missing him?' she asked gently.

Aisling smiled at her. 'Yeah. Lots. I just want to know he is okay.'

'He will be fine,' Millie responded. 'I would worry about who it is he's after.'

'I hate not knowing where he is,' Aisling murmured. 'I know none of us are supposed to know, but . . .' her voice trailed off. Millie leaned forward and turned on the small radio that stood on the window sill wedged between pot plants, egg boxes and a small pine medicine cabinet that now contained reels of cotton, string, scissors and old dried-out rolls of wrapping tape. The sounds of Radio Free Ireland came from the speaker.

'He will be fine,' Millie said reaching for a wet plate. There were five plates and only three of them in the house. The other two were for the pair of soldiers that were down in the tunnels and they were always careful to get any signs of other occupants cleared away quickly.

The alarm system triggered at six points. One in the kitchen, one in the attic, one on the bedroom landing and at three points underground. They were wired into what looked like standard domestic smoke alarms. They went off together, stopped, started again and then stopped again. Finally they went off again for three seconds and then fell into silence.

Millie and Aisling looked at each other. The three signal was a friend, but it had not been used before.

Peter Morris appeared down the stairs, taking them two at a time. 'Someone's coming,' he said. He had a gun in his hand and looked most uncomfortable.

'It's a friend,' Aisling said. 'Three bursts is a friend.'

'Or a malfunction,' he responded.

'Oh, shit.'

Millie walked to the windows and peeked through into the night. 'No headlights.' Her voice was tight with tension. They waited for a few minutes and finally the trapdoor opened and Scott climbed up into the house. Aisling, delighted to see him, broke into a smile and went to put her arms around him, seeing the exhaustion and promising herself that she would make him eat and rest.

He held her for a second or two and then looked at Millie. 'Don't stand in a room with the lights on and look out the window. I saw you from the gate.'

She ignored the comment. 'I'll bet you could kill for a gin and tonic.'

'As long as I can have it in the bath.'

An hour later he closed himself into the tunnel with Morris and they moved down to the ops bunker where they could bring each other up to date, Morris handing the latest high-speed coded transmission to the SAS communications man for decoding. Four hours later Scott eventually called it a night and crawled into his bed. Aisling was awake and as he settled into the warmth she moved closer.

In London the Irish government-in-exile, comprising four senior ambassadors and Professor Kiernan, made preparations to move to Belfast. It was appropriate and as the public relations machine designed by O'Malley began to function in high gear, they would need a shadow capital, somewhere where the thousands of enquiries could be handled, somewhere they could hold press conferences and manage their campaign to liberate their homeland. The thousands of Irish who had escaped in time had their own problems. With cash reserves running out, many banks round the world not accepting Irish punts, and transfers from their homeland frozen as the new authorities clamped down, things were desperate. The problem was that in a matter of a week the Irish currency had become worthless. The Bank of England stepped in and supported the currency, not only guaranteeing its worth, but offering one for one parity with sterling providing the bearer could produce an Irish passport over three years old. The Americans followed suit and with this kind of support the normally cautious Germans also agreed to accept the currency.

The other issue was larger. Kiernan was right. The Irish diaspora were coming, in their thousands. The mood on the streets of Liverpool, London and a dozen towns in Ulster was sombre and silent. As bed and breakfast places, guest houses and hotels filled up the local residents began taking them in. Public meetings were encouraged, but any attempt to organize an armed response was swiftly curbed. At the new Irish and Celtic recruiting offices they were told they would have a role to fill, a worthwhile job to do, but to leave the planning to others. Men with military experience were singled out, and the British were advised that groups would soon be arriving. Seventeen Irishmen in the French Foreign Legion had been given leave for six months, and a group of three hundred Irish Australians in the Australian army had been asked to sit tight in Melbourne for the time being.

In the USA the Marine Corps was very quietly, but very determinedly, reassigning men within its 30,000-strong ranks. Those of Irish descent or who had claimed some affiliation were quietly transferred into new units and papers were prepared to give them leave of absence.

In the Arabian Gulf the aircraft carrier USS *Independence* and her battle group received orders to make for the north Atlantic. Only her captain knew that there they would be joined by marine assault ships and helicopter carriers.

The meeting between the American Secretary of State and the Arab delegation was held in secret in one of the many conference rooms in the massive United Nations building in New York. The message was simple. If America interfered in the internal affairs of Ireland, or made any attack on the new administration, then the Arab world and OPEC would react with speed. All American embassies and diplomatic missions would lose accreditation, all Americans living or working in the Middle East would be expelled, all military bases would be closed. American merchandise would be boycotted and the price of oil would be hiked to double its current rate.

'So you will throw us out? And who will keep Saddam Hussein inside his own borders?' the Secretary asked.

'The Russian Federation would be invited to provide the military security in return for interest free loans and cheap oil. We have reason to believe they will look kindly upon the suggestion. We are serious, Mr Secretary. One American soldier sets foot in Ireland and we will act. Think about it. Withdraw your support for the State of Israel. All we want is Palestine for the Palestinians. Then your Irish can have their country back.'

'And what if they take it back?'

'They might try.' The speaker, a senior Palestinian, waved a hand as if it was of no importance. 'But think about it. You can maintain your Middle East relationships, your presence, maintain a supply of affordable oil for the next decade at least, and get Ireland back for the Irish, if you stop supporting Israel.'

The Secretary knew the Russians would jump at it. A massive standing army, bored and broke. It was ideal. Pure synergy. He stood. 'We will consider the position and respond in due course, but I'll tell you this. Whatever the United States Government does or does not do, we do not and cannot force conditions on our citizens. Many of them are Irish. You have been warned.'

'We are not concerned about your citizens, or their behaviour. Just your government's policy.'

'I'll hold you to that.'

'Please do,' the Palestinian replied.

As the Secretary of State paced from the room one of his aides thought he saw the merest hint of a smile.

The ship that the Royal Air Force Nimrod had spotted leaving Libya was now confirmed to have met up with two others. Five other mini-convoys had been identified and as the first, designated by the Northwood computer 'Contact Sierra', turned for the Irish coast and the exclusion zone a signal was flashed to the fleet. Sierra was now a contact of critical interest and it would be closely shadowed for the next day or two, while Northwood Intelligence learned what they could about the make-up of the convoy and any threat it might contain. Its course would bring it squarely into the patrol area shared by HMS *Dundee* and the Irish ship *Kathleen*. The other four were heading for the Irish coast at different points, but would cross into the total exclusion zone some six hours after Sierra.

In Ireland, Libyans rounding up a group of people for internment as a reprisal, pointed to a woman in the crowd. She refused. An officer shouted to his men and three dashed forward. The woman, proud and angry, tried to fight them off and a soldier, wet, cold and angry, swung his rifle butt. She dropped to the pavement bleeding profusely from a deep compression fracture of the skull, her shopping scattered round her, broken eggs and flour mixed in with the bright red blood. The Libyan officer shrugged. A week ago he would have censured the soldier, but not any more. He pointed out another woman and his men grabbed her. The critically injured woman was left on the pavement, people trying to help, but by the time the ambulance came Katriona O'Sullivan, wife of Patrick O'Sullivan and mother of his children, was dead.

# 10

The party crossed into Ireland just after four in the morning on one of the hundreds of unmarked footpaths that connected Ulster to the Republic. Many of them had been used for hundreds of years but were only known to those who lived nearby. The group comprised six SAS soldiers, one of Joseph O'Reilly's resistance men as a guide, and Maeve O'Donnell. She was dressed as they were, in camouflage, but beneath the military kit she wore what others her age wore, jeans and a casual shirt. Her long hair was up beneath the woollen hat, but unlike them she had not used camouflage cream. As she followed the men in front of her, entering Ireland for the first time since the crisis had broken, entering to begin her part, she felt the excitement rise. They moved slowly, feeling the way, one man way out in front, the rest following in absolute silence, like shadows in the night.

Four other larger groups also crossed that night at different points along the border, both British, like members of the SAS and the Royal Irish Regiment, and Irishmen, a detail of troops that had returned from the Lebanon and men of the Irish Defence Force.

Kiernan had travelled back with the Irish soldiers. The planners, including O'Malley, had tried to talk him out of it, explaining that as head of the resistance he was simply too important to risk in the war zone. His reply, typical and delivered with conviction, was that there was no other place for him to be. O'Malley, the hard-headed businessman, marketer and romantic, explained it to the others.

'It's the Irishness. The saints and scholars. There could

no more be a coronation of an Irish queen without an eminent scholar than without a priest. I now agree with him. Anyway, given the choice, I wouldn't miss it for the world. It's history in the making.'

Then Kiernan had made his second decision – the early involvement of the Irish soldiers who had arrived in Britain. He had insisted that they not only form the bulk of Maeve's bodyguard, but that he would re-enter Ireland with them. It may have been only symbolic, but to him and the Irish it was important.

The twenty-two men had been carefully selected and then taken direct to the 2 Paras' battle camp, where for four days they had been hammered through fitness and skills testing. The instructors, twelve men from the Paras and the SAS lines at Hereford, had been quietly pleased with their calibre, one saying he thought at least six of them could get through the SAS's own selection course, the toughest in the world.

The Irish soldiers were then linked up with their counterparts from the British army's Royal Irish Regiment, men who had been similarly trained but for longer. They would form the defensive perimeter for the danger period, the time they were all out in the open. Scott had surveyed the ancient site at Tara, not as a tourist but as a soldier. It looked easy to defend, with its height and ancient ditches – in fact it had been built there for that reason, on high ground to see an attacking force approach – but it had been selected when men fought with staves and clubs, swords and sorcerers. In a modern context it was exposed without enough real height. Its only benefit was the ditches, deep, almost moat-like hollows that ran in concentric rings out from the ancient stones. Scott knew that even with his small force they could hold it for long enough to get the civilians clear, as long as there was no artillery or air attack, but if that happened it would be a disaster. Too much depended on what was to happen up there.

Another of his men had parachuted in the night before. The man, a keen parachutist and instructor, had done over a thousand high-level free falls and he volunteered to do the jump. Using a tandem 'chute and breathing oxygen from a bottle he had jumped from 26,000 feet, with 315 pounds of carefully packed cargo slung below him in a harness. It had been perfect weather. Still air at height and low cloud had enabled him to land within half a mile of his target unseen.

The resistance were there, as they were in France fifty years before, men and women with guns and torches to receive him and his precious load.

It was a slab, carefully packed in layers of shock resistant foam, the size of a small tabletop four inches thick and for the ancients worth its weight in diamonds. It was part of the Coronation stone from Westminster Abbey, the stone of Scone, what the Ancient Irish had called the *Lia Fáil*, the Stone of Destiny.

The legend said that when a true king was crowned upon it, the stone would roar or tremble. Lent by Murtagh mac Erc to his brother Fergus the Great for his coronation in Scotland, it was never returned and became the stone of Scone. Later, in 1297, it was removed to Westminster by Edward I.

The resistance members had gathered round it, two of them, history students, in awe. It had last been in Ireland in the sixth century and now it was home, temporarily at least. A tractor, its engine muffled right down, lurched across the field and minutes later the famous stone was on its way.

The camera team had arrived the day before and were billeted in a nearby farm. Their equipment with its satellite link was safely stored in the bunkers and the other preparations were complete across the land.

For now the men were deep below ground in the tunnels and bunkers below the farm and Scott left Maeve sitting before the fire chatting with Aisling and Kiernan and went below to see them settled in and redeploy the sentries.

'It's nice to be back,' she said. 'Tell me what's been going on?'

'I thought you would have been getting all the news,' Aisling replied.

'Just the big stuff. I want the everyday things. Real things, you know?'

'Well, we are baking our own bread now and the petrol station in Navan has run out of petrol already.'

'People okay?'

Aisling shook her head. 'No. A couple of the local lads had a go at them the other night after the pub shut. They were taken off. Haven't been seen since. It's happening everywhere. People who challenge them out in the open get rounded up. Everyone's hoping they get released after a few days or something. People stay home if they can, listen to the radio, some places can still get BBC and ITV, and wonder when the Americans or Brits are coming. What's happening out there?'

Maeve smiled. 'They are coming. London, Liverpool, Belfast, Bristol, Cardiff. All full of Irish. The biggest problem now is finding things for them to do, assuring them that something is happening.' She blushed. 'Mr Kiernan,' she looked across at him as he dozed before the flames, 'Mr Kiernan says I will be able to help with that after tomorrow. The crown will be the rally point. What else? . . . There are concerts this weekend. The Dubliners were on tour in Europe. They will be playing. So will the Fureys. U2 are doing one in New York, then flying back to play at this one as well.'

They talked for an hour or so and by the time Scott climbed back up through the trapdoor, a parcel under his arm and dragging an aluminium case, they were like old friends and he knew he was the subject of their chatter.

The pair grinned at him, Aisling's expression one of proud ownership and Maeve's curious and interested.

'Ash has got your kit up in the spare room at the front. There's a couple of changes of clothing, a suit, toothbrush and smellies. The . . .' he looked at Aisling, 'what's it called?'

'A gown,' she answered drily. Kiernan had woken, and sat watching in silence, half a smile on his lips.

'The green silk job is to be worn tomorrow night.' He ignored her. 'There's thermal undies because it's looking like it will be cold. This . . .' he held up the parcel, 'is your cape.'

Maeve looked at Aisling, biting her lip nervously.

'Oh go on!' Aisling said.

Kiernan smiled. 'You'd better see if it fits,' he said.

Maeve stood up, an embarrassed look on her face.

'All of it. Come on, I'll help,' Aisling encouraged, rising to her feet.

'How's Pat holding up?' Scott asked.

'Not well,' Kiernan replied. 'He has locked himself away apparently. He seems inconsolable. I think he blames himself . . . We never had a chance to talk, you and I,' he went on, as the girls left the room. 'You are Irish, are you not?'

'Half,' Scott replied. 'My mother is from Birr.'

'To me that makes you Irish,' Kiernan replied, reaching for a poker and prodding the embers. 'You are what it's all about.'

'Sorry?' Scott said.

'The homecoming. The Wild Geese returning. You were just the first.'

'It's my job,' Scott said.

'That's what you say. But I hazard a guess that if it hadn't been, you would have come anyway. You would have heard the call of the drum.'

'Others have?' Scott asked, partly just to keep the conversation flowing, but also out of interest. Lately he had felt out of touch, isolated by his role.

'Thousands upon thousands of them,' Kiernan replied softly. 'The Home Office estimates there are four hundred thousand of them already. More arrive every day. For years we watched them go. Go to America, Australia, New Zealand, Britain, Canada. And now they are coming home. Answering the call. I don't think,' he said, looking into the flames, 'that I have ever been so proud to be an Irishman.'

'You expected it,' Scott said. 'You planned it this way.'

'Yes. We planned it this way. But never in my wildest dreams did I expect so many to come. I wanted to believe it like all the Irish. Believe that the velvet chain was still strong. But deep in my heart I was prepared for rhetoric, for talk, for public meetings and not much else. The irony is that now that a mighty Celtic but predominantly British army is gathering, and the Irish could have done it. Done it alone.'

'At a hell of a price,' Scott said. Most civilians didn't realize that most of a soldier's training was to stay alive – kill the enemy, but stay alive themselves. Untrained men die at a rate ten times that of trained men.

'Yes,' Kiernan replied. 'A price they were prepared to pay.'

'Sorry,' Aisling said, popping her head round the door, a broad smile across her face. 'Can we have the other stuff?'

Scott handed her the aluminium box, thinking about what Kiernan had said. He had seen green, untrained men face tanks, rocket artillery and air strikes in the Gulf. Young conscripted Iraqis. Some of those that lived through it would never get over the shock of a modern battle. The firepower and noise that left grown men weeping, shivering, jabbering like morons, faeces running down their legs, wild animal fear in their eyes. The terror was simply too much.

'No one should have to pay that kind of price,' he said, the professional soldier slipping momentarily into a tired veteran, sickened by what he had seen.

'You are right of course,' Kiernan replied, sitting back in his chair, his eyes fixed on the flames. 'I was at Normandy.'

'I never thought of you as a soldier,' Scott responded honestly.

'Good gracious me no. Not a soldier. I was something of a linguist in my youth. Spoke passable French and German. Hated the Nazis. I ended up in France. Listening in on their wireless net, listening to telephone lines. Was there with the local chaps when the invasion began. Thought it would be exciting. It wasn't.' Kiernan stopped there, his eyes fixed on the flames as the memories flooded back, the smell, the noise, the roar of incoming shells, the explosions so massive that ears bled, and hearing was damaged for weeks afterward. The drifting smoke and the dead boys, thousands of them along the beaches, bodies bobbing in the surf.

'I was horror-struck and compelled all at once. I was sickened by the ferocity of it, proud it was ours and saddened all at once. I had never felt such mixed emotions. I wanted to run away but I couldn't. I was a historian and this was history before my eyes. So I watched from the farmhouse on the hill. Some Americans came by. We were allowed to stay. I watched as thousands of boys no older than me were blown to pieces or cut down by bullets. Our boys. German boys. I had often thought that if the men who sent others to war had ever witnessed real war they would never do it. I was wrong.'

The last statement was a self-indictment. They sat in silence for a minute, the room silent but for the crackle of the fire, until a movement behind Scott made Kiernan turn, a smile breaking across his face.

'Good God,' he said.

Scott looked round.

Maeve stood at the bottom of the stairs, the light from the hall putting highlights in her hair. She wore an emerald green gown of silk, tailored to her form, with a scooped neck and long sleeves. Over it she wore the cloak that had been made by Pringle in Scotland. Its inner lining was a green cashmere tartan and the outer layer was fine light wool, a deep bottle green. A hood dropped down the back and as she walked into the room the cloak swung back.

She was wearing the ancient gold. The torc round her neck, the earrings and, holding the cloak closed at the point between her breasts, the Tara brooch. Its cast silver surfaces with their gold filigree, inset enamel and amber reflected the flickering firelight.

'You look magnificent,' Kiernan uttered. 'Yes! yes! Every inch the Celtic queen.'

Maeve blushed.

'Where's my bag?' he asked, looking around. 'There's more. Have a look at it all.'

Scott looked at Aisling. 'I'll get it,' she said. 'It's upstairs.'

A few minutes later as they looked at the last items, Kiernan again talked them through the order of events for the following night, but Scott, ever the soldier, was interested in the sword. It was made in Sheffield, hand-made by a man who had used time-honoured techniques of folding heated steel, of tempering, the sword-maker's art, and had combined those with the most modern of alloys. The result was a weapon that was light, flexible and immensely strong. The thirty-inch blade was mounted on a hilt that been modelled on one dug from a bog that dated back to the sixth century. The scabbard was leather and wood, inlaid with worked filigree, and the belt could be worn either round the waist or higher, so the sword hilt protruded over the wearer's right shoulder.

It was the last item that stunned the girls. Kiernan

produced it with a flourish. 'Asprey's want it back when we have finished. Couldn't have a queen without a crown now, could we?'

Maeve gasped softly and threw both hands up to her mouth.

'It's exquisite,' Aisling said.

It was more a tiara than a crown. The band of white gold and diamonds surrounded a single huge perfect emerald that was set in the centre of the arrangement. The gems glittered in the firelight.

'Don't put it on. It's bound to be bad luck or something. We will need to do your hair so it sits properly.'

Morris put his head round the door. 'Aiden . . . good grief. You look magnificent!' he said to Maeve, then looked back at the SAS officer. 'Problem.'

'Speak,' said Kiernan.

'Rory has been on. A group of army officers tried to make a break today. Four were shot. The rest, they have been moved. Trucks. They left at four this afternoon.'

'Palestinians or Libyans?' Scott asked. Already patterns had emerged. If the Libyans were involved, then inefficiency and brutality were the order of the day. Morris's face told the answer.

'Pass the word. We need to know where they are. Any details we can get.'

'They shot four of our men?' Maeve asked. Morris nodded.

'Unarmed men?' He nodded again.

She stood up, eyes blazing with an anger none of them had seen before the tears began to well in her eyes. They were tears of sadness, but mixed with rage and impotence.

'There's nothing we can do,' Kiernan said.

'Oh yes there is,' Maeve answered coldly. 'Get the details on the Libyan officers. Whoever gave the orders. They will answer charges. Leaflets. We need leaflets printed in Arabic and English. They must understand that every one of them, without exception, irrespective of rank, will be held accountable for his actions.'

'Who issues the statement?' Kiernan asked, thinking aloud.

'Tomorrow night I shall be crowned queen,' she replied. 'So from tomorrow night I have that authority. Correct?'

'Yes. Yes you do,' Kiernan answered, looking up at her as she stood in her Celtic regalia before the flickering fire, the tears drying on her cheeks, a new strength coming from somewhere.

'Put it in my name,' she said. Her voice was low, tinged with steely conviction.

'There are other things we should make clear with the same device,' Kiernan said.


## 9 November, the North Atlantic

Commander David Lyall was the boss, the driver of HMS *Dundee* and he was watching the screen with interest. The big slow sweeping radar above and behind the bridge looked out two hundred miles, but they didn't need that range. The blips that were approaching the exclusion zone showed Contact Sierra, their contact of critical interest, only thirty miles away. To the north there was another series of blips, but they were someone else's problem. Sierra was three ships, merchantmen, their photographs stuck up on the bulkhead above the plotting table. If they kept this course they would cross into the zone in two hours' time.

The ship had been at defence watch for three days now, the crew split into two watches, port and starboard, each watch working six hours on, six hours off. It was tiring but could be sustained for weeks if necessary. From defence watch the next stage was action stations, when the entire crew turned out to fight the ship, and that state of readiness took just under ten minutes to achieve.

Commander Lyall looked across at Burnett, his first lieutenant, who had one of the bridge phones in his hand. 'Problem with the chopper, sir,' he said, replacing the handset.

'How long?'

'They aren't sure,' Burnett replied. This put a new perspective on things. Helicopters were not only the preferred method for visually sighting a target ship and delivering their message, but also the preferred method of transferring a boarding party. For the seaman officers they were also notoriously unreliable. Lyall grimaced.

As a captain he was respected by his crew. Calm, measured and thoroughly professional, no one had ever seen him flustered. *Dundee* was his second command, the first having been a submarine. Short and lithe, he was often physically the smallest man on the bridge, but his presence was huge, an almost tangible aura surrounding him. It was more than the three stripes on his sleeve. It was command presence and crew would say they could feel him even when they couldn't see him, when the bridge lights were down to preserve night sight on a dark night.

Lyall stepped over to the chart table and was immediately joined by the navigating officer. 'I want to intercept. At a point three miles off the edge of the zone.' He took a pencil and the dividers. 'Here.'

'Aye aye.'

'Visual when?' the captain asked.

'Vasco' the navigator did a quick calculation. 'Thirteen twenty, sir.'

The captain nodded. He would take the ship to action stations as the watch changed at noon. Both watches could have a quick meal and get settled at their stations. He lifted the secure phone and a few moments later he was talking to the admiral who was aboard the carrier HMS *Invincible*, to their south-east, requesting a change in the Rules of

Engagement. He knew the politicians were still prevaricating in London and getting the ROE changed would not be easy.

Two levels below the bridge Lieutenant Carson, who had been dozing on his bunk, swung his feet over the edge and dropped to the deck. Already wearing his number eights, the flash-proofed blue uniform of all on defence watch, he picked up his flash hood and gloves and made his way the ten steps round from his cabin to the wardroom.

Below in the centre of the ship the operations room was only illuminated by the dull overhead lights and the glow of the radar screens. There were banks of them across the front bulkhead of the space, the air plotters to the left and surface plotters to the right. In the centre of the room was the captain's station. To his left the Air Warfare Officer, a lieutenant commander, had his plotting area and to his right the Principal Warfare Officer, in *Dundee* a lieutenant. From here they would fight the ship.

To the uninitiated the area would seem crowded with men and high technology, the figures in the ghostly flash hoods and gloves leaning over the glowing screens, listening to headphones and speaking into microphones. In reality the sequence is simple. The seamen watching the screens at the forward end of the area are the first to see the threat. Different types of radar and equipment give early warning of threats to the ship or her charges. If the radar finds aircraft or missiles incoming, the battle management computer immediately allocates a number to the trace. The operator calls out the screen he is watching, the number, the bearing and what he thinks it is. The captain and his warfare officers identify the numbered trace on their own screens and one of the warfare officers then takes the ship into action. Only if the captain disagrees with his decision will he intervene. The Royal Navy calls it management by veto and it gives the specialist officer the confidence to fight the ship. In practice the captain would not allow a second's hesitation. If he is in reach of a microphone he would give orders to the warfare team to engage the enemy and to the bridge to put the ship in the best possible position to fight and achieve the objectives. If he isn't, then he knows that management by veto allows his officers to act.

The appropriate warfare officer, the specialist for the threat, calls for control of the weapons he requires, and issues orders to the missile or gun directors who sit behind him and to his left. The design of the operations room allows him to turn his head a quarter turn to the left to see them, the two petty officers and the chief petty officer standing behind them. In action the room is a hubbub of sounds, but once the warfare officer has begun everything else fades, as he and his small team become the focus of 208 other people, an entire warship, and maybe the aircraft carrier she is protecting. Suddenly nothing else seems to matter.

That was why Lieutenant Peter Carson liked what he did. He was a seaman officer, had worked his way up the command chain from midshipman, to junior watch officer, to navigator. Then he had done the warfare courses and his speciality was surface threats and submarines. He was the PWO, the Principal Warfare Officer, on the starboard watch. To him, until he had his own command, this was as good as it got.

At 1115 hours he entered the wardroom to get a cup of coffee. At the table two of the others coming on watch were playing 'uckers', the navy's version of Ludo.

'What's new?' he asked.

'Chopper is in bits again. The boss is pissed off.'

'Fucking gits,' the other officer muttered, moving a piece on the board. The navy, delighted with the fictional Captain Blackadder's terse remark: 'I don't care how many times they go upiddy-up-up, they are still gits!', had overnight labelled all their helicopter pilots with the tag, and every time something went wrong with a helicopter it was the gits' fault.

'So,' the first officer finished, 'we are going to intercept.'

Carson glanced up at the speaker from the hot water he was pouring into his cup. An interception meant the possibility of something to break the tedium of the patrol. The sea boat and a boarding party, possibly.

In spite of the will-we won't-we uncertainty, General Stewart had managed to keep his people focused and his headquarters at Bulford was bustling with preparations. North, at the JHQ at High Wycombe, they kept pace. Every evening they received the tapes smuggled out by the resistance, video footage of everything from the location and array of armour to troop dispositions. They also received copies of the footage intended for the media, odd sequences of resistance attacks, Libyan reactions and some of what passed for everyday life in occupied Ireland. The planning teams watched the tapes over and over, the room crowded each evening as they arrived at the base. High Wycombe was teeming with people, not only the resident tri-service staff but the extras drafted in.

Luckily there had been only one serious clash of personalities. Stewart had reluctantly requested that a senior RAF man be replaced and now he had a team he could work with. Even the Americans had dropped into the rhythm, Stewart impressed by the sheer professionalism of the Marine Corps officers and, like all British, constantly amazed by the technology they could deliver to a tactical problem.

There was also a small section of American specialists who were there to analyse the satellite images that were now arriving daily. Lacrosse, Landsat and KH-11 material now took up three rooms.

Stewart was tireless and although he would rather have been out with his men where they were training hard, the airborne now training to become air mobile, his place was at HQ, directing and redirecting the efforts of many who were working eighteen hours a day. The contingency plans in place for the rapid deployment of the division could only be extrapolated so far and real planning for the sheer numbers of men and weight of equipment took over the dynamics. New plans for an action this size were hugely complex, but now, just before lunchtime on 10 November, he sat alone awaiting the news from the Joint Chiefs of Staff in Whitehall.

He had presented his plan, Williams there and in support, and now he awaited approval. He had been warned by his own contacts in Whitehall. The PM was still trying to pressure the parties with back-room deals and the Foreign Secretary had been shuttling round Europe for a week now on an exhausting series of meetings and favour calling. His next trip was Moscow and his new brief gave him mandate to take the gloves off. He was given new sweeteners and a very big stick. Even so, that might mean another week or more of uncertainty.

In the Security Council of the United Nations, the Americans and British had pulled the French in and closed ranks against the Russians. The Chinese remained supportive of Palestinian self-rule in principle, but had made only bland statements on the Irish situation. The positive shift was in the General Assembly, where the huge support that the Palestinians had built over the years was being eroded by the guilt of association with each reported Libyan atrocity.

The call came through as promised by 12.15 and he almost slammed the phone down on the caller. Continue planning only. Treat as an exercise. Problems, you understand.

*    *    *

HMS *Dundee* was now at action stations and her captain, Commander Lyall, was still talking to *Invincible* trying to get a change in the Rules of Engagement. As far as he was concerned the fact that he was now forced to take his ship in close instead of using a helicopter made all the difference. The admiral agreed and aboard *Invincible* they in turn were talking to Northwood.

Burnett, the first lieutenant, was standing a few feet away, the radio mike in his hand.

'*Ras Ali, Ras Ali*, this is the British warship *Dundee*. You are now entering an exclusion zone. Change your course. I repeat. *Ras Ali*, you are entering an exclusion zone. Change your course.'

Burnett tried each of the three ships in turn but there was no acknowledgement. He lifted a pair of binoculars. *Dundee*'s course had brought them round behind the Libyan ships and just definable to the naked eye away to the east were three vessels. Through the binoculars suspended round his neck on a white cord they appeared much closer, but not close enough. He lowered the glasses and stepped across to watch the closed circuit monitor. Mounted on each bridge wing was a powerful surveillance camera, and its 40-power magnifying capability had proved its worth on stop and search operations in the Gulf of Aqaba. It meant they could sit two miles away from a suspicious vessel and almost lip-read the bridge commands. The three ships were there on the screen, each vessel's broad transom clearly identifiable, with her name and port of registry. He looked down at the controls. The camera was only on 22-power magnification. He cranked it up to 30 and scanned right till he could see the aft decks of the *Ras Ali*.

Tarpaulins covered cargo and figures moved among the uneven lumps, but above the weather deck on the bridge wing he could see a figure standing, looking back at them with a pair of binoculars.

'*Ras Ali, Ras Ali,*' he began again for the eighth time. He looked around as he made his announcement. The bridge was quiet. Only the officer of the watch, the lads and the captain. Everyone else was at their stations. He finished and looked at Lyall.

'I don't like it,' the captain said.

Burnett stepped a pace forward over the green non-slip linoleum covering on the deck, remembering somehow that *Nottingham*'s bridge deck was covered in an opulent red carpet that had begun life aboard the royal yacht *Britannia*. He had his binoculars to his eyes.

'*Kathleen*'s changing course. Gathering speed, by the look of it, sir.'

Lyall took up another pair of glasses. The little Irish ship had been keeping loose station off their starboard bow since they had made the intercept. Now she was moving ahead.

'What's she up to? I don't like it, Number One. I don't like any of it. Start both Olympus.'

'Start Olympus,' repeated the officer of the watch.

'Yeoman. Aldis. Make to *Kathleen*. What is your intention.'

The rating ran out to the bridge wing to the big ten-inch signal lamp.

'Those merchants. Too cocky by half,' Lyall said softly, thinking aloud as he focused the glasses back to the three ships on the horizon. 'I think the buggers are going to do something silly. I am going below.'

Burnett just nodded. He would now be the captain's eyes and ears outside the operations room, moving from station to station, making sure that everyone was where they should be, but now he was watching the *Kathleen*, as the grey sea churned under her stern.

'Mr Burnett.'

The first lieutenant ignored the captain for a second before speaking. 'Stand by, sir. *Kathleen* is signalling.' Below, the two huge Olympus turbines had begun to turn, the characteristic jet engine whistle loud from the funnel and the deck vibrating under their feet.

'Shit,' he said. 'Signal reads "Am engaging", Captain.'

The brave little Irish patrol ship was now racing towards the big Libyan merchant ships, her flared bows taking the oily swells like a thoroughbred over fences.

'Stupid bugger! Keep the messages going.' Lyall looked across at the officer of the watch. 'Forty-five on both levers. Yeoman . . .' the rating had just stepped through the bridge door to report *Kathleen*'s response; ' . . . make to *Kathleen*. Request you do not engage repeat do not engage.'

'Forty-five on both,' the officer of the watch repeated.

'Number One, bring us up abeam the *Kathleen* if you will.'

Burnett looked at the captain. For an air defence destroyer abeam another ship as you closed for action was a close-in defence posture, close enough to engage all systems.

'Sir,' Burnett acknowledged.

With that the captain was gone, down the steep stairs towards the operations room.

Burnett looked round. 'Lieutenant Conway.'

'Sir?' she replied. Her voice sounded dry. This was her first bit of tension. First time the gun had live ammunition in the racks as they closed for action.

'Watch that ship. I don't give a stuff where the ops boys put the camera. If it's not on that big bugger in the middle, then watch it through glasses. Goddit?'

'Yes, sir. What am I looking for?'

Burnett looked at her. 'I'm not sure, Lieutenant. I just don't like the look of her. Those tarps on the back. Steer zero nine zero. Eighty per cent on both.'

'Zero nine zero. Eighty on both.'

The bridge phone went off and Burnett spoke for a second or two then replaced the handset, the deck now rumbling beneath them as the increased torque from the Olympus turbines reached the propellers, the warship gathering pace beneath them.

'That's it. They have crossed into the exclusion zone.'

Three decks below in the operations room Lieutenant Carson, the Principal Warfare Officer, stood over his plotting desk, flash hood and gloves on, earphones over his head. His radar screen, set up for surface actions, only looked out twenty-odd miles, but that was plenty. The three Libyan ships were now just nine miles off the port bow and as the *Dundee*'s speed moved up towards thirty knots they would overhaul them in just over half an hour. The *Kathleen* was only half a mile in front, her trace a big rust-yellow blob on the brown screen display. Across from Carson at the Air Warfare Officer's station the AWO's screen was capable of a much wider view from the big slow scanner and now it was displaying a two-hundred-mile arc round the ship. There were at least four sets of eyes watching the display at any time because in these days of air-launched anti-ship missiles, long range tanks, mid-air refuelling and vertical take-off jets, no ship was safe. The AWO, a lieutenant commander, stood back and watched his screen, one hand up to his earphones listening to the muted talk among the crew.

Behind and above the bridge on the exposed gun direction platform the petty officer, happy with the state of readiness on the starboard side, crossed over to the port and looked down at his ratings. The man who had been manning the local area sight for the deck gun a few moments before had been replaced and an older, more experienced seaman of the other watch was now in the seat, his hands moving, lining up on the ships ahead of them. He nodded silently to himself. That was the way of it.

As they bore down on the targets the local area sight became more important, the rating's eyes through the old-fashioned glass sight visually aiming the quick-firing 4.5

inch gun, rather than relying on the radar. A man's eyes allowed the high explosive shells to be accurately directed at specific targets on command. If they got that close and engaged, then the best man should be sighting the gun. Everyone knew it and the younger man would have given up his station without complaint.

Commander Lyall entered the operations room and moved straight to his position between his two warfare officers. In an old ship of the line he would have stood on the quarter deck, midshipman runners ready to take his commands to any corner of the ship, be it the crowded gundecks below or the marines gathered on the foredeck. He wasn't to remain there. The operations room on a modern warship, a warship built to engage missiles and aircraft forty miles away, wasn't intended for close action command. He wanted to be on the bridge, where he could see his enemy, see their tiny consort, the *Kathleen*.

He gathered the warfare officers round him, four of them now that both watches were present, and briefed them as succinctly as he could, finishing by saying, 'Not sure what *Kathleen* has in mind. As you know her main gun has hydraulic problems. We are moving up. ROE remain the same as does the objective. Enforce the exclusion. Questions?'

There were none.

'Right. I will be on the bridge and I will make an announcement to the lads forthwith.'

Thirty seconds later he was back on the bridge and immediately spoke to the admiral aboard *Invincible*, insisting that his rules of engagement reflect the new threat analysis. Finally, his eyes still watching the surveillance camera monitor, he picked up the microphone and began to speak, his tone friendly and professional as he briefed the entire crew.

A minute later, the three Libyan ships appreciably closer and making no effort to comply with their commands,

*Kathleen* now nearer but still closing on the enemy ships, Lyall let his binoculars drop round his neck.

'Mad Irish bugger. He's closing enough to use his main gun at point blank range or his twenty mills.'

Lyall stepped back to the VHF radio and picked up the microphone. This was the last stage in the procedure, when the captain himself addressed the other ship, raising the game.

'*Ras Ali, Ras Ali*, this is the commander of the British warship *Dundee*. You have entered an exclusion zone. Turn away immediately, I repeat, turn away immediately. If you do not comply I shall be forced to take action. Please acknowledge.'

He crossed to the monitor, manoeuvring the camera to scan the bridge wings and deck areas of the *Ras Ali*. A figure was watching them with binoculars, and men moved with purpose about the lower aft deck. Off the port bow *Kathleen* was still racing ahead, her course bringing her round to overhaul the Libyans at close quarters.

Lyall looked across at Burnett. 'They are going to fight. We can't have that,' he said, unusually justifying himself. 'The *Kathleen* is all they have left. If anything happens to her . . .' He lifted the glasses back to his eyes and took it all in again. 'Full ahead on both levers. Number One?'

'Sir?' Burnett replied.

'We may have to fight the ship.'

'Full ahead on both,' called the man at the helm.

Burnett nodded.

'Then hoist the battle ensigns if you will, please,' Commander Lyall said softly.

'Aye aye, Captain.'

Burnett gave the order and as the bosun's mate darted off the bridge he crossed back to the camera control and zoomed in on each of the Libyan ships in turn, the uncomfortable feeling in his gut stronger than ever. The ship to port and astern of the *Ras Ali*, the *Ras Mohammed*, also had activity on her after decks, but the smaller vessel to her front and right, the *Salladin*, seemed quiet enough.

Ships are small, confined environments and before the white flags with their red crosses were halfway up to the yard-arms the word was spreading. The battle ensigns were up and if it came to it they were going to fight the ship. HMS *Dundee* was going into action. Tired seamen stood straighter, shoulders squared. Above them the battle ensigns signalled their intent and the petty issues didn't seem to matter any more, six hundred years of tradition ingrained deep in their hearts, tradition that had given them men like Drake and Nelson, the famous fighting ships like the *Temeraire*, the *Victory* and the *Agamemnon*, all who fought under the same huge white flag with its red cross.

*Dundee* surged across the oily swells, her 50,000 horsepower turbines driving the huge propellers, her speed exceeding 32 knots. The huge rooster tail of white foaming water churned out behind her, the battle ensigns snapping out from her yard-arms, coming abeam of the little Irish ship, heading her away from the danger like a blue whale with her calf.

Lieutenant Conway, the WREN officer of the watch, was still standing with binoculars held to her eyes. She said something, dropped the glasses to her chest and bounded across to the monitor, cranking the camera round to the aft deck of the *Ras Ali* as she spoke.

'Sir! Covers are off something on the centre ship.'

'Where?' Burnett asked crossing to stand beside her.

'Aft deck,' she replied, 'there!'

They both recognized the pair of square-ended objects simultaneously.

'Oh my God,' she said. 'That's a –'

'Captain,' Burnett called, and as he spoke a cloud of white smoke erupted from the box. 'EXOCET IN-BOUND!'

Lyall was across the bridge beside them in a second, his finger reaching for the microphone switch.

'Longeye! Alarm! Missile bearing 020, track 1237.' The cry from the radar plotter cut across the room and the Air Warfare Officer flashed a look down at his screen, the tiny contact identified by the computer generated number.

'Confidence level?'

'Certain!!'

'PWO—AWO, request Sea Dart.'

'AWO—PWO, you have Sea Dart.'

The captain's voice cut across their headsets. 'TAKE IT WITH SEA DART!'

'Missile director,' the AWO said smoothly. 'Take track 1237 with Sea Dart.'

The missile director sitting just feet from the AWO facing his consoles, acknowledged and as he did so the computer verified the target. Below the display screen there was a vertical row of buttons with two aside the top in a 'T' shape. His finger jabbed at the upper left button.

On the foredeck the launcher positioned between the superstructure and the deck gun snapped upright. As it did so the magazine covers slid back on their greased housings and a Sea Dart missile rose into the launcher. Immediately the launcher dropped on to its active mode, the radar scanners selecting its angle and direction, and half a second later the missile blasted away, searing off into the sky before dropping on to its track, closing with the incoming Exocet at a combined speed approaching Mach 3.

'Longeye! Alarm! Missile bearing 019, track 1238.'

'Take it!' Lyall snapped from the bridge.

Beside him Burnett and Conway watched the plume of white smoke that marked the track of their Sea Dart, the first lieutenant willing the missile on to its target, the first Exocet. He had been aboard *Glasgow* in the Falklands when her Sea Darts had failed. Four Argentinian Sky-hawks were on their attack run and finally, with her Mark

8 Vickers deck gun blazing away at them, *Brilliant*, just across the water, had engaged with her Sea Wolf systems, knocking down two of the Skyhawks. The problems with Sea Dart had been sorted out, but anyone who had been in the Falklands had a healthy respect for the vagaries of high technology.

Suddenly there was a brilliant flash of white yellowish light and as Burnett said, 'Got the bastard', the blast and shock wave swept over the ship. Below them Conway, the adrenalin racing through her blood, watched another Sea Dart rise into the launcher and blast off.

Lyall was now a cool machine. They had initiated hostilities. Rules of Engagement were changed. He pressed his throat mike switch.

'PWO–Captain. Take the centre ship with gun. Try for the aft deck area and bridge. Five rounds HE.'

In the dim light of the operations room the hooded figures moved with precision, the thousands of hours of training now bearing benefit. The Principal Warfare Officer acknowledged and looked across at his Point Defence Controller and the AWO gave him control of the gun.

'PDC–AWO, gun policy service PWO directing.'

'Thank you. PDC–PWO, take track 1234 with gun. Five rounds. HE.'

Now it was the Point Defence Controller's and the Gun Controller's fight.

'Port LAS centre ship. Aim at bridge.'

Up on the exposed deck the man sitting in the local area sight quickly took aim through the glass reticule. 'Aimer target!' he called.

Back in the operations room the Point Defence Controller spoke again. 'Gun Controller PDC follow LAS,' and looked up at the Principal Warfare Officer and nodded.

The PWO leaned forward. 'Gun controller–PWO, five rounds HE. ENGAGE!'

The gun controller sitting at his console pressed the trigger, a spring-loaded pedal beneath his foot, and the self-loading 4.5 inch gun began to fire, a high explosive shell leaving its barrel every second and a half.

Somehow through the smoke and noise Conway was still keeping watch on the Libyan ships. There was movement on the after deck of the *Ras Mohammed*, familiar shapes. She found that surprising, considering that they were in the middle of a battle. Anyone who could would be under cover. She checked her bridge. The rating at the steering position was in control. The *Dundee* was on course. Controlling her own fear, her heart pounding, she crossed to the monitor and cranked the cameras into the aft deck of the *Mohammed*, overriding whoever was on the camera controls down in the operations room. They will be wanting fall of shot she thought. She zoomed the camera in. Jesus! It is!

'Sir! On *Mohammed*. They have tanks!'

Burnett, who had gone out on the bridge wing to see what the *Kathleen* was up to – she had slowed in the water – darted back on to the bridge, the massive crash of the gun deafening as the light door swung open, but he heard the tone in her voice.

'Say again,' he yelled.

'Tank! Its turret . . .' she yelled.

'A tank. You mean a . . .' Burnett interrupted.

'YES! A bloody tank. Its turret is training on us!'

Lyall, his head down as he talked into the secure phone, quickly looked at her and began to move across to the monitor. As he moved the cable connecting his headset to the intercom snagged on something and the connector separated. Burnett saw this, took it in, and, trusting Conway's eyes, couldn't wait in case the men below weren't watching the monitor. He grabbed a microphone. 'PWO–Number One. The ship on the left, the *Mohammed*, take it with gun. Afterdeck. Ten rounds HE. Quick as you

348

can, lad!' Lyall scrabbled to get his cable re-connected and finally as their first shells slammed into the *Ras Ali*, he retook command. 'PWO—Captain. The *Mohammed*. Use Sea Darts as well. Salvo fire. TAKE IT OUT!'

'It's fired,' Conway yelled, 'Incoming!'

'We are out of range!' Burnett answered.

The Vickers gun was traversing as the radar control sighted on the new threat and as the gun stopped it began to fire, the recoil felt on the bridge, the muzzle blast deafening. Behind the gun two Sea Darts rose into the launcher and seared away into the sky. Burnett was grinning: his fist clenched, he punched the air. Across the water *Ras Ali* was on fire, great gouts of smoke rising from her superstructure where the 4.5 inch shells had hit her.

'Good job, Conway,' he yelled, 'now keep a watch on the *Salladin*.'

The *Kathleen* had now crossed behind *Dundee*'s stern and was lining up her bows on the enemy to make up for the lack of hydraulics to swivel her turret. At last in range, her 76 millimetre gun began to fire.

The fires on the *Ras Ali* were burning fiercely, black smoke from her bunkers mixing with whiter fumes rising from burning deck cargo and electrical wiring and she began to slew in the water, her steerage way gone.

Suddenly a massive blast tore through her, hatches thrown hundreds of feet into the air, debris and missiles atop smoking superheated plumes, the blast wave slamming into *Dundee*, deafening the men on the exposed gun decks. Further explosions followed, sympathetic secondary detonations as her cargo began to explode.

'Holy shit,' Burnett said in awe.

Lyall seized the initiative, snatching the microphone up. '*Salladin Salladin*, this is the British warship *Dundee*. Heave to, I repeat heave to, or I will blow you out of the water!'

349

The *Ras Mohammed* was now also burning, her bridge and upper superstructure a mangled, blackened wreckage, smoke from her afterdecks thick and black. Burnett raised his binoculars. A tank turret, part of the deck cargo and possibly the one that Conway had seen training on them, had been blown off its mountings and taken down the derrick between the aft holds, the wreckage now scattered, some hanging over the sides. Tiny figures of men moved in a dazed manner, someone directing them for damage control. She was slowing in the water.

'Strike your colours, damn you!' he said aloud. As he spoke ahead of them the two ships, one burning and one miraculously still afloat, but about to roll over and go down, the *Salladin* had dropped her colours and was also slowing in the water.

'*Kathleen, Kathleen*, this is *Dundee*, request you cease fire,' Lyall said calmly.

In the United Nations Security Council the heated debate raged on, as it had for six hours.

The permanent members, some with sweet hints of cheap oil and lucrative contracts in the Gulf States, and others with threats of the withdrawal of just those favours, were still divided over what course of action to take. Now that the Palestinian offer to negotiate was on the table, their terms for withdrawal out in the open, there was even more pressure from the floor of the still pro-Palestinian General Assembly to do just that. Negotiate.

The early offer was welcomed by many who, although supportive of Palestinian rights and claims to the Holy Land, were embarrassed by the sheer aggression of the takeover of Ireland and, while secretly admiring the sheer audacity of the move, were concerned that the Palestinians had gone a step too far. Many were from countries that were equally vulnerable. For all, the offer to negotiate allowed them to remain supportive under the huge pressure from the British, Americans, Australians, Canadians. The New Zealanders, another small island nation, as vulnerable as Ireland ever was, launched an uncharacteristic attack on the perpetrators, their ambassador shaking with anger across the floor of the Assembly the day before.

In the Security Council the mood was tense, diplomatic behaviour having long given way to plain speaking. The Palestinian delegation and the Libyan Ambassador had been summoned to appear before the council for the ninth time in as many days.

Sir Huw Tristan-Carter, in his shirtsleeves, was speaking, jabbing a finger across the table at the Arab delegations. 'I don't care what you say. We don't negotiate over the sovereignty of European countries. We don't negotiate over who possesses those lands. The last people who tried this were the Communists and the Nazis. Both lost. You will. If you think we will allow you to support your aggression and establish lines of communication and supply you are wrong. Her Majesty's blockade of Ireland will be enforced.'

'We protest,' the Libyan snapped back. 'International law allows freedom of navigation!'

'Don't give me that bullshit!' the American Ambassador snarled. 'How dare you quote international law! You break it more often than you observe it!'

'Gentlemen,' the leader of the Palestinian delegation put his hand up to speak. He was older than the Libyan, with impeccable manners and an old world charm even when angered. 'Let us not talk of blockades and enforcement. We simply want to discuss the way clear of these problems.'

'You know the way clear. The problem was created by you. Get the hell out of Ireland,' Sir Huw answered curtly, leaning back to accept a note passed to him by an aide.

'For fifty years we have been wanting the world's attention,' the Palestinian responded. 'Wanting to be heard, wanting justice. That's all. Wanting just what is ours. Now we are in a position to negotiate,' he made a humble gesture, a simple shrug, as though some happy chance had brought them to this new position, 'and be heard. Let us do that. Enough lives have been lost. We want a peaceful resolution. Let us talk. Agree where we go from here . . .'

'Lives? Peaceful resolution?' Sir Huw interrupted. 'Is that why one of your blockade-running convoys fired an Exocet missile at a Royal Navy ship? In the pursuit of peaceful resolutions?' he finished drily, handing the note to another aide indicating it should be shown to the American Ambassador four chairs round to the left.

Across the table the Libyan Ambassador's eyes narrowed for a second, a fleeting look of triumph, of arrogance. The Palestinian seemed surprised, but he recovered quickly. 'I know nothing of that. I'm sure it is some sort of mistake.'

'A costly one,' Sir Huw replied. 'The Royal Navy responded appropriately. They returned fire. The *Ras Ali* exploded and sank with all hands. The *Ras Mohammed* was also sunk. The *Salladin* took on survivors from the *Mohammed* and is under way towards the west. Make no mistake. The blockade remains and will be enforced.'

The Australian army contingent had arrived and were now billeted on the Isle of Skye alongside the Irish army units which had returned from the Lebanon, Macedonia, Cambodia and other United Nations peacekeeping duties. The Australians, poorly equipped for the cold and rain, were made welcome by the four thousand Irishmen and extra canvas was found to supplement their field tents. The Aussies, casual and friendly, moved among the Irish, seeking those who might be relatives, however distant, and finding someone who knew someone from that area didn't take long. Of all the men gathering across Britain, the men of Irish descent from a dozen countries, the feeling among the Irish Defence Force was strongest. Almost in sight of their homeland, and held back from actually crossing into Ulster, they trained and waited.

Across the bay on the headland of Borreraig was the piping college of the MacCrimmins, hereditary pipers to the Clan MacLeod. The facility, now bursting at the seams, was crowded with men, for every piper in the British army was present. They were there training for their role and the Australians were glad of the water that separated them, for there was much to do and little time and the pipers were up practising all night.

For the first time since the Allied landings in Normandy in 1944 a military force would go into battle with their pipers to the fore. The Celtic Forces of 'Dark Rose', the soon-to-be Royal Army of Queen Maeve, now also had their own tartan, but the men of the Black Watch had already sought dispensation. They had their own, and among the pipers gathered at Borreraig their familiar dark pattern stood out from the predominant bright green of the new tartan. Stewart's orders were clear. Every major formation would have a piper, and two entire bands would accompany Celt Force.

Across on the mainland other regiments were moving up to train alongside the units that they would operate with, and all day every day in the long narrow valleys and glens the huge Chinook helicopters thundered through the leaden sky, troops loading and unloading, their sergeants hammering home the message. Speed, speed, speed. There were other smaller troop-lift helicopters, but the broad bulk of the air mobile work would lie with the Chinooks. With only forty of them in the entire Royal Air Force, they could count on only thirty ever working at once. Ideally a light division in a rapid air–land campaign, the modern version of the 'blitzkrieg', would need double that number to drop sufficient men on to an objective to meet the most basic tactic of every battle: concentration of force. It had been agreed. If the British resources 'attached' to Celt Force came under serious pressure and required more airlift assets for a particular phase, then the Americans would supply the extra hardware from the flight deck of their carrier.

Modern air–land tactics were designed for one task, to isolate and destroy the enemy's formations, and while Stewart's force was only a third of the size of the forces arrayed before them, with his Chinooks he could move his concentration of force where it was needed, leapfrogging forward. Momentum, he kept saying to his commanders, if we go, nothing must stop the momentum.

The tractor had made its way up the hill at Tara that afternoon, the hydraulics that would normally lift a plough now supporting a large flat slab of stone. It approached from the fields to the north up the low green grassy slopes that rose to the flat top of the hill of Tara and the ancient ditches that ran in protective rings round the Neolithic stone structures.

Alongside the tractor three men walked, men dressed as farm labourers, old coats buttoned against the wind, wellington boots on their feet, weapons hidden beneath their coats.

The three men were guards and their leader was Joseph O'Reilly, the resistance commander for the entire north-west. His boldness delighted the people as much as it frustrated the Libyans and Palestinians, and he seemed to go from one strike to the next without sleep or rest.

There was now a £100,000 reward on his head, but the Arabs had yet to find out what he looked like, so he could move through the communities, the public houses and the church congregations with impunity. To all he was Fin mac Cumhal, the legendary Celtic warrior returned. He seemed fearless and utterly invincible, the perceptions having risen from an incident one day where five Libyans

354

soldiers had snatched a youth from a pavement. They were dragging him and kicking him towards their vehicle when O'Reilly had stepped from behind a parked car. He pulled his pistol from his pocket and shot all five men, killing two, disappearing into the crowd that had gathered to hurl taunts at the soldiers. Within days his name was sprayed on walls in elaborate artistic graffiti across the entire northwest, much of it the work of one youthful talented admirer.

He had changed in the last weeks. The hunted look was still there, but he had become, if it were possible under the circumstances, serene, as if he had at last found his role and an absolute unshakeable confidence that what he was doing was correct. His poetry was collected and read by firesides at night, parents telling children not to worry because Fin mac Cumhal and his band were out there in the dark watching over decent Irish people.

A mile away a second band of men waited, watching the approach roads to the hill and its little church and tourist shop. They had erected a diversion sign and expected no trouble. They were Morris's men and some had driven up from Dublin.

While they waited at the road the tractor edged up to the fence and O'Reilly cut the wire. The tractor moved through the gap and a few minutes later it was edging down into the first of the ditches, two heavy railway sleepers positioned the night before now lying across the ditch. Half an hour later it was done. The heavy stone was laid with great reverence on the soft damp earth to the east of the cross, and O'Reilly gently brushed some grass and mud from its flat surface.

'Well, Jamie,' he said softly, 'it's back. The Stone of Destiny has come home.'

'For a time at least,' the other man said.

'Sure. And tonight a slip of a girl will step down from the stone a queen. You can tell your children about this day, Jamie. People will speak of it. Where they were the night

355

Ireland reinstated its monarchy, the night Maeve was crowned upon this stone,' he ran his hands lovingly over its ancient surface, 'the Stone of Destiny, here at Tara, the place of kings.'

'You write it, Joseph.'

'I will.'

'Good,' Jamie replied fondly. 'Then enough of your dreaming, man. Let's go.'

O'Reilly stood and they walked away down the hill. The others would be here just on dusk, with canvas screens, panels, accessories and the tools of the set builder. They would take the sections of sleeper and convert them into what was needed. He looked across at a hill in the distance. The first beacon was there. They were ready.

Scott's sections of men were in place by nightfall. Four teams deployed round the hill. There were three defensive perimeters, the first a mile out from the hill, with resistance men at various positions as a picket line. They would not engage unless authorized, but were primarily there to report on any Libyan movements that might threaten the safety of the party at Tara. The second line was Scott's soldiers. The SAS teams were at the base of the hill, two at the road end, one on the northern side and one at the low summit that would give support where required. The firepower available was intended to simply stop and hold, if it became necessary, long enough for the four Lynx helicopters that would be sitting with engines turning at a base over the border. If they were compromised and things got nasty the helicopters would extract the people while the SAS and the royal bodyguard held the landing zone. They would then withdraw into the night.

With upwards of twenty thousand Libyan troops within twenty miles of Tara, it was by any reckoning a very dangerous endeavour.

The original plan called for everyone to be clear of the

356

hill an hour before curfew, but Scott had convinced them otherwise. If they waited until after curfew to begin the ceremony, then any vehicles on the road could be assumed to be hostile and avoided. Resistance activity had been deliberately stepped up in recent days, with five attacks on occupation personnel after curfew to discourage them. The tactic worked. Within the Libyan ranks morale was down. Whatever orders came down from their high command were now being flouted and patrols that should have been on the roads were parked in side lanes, their men out in a defensive posture. Twenty-two of their comrades had been killed in the last week, no new tactics had been developed to counter the command-detonated land mines or the armour-piercing rockets, and none of them wanted to die on some foreign country road far away from their homes and families.

Kiernan, Morris and the other participants had gathered in three farmhouses along the base of the southern end of the hill and were now approaching in small groups. There were twenty-four of them without counting the men who formed Maeve's bodyguard, who now wore her emblem under the patches on their uniforms.

One of Scott's men touched his shoulder and pointed. He nodded and lifted the image intensifier, counting them, trying not to think too deeply about the ramifications of their being caught or killed.

The entire resistance command was present, as was Ireland's Cardinal, Conor O'Neill, and the Irish President, Mary Johnson, who had been smuggled from her official residence that afternoon. Her guards, who never checked on her once indoors, would be none the wiser till the ceremony was all over. There were three women and three children representing Ireland's families, Father O'Leary and Kiernan. Millie Morris, who had said she wasn't coming, was there, to Scott's surprise. The relationship between her and Peter had become strained of late,

Peter's ever longer absences making things worse, and when he did return to his HQ the bickering was relentless. Now Millie was there along with Aisling, who had almost become Maeve's lady in waiting, and the camera crew, who with their state of the art equipment would beam the ceremony out 'live' to the world. There would in reality be a short delay to allow the party to get clear. As Kiernan said, it wouldn't take a rocket scientist to work out where the place of kings was.

Finally they were gathered, the canvas panels surrounding them, dully reflecting the light of the torches that were fixed in stands. In the centre a simple but heavy wooden chair with a high back and arms was raised on a box that had been covered with a heavy cloth of scarlet. To its right was an altar, covered in a simple white cloth, in the centre of which stood the cross of Cong, the ancient filigree cross that Scott and the British thief had stolen from the museum. Before it was the Ardagh chalice, its enamel and gold filigree reflecting the flickering torchlight, and the children who had seen it harshly lit in its glass case now saw it differently. In the soft light of the torches it became magical, something ancient and wonderful. Off to the left was the Stone of Destiny, flanked either side by a torch in a wrought iron stand .

Cardinal O'Neill, resplendent in purple vestments, cope and mitre, moved forward and knelt before the altar. Kiernan, watching, was struck by the significance of the moment.

Tara, the place of the ancient High Kings, was also the place of the old power, the druids of ancient Celtdom, and it was here that Saint Patrick had worked so hard to weaken that power and turn them towards Christianity. Now, many hundreds of years later, the highest churchman in the land, a man second only to the Pope, sprinkled holy water upon it, rededicating the ground and the Stone of Destiny for the ceremony. Tara, once the place of druids, magic and kings, was again hallowed ground for the same reason, and the same people. Kiernan looked across at the man who represented Patrick O'Sullivan. The Kerry farmer was still deeply affected by the death of his wife and some were saying that he should be replaced as Commander South-West. But his people were loyal and had said they would follow no other. They had taken his orders from wherever he was holed up and had been running the Arabs ragged in their area. Putting it right, as he said. Entire parts of Kerry, Cork and Clare were virtual no go areas after four in the afternoon for anyone but a local. Even the Libyan tactic of putting locals into their trucks as human shields hadn't worked: O'Sullivan's snipers shot at them anyway, always missing the hostages and always killing or wounding the soldiers.

Kiernan looked at his watch. Maeve would be arriving in a few minutes and over in County Donegal four men would have been at her parents' house an hour ago. They would have packed their things and escorted them across the border. They would be safe, at least. Cardinal O'Neill and Mary Johnson would return home and await certain arrest. Both had made that choice, both knowing just how important their role was, both understanding that imprisonment for political or religious actions and beliefs was a price to be paid. Neither could turn their backs, Johnson from the people who had voted her into office, or O'Neill from his God and his congregation. It hadn't been discussed, but Kiernan knew that interned they could become symbols as powerful as the new queen herself.

It was time.

# 11

Suddenly the hushed talk died. Maeve stood at the opening in the screens, Aisling at her left and Mary Johnson to her right. Her hair was down, falling over the back of the heavy cape, and as she began to move forward the cape opened and the green silk gown beneath shimmered in the warm flickering light of the torches. She wore the sword at her waist, one hand on the hilt and the other on the edge of the cape, and the gold torc was round her neck. The three women were flanked by elements of the bodyguard, from the Royal Irish Regiment and the Irish Defence Force. The Royal Irish men were distinguished by the hackle they wore on their headgear, a throwback to their Royal Irish Rangers past. Armed to the teeth, prepared to fulfil their duties, the bodyguard provided a rough contrast to Maeve as the party moved forward. She moved with demure confidence, her step firm but feminine, and the people parted to allow her through, many falling back so as to be able to watch her. Kiernan stepped forward, smiling.

'Just like we practised,' he murmured softly. She nodded, pulling the cloak closer. It was cold.

Cardinal O'Neill turned and faced her, his back to the altar, and asked that everyone line round the screen walls inside the semi-circle of flaming torches. Finally, everyone in place, he beckoned Maeve closer.

'Will you take communion, child?'

'I will,' she replied.

The mass began immediately, everyone aware that each minute they were there they risked capture or death. The Cardinal, resplendent in his vestments, cope and mitre, moved quickly through the reading and the preaching. Then, standing behind the altar, the candles at either end wavering in the snatches of wind that breached the screen, he took the chalice, the priceless Ardagh chalice, and began to pour the wine, moving through the ritual he had performed many thousands of times, taking the bread he had made himself that morning and breaking it as he said the words.

' . . . Take this and eat it. This is my body which will be given up for you . . .' Then the chalice. Kiernan, watching the ritual, was again struck by the way history repeated itself. If Saint Patrick could see us now, he thought. ' . . . it will be shed for you and for all so that you may be forgiven. Do this in memory of me.'

O'Neill beckoned to Maeve and one of her bodyguard stepped forward and spread his jacket on the ground.

She knelt.

The communion over, Kiernan, Mary Johnson by his side, beckoned and Maeve moved slowly in the torchlight across to the stone, the moment rich for all who were present. Finally she stood upon the stone and turned to face the people, now all masked or hooded to prevent their later identification from the television film. Cardinal O'Neill stood in front of her and made the sign of the cross before moving a little to the right to make way for the President. Mary Johnson didn't look at the cards Kiernan had prepared. She had learned her role.

'Maeve O'Donnell of the Clan O'Donnell of Donegal, descendant of the High Kings of Ireland, do you, standing before us on the Stone of Destiny, accept the Crown of Ireland, and Queenship of the Celts and accept the powers, authority and responsibilities borne by that office?' President Johnson asked.

Maeve raised her head, strong and proud. 'I do.'

'And do you,' the Cardinal went on, 'swear before God to faithfully execute the duties of Monarch to the best of your ability, to protect the weak, strengthen the family, and restore freedom to your people?'

'I do.'

'May God bless you this day,' O'Neill again, making the sign of the cross on her forehead, 'may he give you strength and courage for the fight ahead, may he bless you with wisdom and patience, kindness and humility, fortitude and steadfastness. May his love shine through you, now and evermore. In the name of the Father, the Son and the Holy Spirit, Amen.'

He stepped to the right and Mary Johnson to the left and together, representing Church and State, they waited as a small girl, nervous, shy and dressed in her Sunday best white dress and ribbons was pushed forward by her mother, holding out the tiara-like crown.

The Cardinal and President took it from her and each holding one side with both hands placed it on Maeve's head.

Mary Johnson stepped round to the front again, a small gold object in her hand.

'Maeve O'Donnell,' as she pinned the ancient Tara brooch to the cape, holding it closed over Maeve's heart, 'with this crown and brooch, I as President, and representing the people of Ireland, proclaim you our Queen, recognize your authority and pass to you the executive tasks of the President, Prime Minister, Dáil and Senate, to bring freedom to the land and the people and reinstate the constitution as and when you are able. Until then we, your subjects, invest in you the absolute authority to rule by decree and have powers over all laws, matters of state and your subjects as High Queen of Ireland.'

In the soft light the small group gathered could see the strength in Maeve's eyes, but as Mary Johnson took her hand and began to lower herself Maeve looked down quickly, her expression softening. 'Don't, please . . .' she begged in a whisper.

'I must,' Mary replied and the people watched their president go down on bended knee and kiss the hand of their new queen.

'Then rise,' said Maeve firmly, 'and be at my right side.'

She stepped down from the stone and settled herself into the heavy old wooden chair, her cape spread out from the brooch, the tiara twinkling in the soft light, her hand on the hilt of her sword, now the sword of state, that was unsheathed and standing on its point between her feet, as each of the hooded resistance commanders came forward to pledge allegiance to the crown using the names they had been given by Kiernan.

'I, Murtagh of the east, become your liegeman and pledge you my allegiance and that of my followers.'

It was, Kiernan thought, both medieval and magical, of sorcerers and legend. It was a scene that could have come through the mists of time. There should have been a druid, and men at arms and beasts roasting on the fires and mead drunk and music into the night. He hoped the cameras were catching it all. O'Malley's creative people had done a brilliant job. Joseph O'Reilly was suddenly beside him. 'Did you hear the roar, Professor, did you hear the rumble? I did. There is our true Queen.'

'If anyone would hear it, Joseph,' Kiernan said smiling, 'it would be you.'

For each she had a few words, asking of their families, and she surprised Rory McMahon by saying that when it was over she wanted to buy a puppy and would seek his advice. They were all enchanted, even Briget Villiers who was sceptical about the whole suggestion that Ireland needed a queen. Briget also had other things on her mind. Her sister had disappeared from the cottage they shared. She had been left sitting where she usually sat and when Briget returned she was gone. A bag had been packed with a few things so she hoped she was all right.

The last person forward was a captain in the Irish

Defence Force, the commander of her bodyguard. He pledged the unequivocal allegiance of the Irish Defence Forces. As he would be accompanying her into hiding he had no need to conceal his face and in the soft light Kiernan could see he had removed the cover from his new hackle, the three coloured feathers mounted behind an imitation Tara brooch. The royal hackle of Celt Force and the armies of the Queen.

At last the torches were extinguished and the screens and panels dropped and as the people moved away and Maeve's bodyguard escorted her down to the SAS men and the silent, darkened vehicles, Morris pointed a powerful torch at the hillside to the west.

There a farmer and his son, men who had been waiting in the cold, touched a match to the kerosene-soaked wood at the base of a huge stack that reached upwards ten or twelve feet like a haystack. It began to burn fiercely and on other hills a few miles distant other men saw the beacon and lit their signal fires, the announcement of a new queen travelling in the time-honoured way. Inside an hour there were beacons burning as far away as Kerry, Donegal, Mayo and Wexford, and people came out to see the fires on distant hilltops, explaining to their children that, just as the legend said, Queen Maeve had come at last, and as Queen of the Celts she would raise an army and the people would rise up and support her.

In monasteries and churches the bells rang out in the night, the monks and priests passing the word, supporting their people, their new Queen and their Cardinal who they knew would be in internment by morning.

Soldiers arrived at one monastery and, not understanding what was happening, immediately arrested the men ringing the bells anyway. Others stepped forward and they arrested them too. Then others took up the ringing and after the fifth group they shrugged, gave up and drove away.

Those who still had satellite dishes set up their video recorders for those who didn't and sat back to watch, and fifty minutes after the party had slipped silently away from Tara Hill, the BBC, CNN and Sky News interrupted their programming to take a 'live' feed from 'somewhere' inside occupied Ireland. Pre-warned, they had their commentators present, experts on royal procedure, constitutional law and Irish and Celtic history. The cameraman had done well – the occasional jerky movement merely added to the real 'live' feel of the event – and the world watched enthralled. The Irish, having long been told that their problem was an Irish problem, were now applying an Irish solution.

'There's no doubt about it,' one CNN commentator said. 'In this context, the President has transferred power and given a mandate to a new authority. Their Queen. As long as Queen Maeve has the mandate of her people, and the support of her people, she becomes the legitimate authority as with any other existing monarchy. This means that the new government, the Emergency Council, the New Irish Businessmen's Association or Patriots Council or whatever they call it, is now no longer – if it ever was – constitutionally empowered.'

'But in real terms?' the newscaster asked.

'She will have to take over. Force her rule. They are not going to capitulate simply because the Irish have decided to reinstate their monarchy. It will mean civil war.'

'Do you think she can force her rule?'

'If nothing else she becomes a focal point for the resistance, a light in the darkness, a symbol. She could also raise a force. Don't forget, there are now an estimated million people of Irish descent gathered in Britain. Now that number does include women, children, old, weak and so on, but it bears consideration. That group with the support, monetary and moral, of the forty-odd million Irish Americans, plus those that settled in Britain, would be a force to be reckoned with.'

In a small house in County Tyrone in Northern Ireland, Maeve's parents were watching the television. A senior member of the resistance and one of the planners sat discreetly at the back of the room. In front of them on the sofa Maeve's parents sat together, arms linked, hands held tight, her mother blowing her nose into a tissue and telling herself not to be so silly while her father, his heart bursting with pride, occasionally wiped a tear from his eyes.

'She's the queen,' Mrs O'Donnell said, trying to believe it all.

'And a grand queen she'll make, pet. A grand queen.'

One of the two men spoke up. 'Another thing to consider, Mrs O'Donnell . . . this makes you the queen mum.'

The couple on the sofa started to laugh.


In the vast camps on the hillsides and meadows in the Northern Irish counties of Armagh, Fermanagh and Tyrone, as the word spread, huge fires burned into the night. Music played and people, Irish nationals or of Irish descent from America, Australia, New Zealand, Canada, Britain, Argentina, South Africa, Kenya, Zimbabwe, returned expatriates from the world over, celebrated till dawn. A girl working in the mobile clinic at one 3000-strong camp outside Enniskillen shrieked with delight as she watched the television. She had worked with Maeve only weeks before, and was an instant celebrity as she was forced to tell people what she knew of Maeve O'Donnell of the Clan O'Donnell. They loved that. The sheer romanticism of the ceremony captured both their modern hearts and their Celtic souls, and suddenly there was pride in being clansmen with ancient blood ties and allegiances to the new crown of arguably the oldest constant civilization in Christian Europe.


The New Irish Patriotic Council was in heated session. The members, seven eminent Palestinians, were divided over many issues, but on one they were united and facing off against their five Libyan advisers.

Khalil Ashrawi, the elder statesman who had been fielding press enquiries and attending meetings with diplomats and emissaries, was as usual measured and calm. He cut through the anger and tension and brought them back to the agenda.

'Gentlemen, gentlemen. Please? We are making progress. The news from New York is good. As you know, the UN continues its usual fence-sitting. Every day our negotiating position gets stronger. Habash and Arafat are pleased with progress and have assured us of their full confidence as recently as this afternoon. Let's all calm down a little. I suggest we finish the business and cover this instant monarchy and the . . . other issues at the end.'

The 'other issues' had three of his Palestinian colleagues furious, but he ignored them and, trusting their long respect for him would silence them, turned to one of the staff members, an intelligence officer.

'Tariq?'

The young man stood and began his briefing. 'There are significant gatherings of Irish north of the border now. The earlier surge areas of Liverpool, London and Cardiff seem to have abated, because they are now arriving in Northern Ireland.'

'Any troops?' someone asked.

'Australians. Under a thousand. No heavy equipment,' the intelligence officer answered succinctly.

'And the others?'

'So far a rabble. The usual emotional rantings at meetings. Talk. Out in the camps some weapons have been seen, but it's an odd collection of vintage stuff, hunting rifles, shotguns, that kind of thing. I was up there last night. It's all a bit weird. Fires on the hilltops, singing, bagpipes playing, strange bloodcurdling screams. To be honest, the border guards are getting unnerved by it.

There have, however, been troop movements in Britain . . .'

'Sabre rattling,' someone scoffed. 'They have no mandate. They will keep trying to force the UN into some sort of enforceable resolution and that's not going to happen.'

'I just report what my sources are telling me,' the intelligence officer replied.

'Thank you, Major,' Ashrawi said, looking up around the table. 'Now, what do we make of this sudden appearance of a queen?'

'As CNN said,' one answered, 'a figurehead. Although I don't know why. Their resistance has been good. We will all admit that.'

'What concerns me,' said another, 'is the speed with which they mounted their resistance. Within days they were armed and operating. We expected that to take weeks, months even.'

'What of the claim that she will raise an army? We will be expected to make a statement to the press later.'

'That's just the point,' the first speaker replied. 'If they knew enough to set up a resistance in advance, then maybe we should consider their ability to raise a bigger force . . .'

'If she thinks she can raise an army from those drunks gathering at the border and take us on, then she is going to make a fool of herself. Our statement should repeat that we are the legitimate authority in Ireland. This is a republic. With a temporary security problem, true, but we remain an independent republic nevertheless. We recognize a queen no more than the Americans do.'

'What did we find at this Tara place?' someone else asked.

'Nothing. The place was deserted,' replied one of the older men, one of the Palestinian old guard. 'We picked up the Cardinal at his residence. He was waiting for us. Mrs Johnson was as well. They have proved to be subversive and will remain in internment. For the press let's play it down. It will die away if we let it. What's more of an issue is our reaction to the sinkings.'

'Reaction! I'll tell you what our reaction should be. Reprisals!' This was General Mustafa Saad, officer commanding the Libyan armed forces in Ireland. He was a strong man who had been advocating the iron fist from day one.

'No, General,' Ashrawi challenged as diplomatically as he could. 'I also suggest gentle handling of Cardinal O'Neill and President Johnson. We don't need martyrs.'

'Strike back! Enough of this weakness! One for one, or better ten for one. I'd hang the bitch.'

Ashrawi almost sighed. That had been the earlier problem. The Libyans had stepped up their hostage-taking and were now threatening firing squads for civilians. Until now only soldiers from the Irish armed services had been executed for breaking the edicts.

'We need Third World opinion, General, all of us. We still have it.'

'We need tanks, guns and ordnance! We need these scum to respect us! Fear us! Then your negotiations will go smoothly!' the general replied. 'I have been soft long enough. The next time my men are killed while innocently going about their duties I will unleash my reaction force.' He stood, pushing his chair back, the rows of ribbons on his battledress top a splash of colour against the olive drab. 'Enough of this weakness. They will not respect weakness.'

Out in the anteroom Ali Jassem, the Palestinian commander of the southern region, waited to speak to the meeting and as the Libyan general stormed past him, his subordinates following, Jassem's eyes narrowed. He had never liked the man. Too many medals for nothing, too much bluster, too much brutality from his men. The story was that Saad got his medals after a campaign in the south, fighting the rebels in Chad. Tanks and rocket artillery against villages and men in soft-skinned vehicles. That didn't take much courage, he thought, not commanding a slaughter from thirty miles away. The rumour was he was a cousin of Ghaddafi's, which would explain much.

He got up and entered the committee room.

Only four miles away in the Kelly home in Dublin, Simon was doing his best to hold the family together. His mother had still not got over the death of Sinead and he had taken it harder than he thought he would. He took strength from his own children and had laid down hard rules. He was the only one allowed to leave the street. He would find food, provide for them. Sarah and Alan, the bluster gone and now a shell of a man, had moved into the top room. Sue and David shared a room and Simon's two children were topping and tailing in Sinead's bed. They all worried about Mary, but every so often word came back through Father O'Leary that she was well and being cared for. He didn't tell them that she was now active in the resistance. They didn't need to know and would just worry.

Once in the underground network Mary had ceased to be a civilian to be smuggled to safety in the country. She had immediately volunteered for active service and her aptitude had pleased her trainers. She was a ferocious fighter: one cadre commander said she was 'as merciless and single-minded as only a woman could be'. At times she worried her own command. They had seen people go over the edge before and Mary Kelly, now thinner, gaunt, obsessed, her eyes wild with the cause and prepared to die at any time, was ready to take what they viewed as insane risks. She had lost her superficial femininity. Her hands, once stained with paint, were now grimy with gun oil and she carried her rifle everywhere. Her hair, once her pride, was filthy and hung in rats' tails, and her clothing smelled. Her feet, shod in only lightweight trainers, were perpetually wet and the cadre medic was treating her for the classic infantryman's complaint, trench foot, the sores open and bleeding. She cared not. She was driven by something, something unreal, but a few that knew her tale understood. While some resistance fighters lived normal lives, others, a super-hard core of impassioned zealots, lived like rats in the sewers and basements, coming out to strike without mercy. They were dubbed the rat-hole fighters and held in awe even by other members of the *buachailli*. They would strike and moments later they would be back in the sewers, basements or rooftops, having left no survivors. Mary was a hard-core rat-hole fighter and to many it seemed she had no compassion left.

Collaborators were shown no mercy. Six more men had been executed in the Dublin area, two for profiteering from the people, and four for outright collaboration. All had profited greatly from the invaders and thought they could continue safely. Women who had crossed over and formed relationships, however temporary and for whatever reason, were tarred and feathered and chained to a lamppost, a warning that dated back to the Nazi occupation of Europe.

Mary's cell were handed one such woman. Barely more than a child, she was obviously of almost substandard intelligence and barely literate. She had been seduced by chocolates and money, food to take home to her family and, Mary acknowledged sadly, the simple pleasure of a human touch, a few moments' caress when the world was ending around them.

The verdict of the four-member drumhead council was tar and feather and head shave.

Mary stood. 'No,' she said.

The others looked at her.

'Jesus, look at her!' she snapped at them. 'If we do it, we become as bad as them.' She turned and faced the frightened girl, whose normal vacant expression now looked back at her with big, frightened eyes.

'Do you know why you are here?'

'Waa?'

'Do you know why you are in trouble?'

The girl nodded.

'Why?' Mary pressed.

'For doing it with them. You know.' She smiled weakly and thrust her right forefinger into a circle made with her left forefinger and thumb.

'Jesus,' Mary muttered softly, shaking her head. 'That is wrong. Okay? You don't do that any more! Do you understand?'

'Waaa? Wi' no one?' the girl asked disbelievingly.

Mary shook her head, her patience running thin. 'No! You don't do it with anyone till I say you can! LOOK AT ME! If you do I will tell your mum and everyone in your building that you are a whore!'

That didn't seem to bother her. Mary reached out and grabbed the girl's long blonde hair, pulling it out. 'Give me the scissors,' she shouted.

'NO! Waaa . . .' The girl pulled back with a wail.

'If you do, I will cut your hair off! Okay?'

The girl nodded.

'All of it! I will know. People will tell me.'

The girl nodded.

Mary looked back at the cadre leader, her eyes pleading. 'I will vouch for her,' she said. The man was pleased, not for the girl but for Mary. It was like seeing someone come back from the dead. 'Fair play to ya,' he said.

It was John La Touche, another of the rat-hole fighters that facilitated the next change. He took a few of the group into a flat in Tallaght, where hot food, hot water and dry clothing, the first in two weeks, waited for them. In among the pile of things for Mary was her teddy bear, smuggled from her mother's home, a tiny sample bottle of Chanel No 5, a brand new cake of Cussons soap, and a big new full bottle of Head and Shoulders shampoo, something few people had been able to buy since the crisis began.

She sat on the bed, held the teddy bear and tried not to cry. Finally she began undressing, starting with her trainers that were rotting on her feet. They were painful. The medic was coming over later. When La Touche put his head round the door she suddenly knew who had found her her teddy, and the precious luxuries. She looked up and smiled. 'You are a pet. I want to cuddle you.'

'After we have showered,' he replied with a grin. 'I smell worse than you, and that's saying something.'

For the first time since Sinead had died and she had helped her brother kill her lover she laughed. She threw back her head and laughed.


Pat O'Sullivan hadn't shaved since Katriona's death and hadn't eaten anything substantial in the last week. He rumbled round a tiny disused pump shed a quarter of a mile from his command post centred further down the hill. The pump shed was bleak. Before her death, with the huge bounty on his head he never slept there, moving into the brush, sleeping somewhere different each night. Now he seemed to have given up. No longer cared. Damp, his sleeping bag was filthy and at night when he dropped into exhausted sleep he invariably just pulled it round his shoulders. He was a man in torment. The love of his life, his very reason to be was dead. His grief was total and he blamed himself. His fighters came to him for orders, but shielded him from outsiders, bringing notes from his sister who had moved on to the farm to take care of the children. No others were allowed, so when one of his people walked up the hill in the dying light with a visitor the guard challenged them. The fighter, who had known O'Sullivan since she was a child, and cared deeply about him was blunt.

'Look, I'm taking her to see Pat and you can piss off, right?'

'Why?' the guard asked looking at the visitor, wondering what she could offer. She looked equally wounded in some way and the Jack Russell terrier at her feet looked miserably round the wet brush as if it wished it were somewhere else.

The woman fighter was older and wiser than her years. A nurse, she had seen people in grief many times and she trusted her instincts. She was very worried about Pat. He had not cried, not once. It was building inside him and he would either crack, or go berserk and vent his pain on the enemy; either way it was bad. The girl had walked and hitchhiked all the way from Wexford and that earned the right to see Pat.

'Never you mind,' she replied, pushing past him.

O'Sullivan was sitting beneath the overhang of a rock, his coat filthy and wet when they arrived. Jesus, the fighter thought. He looks like shit. He had lost weight, his cheeks beneath the stubble of the new beard were hollow and his eyes were red-rimmed. His hair was filthy and he barely acknowledged them as they sat down beside him.

'You have a visitor, Pat,' she began. There was no acknowledgement. He just stared off into the gathering dark.

'Thanks,' the visitor said to the fighter. 'You can go now.'

The woman looked at them both and smiled. Not a wound in sight, no bullet or bomb, but casualties as sure as those with visible injuries. She nodded and moved off down the hill and the girl settled herself down beside O'Sullivan, the little dog nestling beside her.

'They killed my John,' she said simply. 'It's funny how no one seems to understand. They expect you to just go on. He is with me though. His spirit. I can feel it.' She stroked the little dog's neck and looked out into the dark. It was getting cold now and her coat was light, but she was more conscious of his presence beside her. It was brooding, large, slightly threatening. 'He was my brother. I loved him so much.' She smiled. 'When we were little, he wanted a brother and didn't have one, so he used to dress me up as a boy and call me Bob. I thought this was all normal until someone pointed it out. I pulled the clothes off and went to my room. I didn't want to be a Bob. He bought a farm. They took it. Killed him . . . I . . . I hate them,' she said, her voice cold like the wind.

He looked at her like he had just noticed her. 'Who are you?' he asked, his voice an irritated rumble.

'Sue Villiers.'

'I know a Villiers. She's a madwoman.'

'My sister,' Sue said.

'Well,' he replied, 'that's no surprise. Now bugger off and leave me alone.'

She ignored him and leaned back against the rock. 'John used to tell me to bugger off. He would be playing with his friends and a little sister was just a nuisance . . .' She talked on and it was well past midnight when he looked over at her and shook his head.

'Don't you ever shut up?'

'No.'

'Stupid cow. Here.' He slung her his sleeping bag. She took it and moved closer wrapping it round both their shoulders. He didn't move away. He just looked back off into the night.

'Tell me about Katriona. What was she like?' she asked. He ignored her, his jaw clenching. 'She must have been strong. I can feel her here now. She is with us.'

'What? You are as mad as your bloody sister,' he said.

'Her spirit. She is here beside you. I can feel her. Strong, warm, bright. What was she like? The nice bits now, because she is here listening and we don't want you two to start a scene.'

She picked the little terrier off her lap and placed it on his knees. It barely woke and settled back down.

'I always know when John is around. Think about it, Pat. Think about the things that were Katriona. Think about her thoughts, what made her laugh, her love. Could that just die? No way. The soul lives on. It is indestructible. She is here. Her soul. Her spirit. That thing that made her what she was, that soul that your soul loves, is still here.'

She fell silent then, but noticed an hour later, when his big scarred hand began to move over the little dog's back, the stroking gentle, the touch almost a caress.

'It's funny, I know he is here with me,' she began again, 'and that helps, but dear God, I miss him so much,' her voice faltered, 'and sometimes I want to die too.'

He looked across at her and for the first time since his wife's death a small bleak smile crossed his face.

'Join the club,' he murmured. He put his arm around her shoulders and pulled her closer. 'But Katriona would be giving out about that,' he finished.

'Would she?' Sue asked, blowing her nose noisily.

'Oh yes. She was the most wonderful person I ever knew. Strong. A will like oak and a heart the size of a mountain. Beautiful, too. There was a fella from Dingle who was keen to start courting her, but one look and I knew.'

'Did she?'

'Jasus, no! She thought I was a clod. I was so shy I almost fell over my boots on our first real meeting. She had the good grace not to laugh.'

Sue didn't. She giggled delightedly. 'Go on! Where was this?'

'The fair. I was twenty-two and she was just nineteen.' He quickly looked off into the dark again and she knew the tears were coming at last. A moment later his big shoulders began to heave. 'Oh dear God . . .' and he began to cry, great racking sobs that came from deep within him. The little dog woke and sat up and as his hand reached down to stroke it, it lifted its little head and licked his chin and he cuddled it closer and rocked backwards and forwards, his head bowed, and he wept.

She wrapped the bag tighter round them and she cried too, not for Pat or John or for herself, but for them all. That was the pattern until dawn, tears and talking, long rambling monologues, and when the sun came up Sue felt she had known the woman Pat O'Sullivan had loved. Late the following day she stood up and stretched her legs.

'I want a hot bath and some food. Coming?' she asked.

He nodded and stood up too.

## Wadi Shati, Libya

They had been moving for two nights, marching with their kit on their backs the last forty miles, and now just before midnight they were at the rendezvous. The officer signalled silently back to his men and they dropped as one to the ground. This was the fifth and last group in and the men in lightweight sand-coloured desert fatigues settled down under cover in the base of the gully. It was cold, and several of them had pulled balaclavas down over their faces.

So far it had been a textbook penetration of their much practised method, the silent, fast night march, following insertion by helicopter. The big American Blackhawks had dropped them two hundred miles inside Libya, their pilots following the terrain with night vision equipment, their bellies almost scraping the rocky ground below, three of the big machines with modified long wheelbase Land Rovers slung on very short strops beneath their fuselages. They would far rather have parachuted in or driven over the border from Chad in their beloved pinkies, but the planners had considered the risks of breakdowns or discovery too high. The final plan called for 104 men to arrive at the rendezvous on foot ready to deploy for the assault by 0200, to cover the last mile and a half. Once in position they would move on the target at 0400, eighty-six of the men at the camp, eighteen to take and hold the airstrip. It was the classic Special Air Service operation. Intelligence gathering, followed by a deep insertion and a killing blow, right where it all began in the 1940s with the Long Range Desert Group. For many of the men gathered silently in the gully, the SAS had come home, back to their roots, and they had brought with them their new colleagues, eighteen Irish Defence Force soldiers, rapidly absorbing the skills of the special forces men they were with.

The officers in command of each of the five teams moved forward and as the last of the commanders slid into the hollow the colonel put down the radio headphones he was listening to. His ops officer, an Arabist and one of seven men dressed in Libyan army uniform, took them and kept listening. The last man in the hollow just sat, sipping from a bottle. He was one of the pair that had been watching the camp for three weeks, and the beard, matted hair and filthy clothing said much.

''Allo, Jeff,' one of the grinning newcomers said. 'You need a bath, my son.'

'Fuck you too,' the soldier replied drinking from the bottle again. It was almost an endearment. After weeks sitting in a rat-hole, close enough to see into the Libyan camp, sneaking out at night to put up the aerial and transmit high-speed coded information back, he was pleased to see his comrades. Pleased the job was nearly over. Pleased they were going in. He had seen the hostages every day, inside the razor wire fence, and had been willing them to keep the faith. We are coming. Soon now. We are going to take you home.

'Everyone in okay?' Colonel Forrest asked, ignoring the exchange.

All nodded except a captain. 'Corporal Sowerby. Got a few stitches in his chin.'

Forrest nodded. A few stitches were of no consequence. 'Right. Sitrep. Nothing has changed. Might have an extra handful that arrived in a truck this afternoon, but other than that it's all as planned. Jeff will lead blue team in from the east. I will take in the others. Bob?'

'Sir?'

'Your team can move out now.'

The officer nodded and slid over the depression. His smaller group had the furthest to go, another mile and a half to the airstrip. Even carrying lighter loads – they had none of the belt-fed machine guns or claymore mines – they would have to move to cover the three miles with their fifty-pound packs in under an hour without being seen. The Land Rovers, now painted in Libyan army colours, with skirts and façades to make them look like the Russian four-wheel-drives the Libyans operated, would be used in the camp assault, the incredible firepower they were able to deliver essential to keep a battalion at bay and if necessary engage it.

At a remote airstrip in neighbouring Chad, 270 miles to the south, secured through some very heavy pressure and promises of soft loans, four Lockheed C130 Hercules were preparing to take off. The four-engine short field Royal Air Force transports were loaded, starter units in position and crews in place. Alongside them on the western end of the runway, eight Apache attack helicopters and two scout helicopters had lifted off an hour before, their weapon pods fully loaded. They left as two four-ship formations, each with their scout out in front and each able to deliver the same firepower as a battalion of men, but only for a minute or more. This would be the first action for the new improved minigun mounted in the Apache's nose since the problems in the Gulf War and specialists from the manufacturers were present. The helicopters would shuffle along the Chadian side of the border hugging the ground and slip across the border into Libya further to the west. They would refuel at a dump positioned two days before, make for the objective to arrive at precisely 0350, then stand off and await orders from the ground commander.

Further to the east and approaching at six hundred miles an hour was the cover screen. A force of six RAF Tornado GR3s, the air defence variant, was mixed with twelve US Navy F-14s from the carrier *Forrestal* with her battle group in the Red Sea. One hundred miles out behind them was a Boeing AWACs which would hold over the Chadian side of the border, and a pair of tankers that would loiter over Sudanese territory to refuel the fighters and C130s on their way out.


0340 hrs. The soldiers moved forward through the rocks, silent shadows in the night, towards the coils of concertina razor wire that marked the edge of the detention area. Beyond the wire in the flat glare of overhead lights, three large tents dominated the centre ground. Five Libyan soldiers moved around the tents in a bored patrol. To the right was a smaller canvas structure which they knew was a latrine area and to the left a small water tank on wheels was parked near a long trestle table where the hostages collected their food each day, a glutinous mass of curried potatoes, vegetables and chicken that never varied.

The gap in the wire was to the left, facing the larger military camp half a mile away, and consisted of a pair of four by four timbers crossed at the centre that could be dragged round to provide an opening. The guards were sloppy and recent satellite photos had confirmed the SAS observers' intelligence, that invariably the gap was left open and the duty guards, never more than forty men, walked through constantly. Outside the gap was a small line of lean-to shelters, and some canvas awnings spread over a small prepared revetment. A four-wheel-drive vehicle was parked by the awning, and forty yards down the track to the camp a heavy Mercedes truck sat in the moonlight. The officer pulled up his night vision gear and studied the vehicle. Garish paintwork and rows of brake lights along the entire back end identified the rig. It was most likely a sub-contracted haulier, Yemeni or Egyptian. He might be asleep in the cab or underneath. A second smaller four-wheel-drive moved slowly round the outside of the detention area.

As they watched it stopped at the eastern end and shut down its engine and lights. The SAS men watched as the driver and his companions lit cigarettes and began to talk.

The officer commanding blue team, the twenty-man force about to take the detention area, signalled to the sergeant, pointing at the vehicle and holding up two fingers, then tapping his watch.

The man nodded. Seconds later two soldiers detached themselves from the group and moved round towards the vehicle.

The officer looked at his watch. Although everyone knew what time they were due to hit the target it didn't matter if the pair of soldiers were a few seconds early. It would be absolutely silent and they would hear nothing at the gate or in the camp.

He looked across at his sergeant, nodded, and began to move forward, his section spread out behind him. The sergeant and his group moved further out, to cut the road to the camp.

The other three groups had arrived at the camp and were in position. Two of the teams were spread in four-man sections along the eastern edge, heavy belt-fed machine guns positioned for best advantage. Two of each section would operate the gun, one would shoot from a stand a few feet away, using a high-powered rifle with night spotting equipment, and the last would operate the claymore mines that they had just dug in. On the hill to the south the last team was settled in, with two more heavy machine guns, mortars from the backs of the vehicles and Milan anti-tank weapons to be used in an anti-infantry role against bunkers or trenches that might not have been spotted. Colonel Forrest, about to command the engagement, was also on the hill with his radio operator, operations officer and his number two, Major Busby Grogan.

The claymore mines were in place, the first teams were ready, one at the airstrip, one at the hostage camp and the third outside the communications trailer and command bunker below him. He looked at his watch and as he did so, the radio operator looked up, his head cocked to one side as he listened to his tiny space age receiver that decoded a satellite transmission.

'Choppers are here, boss.'

Forrest nodded. That was the final loop closed. One of the helicopters was equipped with a mine dispenser, and as battle began, if the Libyans looked like breaking out to the west, the Apache would swoop down and sow a minefield. The mines were new. As they hit the ground they buried themselves a few inches and activated. Then proximity tremblers would detonate them if anything moved within three feet. Forrest checked his watch again. Six minutes to go. There were some eight hundred men in the camp below, a reinforced battalion. He had his small force and four helicopters in reserve. He was not concerned. The regiment only failed when someone fucked up or fate took a hand. Mechanical failure, storms, cold, or bad intelligence and bad training. They had got here. The gear was working. His training was thorough and his intelligence was as good as it could get. It was his men that had been watching the camp and airstrip for weeks now. He looked across at Busby Grogan. They had served together for a long time now, seen action in the jungles of South America on anti-drug campaigns, Afghanistan, Belize, Northern Ireland and in the Gulf. Their friendship had been strengthened by adversity, forged the way only soldiers understand, in combat.

'Right, Busby. Let's do it,' he said crisply.

Grogan grinned and pressed a small button on a communications unit. On the plain below them four men, balaclavas pulled down, moved the last few feet to their objective. Two stepped into the communications trailer and with silenced Heckler and Koch MP5s, shot the three duty operators and their officer. It was brutally efficient. Each man died instantly with two bullets in the head. Even as they were falling one of the SAS soldiers was slinging his weapon and pulling wire cutters from his pocket. He cut through each connecting cable between the big transmitter receivers and as they dropped silently to the ground outside, he pulled the cable connecting the trailer to its portable generator, and cut it in two.

Forty feet away in the command bunker the other two soldiers stepped through the tent flap. There were nine men in the bunker and only one got anywhere near his weapon in time. He was the first to die. This was less targeted, bullets hitting men in the chest, but it was all over in seven seconds, one soldier stepping forward and finishing off one wounded Libyan who could still raise the alarm. Then they were out into the night meeting the other two and making their way back to their positions.

At the airstrip, two soldiers entered a Portakabin and took out the duty officer and another man who sat smoking and chatting with him. The bigger operations room and mess area for the duty patrols was in a pair of Portakabins with a connecting door. Four soldiers entered there and with silenced weapons killed the men that sat smoking and drinking tea. A few seconds later the bodies lay on the floor, the blood mixing with spilt tea, scattered sugar and soggy tea bags, the bright yellow labels in stark contrast. One man had fallen forward, his face now resting in a bowl of hummus at the table. One body twitched for a few moments, the man's nerves in their death throes, his blood pooling on the pages of an Arabic newspaper he had been reading.

The SAS officer entered and did a quick body count.

'Four to go, boss,' one man said.

'In the vehicle,' the officer replied. That was the full tally. They waited in silence as the old Toyota Land Cruiser made its way back to the cabin area and as it pulled to a halt its four occupants were dealt with. The airstrip was now in the hands of the SAS, and ten men of the team began to move down the road to the camp to set up a defensive position as four of the remaining eight pulled the bodies from the Toyota and drove away, their battery operated runway markers in the back.

The officer pressed the button on his communications device and with two men left at the Portakabins he began to make his way down to the defensive position, the last man left checking the aircraft start-up unit that was sitting on the oily dirt apron.

Blue team at the camp had been waiting for the signal from the airstrip and now made their move.

Five men crossed into the area covered by the awnings outside the gate, a sixth moving very quickly up to the parked truck. Three sections of four men slid through gaps that they had cut in the razor wire moments before, two of each section moving towards a predetermined tent, the remaining two sweeping outside in a carefully planned and well rehearsed manoeuvre. The six men, two outside the left line of the tents, two inside and two outside on the right, moved forward at a slow jog, using the shadows, looking for the guards who were patrolling the camp. Inside the tents the SAS men, night vision goggles heavy on their heads looked for targets among the sleeping forms on the rows of mats on the floors. In the middle tent, a guard dozing in a chair at one end was knocked senseless by a punch to the base of the ear. He collapsed on to the floor, an untidy heap.

Outside the action had begun. The two SAS men at the eastern end engaged three guards smoking behind the canvas latrine, their silenced actions clicking in the night. One of the pair of soldiers that had taken out the men in the vehicle two minutes before fired three aimed rounds into the camp through the wire when another man walked out of the latrine buttoning his trousers behind the pair that had just killed his comrades. At the eastern end of the camp two SAS soldiers opened fire on a group of men standing at the water tank. One of them had his hand on his rifle, his finger inside the trigger guard, and as his comrades were falling around him, he managed to squeeze off a burst. They went high, but the full muzzle blast from his Kalashnikov assault rifle cracked across the camp. He died a second later.

Just then a vicious fire-fight developed in the sandbagged area beneath the awning at the gate. There were more than twenty men in the immediate area and some of them, behind sandbags when the SAS assault began, had survived the first critical seconds. Tracer rounds arced into the sky, men screamed and yelled, unsure of what they were shooting at. One of the shadowy attackers flung a pair of stun grenades into the middle and seconds after the blast two of his comrades moved in to finish off the resistance up close.

As suddenly as it had begun the firing stopped.

In the tents the hostages, woken by the gunfire, were confused and terrified, some standing, others crawling away from the canvas sides. In the western tent, the nearest to the gate, a burst of fire had lacerated the tent wall.

'Quiet,' snapped an SAS man, as yet unseen in the corner. 'We are British army. Lie down on the floor! Lie down! British army! We are British soldiers. We have come to take you out of here. But first lie down!' His voice carried command. People dropped to the floor. 'Check yourselves. Check your neighbours. Anyone been hit?'

'Oh Christ,' someone said, 'you're here . . . We have been waiting for so long.' Someone else began to cry.

'There's time to talk later. Only speak if you have been hit!'

'I think I am,' someone said. 'It's warm . . . sticky. Oh I am!'

The other soldier crossed to the speaker, snapping up his night vision goggles. It was Jeff, the bearded, dusty man who had met the newcomers. He dropped to his knees, switched on a tiny Maglite torch and held it in his teeth as he bent over the lad on the floor.

'Flesh wound. You'll be okay,' he said around the torch. Breaking open a battle dressing he quickly and expertly staunched the blood flow from the entry and exit wounds in the boy's calf. He lifted his head to look at the boy's face. It was pale. He was going into mild shock. 'Relax, son. I've had about four wounds like this. Leaves a scar that impresses the girls no end.'

'Really?' he asked weakly.

'Promise. The doc will clean it up a bit on the plane. Take these.' Jeff passed him two tablets and a water bottle and as the boy took the tablets he pulled a drip from his kit.

'We were waiting for someone to come. Well, hoping,' the lad next to him said.

'Been here for weeks, sunshine!' Jeff said cheerfully, the torch now in his hand shining at the speaker. 'You go to the loo every day at about four. Your other shirt is blue.'

The boy's eyes widened and a smile broke across his face.

'Listen up,' the other soldier said, listening in the lightweight headphones he was wearing. 'We are going to move out of the tent, towards the back of the compound. Quickly and quietly. No talking. Let's go.'

'You're Irish,' one of the children said in delight.

'And what else would I be?' he replied with mock severity, then reached out and ruffled the boy's hair. ''Course I am, lad. We're taking you home.'

In the middle tent, the women's tent, the two soldiers

were having trouble keeping them quiet. The shout of 'British army! Lie down!' as the fire-fight at the gate erupted had only kept them down for seconds before they were up kissing each other, throwing their arms round each other, laughing, crying, and trying to hug the soldiers. Unhooking a girl from his neck the corporal bellowed, 'BLOODY SHUT UP!'

They did. There was a stunned silence.

'NOW DOWN ON YOUR FRONTS!'

They did.

'Anyone hit? Anyone hurt? Check yourselves. Check the person beside you!'

At the camp battle was joined. Libyans woken by the brief fire-fight at the gate began moving round the camp, junior officers running towards the command bunker or their sections. Someone fired into the air and a bellowing non-com ordered cease-fire. Men were running towards trucks, pulling on kit, when the SAS sections opened fire.

As the heavy machine guns poured their scything fire into the lines, claymore mines were detonated, the small curved backplates almost blown out of their mountings as they spread thousands of ball bearings out in an arc, cutting down running men and canvas with savage equality. SAS snipers picked off the officers as they approached the silent, darkened command bunker seeking orders they would never receive.

On the hill they spotted a truck begin to move and second later it burst into flames as a Milan anti-tank rocket exploded in the engine. The crew from the same SAS vehicle began to drop 81mm mortar rounds into the camp, one bomb leaving the barrel every second and a half, the mortar's baseplate dug into the dirt beside the vehicle. Tracer rounds arced through the night as the Libyans began to return fire, some small areas of concentrated activity pinpointing the locations of the officers for the attackers. Milan rockets took out the positions. A minute later the blast of the high explosive mortar rounds landing in tent lines that had been peppered by the claymores was enough and Colonel Forrest signalled the cease-fire and passed his adjutant the microphone for the bullhorn speakers, himself talking into a second microphone, this time to the Apaches that were loitering a mile back over the ridge. While he spoke his eyes continued to take in the devastation below in the camp. Men lay dead and dying in the light of the burning tents and bedding, upended tables and destroyed equipment. This was the face of modern warfare. Concentration of power.

'Brave soldiers of the Libyan forces, here is a message for you all,' the ops officer began, speaking in classical Arabic, his voice booming out of the speakers. The return fire below began to peter out. 'There has been enough killing. We will let you collect your wounded and treat their injuries. But if any man picks up a weapon, if anyone acts in a hostile manner, you will all die. Stay inside the camp. Do not leave the perimeter.' His voice cut across the night into the stunned defenders. 'O Arabs, brave Libyan soldiers, the book says it is wrong to treat others badly or to be cruel. There is no place in paradise for those who have broken the laws of God. We have come to take our children home. Do not try to stop us. Look to the west and see what awaits those that try.'

Below in the camp a man either insane or fanatical had snatched up a rifle and was running toward the ridge shouting words that were unintelligible. He was shot dead with one bullet. Forrest ignored it and watched to the west. An Apache had shuffled forward, to the ridge top, its pilot using night vision equipment, but careful not to look at the flames in the camp, keeping his eyes on the target area to the west. He pressed the triggers on his weapon systems, rockets streaked from their pods and the minigun began to fire, the multi-barrel gatling gun pouring thousands of rounds into the rocks. In a second and a half the Apache had torn up an area the length of a football ground and the message was clear to all.

'Treat your wounded and do not attempt to interfere with us,' the adjutant finished. It would not stop all resistance, but it would certainly make it difficult for the few remaining officers to rally a counter-attack.

'Okay. Clear the aircraft to land,' Forrest said to Grogan. 'Orange and green teams remain on site. Vehicles okay?'

Grogan nodded. They now had six Libyan soft-skinned vehicles which meant he could hold their own Land Rovers for his two rearguard teams. 'They have a bloody great truck over at the compound, too. Loading now,' he finished, lifting the mike on his radio.

'Long reach, long reach, this is Chieftain.'

'Chieftain go.'

'Long reach, caramel caramel caramel.'

'Roger, Chieftain, we have caramel.'

Grogan looked up at Forrest. 'Inbound now.'

'Right. Casualties?'

'Four. Two down below in my team. Both minor. Two at the camp. A hostage took a round in the leg, seems okay, and one of ours. Horrocks. That's a bit more serious. Flash burns, and a bad neck wound. He is stable, but the medics want him at the airstrip and on his back.'

'Get him loaded now. I don't want anyone being bloody heroic,' Forrest said, rising to his feet and signalling to his command vehicle driver to get started up. 'See you there.'

At the hostage compound the SAS men in blue team had left the Egyptian truck driver tied up at the roadside and had driven his old Mercedes with its forty-foot high-sided trailer round to the eastern end of the compound where they were lining up the Irish hostages, seating them in rows. The little ones, some as young as eight or nine, were grouped together with several of the older girls, one of them with clear pre-established authority. They learned she had insisted that the captors allow lessons for the young ones, and she and several others had taught classes each day. She had set up a junior section and also insisted that she and two others be allowed to sleep with the children. The Libyans had agreed, but otherwise males and females were separated in accordance with Islamic standards. There had been other victories, small but significant. She had negotiated for vegetables daily, fresh fruit once a week at least, vitamin supplements and enough of the desalinated water to be on hand for them to wash every two days.

Now she moved down the two rows of younger children, chatting to them, easing worries and the fear of being woken in the middle of the night by shooting and more men with guns. In two instances brothers and sisters had been reunited and they sat huddled, smiles of contentment on their faces. The section medic moved down the line doing rapid checks on each child, separating those with minor cuts, three with early signs of dysentery and two with chest infections, and sitting them with the lad who had taken the bullet through the leg. He had got over the shock and was now a minor celebrity among the others, the older ones having helped it along by asking for his autograph and making appreciative noises about the saline drip that was plugged into his arm. He had limped over to the truck supported by a Libyan rifle, bayonet end down into the dirt, before they were settled into rows. Most of the soldiers had stripped down and handed their jackets and fatigue shirts to the smaller children who were feeling the cold. There would be blankets on the aircraft and one of the Hercules carried a trauma team. So far they had got off lightly with only one serious injury, the soldier with the messy neck wound, who was now breathing through a tube into his airway, a drip in his arm.

'How many?' the officer asked.

'I make it one sixty-two, boss.'

'More than we thought. Anyone missing?'

'They say not.'

'Then start loading them. Get the den mother on to it. Little ones first. Cram 'em in. There's a couple of Land Rovers coming over. I want as many as we can get in the first trip. One pinkie in front. Move it.' As he finished speaking they could hear the first of the Hercules on final approach at the airstrip.

Forty miles to the east was the town of Sabha. From there the main trunk road swung round to the north as it wound its way to Tripoli. To the south-west was Awbari, and both towns had sizeable garrisons and all-year air bases. The Hercules would have appeared on radar from the south, from Chad, where the historical hostilities would ensure it was treated with suspicion. They were now compromised.

The first Land Rover drew to a halt beside them, fresh from the battle at the camp, the men in goggles with scarves pulled tight round their faces. They had dropped the skirts and façades somewhere and the vehicle was back to its standard angular SAS profile, made up of bullbars, roll cage, machine guns, both heavy and light, and rocket launchers. The rest of the frame was taken with other kit – camouflage netting, radios, fuel cans, shovels, ropes, spare tyres and sand tracks. There was very little room for extra people, but some of the SAS men scrambled aboard anyway. The following two were different. Standard Libyan army equipment, they could load at least fifteen people into each and they began immediately, Forrest pushing on in his Land Rover for the airstrip road. The Mercedes truck pulled out after them, the final 130-odd people crammed into it. They were hanging off the sides, seated on the roof, four people inside the cab alone. The SAS men scrambled on where they could, some riding on each of the three vehicles as they pushed up the rocky road towards the airstrip where the third aircraft had just landed.

On the dirt apron a soldier stood, a pair of neon signal beacons in his hands, working the last aircraft to where they wanted it parked. As it turned, four engines still running, its rear loading ramp was already lowering. Inside, the doctor and three medical orderlies were already setting up their equipment. In all three aircraft, blankets had been laid out on each of the hard canvas seats, and on each seat a litre of water, a carton of apple juice, a piece of fruit and a pack of fresh sandwiches awaited the arrivals.

The fourth Hercules was standing off a few miles away – it would not land unless they had problems with one of the primary three – and one of the helicopters was now over the airstrip perimeter in its hunter killer mode, the pilot with his forward-looking infrared equipment scanning the area for any threats, one of the tiny scout helicopters moving a mile out in front, popping up behind rocks and ridges to look ahead with a periscope camera.

As the convoy approached the waiting aircraft, the Libyans back in the camp had overcome their initial confusion and mustered some sort of command. Sporadic firing had broken out. The Libyans weren't sure where the enemy positions were and were raking the desert with tracer fire. At the northern end of the camp a heavy machine gun opened fire, and the nearest SAS team quickly moved sixty yards to their right and fired a Milan anti-tank round into the position, silencing it. Grogan decided it was time and called the helicopters in to suppress the camp while they made their escape. There would be two vehicles coming back from the airstrip, and with the two they had, no one should need to cover the distance on foot. He gathered up his handful of men from the ridge and they began to move down to the teams at the eastern flank, who were now returning the sporadic shooting with aimed sniper fire using night vision equipment. Each time they hit a target the firing died down as the Libyans wisely took cover or retreated to what few sandbagged areas they had.

Once at the bottom, Grogan left one vehicle with twelve men and as the Apaches advised that they were now in position, standing off two miles away, silent and dark in the night sky, he signalled to the driver and they moved off.

At the airstrip the mini-convoy had arrived and soldiers and airmen were shepherding the hostages towards the aircraft. The prop wash from the big variable pitch propellers was blowing back into the groups from the one engine that each pilot had kept running. A triage was operating as the Irish Defence Force doctors examined each person, selecting some to travel with them and the earlier cases in the third Hercules. This was a Royal Air Force 'aeromed' equipped version, with a full team of medical staff under the command of a female wing commander and able to deal with most battlefield traumas.

One hundred miles back the AWACs had spotted activity at two air bases and thirty thousand feet above the ground and twenty miles away to the north the F-14 Tomcats took up station and illuminated their weapon radars, obvious, there to be seen, there to intimidate, daring the Libyans to approach or retaliate. To the east a pair of Tornadoes stood sentinel, preventing take-offs from Sabha while to the south-west the second pair stood off from Awbari.

On the ground the SAS men were now in a defensive posture round the three Hercules, leaving the perimeter security to the Apache gunship and its little scout. Forrest scooped up his radio handset to advise Major Grogan that the transport for the last of his men at the Libyan camp was on its way.

Grogan and four men in the lead vehicle were approaching the junction in the road, a natural rise where they could cover the withdrawal of their comrades. Grogan was half-turned, his right shoulder over the rear of the seat, putting the radio handset back when the front wheel hit something on the road. The steering wheel was wrenched from the driver's hands and the Land Rover spun left and slammed into a rock the size of a house. Grogan was thrown into the dashboard, his face striking the handles of the machine gun, his left shoulder and jaw broken, shards of bone driven upwards into his cranium. The driver, a veteran corporal, was thrown forward into the steering wheel, his chest crushed, and his spine snapped when the mortar baseplate, loaded in haste and unsecured, struck him in the back. He died instantly. In the back the other soldiers, standing either side of the 30mm cannon above the roll cage, were thrown clear, only one suffering a debilitating injury with multiple fractures in his right arm.

By the time the commandeered Libyan four-wheel-drive arrived two minutes later, the survivors had dragged Grogan and the dead driver clear of the wreck, administered first aid, advised Colonel Forrest and set up a defensive perimeter. They waved it on to bring the remainder of the squadron out that far at least. Another vehicle would leave the airstrip for them.

Fourteen minutes later, the wrecked pinkie burning fiercely a mile from the airport, the last Hercules powered its way down the dusty runway and lifted into the sky. This was Aeromed One, and the trauma team now had their hands full. As they worked trying desperately to stabilize Major Grogan, the young hostages watched as the green screen flapped back occasionally, the green-garbed medical staff over the operating table now set up on the flat mid area. The joy at their freedom had been short-lived. Thirty-one of them sat, not sure where to look, or how to behave, some of them quietly drinking their juice, but missing the taste, missing the sweetness, aware that one of the men that had come to save them was now in the black rubber bag at the back and another was dying before their eyes.

The doctor looked up at Forrest.

'Six hours to Cyprus?' he asked

Forrest nodded.

'I'm sorry. We will do our best. But without a neurosurgical team, and the facilities, I don't think he will make it.'

A few moments later Forrest was on the flight deck and with a heavy heart he pressed the button on the radio mike.

'Mother Hubbard, Mother Hubbard, this is Chieftain.'

'Chieftain go.'

'Blue Peter, repeat Blue Peter.'

'We copy Blue Peter. Well done, Chieftain.'

Tornadoes alongside and the F-14s above them, the four C130 Hercules moved eastwards over the Sudan towards the Red Sea. The tankers that had refuelled the fighters and topped up the tanks on the C130s now turned for home and eased their throttles forward into an economical cruise.

Busby Grogan, soldier, father, and friend to many died as the aircraft they were travelling on called long finals at Akrotiri air base on Cyprus. His body and that of the corporal who died in the same accident were transferred to one of the other aircraft with the other squadron members and as soon as they had refuelled at the far end of the runway, a fresh crew came aboard and the three aircraft took off again for RAF Brize Norton.

The children were met by teams of people who were well prepared. News of loved ones for most, clean clothing, good hot food and endless hot water did more than the medical and welfare personnel could have hoped for and the following morning, their rescue still unknown to the media, they were cheered on to an Air Lingus 747 by the crew, all Irish, who had been in New York when the crisis erupted. Messages smuggled from family were handed out and on the long flight back to the British Isles they were told they would not be going all the way home, not just yet.

General Stewart stood, half a dozen senior officers around him, on the hilltop and surveyed the soft gentle valley below him. The picturesque view of trees, lush green pastures and little settlements had fooled many observers. This was the Irish border. A thousand crossing points, every one used by the IRA, had driven the British authorities to bizarre lengths over the years. There was no fence, no markers. Roads were blocked with steel barriers, but people had learnt to simply drive round them and they were not stopped. Since the cease-fire many of the crossing points had been reopened, but closed just as rapidly when the crisis flared. British army patrols appeared every so often, small groups of soldiers moving slowly, settling every few feet into a defensive posture behind cover, while the local residents walked past ignoring them. The Royal Ulster Constabulary manned checkpoints on most roads and the local people had become used to it over the years.

Every so often along the border a tall tower dominated the British side, its steel structure supporting sophisticated listening equipment, electronic eyes and ears in counter-terrorism operations. Now they were listening to a different enemy, the signals beamed directly back to GCHQ at Cheltenham, but that was not why Stewart was here.

He lifted a pair of binoculars to his eyes. The border was to his left, but across the valley looking west along the last patches of British Ulster the hills were alive with people. Tents sprawled in haphazard lines, a mish-mash of shapes and colours, everything from bright blue and red igloo-shaped camping tents to big old canvas spreads grey with age and mildew and more modern field green army surplus twenty-man tents. There was occasional order in the scene that greeted him, small enclaves of regularity where field kitchens, messing facilities, administration offices and ablutions blocks provided services to the ever-increasing numbers.

It was like this all along the border. Groups of Irish gathering to volunteer had found the hotels and guest houses full and had ended up here, along with the more hostile and more warlike who wanted to be close to the action, or those there simply to look across at Ireland, the old country.

Stewart swung his glasses across and looked into the Republic, unable like any soldier, this close to the enemy, not to study them, to seek out their deployments, their lines and positions, their array of battle. He had the aerial photos, the miles of video footage, the intelligence that poured over the border, but this was different. There was nothing like seeing them, feeling them, allowing his instincts to rise and his training to assess the foe deep in his soldier's heart. Across the trees and behind the new minefield there were observation posts and military vehicles moved along rutted tracks.

The brigade intelligence officer came over. He was a old Glosters officer, his regiment having moved up to the border to provide a visible British military presence within hours of the crisis erupting. This was their sector, from Crossmaglen through to where the B32 crossed into the Republic from Keady.

'They have stepped up patrols sir, as we expected.'

'Good,' he said, then looked back at the crowded hillside. 'Are we ready over there in that horrible-looking mess?'

One of the civilians stepped forward. It was a man attached to O'Malley's creative team and his real job was directing movies.

'We are,' he replied. 'We have moved the old, the very young, the pregnant, the sick, the arseholes and pretenders back. Yesterday your people started trying to pull them together, and we will have enough going on to keep,

397

ah, any observers interested. Believe me, General, it will look like it should do. A vast rabble, with all that you would expect from thousands of ill-disciplined louts, but fast becoming an army.' He grinned. 'My guys have some real magic in store.'

Stewart nodded, but sceptically. 'I shall look forward to seeing it work.'

He lifted the glasses again. Down in the shallow valley professional soldiers were trying to instil some order in groups of volunteers. As Stewart watched one stout fellow fell out of a column running round a square and just sat down on the ground. The instructor ran back and stood over him, his pace stick in his hand, yelling something that could not be heard from that distance, but the fat man just sat, too exhausted to stand or reply.

In another group a fight broke out and as the instructor moved there to break it up he too was punched as more men joined in. Other groups were drilling with wooden rifles, but everywhere one looked it was obvious. There was no discipline, no martial skills, no order. It was chaos.

'General,' the director said, 'you are a military man. I am not. But creating illusions is my business and I am normally paid great amounts of money for it. I am paid great amounts of money because I am very good at it. It will work!'

'I expect it to,' General Stewart replied, 'because this isn't to make Arnold Schwarzenegger another five million. This is lives we are talking about. Potentially hundreds of thousands of lives. This had better be the crowning achievement of your career.'

'You a betting man, General?'

Stewart who had never placed a bet in his life turned to look at the American.

'I know my audience. I will get the desired reaction from them. You like good claret, I believe. So do I. I will put ten cases of Petrus on it. Every bottle I have.'

Stewart laughed out loud. 'One bottle will do. Always wanted to taste the stuff,' he snapped.

'And I?'

'You?' Stewart replied his voice crisp, his delivery the characteristic staccato burst, 'You get to see the main feature, and . . . ' his eyes narrowed, 'it will be no illusion. It will sicken you to your stomach, sir!'

If we go he thought. If we go.

That night, after the normal patch-through to the BBC for the news, the Voice of Free Ireland broadcast their usual messages for the resistance. At the end of that segment came the message many had been waiting for. The announcer paused. 'Here is another message for a special group among the people of Ireland. The wild goslings are safe. I will repeat that message. The wild goslings are safe.'

In the prime minister's official residence Colin Mahoney didn't hear the news for a hour, not until the housekeeper, who had a small radio undiscovered in her room and had been briefed by the resistance to listen for the message, found an excuse to enter the private apartments. She made sure the guards were clear and entered the drawing room.

Mrs Mahoney looked up. 'Yes, Mrs Emery?'

'On the radio, Mrs Mahoney. A message. The wild goslings are safe.'

Mahoney turned from where he stood looking out of the windows, his heart pounding in his chest.

'It means they have the children back. Our boys and the British. Tom's safe, Mrs Mahoney.'

'Are you sure?' Mahoney asked.

'Yes, sir. If there were any left behind,' she crossed herself dramatically, 'or killed, the message would have been different. He's safe.'

For the first time since his son had been born the Taoiseach allowed himself to cry, and they stood, holding each other, one pair of parents among many that night thanking God and their friends for their help.

Next morning he was arrested and interned after refusing any further co-operation and punching the senior adviser in the face when asked why. The Taoiseach who had played rugby for Ireland in his day knew how to punch. The adviser was taken to hospital with a broken jaw.

What the Libyans and Palestinians didn't know was that he had made a videotape during the night. It was a 55-minute impassioned address to the world and the tape was with the resistance by the time his car arrived at his office. That night, in a statement issued by the White House, the news of the rescue was released to the media, Mahoney's address broadcast at the end. The British were as unwilling to discuss the role of their special forces as usual, but did say that they had made equipment and some advisers available to special units of the Free Irish Defence Force. The BBC and the Voice of Free Ireland gave massive coverage to the events and the surge in Irish morale was only matched in scale by the vitriolic Libyan reaction.

# 12

General Mustafa Saad's iron fist had descended. The loss of the hostages on top of the naval blockade, the stiffening resistance and the appearance of a queen with growing support was the last straw.

Army officers who had been interned in various camps were re-sorted and anyone over the rank of captain, from whatever branch or discipline, was moved to a new camp outside Roscommon. The camp, hidden in a stand of trees in the centre of a no-go area, was as brutal as it was simple. A concertina of razor wire fence surrounded a flat boggy piece of ground. A second fence ran outside the first and mines had been laid in the six-foot gap. Guards' huts with machine guns dominated each corner and lights illuminated the fence line at night. Inside the wire the Libyans had provided nothing. There were no ablution blocks or toilets. The men used a hole in the ground at one end. There was no running water, each man taking a daily ration from a water tank before dawn. The camp's only permanent structure was an old corrugated iron shed that had once housed a pump. This became the camp hospital, the sick lying at the drier end of the wet mossy concrete floor. All other prisoners sheltered under the rotten leaking canvas they had been allowed to carry in with them from other camps. It was cold, damp, and the air was permanently wet, with mist and fog coming off Lough Ree and the bogs around the Shannon.

The men, as part of a regime of discipline and exercise, trudged round the inside of the wire, their boots wet through, ankle deep in mud, each following the man in front, a leader keeping them in time, but they were listless, their shoulders slumped, somnambulists going through the motions.

Three medical officers, themselves thin and run down, knew that the men, already weak, would quickly fall to chest infections, pneumonia, every kind of dietary condition and eventually the dreaded results of poor water and crowded conditions, typhoid, cholera and tuberculosis.

'Those that survive the cold,' the senior medical officer, a lieutenant colonel, finished. The man he was talking to was also a colonel, but an infantry officer, the senior survivor from those who were in Ireland when the crisis began. The handful of more senior men had disappeared. He had arrived that morning, driven in the back of a truck with eight others past the checkpoints and through the stand of pines. They had been planted in ordered rows years before and now, in this clearing, they held back the sunlight for most of the day, the sunlight that would have helped dry the ground and clothing. It seemed a perpetual shadow hung over them; the trees that should have looked Christmassy now just reminded him of Germany and Poland, places like Belsen and Auschwitz.

'What do you need?' he asked, knowing it was hopeless, but also knowing he had to try.

'A dry area, something we can heat, and a heater to do it with. Facilities to wash and boil water. Better rations and vitamin supplements. Drugs, basic stuff. Antibiotics. That's for the hospital. For the others, decent tents, blankets, ground sheets, coats and food. We need more food. I can't keep these men alive on this, not with winter coming and run down as they are.'

'What are the rations?'

'So far? Rotten potatoes, cabbages and some turnips yesterday. The day before nothing. Today, so far nothing. We managed to save a bit for today but it's no more than a mouthful per man and to be honest, so disgusting that some of them wouldn't eat it yesterday let alone today.'

'Two hundred and eighteen men,' the colonel said.

'Plus your group. Two two seven,' the medical officer corrected him.

The colonel nodded and looked around. The camp was seventy yards long and sixty deep, a wet quagmire crowded with thin, hungry, dispirited men, men he had to keep alive. He walked to one corner and looked up at the guard on his steel platform.

'I want to see the officer. You understand?' he called, then breaking into one of the few Arabic words he had learnt, 'Mudia.'

The guard waved him away but he persisted, tapping his own shoulders where his badges of rank would have been and insisting. The men walking the perimeter stopped and began to gather behind him. Eventually, uncomfortable with the way things were moving, a guard went back into the trees towards a group of wooden-framed huts. A stove pipe smoked from the roof of each and to the men behind the wire they looked warm and cosy.

Finally a Libyan officer walked back towards them, his heavy coat flapping open in the chill wind, a detail of guards at his side. He was a heavy man, his bottom lip thick and set into a wide, square primate's jaw. Bareheaded, the wind plucked at the hank of hair he had brushed over his bald spot and below his low forehead his eyes were angry.

He stopped outside the wire, feet planted in the soft boggy grass and glared in at the prisoners.

'I am the senior officer here,' the Irishman began. 'The Geneva convention requires that we receive adequate food, shelter and medical care.'

A soldier quickly interpreted for him and the Libyan officer grunted and pulled a piece of paper from his pocket.

'The captain says that this not Geneva.' The soldier screwed up the paper and threw it over the fence. The Irish officer picked it up and quickly read the message. It was in English and Arabic and was a warning that crimes against individuals or humanity by occupying forces would be severely dealt with, signed by Maeve, High Queen of Ireland and Queen of the Celts. The colonel's heart soared. He understood immediately. The resistance now had a voice, a leader. The note had this one rattled. Why else would he have bothered to keep it? He tried to keep the delight from his eyes, as he passed the proclamation to the men beside him and looked back at the soldier through the wire.

'The captain says that when we catch this rebel queen he will fuck her up her fundament like the Turks did to your Lawrence. He will then give her to the men.'

The colonel, feeling his opponent through the interpreter, decided to change tack.

'Tell your captain that Lawrence was English, not Irish, and I want to discuss conditions here. Surely such a warrior as he would not deny mere captives food and shelter before the eyes of Allah?'

The soldier spoke quickly, the officer's eyes narrowing as he finished. The reply was short.

'No extras. Rations for today are withheld.'

The Libyan had turned and was walking away when the Irishman spoke again, his voice low, menacing.

'Tell your officer this. Tell him that when the queen comes he will be accountable. He will be held responsible for his actions.'

The Libyan officer turned, pulling a pistol from his pocket, and walked heavily back three steps, his fat thighs rubbing together, raising his arm and taking aim. The Irishman stood fast.

They faced each other, ten feet, razor wire and two cultures dividing them, the tension rising, palpable in the cold air. Seconds passed. Then the Libyan lowered his gun, turned and began to make his way ponderously back to the warmth of his quarters.

That evening he returned, drunk and angry, his eyes glazed with alcohol and something malevolent. The guard who spoke English called for the Irish officer to step forward. The colonel, who had been sheltering in a leaking tattered tent with many others came to the wire, the medical officer and one young commandant, the Irish army's rank equivalent to major, a few paces behind him. The commandant was Andre Hyland, the man who had scored the winning try for Ireland in the five nations final only eight months before. He was a shadow of his former size, thin and hungry like all of them.

The Libyan glared through the fence, muttered something in Arabic, pulled his pistol from his belt and fired through the fence. The first shot missed, but the second and third hit the colonel, the first bullet in the lower abdomen and the second full in the chest.

His body shuddered as each bullet hit, but he fell forward, down on to his knees in the mud and slowly, his arms covering the two wounds, he raised his head. The medical officer and the commandant both ran forward, but the colonel waved them away. Even the Libyan guards were shocked and one looked away, either embarrassed by his officer's conduct or revolted or both. The Irish officer coughed a gout of blood that ran down his mouth and neck.

'I will see you in hell. Tell him that.' He coughed again. 'Tell him I will haunt him till then.'

He died ten minutes later, lying in the mud, rain washing down his face, the young Andre Hyland holding his head, the doctor trying to stem the flow of blood, but knowing that it was all pointless with the massive internal injuries.

As he died Hyland swore to live, to survive no matter what, to hit back, the anger deep in him, cold, calculating, quenchable by only one thing. Justice.

\*　　\*　　\*

In the cities and towns the curfew was brought forward and now ran from 8 PM to 6 AM. Checkpoints were increased and armed patrols with a new stronger mandate were stepped up. The efforts to completely jam the BBC signals were ineffectual and the troops had begun searching houses and private dwellings, confiscating radios and smashing television sets that were too big to carry out. Satellite receivers were torn down and those that were too high to get to were shot at.

The Libyans had tried mixing loads on vessels, but the Royal Navy remained vigilant. The few purely humanitarian ships that were allowed through the blockade could not meet the demand and there were now severe shortages of most things. People standing in lines for bread, fruit and tinned goods could expect to wait hours to be served. Only milk, meat and potatoes were in full supply. But there was no despair on the faces. No resentment. Shoppers put on a smile for each other, sang songs quietly, and waited their turn. As the sanctions and blockade bit, if it was hurting them then it was hurting the Arabs and that was grand. Petrol was rationed, and only the transport companies and farmers were allowed diesel. Rumours said there was plenty of petrol: the rationing was to try and limit the movements of the resistance. People took to bicycles and the oldest relics were dusted off. Newer bikes were in high demand and only the rich could afford the price of a mountain bike. Tobacco was also rationed and the country's few drug addicts were on hard times. Their sources had dried up along with the airport traffic and the other method of smuggling drugs into the Republic, over the border from British Ulster, had been closed down with the ever-increasing Libyan presence on the frontier. Prices of whatever was available were now ten times those of a year ago and addicts began resorting to crime to meet the need.

Public houses had run out of all imported drinks and

now only served whatever was produced locally. This engendered a curious pride and much to everyone's delight the last shipload of materials for the Guinness factory had been allowed through the blockade in record time. The Palestinians chose not make an issue of it and in fact many suspected they avoided telling the Libyans at all. The division between the two groups was now apparent, even to the people on the streets. Only the day before Palestinians and Libyans had faced off, fingers in trigger guards, over an incident in Blackrock. The Palestinians had won the day, finally persuading the Libyans to leave the busload of schoolchildren alone. There had been abuse of the searches, some said, and girls had arrived home distraught and crying. The Palestinian commander, a woman, her black and white headcloth round her neck, had then put an escort on the bus for the last mile of its journey, and that night the local priest thanked her.

People who stopped for a drink on their way home before the curfew now had every pint served with the feathered Tara brooch emblem of Queen Maeve drawn into the creamy head, and toasts were made to the *buachailli* and their new queen, long may she live and bless her heart. This simple part of Irish life combined with the strength of the family unit and the ever present church gave a solidarity, a oneness that Ireland hadn't seen in recent history, not even in the rebellion against the British; and it was different to the joyousness of being Irish in the fever of last summer's World Cup.

At the time of the last invaders, the English, the church had been largely spared, but now the priests, the holy brothers and the nuns were suffering as much as any. The harder the occupiers tightened down, the more the Irish people welded together and the *buachailli* owned the night, moving among them like Mao's proverbial fish through water. There were now mounting resistance casualties. Fourteen had died in a series of skirmishes on Dublin's North Side in the last week and a half.

Mary Kelly, now commanding her own team of fighters, had exacted revenge for those deaths. The Palestinian fighters, with grudging respect, had dubbed her *korbaj*, the Arabic name for a short leather whip, but the Libyan troops in her area of operations knew her as the devil woman and their masters put a price of £50,000 on her head. As with Joseph O'Reilly they had no accurate descriptions, no photographs and no name other than her given name, as common as any. Even her family, still held together by Simon, had no idea what she was doing for the cause.

Three more *buachailli* had died when their vehicle overturned while escaping the scene of a successful ambush in County Mayo, and in Cork a Palestinian sweep through a farming community had netted two armed men in hiding. There were now areas that were almost considered liberated and certainly no-go for the invaders even in broad daylight. These included the Wicklow mountains, areas of Kerry, huge tracts of County Offaly, the banks of the Shannon and County Mayo. In most rural areas the night belonged to the resistance. There were reprisals, soft and hard.

The latest soft reprisal was the blackout. Any area where resistance activity was recorded would suffer blackouts for the following three nights. Again it became a weld in the seam, people unconcerned and joking that the next thing to run short would be candles. There were other odd things that were now in short supply including matches, newsprint, paper, soap, cooking oil, floppy disks. Magazines were unobtainable, as were new tyres, most motor spares and wine. Coal, gas and heating oil were very scarce and people had returned to burning peat in their fires when the blackouts would have meant a cold house.

Simon Kelly, out trying to find food, was taken from a line outside a bakery. The round-up was a reprisal for a *buachailli* attack, and he was herded on to a truck with fifty others. He managed to wave to someone he knew and they nodded back. Word would get back to the family.

It wasn't the first time one of them had been grabbed in a round-up, but luckily that was one of the rare occasions when human decency came to the fore. The week before, Moira had been in a line at the shops and a Libyan truck had pulled up. Soldiers jumped down and selected the last ten in the line, Moira included, and were moving them at gunpoint back to the rear of the truck when three Palestinians in a Land Cruiser, the black and white chequered *keffiyehs* wrapped tight round their heads against the cold, screeched to a halt. There was a quick conversation among them and a young man climbed out of the Land Cruiser and walked over to the Libyans. He pointed to Moira, talked for a few moments and then led her back to their vehicle. They drove away, stopped round the corner and asked her where she lived. She didn't want to tell them in case they were after the others, but Simon had said, if you are caught out then co-operate, always co-operate with them. If you don't they will react violently. She told them and then to her complete surprise, they drove her to her door and indicated that she should go. As she stepped down on to the road the driver wound down her window and pulled back her scarf.

'Remember me?'

The light was not good but Moira, even very nervous, had never forgotten a face in her life. She nodded. 'Yes.' The sale at the church hall two months ago. It was the girl she had given the chocolate cake to, the one who said she was from Madrid. Raishma.

She smiled. 'The cake was good,' turning and saying something to the young men she was with. They nodded and beamed and grinned at Moira. 'Cake good,' one said, kissing his fingertips like a Frenchman.

'If I had known who you were,' Moira said, straightening her shoulders, 'I would have poisoned it.'

'No you wouldn't,' the girl responded, her smile small and sad, wise beyond her years. 'You are kind. It will get worse. Stay off the streets. Stay with your family.' She jammed the vehicle into gear and drove away.

Simon was not so lucky and so David was man of the house now. That night the young man knelt before his mother and tried to reassure her that Simon would be okay, that there were camps all over and many people were hostages. He then reminded her that the children were in the house and would be looking for their dad and she was to be strong. She nodded and went to the kitchen. There were mouths to feed and enough food for a day or so, before someone else had to go out on to the street.

The following night the remnants of the family sat round the table eating the evening meal. It could have been bland, but Moira's skill had made it tasty. Cheap cuts of meat had been stewed with potatoes, carrots and herbs from the garden, and David had found celery and turnips, some Cox's apples and a few pears at one of the many roadside stalls that had sprung up as farmers tried to sell their produce. He had met a friend and already word had come back. Simon was alive and in a new detention camp at the old bus station. Tomorrow he would go down there and maybe see if he could pass some food through the wire.

Sarah was increasingly distant these days, no doubt, David thought, still thinking about her lovely home in Fox Rock, the foreclosure on the mortgage, the people at the tennis club and what would they say, the end of her illusions.

Alan sat on the other side of the table eating with gusto. He seemed to be trying to rise into the vacuum left by Simon, big silent Simon, gentle as a lamb, as male head of

410

the family. Alan had never liked Simon. Never understood where his quiet strength came from and, never understanding him, was always a little wary. They were chalk and cheese. Simon, steady, solid, dry-humoured and modest was the opposite of shallow, brash, avaricious, pompous Alan.

'I should think he will be all right,' he said, stuffing a piece of Moira's bread into his mouth. 'I know a chap.' He grinned. 'Might be a good contact. Maybe get some decent beef and fresh vegetables.'

David looked up at him. 'And who might that be?' he asked evenly, not liking the implied reference to his mother's cooking any more than the suggestion.

Alan tapped his knife to the side of his nose in a smug, irritating gesture. Ask no questions, lad.

'One of the people you met through the factory, darling?' Sarah asked.

'Yes, as it happens. He is now a quartermaster. Should be use—'

David slammed his fist on the table, his eyes blazing, with a look only Mary had seen before. 'You fookin' edjit!'

'Davey!' his mother admonished.

'No, Mum. Enough, by Christ!' He stood, shaking with fury. 'You children, up to your rooms,' he said, his voice barely under control. 'NOW!' he snapped.

Sue, knowing her brother better than most, quickly stood and swept them out of the room as their mothers sat stunned, Sarah wiping her lips on her napkin.

'Now you, you bastid, you fookin' listen to me once and for all.' He jabbed his knife across the table. 'You are not the head of this household so don't you sit there like some fat gutless parasite stepping into a better man's shoes. Until Simon is home I am the head of this family. We take nothing from those bastards. You go to them for anything and I'll deal with you. It's people like you that allowed this to happen.'

411

'Now just hold on! I want my say.' Alan pushed his seat back and tried to rally a defence.

'You don't get a say,' David rasped. 'This isn't the fookin' Rotary Club. You are only here because my sister loves you and you are the father of my mother's grandchildren. That's where it ends and don't you forget it.'

He sat back and surveyed the stunned people round the table. 'Tomorrow I am going out. I will get some food to Simon. You will all stay in the house or the back garden. With these round-ups no one is safe. You will stay off the streets.'

The silence round the table was absolute and when Sarah caught her little brother's eye she dropped her head. Sue, who had been at the door, came back into the room smothering a smile and Julie, Simon's wife, raised her head proudly and smiled across at his little brother who, she thought, had just come of age with a vengeance.

'I have some fruit,' Moira said getting up, ever the peacemaker. 'Who would like some?'

'I'll have some, thank you Mum,' David said evenly and Moira walked into the kitchen, her heart bursting with pride in her young lion. She knew where he would rather be. Out on the streets with the *buachailli*, with a gun, facing them, but his responsibilities were here, taking care of the family, and he knew it.

While they finished their meal a group of youngsters gathered with some drink at the home of one of them. One who had overheard the Palestinians talking about one of the local *buachailli* began to chant: 'Ooh . . . Aah . . . Maree Korbaaa, Ooh . . . Aah . . . Maree . . . Korbaaa', the old football chant now in honour of 'Mary *Korbaj*' and her latest exploit. Within days it would be chanted softly in pubs and wherever people gathered to talk or pass news.

Trading in the Irish pound from occupied Ireland had ceased, but there were ways that companies could continue to import goods. In London a new organization called the Free Irish Trade Office vetted applications for currency transfers. If the company was a bone fide operation registered with one of the old Chambers of Commerce they could apply to buy foreign currency, the transaction channelled through one of two major British banks and one American bank. The transaction could only be completed once the Free Irish Trade Office had agreed that the goods were of no use to the occupiers and were for the benefit of the man on the street.

In the countryside barter had returned. People swapped eggs and milk for greenhouse vegetables, hand-churned butter for cigarettes or chocolate. To conserve their petrol ration they walked or rode horses where once they would have driven and the smell of peat smoke rose on the evening air.

Maeve O'Donnell, High Queen of Ireland and Queen of the Celts, had in the hours since her coronation become the instant focus of the media, but efforts to portray her as a mere figurehead, however beautiful, alluring and pure, failed from the very start. The intensive training intended to provide her with the skills to meet the odd awkward question or hostile interviewer had given her a confidence that a few of her advisers found unnerving. There had been the usual difficult reporters from the word go, questioning her right to a throne, her right to lead the Irish resistance, her right to speak. In the first press conference her advisers and aides covered her flanks, but in the second from her base in Ulster she waved aside her counsellors and took questions direct from the floor. Her answers were lucid and direct, and delivered with passion. One reporter, a freelancer who specialized in sensationalism, suggested to her that she was just there to look good. She had been warned and told a little about him.

'I mean,' he finished, 'this isn't some sort of political version of the Eurovision song contest. This is serious. Don't you think you should leave leadership to the professionals?'

Two of her advisers leaned forward to the microphone, but she waved them back and stood up, her eyes flashing, her thick hair moving like a living thing.

'It was the professionals and the system they developed, that you make the pretence to admire so much, who allowed this to happen! But as we all know, you don't even admire them. You admire no one. Your life would seem to be bereft of any cause. Now here is something that even a man like you can believe in. If not, then shame on you, Mr Harpen. I am here to see my country and my people free. Nothing more and certainly nothing less. I will use every skill, every talent, every friend that my people can throw into the fight, and I will not cease in that endeavour!' Flashbulbs were popping round the room, and the television cameramen were recording every second, some cutting back to take in an image of the reporter who was now shrinking under her onslaught, but most on Maeve, standing proud, angry and beautiful on the small stage.

'I am not here to look good. I am not here to provide photo opportunities. You have made mockery of your own royal house. They have, with all the patience in the world, put up with it. Well I'm not here to provide an institutional target for your attacks. So don't make mockery of mine! Now, unless you have a sensible question to ask, keep quiet or leave!'

There was a smattering of applause from some parts of the room, and a good deal of nervous laughter at the expense of Harpen. A woman from ITN raised her hand.

'Your army is gathering along the border. But even to the uninitiated it seems untrained and ill-equipped. When do you expect you can act?'

'True we need more training and we are sorely short of the right equipment, but we are motivated and have the will to win. If the PLO and Libyans don't take us seriously then all well and good!' she replied with a confident smile, her style taking everyone in the room into her little secret, making them confidants yet telling them nothing, like a seasoned politician.

Fifty miles to the south beneath the County Meath farmhouse, Scott finished his debriefing and sent his men to rest. The movements had started the night before, columns of tanks and artillery, with support vehicles moving north towards the border. The array looked like being typical of the old Soviet bloc tactics. Main echelons of combat-ready troops thrown into the divisional front with their support and reinforcements very close, allowing their sheer weight of numbers to wear down their opposition by attrition. There were no long supply lines to worry them. Their matériel was on site, being moved up hourly now. The resident SAS men would move back within reach of their positions before curfew, their dress and papers supporting their identities as local men.

Elsewhere in the country Scott's other men, based with the local resistance, were reporting in twice a day with high-speed coded transmissions. Their intelligence supported everything that Scott was seeing and he silently blessed the laws of serendipity, that had allowed him to position his base so close to the troop build-ups just to the north of the farm.

Aisling and Millie now stood twelve-hour shifts in the attic. The equipment that signalled the arrival of inbound data was faulty, so one of them was in the attic with the hardware satellite receiver and all-important decoding software at all times. GCHQ at Cheltenham would decode simultaneously, but Scott needed his own access to be able to brief the resistance on the overall picture and redeploy his own small resources to keep track of the ever changing scene. For all the satellites and J-Star systems overhead, everyone knew there was nothing like a trained observer on the ground, close enough to see unit markings, hear men speak, see the state of equipment and the readiness of the troops. The latest intelligence coming through involved the deployment and use of the Libyans' Russian built Mi-24 Hind attack helicopters. They had been operating over the Wicklow mountains and the south-west on search and destroy missions and were now also escorting convoys. They were becoming a problem.

He finished his own briefing on to the tiny tape encoder-condenser and moved back up the tunnel towards the house. He was in this evening. The last time was the night before Maeve had been crowned at Tara. There were troops there now. They had taped off the monuments for some reason, bright yellow tapes running between pegs. A couple of bored soldiers squatted under a lean-to canvas shelter by the church and people who tried to visit the site were refused.

He climbed the four steps to the trapdoor and let himself into the house.

'Hello, stranger,' Aisling said warmly, moving into his arms.

'Hi yourself.'

'I'm off till six in the morning. Hungry?' She looked into his eyes.

'Yeah?' he grinned his hand running down her buttocks.

'For food, you fool,' she replied, pleased with his desire.

'I am. Munchability, please.'

'When was the last time you ate vegetables?' she asked.

'Dunno. Over in Longford a few days ago. A widow woman. Bit of a reputation so they say,' he teased, one eyebrow raised.

'I'll cut it off,' she warned.

'No you won't. You love him.'

He sat at the kitchen table, a mug of tea before him and they chatted as she cooked dinner, both of them enjoying the domesticity of it, the ordinariness of being together in a kitchen while pots boiled and delicious smells came from the oven. Scott liked watching her move, the swing of her hips, drinking in the feminine gestures he missed so much, the hand brushing hair back over her shoulder, the finger dipped in the gravy and lifted to her lips to taste.

There were vast amounts of food, four chickens, a whole cabbage, twenty carrots, sixty roast potatoes, pints of gravy and great wedges of fresh soda bread baked on the farm by Millie that morning. Home-made ice-cream would finish it off and the lads would wash up their own dishes down below. They appreciated the fresh food after days and sometimes weeks on re-heated and dehydrated rations and the six of them would plough through half a chicken and a plate of vegetables each.

Scott passed the food down when it was ready while Aisling took a plate up to Millie in the attic, then they sat down, just the two of them at the kitchen table, and ate their own meals. They shared a shower later, before bed, making love against the wall while the hot water washed shampoo from Aisling's hair, her head on his shoulder, the foam running down Scott's chest.

An hour later they lay in the dark, Scott smoking a cigarette. Aisling reached for the packet.

'Since when?' he asked.

'Since cancer doesn't seem to matter much any more,' she answered drily.

He chuckled. 'I was in the Gulf at Muharraq when the RAF guys arrived. They had all taken up smoking, too.'

'When are you going away again?' she asked, sitting up, pulling the duvet up over her breasts in the dark.

'In the morning,' he answered.

'Do you have to? I mean can't you . . . just a day, Aiden? It's been weeks since you had a day off.'

'No,' he replied, running his hand down her back. 'There will be time for that when it's finished.'

'Then you will go back to England,' she said quietly.

'Just for a while.' He sat forward. 'Why don't you come with me?'

'Live with you?'

'Mmmm.'

She was silent for a second or two, wanting to say yes, wanting to be with him, to be seen as his to the world, but her Irish upbringing rising, the thought of what her parents would say, what others would say, disappointed that he hadn't proposed, that he didn't think enough of her to want to marry her.

'What if something happens?' she asked. 'Then we will never have had any time.'

'Nothing is going to happen,' he said, realizing it sounded stupid as he said it.

She laughed softly. 'Oh no? Christ, Aiden, there's a war out there, and I just want my little slice of happiness. I know it's selfish, but every now and then I don't give a stuff about everyone else, just about us.' And she began to cry, silently in the dark. He took her in his arms and held her and finally they fell asleep.

In the cold dark before the dawn they made love again and as Scott dressed silently and Aisling slept, warm under the duvet, nature worked its miracle inside her and she conceived their child.


It took him most of the day to travel down into County Kerry. His papers identified him as a civil engineer on the job for the new administration, and with much of the country without electricity and with sewage backing up into various garrisons, he passed through the nineteen checkpoints without incident. By nightfall he was with O'Sullivan's second in command, a short, wiry woman in her thirties, who was a pharmacist during the day and

418

after dark assumed her other persona.

Pat O'Sullivan's resistance cell had expanded tenfold, many of them members of the army reserve and a handful of those Ranger reserves. The Ranger company in the Irish Defence Force was not true light infantry. They were Ireland's fighting élite, their training and role more like that of the American Special Forces or the British SAS – not as well trained or as well equipped, but certainly the very best the Irish could warrant and in their counter-terrorist role as good as any force in Europe.

Seven of them waited for Scott in the warmth of a cowshed near Newmarket. They wanted to present a plan and even O'Sullivan, the most audacious of the resistance leaders, was uneasy about this one. As technical adviser, the decision would depend on Scott's recommendation to O'Sullivan and now he sat with the Kerry farmer and his pharmacist number two not a dozen miles from the man's house and the room in which they had first discussed the formation of a resistance in the south-west. It was a flat over a garage, the damp, crumbling walls covered in mildewed calendar girls and old posters for Castrol motor oil. A tea room for the mechanics, it was now deserted and Scott sat at the table, grimy from years of greasy overall sleeves rubbing its surface. The change in O'Sullivan was gratifying. The big, strong individual was back and back with a vengeance, all, Scott heard, down to three days spent with him by Briget's sister. The girl had worked a miracle, but then as Aisling had said maybe they had helped each other through their darkest hour. He was as relentless as ever, but there was a softness now, a compassion, and each time hostages were taken in reprisal for one of his raids he felt it deep inside him.

A big chipped enamel teapot was placed with cups in the middle of the table, and O'Sullivan sat down and began to pour.

'I used to bring my car here for the big jobs. Now there's

no spares and no bloody petrol. Anyway. As I was saying,' he continued, 'the bloody things are making life difficult.'

'When did they start?' Scott asked.

'Four days ago. I can't afford to lose people, Aiden. Three last week. Good people. One was a slip of a girl, but she could shoot.' He took his cup and sipped at its steaming sweet contents. 'If I have to be watching above, then I can't be watching the ground,' he finished simply.

Scott was thinking, racking back through his training. The Mi-24 Hind, a big mother of an armoured gunship, had created havoc in Afghanistan. Capable of a weapons load including anything from rotary cannon, ground strike rockets, to anti-aircraft missiles, Swatter or Sagger anti-tank missiles, it also had chaff and flare dispensers and some of the later models were fitted with infrared shrouds on the engines, as well as infrared jammers in the counter-measures pod. In theory it could be downed with a Stinger or a Javelin anti-aircraft missile, but if the pilot was on the ball, and the Soviets operated them in pairs or fourships, the chances were if you got close enough to use a Javelin the wingman would nail your location within seconds of the missile lifting off. It was a nasty-looking beast, big and heavily armoured, its weapon systems mounted on pylons that stood out from the fuselage like mini-wings. The winglets were aerodynamically sound and in fact provided up to a quarter of the aircraft's lift while in flight. It could also transport eight troops in the cabin behind the pilot. If it had a limitation it was its range. One hundred miles was its combat radius, but in Ireland a hundred miles was a long way and they were tough to kill.

'The lads have been watching the base. They want to lure one up a valley somewhere and have a go at it with the rockets you gave us.'

'SAM sevens,' Scott replied, 'not much good against this one. It has missile counter-measures systems. Infrared, heat-seeking and radar guided. For heat-seekers like the seven it will be blowing flares and while your missile is ranging in on a thirty-dollar flare, the Hind will be coming in at you.'

'What do you suggest?' O'Sullivan asked. He was always ready to take advice, unlike some of the other local leaders.

'Let me talk to your lads and see what they are made of. In the first instance my advice is do it before it takes off. The best place to take out an aircraft is on the ground. There they are cumbersome, vulnerable and burn like a bastard.'

O'Sullivan grinned. He liked the thought of them burning like a bastard. 'There's six at this base.'

'What?' Scott looked up. Someone had screwed up, screwed up badly.

'Six of the buggers, yer man tells me,' O'Sullivan repeated. 'I don't like it. Not in my patch.'

'I want to see them,' Scott said. 'Pat, the Libyans only *have* ten of these things. Even if they have all of them in Ireland, and I doubt that, if we can hit them on the ground, we can take out six-tenths of their ground attack force in one go.'

O'Sullivan grinned again. 'I like the sound of that,' he said. 'That would help make it right. We can have a look tonight,' he finished happily.


Four nights later Scott was back on the low hill that overlooked the base. In terms of hurried preparations this operation took the record in his experience. The whole SAS mentality was to make thorough plans and train, train, train, till there was no room for error. But this target was different. The defences were rudimentary and someone was going to wise up soon – spread the deployment of the expensive helicopters, or beef up the ground defence. Either way it was too good a target to miss and Scott was trained to take advantage of serendipity, always ready to take opportunist actions.

The hill on the other side of the valley was covered by the seven reserve rangers with a ten-man section of resistance giving them covering fire. They had dug the mortar baseplates in the night before, and at dawn, with the sun off to the right, they had used spotting equipment to carefully estimate the range and calibrated their mortars. Their escape route was back over the hill, back-up units were organized on the route out and they were happy with their arrangements.

Scott's prime concern was his own men. There were twelve of them and they were only 1100 metres from the Libyan base below. That was why they were waiting until dusk, to give themselves the hours of darkness to get clear. There were no support units or men to provide covering fire for their withdrawal. The risk of blue on blue kills was too high and the SAS men knew they could fight their way out if things got hairy. The precious Milan launchers would be carried out – they were light and too valuable to leave.

The short patch of ground that housed the Hinds was bordered by a high wire fence. A camp with tents and some semi-permanent structures dominated the far side, the maintenance area, and barrack lines for the air crew, support staff and airfield defence.

They had sat there in the brush on the hillside, invisible from more than a metre away, and watched the base. Four of the Mi-24s had lifted off during the day, returning forty or so minutes later. One of the Hinds was in pieces on the grass pan and the last was parked, its tail rotor off for some reason. Scott looked down the line of his men's positions, unable to see them but knowing they were there. The last pair had had to move several hundred feet to the left to get a clear line of fire on the last Hind and as long as the Libyans left them where they were, they could hit all six from their position. The launcher was just over sixty pounds, but they could deliver a three-pound high explosive anti-tank round through forty inches of armour at 2000 metres. Because they only had three missiles for each launcher it was worth lugging it through the bracken to get the shot right the first time, and if they could take out the helicopters, it was worth the risk. Getting out would be a scrambling, running withdrawal to the vehicles, lugging the launchers on their shoulders.

Scott lifted his binoculars and gazed across the valley, hoping like hell he would not be able to see O'Sullivan's men. Mortars were an indirect weapon. They could be fired out of line of sight of the enemy, but the resistance men had opted for direct sight and get it right. They were Irish Rangers, so seeing them was extremely unlikely, and after scanning the position he knew them to be in and seeing nothing he settled back to rest, his mind flashing back to Pakistan, the last night before he flew back to Britain. That was waiting above, waiting for it to happen. This time, however, he would be starting the fight.

He checked his watch. The wire-guided infrared missiles were all very well at night if your target had a hot engine, but at least two of the choppers hadn't turned their engines over all day. They would have to hit as the last edge of daylight faded. He gazed through the viewfinder. Four minutes according to the schedule, but the light was fading fast.

He nodded to the man next to him.

'Thirty seconds, Taffy.'

The soldier nodded and pressed a button. In each position on both sides of the airfield and camp, lights twinkled on black panels and everyone moved forward over mortar tubes and missile launchers.

Across the valley the reserve ranger chosen to start the action took the first bomb and looked up. His partners had the next ready, one looking at his watch.

'Go,' he snapped.

The other grinned and dropped the first bomb down the tube and as it blew outwards powered by its own charge he dropped the next into the tube, very quickly gaining a rhythm. The first four mortar bombs were away before the first one hit the camp and the preparations paid off. It hit dead centre, the following three bracketing its fall. Bombs from the two other tubes followed them in and as men began running for cover in the camp below, the SAS men across the valley engaged their targets on the airfield.

Scott's was the first Milan away, blasting out of the bracken, its searing tail flame pouring white smoke into the dying daylight like the breath of a dragon. Scott kept his eye on the target through the reticule, the missile on track, knowing that he could alter its track back on course if necessary. He heard two other missiles launch and then his hit, a satisfying white orange flash and then a blast in the target Hind's engine that threw debris into the air, the concussion wave followed by white smoke. There was a secondary explosion and then fuel began to burn as two more Milans hit their targets, one in the cockpit and the second just below its main rotor.

He rolled back to allow his partner to reload the next missile and then rolled back, the launcher ready. The fourth Milan had missed, slamming into the ground forty metres beyond the target Hind, bits of the missile careering off into the dying light, the warhead exploding. Scott leaned into his reticule, seeking the undamaged Hind, fire now raking up from the camp as the defenders finally began to get organized.

He pressed the trigger and the missile blasted away, tracer now arcing up into the sky, mixed bright rounds betraying the gunners' location.

Hit 'em, Scott thought, hit 'em, his own missile streaking in to its target, his eyes glued to the launcher's optics, the tracer now getting uncomfortably close, someone to his left targeting the gun position with an American light fifty sniper rifle, its unfamiliar muzzle blast echoing across the valley, his missile hitting true and the helicopter burning fiercely.

'Let's go,' he said, snapping 'go, go, go!' into his tiny hand-held radio. Although one helicopter was still un-damaged, five were hit, the camp was in turmoil and discretion was the better part of valour. They evaporated into the bracken and brush, moving as fast as they could up the hill, the six men carrying the missile launchers, leaving nothing but tracks on the hillside.

Across the valley the resistance men did the same. Leav-ing the mortar baseplates, they lifted the tubes and moved away as quickly as they could, into the gathering darkness. Above them their support group encountered a Libyan patrol and a fierce if one-sided fire-fight developed. The Libyan patrol, only six men strong, had hidden when the attack began and, confused and frightened, had waited for the firing to stop before moving back into the open. They sighted each other across a clearing in the dark, both sides moving fast, both sides having forgotten the basic night patrol tactics of stop, listen, move, stop, listen, move.

The Libyans fired first, their bursts going over the heads of the resistance group, who were spread out single file further down the hillside. They had made the classic error of poor light and downhill shooting. The Irish returned fire, pouring rounds into their attackers. Better motivated, with superior numbers and with more to lose, it was over very quickly. Three Libyans were left on the damp slippery slope, one dead, and the other three retreated. The resist-ance moved on, this time more carefully, but buoyant on the adrenalin and success of the strike. They had one casualty, but he would live to fight again.

After hiding their vehicles the SAS section split up and moved into prearranged safe houses, some as far away as Dublin. They knew they had stirred up a hornet's nest and that the locals would bear the brunt of any reprisals. Scott had stressed the risks to O'Sullivan, but the Kerry farmer overrode his feelings for hostages.

'They are Irish,' he had replied, 'and this is Ireland we fight for.'

General Saad reacted quickly to the loss of his precious helicopters. Three hundred people who lived within twenty miles of the destroyed base were rounded up and interned within its wire perimeter, to live in what was left of the camp. As the cold winds swept up the valley, they huddled wet and miserable beneath the tattered remains of the tents. There was no heating, no hot food and no blankets. There was also no capitulation. The people gathered inside the wire looked across at the burnt wrecked Hinds and most felt it was worth it. In the face of this support the few dissenters kept silent. On the night of the first day a priest arrived and demanded to be interned with his congregation. The Libyans refused, beat him and had him driven back to town. The priest returned to his church, sat down outside, bloodied, his injuries obvious, and began a hunger strike.

Stewart's plan was to draw the Libyan armour into the north-eastern counties, cut it off and kill it, before sweeping westwards and south to liberate Dublin and link up with the Americans. To lure the Libyans into the northeast he had used the sprawling thousands of volunteers and the ruse had worked. The movements, deployments and training over the border in Ulster had attracted the right kind of attention. The early Keystone Kops days of the training, with the drunken fighting, the desertions and the complete lack of discipline had fallen away and now units moved with some precision, some cohesion. They were starting to look like soldiers and behave like soldiers and they had begun cross-border patrols.

The Libyans, seeing the change, had begun moving more units north, more armour and the motorized infantry supported by anti-aircraft units, to oppose the growing strength of the Celts.

The Irish and their Celtic clansmen were in sprawling battalion-size formations from Newry through Cross-maglen all the way to Aughnacloy and south-west to the bog country south of Enniskillen and as the days went by the Arabs watched, the Libyans with their military intelligence structure but the Palestinians more subtle, with silent observers along the frontier. The Libyans had powerful thermal imaging equipment mounted on rapidly built watch towers and they were supported by cameras mounted in the doors of two light helicopters that had appeared. The helicopters, commandeered from an airfield in the west of Ireland, had been hastily painted, but their original paintwork showed through. The resistance, flushed with their success after taking out the Hinds in Kerry, considered shooting them down, but the real owner reassured them that they were in dire need of mainten-ance and the spares weren't available in Ireland. He advised they wouldn't be flying much longer and with a bit of luck would malfunction in flight.

The first Libyan armour had moved into the prepared revetments, companies of the same armoured regiment concealed in groups of four in the trees. These were the same revetments Scott's people had found months before, and advance units of engineers had scraped them deeper and pumped the rainwater out, cutting drainage channels.

Two of Scott's men, concealed in spider holes in the forest, watched with disbelief. The drainage channels and deep track marks in the soft ground led back to the tanks' hiding space like arrows on a map. While the men watched and reported their intelligence was supported by satellite reconnaissance photos that picked the armour out effortlessly.

American J-Star surveillance systems positioned one hundred kilometres to the north, well over British territory, supplied yet more information and were able to track movements along the entire divisional front hour by hour.

Her Britannic Majesty's Secretary of State for Foreign Affairs, with his counterpart the American Secretary of State, had their final meeting with the Russians in Helsinki. In exchange for cast iron guarantees on soft loans, massive economic assistance, western expertise and favoured nation trading status, the Russians capitulated. They would not accept the Gulf States' offer of defence contracts and eastern versions of the Peace Shield programme that the Americans had worked on for years with the Saudi government. The Gulf States were huge weapons buyers and the possibility of forming a defence agreement with Russia, troops and equipment on the ground, all at set rates, should the Americans be thrown out, was tempting beyond belief. Only this western offer was better and six hours into the simultaneous meetings between economists, tradesmen and bankers, the Russians finally agreed.

'We shall advise them immediately,' the Russian politician said, very pleased with the deals his negotiators had hammered out, the contracts in his hands as he spoke.

'No,' the American Secretary of State said. 'No you won't. You won't tell them anything till we say you can or, my friend, those deals in your hand will be just so much crap wrap, and your political career will be over.'

General Stewart received a phone call at his command at 09.27. The last diplomatic effort in the UN had failed. The last of the doves in the cabinet and Whitehall, appalled by General Saad's iron fist and perhaps weighed down by collective guilt over Britain's actions in Ireland over three hundred years, crossed over. Dark Rose was no longer an exercise.

It was on.

His staff rose to the challenge and tired officers found something as they always did when the situation demanded it. The pace was frantic and it seemed that each new detail spawned a dozen others. The planning room, dominated by maps, was active twenty-four hours a day. As intelligence arrived and was vetted, analysed and applied, the information laid out grew.

There were high tech versions, computer screens showing tracked troop positions, extrapolated patterns, computed results against ratios, but Stewart liked the real version.

He would sometimes pace up and down, stopping to look at the orange figures that represented enemy forces, his brain absorbing the detail of the terrain, running the tactics over in his mind. At other times he would be in his office off the operations room, surrounded always by aides, staff officers, liaison people and his tri-service commanders.

The early inter-service problems had been overcome by Stewart using sheer force of personality. He was a natural leader, a man who commanded instant respect, and he was tireless, sometimes going through three teams of aides and planners on eight-hour shifts before allowing himself to sleep, and always he was concerned about his people, remembering Christian names and the last time a person had eaten or had an hour off.

Today was crunch day. Today was the day when his troops would be told what they were training for and given the option to back out.

Kiernan, O'Malley and their young queen would join his road show that would tour the regiments in their battle camps over the next seventy-two hours, ending up in Scotland on the Isle of Skye. After each visit that regiment would remain out of touch, the regular forces mail being the only routine contact they would have with their families. Any personal phone calls for compassionate reasons would have an officer present.

'Well, Brownie?' Stewart, dropping into a seat, slung his cap and baton on to the chair beside him and looked down the group gathered round the table. This would be the last briefing in this room for a few days. After this it would be wherever they were. 'What's the latest?'

Colonel David Browning, his intelligence officer, stood clutching a handful of papers and acetates. The clear acetate sheets were from a state of the art colour printer, representations of the latest fixes on the Libyan and Palestinian movements of the computer.

'More of the same, sir.' Browning dropped the first acetate down on the overhead and flipped the light on. The image thrown on the wall was a map of counties Monaghan and Cavan, the greens and yellows of the terrain and towns dotted with the red unit symbols of the tactician. When the representations were in black and white the enemy units had double borders.

The shape inside each square red box identified the type of unit. Armoured units were an ellipse, mechanized infantry, never very far from armour, an ellipse with diagonal lines crossing in the centre. Monaghan and Cavan were a sea of boxed eggs.

Because the area was so small, the normal big picture view was forsaken for the tactician's dream, micro-plotting of individual units. Companies and battalions were laid out according to their disposition and array, the armoured and mechanized units interspersed with self-propelled artillery and infantry units. There were two lonely little air defence designators in the centre along with a command area.

'More units positioned in here last night,' he pointed to a spot on the map with his pen, 'just west of Emyvale. A company of tanks with mechanized support. Refuellers and workshops have positioned themselves down here at Kingscourt.'

'That top end must be getting rather crowded,' Stewart observed with a wolfish grin.

To all the men round the table it was a classic concentration of force. Intimidate the enemy with your power and then crush him with overwhelming odds. The Libyans had two divisions in what for a NATO commander was a two-brigade front. The old Red Army doctrine exported to much of the Third World died hard, even as the Red Army itself was decaying in the new Russia.

'They must be taking it in turns to stretch their arms. What about friendlies?'

'We now believe there are no civilians left up there. They have been moved out, some turned up in Drogheda last night. They are debriefing them now.'

Queen Maeve had spent the last four days visiting parts of Britain on her own agenda. She had insisted on travelling with a minimum of support, relying on her ability to look like just another nineteen-year-old to move without being recognized. Special Branch put two policemen, diplomatic protection officers, in a car behind her and two men of the Royal Irish Regiment, men of her own bodyguard, travelled in her car. Two other lads had joined them, boys Maeve had been at university with and busked with on Grafton Street. Kiernan had agreed they could accompany her. A little bit of home would help.

She toured Wales, stopping in Cardiff and the small towns in south Wales, the home of the Royal Regiment of Wales. She had entered their barracks and been shown around, drawn by the history, the heroic tales of the defence at Rorke's Drift by the 24th, now part of that regiment.

From there she moved on to Scotland, through Perthshire, Fife, Aberdeen and Banffshire and finally into the highlands of Sutherland, Caithness and Inverness, the land where Celtic blood ran with that of the Picts and Norsemen, the recruiting grounds of the British army's Scottish regiments. She stopped in each place, talked to people, visited pubs and clubs and shopping streets, feeling the places that the men she would be talking to had come from, where their families lived, worked, drank, gambled, laughed and worshipped. She found the favoured haunts of the men, drank a pint with the landlord, and talked.

Finally it was finished and as they drove southwards, the two lads asleep in the backseat with her, the two soldiers in front, Maeve sat awake and thought about what she would do. Kiernan had given her a script, told her what to say, what to wear, told her to let the powerful visuals and the regiment's officers do the work of gaining as many volunteers as they could. But now, having walked through their streets and drunk in their pubs, she felt closer somehow, close enough to want to follow her instincts. This was what she had been schooled to do. This was the most important thing she could accomplish.

She met up with General Stewart, Kiernan, O'Malley and their party and they drove on together out of Inverness. Darkness was gathering and somewhere to the west, away from the ghosts that still walked Culloden, the men of the Parachute Regiment were in their battle camp. A small stage had been set up against the stone wall of an ancient fortification, and acres of canvas ran back on poles. There was space for most of the regiment to crowd in, and when they arrived the men were there, in clean kit, after their first shower in days.

Thirteen hundred soldiers, the men of 1 and 2 Para, gathered together under one roof for the first time in many years, leaving only a handful on picket duty, sat on the canvas-covered floor, smoking and chatting with their mates, the tension rising. The tribal nature of the British army conflicted with its operational usage. The Parachute Regiment was a regiment in name only, because the three battalions were never deployed together. They fought as battalions of a regiment, but were recognized as very distinct units and were notoriously competitive, 2 Para having had the latest blooding in the Falklands. Now gathered under one roof they knew something was afoot. The rumours said everything from an Ulster tour to peace-keeping in Macedonia, but the most prevalent rumour was Ireland itself. It had been on the news. The Libyans building up in the north. Some said they were going to try and take the rest of Ireland, the British bit. Well fuck that, said one. Let 'em try. We turfed the Argies out of the Falklands, and if these camel fuckers fink there be'a, they've gotta nuvva fink comin', no wot I min?

Lance Corporal Bonner, whose mother was Irish, agreed, but sat silent. For him the problem was a lot closer than the Falklands. His aunts and uncles and his cousins were all there, scattered across West Meath. For him it wasn't simple jingoism, or pride in Britain. It was personal and where the others showed their passion, he showed nothing but ice. Given half the chance he would go in there tomorrow. The others in the section accepted that they would find out in due course and sat back, the stoic solid squaddie of Kipling, who accepted the hurry up and wait nature of the army as the natural order of things, told filthy jokes, and complained about the lack of chairs. 'I'll get piles,' one said, 'I know I will. My mum said so.' The soldier whose mum was a known authority on absolutely nothing frequently quoted her with a dry left-handed humour. 'She said that sitting on canvas floors in fucking jock land gives a lad piles. Know what else she used to say?'

'Mums know best,' the others chorused. The banter was easy, built from old familiar jokes on a foundation of comradeship. The manner was relaxed, all at ease with each other in any situation. This was a section, of a platoon, of a company, of a battalion, of a regiment. Trained to fight and survive together, there was no falseness, no room for doubt. When it went down they didn't fight for queen or country. They fought for the regiment and they fought for their mates.

433

''Ere, something's up,' one said. They turned to look at the stage. Earlier a trestle table had been set up and video screens lined the walls. Now a group of people were moving towards the table that faced the room.

''Ere, that's fucking Stewart, innit?' They all knew him by sight. He had been there, three weeks before, in the mud with them as they trained for air mobile, dropping from helicopters and going straight into the Milan drills, watching, an encouraging word here and there. He was a soldiers' commander. But it was odd. He, a general, had just entered the room and yet there had been no command to come to attention or even to stand. Across the tent the RSM waved a hand at some soldiers who had stood up, signalling to them to sit down.

The colonel of the regiment was with Stewart. Behind them their battalion commanders, both colonels, stood against the screens at the back of the stage. There were also two civilians, one an old bloke and the other a young girl. She was beautiful. Any soldiers who hadn't been watching now were. The soldier with the relatives, Lance Corporal Bonner, recognized her instantly, the pieces falling into place. Jesus. That's Maeve. We are going in. Please God, please, please, please, let it be us. Let it be the Paras.

Colonel Chard, the colonel of the regiment, waited till the others had settled at the table and then moved up to the microphone in the centre of the stage.

'Good evening, gentlemen!' There was a chorus of response and he continued. 'You all look cleaner than this afternoon! Now then, I would like your complete attention for about thirty minutes. You will see a presentation and hear from two speakers. I ask that you listen and watch. Finally you will hear from Lieutenant General Stewart. At the end of the evening you will be asked to make a decision. Each of you as individuals. This is your choice. Regardless of what your mates may do, or say, you will each decide for yourselves. The first speaker is

Professor Kiernan, a noted scholar from Ireland and head of the Irish resistance.'

Kiernan moved forward to the microphone as Colonel Chard stepped back.

'Thank you for coming,' he began. 'I realize that you may not have had a choice over that, but thanks anyway.' The simple gesture worked wonders and the troops settled back.

'You all know that my country, your neighbour, has been invaded. Cleverly, secretly and viciously invaded. Decent people, ordinary people, people who go to work to put food on the table and pay the rent, people who go to the football or the rugby on a Saturday, go to church, people just like you and your families . . .' he paused, looking around the crowded draughty enclosure, 'well, maybe your mums go to church.' They laughed and Kiernan continued, warming his audience.

'Decent people,' his hand pressed the remote control switch in his hand and the screens flickered into life, 'now living like this.'

The first images were of one of the camps. Resistance people had videoed thin faces at the wire, filthy children, some obviously sick standing before gaunt adults staring out through the fence. O'Malley's creative team had done the editing, piecing together the dreadful realities of life in occupied Ireland.

'Can you imagine your mother or your child in a place like this?'

The tape continued, the scenes changing to reveal other horrors, bodies in the streets after a brutal reprisal only the day before in County Clare, the body of a child run over by a half-track, queues of silent people waiting for bread and everywhere the heavily armed invaders. There were before and after sequences, images of a happier time and then the more recent footage, a greyness, a sadness overpowering everything. Kiernan supplied a commentary where necessary, but for much of the programme he was silent. Maeve, seeing the footage for the first time was visibly upset, tears on her cheeks. The pictures said everything. There was footage shot during a round-up, rifles swung like clubs at cowering people, any defiance brutally suppressed, and when the screens showed two soldiers kicking a woman on the ground, a groan rose up from the assembled men. It was collective anger coming from men who had society's basic codes of conduct and were witnessing them breached. It was coming from deep within them and it was menacing.

Finally the screen went snowy and as Kiernan walked back to his seat the tri-coloured hackle of Queen Maeve's Celt Force came up on the screen. The silence in the crowded room was so complete that those at the back heard his chair scrape the floor.

Maeve stood and walked to the edge of the stage and the microphone.

'I am Maeve O'Donnell of the clan . . .' she faltered there, swallowing hard. 'I'm sorry. Those are my people,' she began, wiping a tear from her eye, then looking out at them.

'They gave me a speech to read.' She was holding up a bound document. 'I am new to all this. But . . . I can't read it.' She paused, looking out at the hundreds of faces that silently watched her. Behind her Kiernan was leaning across to talk to Stewart. They hadn't planned on this, Maeve breaking down. She was supposed to be strong, allowing Stewart and Chard to close the evening in a fitting manner.

'My people are in trouble. They are dying not a hundred miles away from where we sit tonight. Civilians. Women. Children. Babies. The young and old. We are a small country. There's only about three million of us, less than a quarter the size of London. We were never prepared for this and . . . we are doing our best now, but we can't do it alone. We need help from our friends. Our neighbours. Our family.'

She lifted her chin and shook her hair back out of her face, her shoulders squared.

'The Paras,' she began again, 'I hear you are the best.' She paused again, letting it sink in, wondering if she was making sense. Behind her Colonel Chard, second-guessing her next words, pulled his beret from his pocket and squared it on his head, the bright orange, white and green of the new hackle in stark contrast to the maroon colour of the beret, the battalion commanders following suit.

'Well, we need a few good men,' Maeve finished, 'so I have come to the best.'

The silence was absolute. Kiernan could feel his heart beating in his chest. The men hadn't been told they were cleared with the MoD, they hadn't been told they were fighting with Stewart, or other British forces, supported by the RAF. There was just a video and a crying girl. It wouldn't be enough.

Thirty rows back Lance Corporal Bonner, the man with relatives all over County West Meath uncoiled himself, stood up and came to attention. His section, his mates, looked up at him and one by one they stood. Others across the room began to stand, men with relatives in Ireland, men who had been there, men who had kids or men who just didn't like what they had seen on the tape. Others, seeing their colonels wearing the new colours, joined them, men from their fire-teams, their sections, their platoons stood too. Thirty seconds later, almost without exception, the two battalions of the Parachute Regiment stood at attention.

The Regimental Sergeant Major of 2 Para had drawn the straw and had been briefed by the adjutant, but this wasn't in the brief. He was supposed to report what percentage of the men were volunteering at the end of the night, after General Stewart had spoken, after they had had time to hear the details of their secondment. He counted to ten, saw nothing was happening, marched forward to the edge of the stage and snapped up a textbook salute. He flicked a look at his battalion commander. The colonel nodded quickly.

'Ma'am,' he said, deadly serious, 'you have a few good men. The Paras are in.'

# 13

She handled each group differently, but each group honestly. From the Parachute Regiment base outside Inverness they journeyed westwards to find the Royal Regiment of Wales who were billeted not a dozen miles from the commandos of Royal Marines on the island of Stornaway. The Welsh regiment heard the full presentation and then were asked to think about it overnight. Maeve asked to stay on with them. She settled in with the men in one of the company positions and ate what they ate. Someone had piled wood on a fire and in C company's lines they sat and chatted with her. Maeve, in jeans, sweater and wearing a camouflage smock that someone had given her, sat on a kerosene tin, with many of the men in a loose circle round the fire. They talked of their homes, Maeve impressing them with the fact she had visited their towns and communities, and was honest enough to admit it was because she knew she would be visiting them.

The singing from up on A company's lines began soon afterwards, the regiment like all those from Wales famous for its choir, the harmony drifting down to them.

Her bodyguard were relaxed and moving among the men chatting with those they knew when someone asked the inevitable. It was a scarred, wiry little chap, a man who had served with the regiment most of his adult life.

'Do you sing, lass?'

A couple of the men gave him odd looks. You don't call a woman officer lass, let alone a queen, but those nearest turned to hear her reply and happily threw down the gauntlet. 'Give us a song, ma'am.'

'No, I couldn't,' she replied.

They heckled her gently. 'Not unaccompanied,' she responded at last. 'But there are two boys at the guest house. Old friends of mine. If you could get them here?'

'Good as done,' someone said.

Half an hour later they arrived and, pre-warned by their escort, they had brought their instruments. One sat on the ground in front of her, passed her a flat tambourine-like drum, a bodhran, and took up his fiddle; the second was found another kerosene tin beside Maeve and, just as they had done in Grafton Street only months before, he pulled his Uillean pipes from his bag and settled back.

The word had travelled down the lines and men from the other companies were now gathered round the fire. Maeve nodded to Tim, the young man with the pipes, and lifted her head and began, tapping out a rhythm on the drum. Her voice, a bright, clear, clean soprano carried across the fire and the talking died and she sang of her homeland, the dry rhythmic rattle of the drum and the sad haunting cry of the pipes under the words of 'Come by the hills'. Kiernan nudged Stewart and they retired down the lines as she followed the first song with two songs with Irish words. When she launched into 'I'll take you home Kathleen' some of the men joined in, a seventy-man bass section, fifty in tenor, but softly so as not to drown her voice. When she sang the 'Anniversary Waltz', choosing a song they would know, they all joined in. An hour later, her throat hoarse, they finally let her stop and decided that she should hear the real thing. The choir was mustered. When the sounds of 'Men of Harlech' carried up to where Kiernan and Stewart were they looked at each other and smiled. They wouldn't sing to her and then say no. She had done it again.

The next day the Royal Marines agreed. It was quite simple. They never even heard the presentation. It was let slip that the Paras had volunteered to a man and three marines met Stewart's party on the road and on behalf of the three entire commandos they volunteered. The age-old rivalry between the two regiments had done enough. The following night Stewart and Maeve and her party moved eastwards towards the Scottish regiments who were deployed inland from Peterhead.

She did the same with them after the presentation, sat and talked of the places they had come from. They had heard she had sung for the Welsh and she had done her homework. Beginning with 'Flower of Scotland' she sang songs they would know, songs from their childhoods, songs from Cat Stevens, the Carpenters and raunchy, throaty Willie Nelson songs. Some of the lads from the regiments who had musical instruments made up the numbers until there were ten or twelve of them performing round the fires. Then she began to tug at the Celt in their souls, with songs in Irish Gaelic. Miles from home and their own people, they loved it.

The Irish units came across en masse as expected, some taking Maeve for a ride in one of their Warriors. By the end of the tour and a short stop with the specialist units of armour, engineering, medical units, logistics and the air corps, the volunteer rate was well over ninety per cent, with most of the refusals genuine. There were a few that had babies due any day, medical conditions and the like, but by and large the regimental system had worked. For the men, if the regiment was going, their mates, then they were, and besides, Ireland was close to home and this was right. For an army that had gained its honours in far-flung places and foreign fields this campaign had more justification than most, and lastly they were soldiers and this was what they did.

In Ulster the psychological operations people had stepped up their work on the border. Huge speakers were mounted on watch towers and the skirl of bagpipes was blasted across at the Libyan positions night and day. The only breaks in the music were for messages in Arabic to tell the invaders that when they heard the pipes for real it would be the sound of death's wings. Cross-border forays were increased with a Celtic barbarity out of the realms of fiction. Patrols often left Libyan dead with sword wounds and faces painted blue. Letters were left at nearby positions telling them they were next. Behind the lines in Ulster newer tent camps had been set up, but these were three to five miles back, with deep reinforced trenches and bunkers. Ahead and behind them were other earthworks. Covered in camouflage netting during the day, these positions were ready for the heavy guns.

In the occupied Republic Maeve had returned and to Kiernan's horror insisted on meeting people in their homes and communities. Her bodyguard was trimmed down, three ex-Irish Rangers and four SAS men charged with keeping her safe. Even considering the competence of those men she seemed to lead a charmed existence and every time she appeared in a church congregation, or in a public house, moving among the people, reassuring them that help was coming, her stature grew, the stories told for days afterwards, the legend told only weeks before taking form and substance.

Her bodyguard kept her moving, not because they were fearful. They knew that anything short of a platoon strength attack against them would fail and at night the patrols kept moving, but they knew that if they did have to fight to protect her, then innocents would be caught up in it, at worst killed, at best interned as hostages. She appeared three times in one evening in the north-west, deep in Joseph O'Reilly's territory, his resistance people scouting ahead of her group. In each place, two pubs and a church meeting of an over-sixties club, she made a short speech, standing on a chair, her oratory fiery, her passion for the cause as real as she was. Her message was simple.

The clans are gathering. The Celts are coming. Wait for word. Listen on the radio.

### 3 December, D−6

In the dark of the night pre-dawn along entire sections of the front, the thousands gathered in the tent camps were moved back to the newer bunkered positions. Marched back down the roads with a darkened escort they left behind tents and towels and personal effects. A skeleton group would remain there, to provide movement for the watching enemy eyes. It was a deception on a massive scale, as large as some in World War Two. As the civilians moved back, leaving only the hard-core volunteers, Royal Engineers moved forward and began bulldozing revetments, the huge machines silenced down with baffles. Ready to move forward, the men of the Royal Tank Regiment rolled their steel monsters silently into position twelve miles behind the border and settled down to wait. Challengers, back in their European theatre green, but proven in battle in the sandy pink of the Arabian deserts. This was not Celt Force, but the British army in the field. Their rules of engagement were simple. If one shell or one bullet was fired at them they were 'to return fire sufficient to repel any attack, now or in the future.'

The titans that had helped destroy the Iraqi Republican Guard were supported by mechanized infantry. Behind them and ready to move forward, hidden in factories, sheds, and under netting, were the big guns, self-propelled and towed, and multiple rocket launchers of the Royal Artillery. Further back again in the support areas the Celt Force Lynx battlefield helicopters had arrived, flown over the Irish Sea below radar cover the night before, along with three squadrons of the Royal Air Force's Harrier jump jets. The aircraft had all been repainted, the familiar RAF roundel reduced to a quarter its normal size and replaced with a large Irish tricolour and the three-feathered hackle up on the tail. Nose art had appeared, the Harriers' pointed noses already sporting long-legged blondes, pirate flags and, on one, a mammoth pair of breasts and little else. The name painted in black beneath the pink circles was 'Dr Feelgood'.

The Free Irish Airforce elements of Celt Force also had Jaguars and Tornadoes, but needing full-length military runways and their beloved hardened shelters and home base maintenance, they would remain on the British mainland. In the planning rooms the operations officers were taking the latest satellite data and the humint coming from the SAS and overlaying maps of the theatre of operation, laying down the order of attack, what one of them called the 'party-planner'.

The Americans had offered their Pentagon facility to produce the 'frag', the computer generated order of events that could co-ordinate thousands of aircraft to leave twenty airfields at varying times, arrive into target zones, to attack and egress the theatre in a deconflicting order. The frag was produced twenty-four hours before each day's air assaults.

The RAF refused. They had spent a lot of time and money training their pilots to plan their own missions at wing and squadron level, pilots using pinpoint navigation at fifty feet if necessary to get in, hit the right target and get out. Besides, someone said, we need the flexibility to change plans at a moment's notice, and anyway we don't have thousands of planes.

The other reason was that the frag report demanded that every aircraft stay in position. Like cars on a crowded motorway, if one drifted or took evasive action it could hit another. The RAF experience of the frag report in the Gulf War was that it was fine until the report required that many aircraft took the same egress route over time. You didn't need a genius after the second pass to work out that there might just be another and if you point a surface to air missile that way and wait for a while you might just bonk the first one of the next wave.

The fleet was at sea.

The Ministry of Defence had advised that the navy would be increasing its strength on the blockade lines around Ireland. In reality auxiliaries, landing ships, helicopter carriers, chartered merchantmen and warship escorts of the Royal Navy were making rendezvous at various points, all having slipped moorings with very little fuss in the last few days. They would link up with three chartered ferries that normally ran across the Irish Sea. The ferries were already making their way north, their bows into blustery freezing winds off the polar cap, the landing ships not far behind, to various points on the coast of Scotland.

In Scotland, the men of the Celt Force ground elements were making final preparations, moving tonnes of equipment to their points of embarkation. Every man would carry his weapon, ammunition, rations and gear. Belts for the section machine guns, Milan missiles, and rockets for the Carl Gustavs would be shared out, but even so there were tonnes of gear. Armies in the field are consumers of more than life. Everything from tents and radios and section medical supplies through to spares for the Warrior fighting vehicles, fresh food, camouflage cream, spare torch batteries and toilet paper had to be moved. Much had been positioned in Ulster over the previous weeks. The men would carry hundred-pound packs and be self-sufficient for a week before requiring re-supply of food. Ordnance, the ammunition for their various weapons, would be the only thing moved forward in the first hours of the campaign. Without that they couldn't fight.

## 6 December

The USS *Forrestal* and her enlarged battle group arrived on station 160 miles off Galway at 3.56 on the morning of 6 December. The familiar silhouettes of the huge carrier and her escort of destroyers and frigates and their supply ships were joined by an Aegis class cruiser, four marine assault ships, four helicopter carriers, and a further three air defence destroyers.

The entire group, supposedly made up of Irish Americans, was a truly American gallimaufry. One was a six foot seven inch black marine who said he had once known an Irish barmaid. Another had the most un-Celtic name of Kawowski, and not a drop of Irish blood in his veins. He just liked soldiering and loved Guinness and if he could combine the two, then why not? Even one of the marine liaison officers attached to Stewart's staff was so obviously a Latino no one bothered to comment.

Major Lopez was at Dark Rose HQ as the weathermen delivered the news the planners had been waiting for. Conditions for 9 and 10 December would be bright, clear, crisp, cold with northerly winds at six knots gusting to ten. There were two plans for fine weather. The first called for the attack to commence in the dark before the dawn, the second just after first light, at 0815 hrs.

The group captain began to present his case, Air Marshal Williams looking at his notes. He had already heard the presentation.

'Gentlemen I will be blunt. Good as our kit is, if we have any cloud cover we might as well be bombing from thirty thousand as one thousand. Lasers don't like cloud. Eyes can't see through it. Battle damage assessment is difficult. Now we do have a night capability, but there's nothing like letting your pilot see his target. It's going to be low. Fast. Targets hidden in trees and revetments. We want the later option. Give us daylight for our strikes and time is no

446

longer an issue. We will give you the time you need. Ask us to go in in the dark and we can only assume that we have hit everything you have asked for.'

The air force officer was desperately hoping they would go for the daylight option. This was an air–ground tactician's dream. Two enemy divisions of supported armour bottled up waiting to be killed. He wanted to let his boys do the job properly. Everything hinged on that, but the gunships, the troop transport helicopters, the LCs and ships at sea, all would be visible in daylight.

Stewart thought it over for the thousandth time. Dark had its benefits. Its cloak covered many things. Light allowed his people to see to work. They had gone over the issue a hundred times. No beach master even wanted to consider a night landing, yet no ship's captain wanted to be in sight of the coast in daylight. Not when they had anti-ship missiles. When dawn broke the gunline moved back to sea.

'How much time?' he asked.

Williams cut in then, keen to get his people their best options and dropping his four-star hat for a moment. 'If we are allowed to wait till dawn to attack and the weather holds out, we will give you four hours at worst, eight hours at best. Nothing substantial will be able to move in that time. In the dark, no guarantees.'

'Done,' Stewart said. 'We attack at dawn.'

## 9 December 1995. Operation Dark Rose: The Battle of Ireland

The Buccaneers raised their heavy snouts and lifted off the runway at five-second intervals, their engines at take-off power screaming in the night. Lossiemouth and the nearby town of Elgin were used to the noise from the air base and normally it would have been unremarkable. But some of the people in the town, families of men at the base, knew otherwise; as the 'old ladies', as they were affectionately called, lifted off into the night some said a quiet prayer, while others raised a glass. One woman consciously counted them out, so that she could count them in. She would not sleep until she had done that. She would wait to see them home, like the ground crews at the base, as a nation had done fifty years before when another invader had threatened Europe.

It was the same at a dozen air bases across Britain tonight. People who knew were waiting. The Tornadoes lifting off from RAF bases at Honington, Scampton and Brize Norton would link up with the Buccaneers from Lossiemouth and Brawdy to be the first critical strike.

The Buccaneers, also called 'banana jets' from the original coded name for their design, were over thirty years old, but beloved by the men who flew them. Over-specified many times, they were, some said, the toughest aircraft ever built. They were very hard to spot, very fast and could deliver big loads of bombs over long distances. They were also, as one navy weapons officer ruefully admitted after an exercise, very hard to kill, and although two of the four Buccaneers lifting off were loaded with smart bombs, the other two were carrying only their laser guidance systems. They were going to do what they did best. Anti-Maritime Operations. They were going to kill a ship.

Lifting off further to the south were the Tornadoes. Six of the variable wing fighter bombers of 617 squadron had JP233 runway denial weapons tucked beneath their fuselages and each pilot was a qualified weapons instructor who had done at least one tour at the Weapons School at RAF Brawdy. The JP233, little more than a munitions dispenser, scattered concrete penetrating bombs and smaller mines along the runway, making the surface useless, the mines scattering around it, some exploding, some lying in wait. If repair crews tried to patch the hole, they would first have to get to it through a small minefield laid down around the damage area. Three Tornadoes had more basic cluster bombs, and six of the GR3 air defence variant would provide top cover for the mission.

The Buccaneers from Lossiemouth would be first over Dublin. Forty seconds behind them the Tornadoes would sweep through, one eliminating the radar controlled SAM 6 battery with an ALARM missile and two attacking the runway and the last dropping cluster bombs on the dispersal area, to destroy as many enemy aircraft as possible.

The other eight Tornadoes would attack the other two airfields the enemy had deployed on. The Libyans had their aircraft scattered. Nine were based at Shannon, twelve at Dublin and fourteen at Knock.

The Shannon and Knock missions would approach from the west, but the Dublin mission would come in over the Irish Sea and there was a problem. The approach to Dublin from the east was now protected by SAM batteries the Libyans had put on the deck of a ship moored in the harbour. Intelligence showed there were three SAM 6 systems on the upper decks of the ship. The three launchers, normally land-based, each with three missiles in the racks, were supported by long track radar, normally a divisional defence arrangement.

They had seen the photo-recce, the images from four angles in daylight and darkness. Up to nine missiles on the launchers and the long track radars could be sweeping.

The Buccaneers were going to kill the ship and the missile systems.

They cleared the land and dropped to 300 feet over the sea, pushing the speed up to 540 knots. The pilot of the lead bomber, Squadron Leader David Chappell, pushed his aircraft lower and his wingman dropped down with him. In daylight they would be so close to the surface of the sea that the pair behind would stay a few feet higher to clear the vortex of spray that the Spey jet engines would be throwing out behind the lead aircraft, but in the dark, with no visual references, 300 feet was as close as they liked to go.

The night was bright and clear, the moon reflecting back off the water, the pilot now flicking a look down at his instruments as they blasted down the Irish Sea, the North Channel behind them. Off to the right they could see the invasion fleet, dark hulls on the water, a destroyer screen scattered round the troop ships and helicopter carriers. Their squawk, the IFF (Identification Friend or Foe), would be broadcasting to show the warships they were friendlies, but even so Chappell could feel the big radars seeking him out, aware that twenty sets of Sea Dart weapons systems could be trained on him if his IFF failed.

'Forty miles to target, boss,' his navigator said, 'turn in sixty seconds, fifty-nine, fifty-eight.'

'Roger,' the squadron leader responded, feeling the aircraft move beneath them, stable like a locomotive on tracks, feeling the adrenalin rising. They had the bombs. The aircraft behind their port wingtip the laser designator. Please Lord, don't let me fuck up, approach five-forty knots hard on the water, the target a black blob against other black blobs.

'Five . . . four . . . three . . . two . . . one . . . Now.' The navigator's voice came through clear and calm. The turn steady and gentle, keep the nose up, the needle swinging, shit Andy, you're only twenty-five years old. You have no right to be this calm as we go into action. I am thirty-seven. I have done this shit before. I know to be scared. Parallel to the coast until we turn on to the target bearing.

They made a long gentle turn putting the Irish coast off to the right, its dark shape rising from the sea and twinkling lights familiar but threatening. The navigator was using INS but working pinpoint references at the same time and finally he spoke through the intercom.

'Commence your turn in five ... four ... three ... two ... one ... now.'

Chappell turned the big jet to seawards first then round to the right, a perfect fifteen-second turn.

'Two seven six,' he said.

'Confirm two seven six,' Andy said, 'and confirm I have stations set.'

He was ready, the bomb release switches set. Ready to pickle it. The navigator had handed control over to the pilot. He would simply squeeze a lever on the throttle and the bombs would fly clear of the hard points automatically.

'Target is on the nose. Sixteen miles.'

The designator aircraft would begin designating after he released his bombs, but its powerful camera would be seeking out the target already, the system ready for lasing, the navigator's fingers on the little ball keeping the cross-hairs dead centre.

Out behind them the Tornadoes were on their run-in. No mistakes. Not with SAM batteries. Defence suppression. I hate this shit, Chappell thought. But it's a ship and I am good at killing ships.

'On the nose fourteen miles, boss. I have the harbour. Target is the contact dead centre.'

The squadron leader said nothing, his concentration absolute. Behind him his wingman, the designator aircraft, clung to them like glue. Three miles to their right the other pair of Buccaneers were searing in, at a forty-degree angle, converging on the target as they were.

Three miles from the ship, airspeed still at 540 knots, the two bombers would stick back, point the nose up 30 degrees, blast up to 2000 feet and lob the thousand-pound bombs towards the target. As the bombs flew clear of the hard points and began to fall, sensors would be seeking the laser beam. The other aircraft would begin to 'lase' the target and the bombs, locked on to the laser beam from the other aircraft, would run in to the target. The bombers would drop back to the water, wing over, nose down, blasting it, evasive manoeuvre, assuming missiles inbound, blowing chaff to disrupt hostile radar signals, and if they had heat seekers inbound then flares, dropping below radar view. The whole thing would take twenty-four seconds.

'One minute to pull-up. RWR is clear.' The voice tense now, excited.

'*Pluto happy*' across the radio net from the other aircraft. Their navigator could see the target on his video and was now manually tracking it.

The squadron leader thumbed his mike twice. The clicks would acknowledge to the other aircraft. Steady boy, steady, straight and level, thirty seconds.

Chappell knew that in the other aircraft the navigator watched the small screen, the black and white image of the ship dead centre, the crosshairs of his seeker head steady on the centre of the image.

'Five miles,' the navigator said, 'on the nose.'

'I see the harbour . . . where is the bastard?' Chappell replied.

'On the nose! Must be dead centre, boss. Huge contact on my screen!'

There! The black shape against the lights. Yes! Got you, you motherfucker!

'I see it. Five seconds!'

Don't let me fuck up now, please, twenty, silhouettes against the city lights, ten seconds.

'Stand by boss, we are ballistic in three, two, one! Pull-up!'

Chappell pulled the stick back, jammed the throttles forward, and the big jet streaked upwards towards the black heavens above.

One thousand, thirteen, fifteen, sixteen . . . 'We are illuminated!' Andy called. Eighteen hundred. 'Blow chaff!' he responded, the altimeter flicking over. Two thousand.

The aircraft jolted as the two thousand-pounders left the hard points.

'That's it!' he snapped. Andy confirmed the lights on his bomb station selector had gone out and called, 'Bombs gone!' Chappell thumbed the mike: *'Bananas! Bananas!'*, the Buccaneer's war cry, looking at his watch, the bombs' tone loud in his earphones, stick forward, power on, right wing over to 150 degrees, racing for the sea below, chaff blowing out, listening for the howl of radar locked on from the ECM units, Five, six, seven, eight, nine, ten, please, please, thirteen.

In the designator aircraft, the Spike, the navigator watched the screen, counting aloud fourteen, fifteen, the bombs now clear and flying, looking for the target, he thumbed his laser switch, the beam firing at the ship, hitting in the crosshairs of his video display.

'Lima on,' he said calmly, 'and I am lasing and I am happy . . . yes . . . good lima.'

'Roger,' his pilot said, 'turning now.'

'Nice and steady, please,' from the navigator, a Gulf War veteran, the experience showing. 'Tracking . . . tracking . . .'

'Five seconds,' from the pilot, turning now to the right, letting his laser tracking head and camera under the left wing have a clear uninterrupted view as he began to clear the area, careful not to exceed the roll limit for the laser head.

'I'm happy,' from the navigator.

There in the sight a flash, and a second, silent huge billowing black and brightness, and over the left wing a double flash down on the water, night into day, like lightning in the night sky. The four thousand-pound bombs had hit the ship, two hitting the aft deck just below the bridge and dropping twenty-odd feet into the hold area before detonating. The third slammed into the side of the ship two feet above the waterline and exploded in the engine spaces, breaking the ship's spine. The fourth blew the bridge into oblivion.

'Direct hits! Cor fucking lovely!' said the navigator. As he saw the second two flashes as the other pair of Buccaneer strikes hit home, two seconds after theirs '. . . and again! D.H.s ! Jesus! That'll make their eyes water!'

'Right. Let's get outer here!' and he too tightened his turn, dropping his wing, racing for the sea and safety.

'*Bulldog bulldog bulldog.*' This code word to the Tornadoes inbound behind them and to command at Brize Norton and on to High Wycombe.

'*Thank you, Pluto,*' from the Tornado leader.

In Dublin the blasts shattered windows in the port area and woke people from their beds up to three miles away. Some got up and went to the windows, others stayed in bed listening, hoping it was help coming and not more of Saad's iron fist. They never heard the first Tornado.

The defence radar at Dublin airport was atop the same tracked vehicle as the missiles. A SAM 6 unit, it was the airfield's prime air defence, supported by four triple A units on the eastern perimeter. As expected, the blast from the port had been noticed even at the airport and twelve seconds later the SAM radar crew cranked out their signal, the scanner searching the sky for threats.

The first Tornado, his approach very low, pushed his throttles forward and pointed his nose at the sky, hitting his afterburners and blasting upwards. His ECM told him he was illuminated, tracked on hostile radar almost immediately, the pilot listening for the warning tone that a missile was launched at him. His nose attitude correct, he hit the launch button on his weapons pad and the ALARM missile seared away from the underwing hard point.

It streaked straight up into the night and he turned, dropping back to the deck, wing over like the earlier jets and running for the deck, blowing chaff but holding his flares — they were too visible until he had a heat seeker inbound — back to deck level where his state of the art avionics allowed him to fly to the contours of the earth away from radar and chasing missiles.

The ALARM, an anti-radiation missile, peaked its climb at thirty thousand feet, its sensors activating as its motors retarded, seeking an active radar signal. It locked on to the SAM 6 site in half a second and homed in, unpowered, its flight path a perfect parabola in the night sky, streaking down the radar signal.

The men manning the missile battery never knew what hit them, the missile coming in so fast they could do nothing. Proximity fused, the missile exploded over the radar scanner, showering the vehicle and its delicate electronics and dish with thousands of pieces of shrapnel. Three of the four crew died along with the radar's sweeping electronic eyes. The missiles in their launchers were now useless. The jet that had launched the ALARM took up station and loitered over the sea, its delicate instruments feeling for another radar probe, however slight the illumination.

The next two Tornadoes came in at low level at 500 knots from the opposite end of the airfield, one twenty-four seconds behind the other. Beneath their fuselages on the hard points the long casing of the JP233 held 30 concrete bombs, the cratering munitions, and 215 area denial mines.

The lead pilot flicked his aircraft over to line up on the runway and, allowing for forward momentum of his munitions once in the fall, he triggered the dispenser, the black strip of the main runway of Dublin International airport racing away beneath his vision, peripheral vision now, the bombs falling away below. There were lights on in the maintenance area. Images. Two fighters on the pan? People running, a vehicle racing away.

The pilot in the second Tornado followed his leader in,

but delayed his thumb on the trigger, watching the bombs from the lead jet hitting the runway, bright flashes, turbulence now under his wing, but clear of the debris hemisphere, the blast waves, now finger on the trigger, the dispenser activating, listening in his earphones for the warning howl of a missile lock. Away to the right triple A arced up into the sky, bright orange tracer rounds.

The pilot in the lead aircraft spoke into his intercom.

'Dave, did you see anything on maintenance pan?'

'Roger that. Two, I think. MiG 23s.'

*'Green two, bogeys on the pan at left, going to guns. Conform on me.'*

*'Roger one.'*

The lead jet pilot eased his left rudder pedal and pulled the stick over, taking him away from the anti-aircraft artillery, but round again. Behind them the fourth jet would be running in for his attack, his cluster bombs aimed at the main dispersal area. He didn't know about the two Libyan jets across the other side on the maintenance pan. The pilot flicked his weapons switch to guns and armed the twin 27mm cannons, looking out now, the lights below, back to the instruments, where is he, must wait, let him in, he is expecting a clear run, the Tornado now on a long curving downwind leg, still on mil power, bleeding the speed off on the turn, the G forces pulling him down into the seat, must be past now, bit of power, wing over, nose up, his wingman behind him and below, following him into the turn, level, power on, there ahead, the other Tornado, bright flashes as his cluster bombs hit the dispersal area, a massive secondary blast, orange in the night, fuel, he has hit fuel, in we go left a bit, shit I hate this stuff, never strafe an airfield unless you are sure it's only lightly defended, am I sure, am I shit, skoshey, very fucking skoshey, four-fifty knots, seat pressing into his back, adrenalin pumping, fuck, fuck, fuck, as the aircraft juddered beneath them, the triple A coming their way now, sights up in the HUD, images of the target illuminated by the fuel burning across the airfield flashed at him, there! Triggers pressed, bright flashes and shudder as the twin cannons opened up, walking the rounds in, classic strafing, hits, nose up.

He went on to re-heat, choosing to be visible for a few seconds rather than slow egressing the theatre, the bright flare of the afterburner on for just four seconds.

As the following jet ceased firing his cannons, the pilot lit his afterburners, following his leader out ahead, the flame from their engines a pair of bright orange streaks in the night as they dropped down to two hundred feet and blasted out for the Irish Sea, not the obvious route, but a longer swing to the south, the lights of Dublin streaking past below them, their terrain-following radar now active.

In Ballyfermot, Crumlin, Rathgar, Rathmines and Milltown the fighter-bombers, at low level, afterburners on again, searing through the sky above their rooftops left no one in any doubt. People tumbled from their beds to look out, but saw nothing. Too excited to go back to bed they stayed up and ten thousand kettles were stuck on.

'What do you think?' Moira Kelly asked David, quickly tying the cord on her dressing-gown.

'They've come,' he said simply.

'Who?'

'Does it matter?' he asked. 'They have come, from across the water, from America. Who cares? Someone has come.' He began to do a little dance in his pyjamas on the kitchen floor. 'And they are killing the bastards. Yes!' his fist punched the air like a footballer.

Dublin airport was closed, the runways shattered and beyond immediate repair while the mines lay scattered round the sixty craters down its length. The runways at Shannon and Knock were in a similar state.

At the Libyan Command and Control centre in Dublin's old Cathal Brugha barracks in Rathmines, the Libyan command gathered as news of the airport attacks arrived. General Saad, bleary after a night's heavy entertaining and several bottles of port, arrived late and so missed the Buccaneers' second strike of the night. A fourship of Pavespike and bombers out of RAF Brawdy in Wales placed four smart bombs in a textbook attack. The first two went straight into the Libyan army's prime communications centre for the entire country, the third into the command centre and the fourth, with the perverse serendipity of a bomb that failed to hit its intended target, into the adjoining building that housed the satellite and decoder link with Tripoli.

Fifty miles north, the northern area command, fourteen miles from their nearest units along the front, were none the wiser about the runway attacks and the loss of their air cover, or the fact that they could no longer raise their command in Dublin. The divisional command officers slept on blissfully.

Roughly twenty-five miles to their east, at a point just to the north of Clogher Head, men of the Special Boat Service, Britain's maritime version of the SAS, had been ashore all night. One team had marked out the beach all the way to Dunamy Point some five miles north again. The other had moved inland and with their SAS counterparts had silently taken three Libyan guard positions and the two roads south to Drogheda. The N1 and the L6 had been closed, with diversion signs and defensive positions set up. They were ready for the lead elements of the Royal Marines, their reconnaissance commando, to take the beachhead and establish a defensive perimeter.

One SAS man, perhaps the loneliest in Ireland that hour, sat just one mile from the Libyans' sleeping Divisional Command (North). Dressed in a ghillie suit and positioned halfway up a tree, he was absolutely still as soldiers on a bored perimeter picket wandered round the base of his tree every thirty minutes.

Slung round his neck was a heavy sight mounted on

what looked like a rifle stock, a battery pack at his waist. The sight was a laser designator, smaller, less powerful than those on the Buccaneers but suitable for the job. At 0630 exactly, for five minutes he would sight his laser on the command centre trailer. The trailer was hidden inside a barn, along with three armoured personnel carriers and a communications unit. The farm's outbuildings were used for messing and accommodation and movements were kept to a minimum. The men who had chosen the site had been looking for concealment, looking to hide the command structure, rather than dig it deep or go for hard shelters. If they were attacked they could be in the heavily camouflaged APCs in minutes and moving. But not this morning. They were crowded together. They were soft. They were found.

Two thousand-pound smart bombs would do the rest. Anything within a hundred yards would be blown to bits, including the accommodation trailers, messing facility, and other support areas for the division command. The SAM battery was a bonus. Some fool had deployed it close to the command. That would go too. At a mile he should be safe. Without the straps he would probably be blown from the tree, and as long as he didn't catch some shrapnel, he thought the worst might be bleeding eardrums from the concussion. He hoped so.

Twenty miles along the coast from Cork, at Ballycotton Bay, and on Inishmore, the largest of the Aran Islands in Galway Bay, small groups of men came ashore. Preceded by hi-tech special forces Pavelow helicopters, the men were United States 'recon' Marines and they hurriedly laid out markers for their own men who would be following in an hour.

The group on Inishmore were the first to be able to apply the first axiom of modern battle, flexible planning and mission analysis. The recon force found the Libyan garrison on Inishmore smaller than they expected. Instead of waiting for the main force to come ashore in two of the big LCAC hovercraft, they called for and were given smaller extra force immediately, and with a fourship of Marine Cobra gunships loitering quietly at the western end of the island, they took the sleeping garrison, silencing the communications and capturing the officers who were still warm in their beds. The fire-fight was as brief as it was brutal and sixteen minutes later the small force of marines were taken aback to find themselves in charge. The first part of occupied Ireland had been liberated, the first strategic objective met a full two hours ahead of schedule.

Dark Rose had begun.

It was now 0608 hours on 9 December.

News of the Aran Islands objective being taken was flashed to the USS *Forrestal* and then to Stewart on board the landing ship *Sir Galahad*. He grinned widely and punched the message flimsy with his fist.

'If you believe in omens, this is as good as they get!' he said.

He had prayed that night, prayed for success, for victory, for the lives of his men. Now as they waited for the dawn he looked up at the dark sky and nodded once. An acknowledgement. A thank you.

He stood on the bridge wing, breathing the salty air, his tam o'shanter on his head, feeling his destiny approach as clearly as he could feel the movement of the ship beneath his feet and the gentle vibrations of the engines. His fleet was spread out around him, the best light division ever fielded by the best army in the world and without question the most powerful Celtic invasion in history.

Fate had put him here. So be it. Let battle be joined. He moved back towards his ops room to await his Commander Air's updates.

The operations planners attached to the Free Irish Airforce

had been up all night, poring over weather reports with the specialists. The battle area had been divided into railway tracks, strips three miles wide running north–south and east–west. The entire front from Dundalk through to the bog country west of Cavan was overlaid with the grid. At 0300 the planners presented the Air Marshal with the weather and the alternatives. The Joint Commander would make the decision over the direction of the attacks depending on the weather. The force had been beefed up for the first day of Dark Rose. Stewart's ruse had worked, worked brilliantly. The Libyans had moved their heavy forces north, to counter and antagonize the growing, sprawling Irish army on the other side of the border. There were now twenty thousand mechanized troops in the two armoured divisions bottled up in the northern end of County Monaghan. The commander who deployed his forces in such a manner in modern times would not have passed even the first elementary class of tactics. It presented Stewart, a fine soldier and a first-class tactician, with the opportunity to truly wage war on the enemy force, to kill it in the field. He had pleaded his cause and Whitehall had heard. His original force of six squadrons for the first twenty-four hours was now enlarged to ten squadrons, 118 aircraft, 33 of those close battle support Harriers. The force was top heavy with the most experienced men that the Royal Air Force could provide, including a clutch of group captains in the back rooms and wing commanders in charge of every squadron. With his enlarged resource he handed the operations over to his Commander Air with a clear set of objectives.

The problem for the air force officers was smoke. If the wind, however gentle, shifted the smoke of the first strikes of the battle, then that would determine the strike direction. Having convinced Stewart to wait for daylight, it would be lunacy to create their own visibility problem. In

461

addition the Libyans, like the Iraqis in the Gulf War, would generate their own smoke.

The wind was seven knots gusting to nine knots from the west. The met people said that it would veer by morning to come from the north.

Everything hinged on the first strike. If the first ground strikes came in to attack the western edge then move the battle lines along to the east, the army Chinook helicopters would have to cover relatively short distances to complete their mission. If the strikes began in the east, then the job of closing the gap to prevent the Libyan armour escaping would be directed to the west, much further away. The big, slow, twin-bladed Chinooks were vulnerable. They would prefer to have the shortest penetration possible, the least time in the air or unloading their precious cargo. But the air force's job was to kill tanks, armour, mechanized infantry before it escaped. The joint commander at High Wycombe consulted his staff and made his decision at 0400. The information was flashed to Ulster and to Stewart's Celt Force at sea and the tri-service liaison teams moved into action. Whichever direction the air force chose determined the actions of many others in the first six hours of the battle. As the decision was made all commanders in the field were told to open the blue orders package and to destroy the other.

Briefings at nine air bases began immediately. The ground crews, the men and women armourers and technicians, had been preparing their aircraft all night, the tension rising. Now the strike aircraft sat heavily laden, the Tornadoes and Jaguars in their hardened shelters as the doors were rolled back. Vehicles carrying the crews arrived, the pilots in green flight suits, a Royal Irish flag with its Celt Force hackle over a Union flag on their sleeves, wearing G suits and lifejackets and carrying their helmets under their arms. No banter. No joking.

They were going to war. There was every chance some wouldn't be coming back.

Police had closed roads that skirted air bases, diverting traffic away. Once the first missions had lifted off and the news broke, there would be the inevitable well-wishers, aircraft spotters eager to see a fighter bomber go to war for real, and the gawkers clogging up the roads and presenting security problems.

In Ulster thirty-three Harriers, the operational aircraft of three squadrons, had arrived the night before. Deployed close to the battlefield in wooded areas, farms and urban sites, the short distance into the battle would allow them to fly with minimal fuel loads and every hard point loaded. Their ground crews had arrived three days before and the logistics people had moved in massive supplies of fuel and ordnance. First take-offs would be from roads, but later as the battle moved forward the aircraft would move with the action, staying as close to the FLOT as possible, using their full vertical take-off capacity from clearings and fields. Close to their crews and supplies of fuel and bombs, the pilots could fly sorties until physical exhaustion stopped them, twelve a day. One squadron could pin down and keep attacking an armoured division almost continuously.

Twenty miles off the Irish coast, sheathed in the pre-dawn darkness, thirty-one twin-bladed Chinook helicopters were being marshalled for loading. During the night 1316 men of the two Para battalions had been re-positioned, along with almost 600 men of the Royal Regiment of Wales. The Paras would go in first, with the Welsh following in the next wave.

Below decks on the helicopter carriers thirty-two of the army's Lynx close support and tank killer helicopters were armed and fuelled. As soon as the big transports lifted off, their mighty rotors clawing at the sky, the AH-Lynxes would be lifted up on to the flight decks by hoists. Most were armed with quad TOW missile launchers and the roof-mounted sight in their anti-armour role, but others had DAT mine dispensers and still others were equipped for infantry support with rocket launchers and 20mm cannon or 7.62 Emerson minigun. Five of the Lynxes were equipped with Hellfire anti-tank missiles. Their role was crucial. As the battle began Libyan units, their field commanders realizing what their generals had not, would attempt to break out to the south.

On the ground would be the Milan equipped Parachute Regiment with the Welsh covering their rear. Their stop group line had been carefully chosen to use natural features. Lakes, wet ground, rivers and other obstacles would force retreating Libyans into choke points and bottlenecks. But even using the geography, 1900 men to cover a 27-mile front for several hours was almost impossible.

They would need support.

Firepower.

The Paras, from their high points and concealed positions, could call in Lynx support while pouring Milan fire into approaching units. The tactic, to kill lead vehicles and block routes, was as old as armour itself.

Behind them the Welsh would take the major roads north, the N3 and the N2, and close the secondary routes north from Bailieborough and Carrickmacross, defending their rear. The two units with the air support would then hold the Libyans until the division was ashore. Stewart wanted no armour breaking south while he was establishing his beachhead, to maul his flanks and have to be cornered and engaged another day.

Across on *Sir Galahad* one of Stewart's staff officers was summoned to a phone. HMS *Brazen*, now patrolling the fleet's eastern perimeter, was pleased to advise that she had three inbound friendly contacts on her radars. The last preparatory strike of the morning was inbound and on schedule. He looked at his watch. It was 0625.

The pair of GR1 Tornadoes crossed the Irish coast at 200 feet, their terrain-following radar active, their speed over 500 knots and increasing. Each had two thousand-pound bombs on their hard points and each navigator was ready, switches armed. Forty seconds ahead of them and pushing his speed up was the third, armed with a pair of ALARM anti-radiation missiles.

The SAM battery was the problem. The MEZ, the missile engagement zone, was extensive and although there was no hostile illumination at present it could be activated very quickly. Sixty miles to the north of the border safely over Ulster at 30,000 feet an American AWACS aircraft stood sentinel. Staffed by British fighter controllers under the command of a group captain, they would control any air battle that morning. Their radars had seen nothing, their electronic counter-measures detected no trace of hostile radar activity. Neverthless, the SAM battery had to be destroyed before the mission came through. As the two bombers swung south, hugging the contours of the ground in the valley around Lough Ramor, the lone defence suppression Tornado streaked in towards its target. Over Bally-hoe lake just east of the cross-roads at Kingscourt, the pilot pulled the nose up and streaked towards the heavens before launching one of his ALARM missiles.

The big missile left the underwing hard point and blasted upward in a long parabolic arch, its trajectory taking it to 40,000 feet before the rocket motors burned out. A small parachute deployed and instantly its sensors began sniffing for a hostile radar trace on the enemy's frequency. If it found an emission, it would release its parachute and drop down in an unpowered flight, homing on the radar scanner.

The pilot pulled his wing over, dropped back to a safe level and headed back towards the sea, his navigator watching for missiles or anti-aircraft artillery.

The two bombers were now in a long low-level turn and heading back in towards their target. They were moving fast and very low indeed, skimming the ground. The navigator in the lead aircraft spoke as the second peeled off and began a second turn. He would loiter. If the first aircraft got hit, or had a UXB, an unexploded bomb, they would come in on a second strike.

'Right. Right a bit. Good. On the nose eleven miles. Seeking as of now.'

'Roger.'

The tension was palpable and rising. They were doing almost 600 miles an hour in the dark, low enough to slam into a hillside, over hostile territory, approaching a target defended by SAM 5 systems.

'Seven miles on the nose.'

The Tornado's complicated guidance avionics were flashing information back to the navigator, but every now and then he looked out, up at the sky, down at the ground, like his pilot, seeking out a threat, an enemy fighter, ground to air heat-seeking missiles, anti-aircraft artillery.

'Five miles on the nose.'

'Roger. Stand by for nose up . . . Now!'

The pilot pulled the stick back and the aircraft blasted upwards, gaining height for the attack. It covered the next mile and a half in seconds, climbing, his hand against the throttles. Above him and falling slowly under its parachute the ALARM missile fired by the first jet was still seeking hostile radar.

'I have a range readout!' from the navigator. The avionics were picking up the laser signal from the ground and the navigator silently thought of the operator, the SAS man, alone and exposed perilously close to the target. The pilot squeezed the bar and waited for the bombs to fall away.

'Wait for it . . . wait for it . . .'

They both felt the jolt and half a second later the navigator called, 'Bombs away!'

The two thousand-pounders were falling and the Tornado flicked over its left wing and began to race back towards the safety of the valley floor. The smart bombs' sensors found the laser signal and, using the momentum of the lob and gravity, they glided in on the target.

The SAS soldier, camouflaged in his ghillie suit, stared through the laser sight. He had tied the device to the branch, in case he wavered at the crucial moment. A waver multiplied over a mile range would mean a complete miss. Wedged into the branches eighteen feet up the tree, tense, absolutely silent, he heard them coming. No noise from the attack aircraft. They had turned away three miles away. Just the sound of the falling bombs. The whistle.

Then they hit. A bright white flash, daylight for a millisecond, the massive concussion of the blast wave and sound hitting him at once, blowing him back against his straps, ears ringing, secondary blasts as the SAM battery and fuel tanks exploded, orange flames and thick smoke curling up into the air. Direct hit. He reached for his comms pack, a small paperback-book-sized transmitter, fumbled, shook his head, his ears ringing and pressed the button three times.

In the AWACS aircraft they heard the signal and called both aircraft home. The two crew loitering in the second GR1 had seen the flash in the night and the crew of the bomber that had dropped the bombs knew that they had struck something, but not that they had been direct hits. They raced for the coast, sparse triple A arcing up to the north as nervous gunners on the ground reacted to a threat they couldn't see.

The first of the big Chinooks were loaded and hovering low over the sea as men loaded with weapons and ammunition piled into the second wave, a manoeuvre they had practised fifty times in the last weeks. On the troopships and landing ships the main brunt of Celt Force, the sweeping blade of Operation Dark Rose, was assembling on the loading decks. From the east as the first rays of daylight brightened the smudged horizon came the squadrons.

Dozens of pairs of aircraft, they seemed so low as to be in danger of striking the masts and yards of the mighty fleet as they blasted past, skimming the sea like huge flying sharks. Their underwings were bristling with hardware, the smooth rounded edges of cluster bombs clearly visible to the men on the ships. Some men cheered, some raised a thumb and others just watched. If the force loading for the marine assault on the beach was the blade of Dark Rose, then this was the hammer. One hundred and eighteen bombers, ten squadrons of the front line attack aircraft of one of the best air forces in the world. These soldiers had all seen the firepower displays and many were veterans of the Gulf War and the Falklands. They had seen what air power could deliver. They had seen land–air warfare.

They were the silent ones. They knew.

'Jesus Christ . . .' someone muttered almost sadly.

'I think someone is going to have one of life's shittier experiences,' his mate said.

'Just be fucking glad they are ours,' a sergeant snapped. 'Now get your arses into that LC.'

Above the battle area were five Celt Force aircraft in advance of the main force. Two Tornado GR3 air defence fighters escorted the only American aircraft in the northern zone, a pair of defence suppression F4 Phantom Wild Weasels piloted by Irish Americans. The old Vietnam vintage jets were crammed with complex electronics that could seek out the most elusive hostile radars and send HARM missiles down the trace. If the Libyans illuminated the inbound bombers, even for a few fleeting seconds, the HARM missiles could destroy their transmitter and receivers and the radar-guided surface to air missiles they directed.

The other aircraft was a lone Tornado fitted with a recce pod. The advanced cameras and recorders mounted in the pod allowed the navigator to zoom in on ground targets, freeze the images and even replay them. This was the forward air controller. The aircraft was alone, unarmed, vulnerable to attack, but doing a vital job. As the first wave passed through, the FAC could do real time battle damage assessment and redirect the following strikes.

If the Libyans established he was there they would direct every effort to knock him down. The FAC crew, both volunteers, were said to have balls that clanged when they walked. Stooging round over a battlefield, with thousands of small arms and light anti-aircraft weapons to be aimed at you and in the middle of a missile engagement zone, was not something most pilots liked to do. The navigator sat, his eyes scanning his instruments for a hostile threat, his ears for the howl of a missile locked on to them. The GR3s would come running if they were jumped by an enemy fighter, but there was little they could do to a fast salvo of SAMs. Then everything would depend on the man in the front seat, the pilot. He was good. Very good. Nerves of ice. Reactions like a mongoose. Used to be part of the synchronized pair in the Red Arrows display team. Veteran of the Gulf War. If you had to be the idiot backseat man who volunteered for this shit-fight then you would want a driver like this. He sat sweating and wished he could smoke. Forty seconds.

With the wind from the north as the met officers had predicted, the attack began at the southern end of the horseshoe-shaped front, sector Hotel One, a three mile by three mile box, along the track to Hotel Nine. The 'H' strip, twenty-seven miles long and three miles wide, would be hit by twelve bombers working in pairs. Each pair loaded with a total of eight cluster bombs would seek out their pre-determined target. Later they would go in as armed recce, to seek out targets of opportunity, tanks, armoured personnel carriers, command vehicles, trucks, tents, manned positions or any enemy men or matériel in their strip, and destroy whatever they found. But on this first run they were hitting specific targets.

The aircraft, the defence threat unknown, came in low and fast, the leader following his navigator's instructions coming off the global positioning system, inertial navigation systems, and the pre-recorded tape to bring them in on a perfect attack line. He checked his HUD, the head up display, listening to the voice from behind him.

'Just off the nose. Four miles. The hill. Stand of trees at one o'clock.'

'I have it.'

He shifted the aircraft to bring the trees into the target line on the HUD and decided on 1/250th of a second on the bomb release. His cluster bombs would scatter 140 bombs across a path, if he got his angle right, of 220 feet. The delay between bombs would give him a twenty-foot overlap, but give him a double footprint, some 400 feet. The satellite photography had shown the four tanks hidden in the trees to be within that distance. He pulled up, 'pickled' the two bombs off his underwing and dropped back down again, the navigator now blowing chaff and flares, his eyes and ears glued for a howl from the radar warning receiver as the aircraft jinked sideways and did a sharp left turn to clear the battle area for the next aircraft, his wingman.

The tree line erupted in a series of simultaneous explosions, branches and leaves shimmering as the blast wave and shrapnel tore outwards. Something else exploded, then another, bright orange flames billowed outwards, and ammunition began to go off, secondary explosions indicating to the pilot he had hit at least two of the tanks in the trees.

The second Tornado lined up on his target half a mile further on, and let four bombs go as the first aircraft pulled in behind him and began seeking his second target of the sortie. The rest of the squadron were behind them, the nearest twoship only thirty seconds out.

To the north, along Golf sector, upwind of the first smoke of the battle, the lead elements of a Jaguar squadron came in. Off to the north-west a Libyan unit began firing rounds to the north and another began making smoke to try and conceal itself from attack. It was a mistake. All it did was show their position. A loitering Harrier on an armed reconnaissance swooped like a hawk and attacked the position, destroying two tanks and a refuelling truck. As the jet pulled up the smoke changed from white to black, a funeral pyre on the edge of a field of green.

As the first squadrons passed through the southern sectors and headed back to base to refuel and rearm the northern areas were taking their first preplanned attacks from the Harriers.

The jump jets, with minimum fuel loads and every hard point loaded, were doing a sortie every twenty-five minutes, the pilots sitting in the cockpits as armourers and technicians crawled over their aircraft. Then, ready for action, they would roll on to a short take-off and be back in the battle, killing tanks within eight minutes of lift-off.

As the last of the first wave of aircraft, their hard points empty, headed for their bases the AWACS cleared the recce Tornado to make a series of high-speed low-level passes to make separate battle damage assessments. Twelve minutes later the aircraft cleared the area and the AWACS advised Dark Rose Command.

Seventy seconds later, the massive guns of the British army, the heavy artillery, rockets and dug-in tanks that had moved up the night before, opened fire along the front. The Libyans had fired at them. Rules of Engagment called for return fire. This was no long-range artillery duel, not just supporting fire by a battery. This was heavy warfare, sustained concentrated fire by more than a hundred heavy guns and six Multiple Rocket Launcher Systems, directly into the positions so carefully plotted with satellites.

The positions were crossroads, dry ground and the soft belly of the enemy strength, the support units, the infantry, the communications, repair, engineering and supply units. Two of the MRLS had their fire control computers targeting the salvos in deep. They were firing the new German mine dispensing rockets, sowing minefields across the higher dry ground that would support a fast armoured retreat away from the incoming artillery and the aircraft.

It was hoped that the armour that had survived the first strike wave would not venture out of their revetments while artillery was bracketing them and hitting the escape routes south. It would be decision time for the individual Libyan unit commanders. They knew the aircraft would be back. They could hear the mayhem on their radios from the units in the north where the Harriers were still hitting them. Leave now and risk running through the artillery that would destroy anything it hit, including their support elements, and risk also being caught on open ground, or wait till the artillery stopped and the aircraft came back? Because they knew they would be back.

To the south along the geographical contours that gave best advantage, the men of the Parachute Regiment were deployed, quickly digging into their positions and concealing themselves. Above them the Chinook transports were back off the ground, their huge rotors making a dull whumping noise as they flew eastwards towards the fleet.

The men on the ground ignored them, the officers moving pairs on to observation points out ahead and positioning their Milan launchers, the weapons teams scraping the soft earth back, digging themselves in. Every so often one of them would look up, unable to ignore the action to the north. Huge plumes of black smoke were drifting south to their positions and they could hear the artillery coming in, some as near as three miles away. For most it was the first time they had heard a sustained bombardment. It was a constant rumble like thunder, the ground shook and trembled beneath their feet, and for some it brought mixed emotions. They were pleased it was their guns they were hearing, but they felt that no one should have to go through the mind-numbing Dantean terror of incoming artillery.

Behind them, with the Welsh guarding their rear, the first Lynx anti-tank helicopters had arrived and were hidden, engines running, in a stand of trees, waiting to be called in. Other helicopters were already moving north and once ahead of the thin line of Paras they would activate their DAT mine dispensers, laying minefields to push any retreating Libyans into missile range of the hidden Paras and the ferocious firepower of the other helicopters.

The news broke to the world at 8.34 AM, when the Voice of Radio Free Ireland's announcer asked for everyone's attention and dropped a cassette into a player.

'People of Ireland, this is Maeve O'Donnell of the Clan O'Donnell. This is a momentous day in our history. Irish, Celt and Clansmen have heard the call of the drum and battle has begun. Today your armies, the armies of a Free Celtic Ireland have begun the campaign to free our homeland. We shall wage war with decisiveness in the belief that our cause is just and we shall not rest till the invaders are vanquished and the Republic of Ireland is again free. Stay in your homes. Stay with your families. We will be there soon. God bless you all.'

The BBC and CNN carried the broadcast as their embargoes on the main story broke.

473

The BBC simply announced: 'A large force of free Irish has launched an attack on the invaders of their homeland. It began . . .'

On the airbases in England the returning bombers were marshalled on to their pans where ground crews were waiting. A thumbs up from the pilot brought cheers from the men who had prepared the aircraft and loaded them with the deadly bombs. As the jets were refuelled and rearmed by double strength ground crews, the air crew were rushed into debriefings with intelligence officers who were recording damage assessments, taking claims of tanks and armour killed, viewing gun camera tapes of the action to put together a picture of the battle ready to brief the next sorties.

Fresh crews were waiting. The average of 1.6 crews per aircraft would not provide complete coverage, but no crew would have to fly more than two sorties back to back and those who would be returning immediately were de-briefed first and allowed to go and get a cup of something hot, smoke a cigarette or two and move back to the briefing for the next sortie.

On the battlefield the Paras were about to go into action.

# 14

The landing craft, crammed with men and two armoured vehicles, shouldered its way through the small waves past HMS *Dundee*.

The destroyer that had fired the first shots of the conflict was now in the gunline, just three miles off the beach, her 4.5 inch gun trained on the land, waiting to go into her gunfire support role. Her captain wasn't happy being this close. The old navy definition of dawn was when you could see a grey goose at one mile and that was when you stood off. In modern times with shore to ship missiles the adage was truer than ever and ideally he wanted to be at least twenty miles off the coast, but he could offer little direct support from that range. Now every radar scanner and lookout searched the skies for any threat to his ship or the fleet, while his gun crew waited for fire orders.

As the landing craft passed *Dundee* dipped her colours, respect for the man standing in the bows. General Stewart wasn't waiting for a perimeter to be established. The Royal Marines were five minutes ahead and for him that was quite enough. He stood, his legs braced against the sluggish roll of the flat-bottomed craft, his eyes on the flotilla of similar vessels ahead. The main force of Royal Marines were crammed into the LCs, moving on to the beach where their recce elements had already stormed out of the three big American hovercraft they had borrowed.

He was pleased. All objectives had been met, most before time, and the hundreds of hours of training had paid off. They had rehearsed this landing six times in remote Scottish bays and every man knew exactly which craft and which wave he was assigned to. So far the landing had been unopposed. Now to get Warriors ashore. Already there were Lynx anti-tank helicopters covering the sector between Carrickmacross and Dundalk, protecting the exposed flank until the division was ashore. The helicopters were formidable and they could close the gap to anything but a full tank regiment trying to break out.

An aide passed him his binoculars and pointed to the high ground at the southern end of the beach. There was a group of figures standing on the low headland. He focused and his face broke with a tight smile. It was Maeve. She had said she would be there. Everyone said no, don't do it. It will be very dangerous. She had just smiled and said good morning and left. And here she was. On the headland, watching Celt Force come ashore, the breeze blowing her hair and the heavy green cloak out behind her. He could imagine the sword of state between her legs, her hands on the hilt. Behind her stood a piper, his pipes up at his shoulder, and three or four other figures in the background. He couldn't see her security. They would be there somewhere. He had been as moved as any by the ceremony at Tara, and if any doubted her right to be queen, they were wrong. She had proved it again and again, earned it again and again in the last few weeks. The men he commanded were going to fight for her and what she stood for. And some of them would die. That was a certainty.

He swung the glasses back to the beach where the first landing craft were nudging up on to the shingle and sand between the markers, the men pouring off the front end into the cold water, their huge packs weighing them down.

The first of the returning aircraft were passing overhead now, this time a good deal higher, for medium-level bombing. Away to the north, somewhere on Dundalk Bay, intense anti-aircraft fire was lifting into the sky and almost immediately out on the gunline HMS *Nottingham* and HMS *Dundee* opened fire, their rapid-firing 4.5 inch guns seeking out the anti-aircraft battery, their aimers using the local area aiming device, but directed by someone on the 40-power cameras on the bridge wing. The anti-aircraft fire stopped, the battery either hit by one or more of the shells or the gunners thinking twice about advertising their location. Stewart didn't care which, as long as his pilots were safe to do their job, and made a mental note to commend the man who had acted.

The water's edge was now teeming with men, packs and equipment, with Royal Marine beach masters working through the confusion, as LCs reversed seawards to return to the fleet and the landing ships that were now moving closer. One LC was aground on something, its propeller churning in its housing, and finally someone threw the coxswain a line and it was towed off.

Stewart's barge touched bottom and as the front end dropped into the surf with a splash, he jumped down and waded ashore, his beret with its bright Celt Force hackle square on his head.

'Hello, sir,' a grinning marine shouted from beneath a huge pack.

'Morning, chaps,' Stewart barked, with a grin just as wide. 'Nice day to be at the seaside, what? Seen any of the enemy yet?'

'Not yet, sir,' one replied.

'Everything all right?'

'Fine, sir,' another responded.

'Good. Carry on, then.' With that he strode off up the beach as though he owned it, his aides and staff officers following, one smaller than the others and encumbered with a huge radio, struggling to keep up.

The first brush with the enemy was a few minutes later. A patrol of men from 45 Commando came across a group of Libyan vehicles moving rapidly south along a quiet country road. The marines officer yelled 'Hit 'em!' and his men opened fire from the roadside ditch where they had taken cover. The withering hail of bullets and two well-placed rounds from their Carl Gustav had the lead vehicles crashed and in flames. The officer called for his men to cease fire a few moments later. One of the marines was wounded, a light flesh wound from shrapnel, but the Libyan force had taken a beating. There were nine dead, seven wounded and twenty-six now sitting down on the road with their hands behind their heads.

The young officer looked at the prisoners. What to do? He called his radio man over and a moment later gave him back the mike.

'Corporal Davis.'

'Sah.'

'Take someone with you. March 'em back to the beach. Give them to some wally and catch up.'

'Yes, sir.'

The officer watched as the young corporal chose a soldier and they began to line the prisoners up in two ranks. It was their first action, for almost all of them. He had hoped that his non-coms and men wouldn't notice when it happened. His father had warned him. Afterwards your hands shake. You get scared before and afterwards. He reached for his cigarettes in his shirt pocket and his hand was shaking as he lifted his lighter.

Beside him was one of the bodies, its face shot away. Suddenly he didn't care any more. Didn't care who saw his hand shake. He felt sick.

His father never warned him about that.

The US Marines' objective was simple. Take and hold Ballycotton Bay, establish a defensive perimeter in such a manner as to convince the enemy that a major landing had taken place and then use the area to mount helicopter operations against the enemy with vigour at every opportunity.

The officer commanding the marines, General James Elroy Murphy, didn't like playing second fiddle in any operation, especially after his beloved Corps had had to provide the diversion in the Gulf War as well, so he took to the second half of the orders with a vengeance.

His advance elements had already thrust inland and cut the road between Youghal and Midleton and the smaller roads at either end of the bay. His main force began arriving ashore in dramatic fashion in eight of the huge LCAC hovercraft. The fast approach landing craft were capable of carrying armoured personnel carriers and fighting vehicles, but the first load was men and their gear, a classic Marine Corps amphibious assault. Lethal-looking Cobra gunships buzzed overhead and already on the helicopter carrier the big transport helicopters were loading with their precious cargoes of fuel, stores, and air mobile artillery, their beloved 155mm howitzer guns.

The general's intent was to be able to report that his shore firebases, one at Ballycotton Bay and a second on Inishmore, were operational by mid-morning and he whipped his people along to achieve that. In all his career, a career than had seen him serve in Vietnam, Beirut, Grenada, and the Gulf, he had never fought a campaign that he had believed in as totally as this, and he felt there had never been a conflict that America should have been more willing to fight. His mother's people had come from a place not thirty miles from Ballycotton Bay. For General Murphy this was the old country, a place that lived in song, verse and tales at his parents' dinner table, and his staff reported his progress through to Stewart and High Wycombe with glee.

The 2 Para C Company command position was set back off the road at the western end of Lake Sillan, two and a half miles from the nearest of the positions that the air force were about to start pounding again, and half a mile away from where a young captain was dug in with his two sections. He was camouflaged like his men, lying in the morning shadows of a hedgerow, his binoculars to his eyes. Captain Mackay's observation point had just radioed in. A small column of tanks and trucks were feeling their way down the road.. With the powerful spotting scope they were using they had a little time. He looked quickly down at his map. He knew it backwards, every road, every stream, but referred anyway to give himself time to think. A line of small lakes ran for ten miles along the southern end of the battle zone. The only way through their sector was on either the R181 or the R162 down towards Shercock. He ran his finger down the yellow lines on the map. The observation point said they were heading towards the right-hand road, the R181. Would they turn and then stay on the road? They had to turn. The minor road they were on ran parallel to the battlefield. They would want to put some country between them and the incoming artillery and the certain to return aircraft. They had to turn and then they had to stick to the new road with its hard surface. Leave the road and the heavy main battle tanks could sink in the wet, boggy ground. The trucks certainly would. His section was sitting midway between the roads and from his vantage he could see both and command both.

'Sar'nt Collier,' he said. 'Stay here and be ready to reinforce Miller's team. Take a third Milan with you. I'm going over to Smith's team. The buggers are coming down that road. They may come down the other, too.'

As the young officer bent over and began to move down the rear of the hedgerow with his radio operator the sergeant, a Falklands veteran, looked across at two soldiers sitting huddled beneath the bracken of the hedgerow. Shit. The Milan was well hidden. with a parapet of small stones

480

and top cover. Now they had to bloody move it again. 'You two. Be ready to move your Milan and follow me.'

Mackay slithered into the long natural ditch his men had positioned themselves in and snatched up his binoculars. The tankers would be in turmoil, he thought. If they left the road they risked getting stuck in the boggy soft earth and they would certainly lose whatever support the motorized infantry could offer, assuming that the trucks were carrying men, of course. On the other hand as long as they were on the road they were exposed, every attack pilot's dream. A column of armour out in the open. They must be desperate. Terrified. Under pressure. People under pressure fuck up. He will stay on the road and hope that the speed its hard surface allows will make up for the exposure risk. Out here there was nowhere to hide MBTs anyway. He made a decision and radioed in again.

His company commander was half a mile away to the east.

'Sunray I have armour heading my way. I'm going to move my section on to Juliet. That will leave India wide open for the time being.'

'Ah, roger five three, stand by . . . okay five three, how many heavies coming your way?'

'Five one confirm figures four repeat four mike bravo tango with three, repeat three soft-skinned transports.'

'Roger five three. Agree with your intent. Angel will hold India.'

Fuck me, Mackay thought. They were moving the Lynxes up already and he had a two-man observation point half a mile out in front of them. If the Lynxes started shooting then his boys were going to be very close to the action.

'Five one. I have an oscar papa out in the open there.'

'Roger three. They can advise on the company net then keep their heads down.'

'Roger one,' Mackay answered dropping the radio mike. 'Get on to Collier,' he said to the radio operator. 'Get him and Miller's team over here on the double. Then get on to the OP. Tell them that if they have traffic down India advise on the company net and get hunkered down. Helicopters will be the heavy mob. Got it?'

The radio man nodded and lifted the mike. Mackay moved down the line to his men where they were positioned with their Milan launchers, twenty metres apart. Three teams each of a loader, an operator and a spotter with a powerful optical sight were deployed along the ditch line below the summit of the low rise. Mackay barely saw the first group till he was on them, so well were they camouflaged, and one of them had his rifle pointed at the ready.

''Allo, sir,' Corporal Smith said, pleased to see his officer. 'Confirm we have them coming this way?'

'That's affirmative. I have Sar'nt Collier and Miller's team coming in. I am going to put them along this slope.'

'Western end would be good, guv'nor,' the corporal replied steadily. Mackay looked down to where the man had pointed. In the British army when young officers, fresh from Sandhurst clutching their aide memoire, didn't listen to the advice of their experienced NCOs, they usually screwed up badly. The western end of the slope was further back from the road, adding a hundred metres to the missile flight, but it offered cover behind a stone wall and hedges and would give a different firing angle to a missile team hidden there. He would have chosen it anyway, but give the corporal the credit. Tactically it seemed as good as it was going to get.

'Thanks, Corporal, I'll take your advice.'

Collier and the remaining ten men had run the distance behind the brow of the low hill and, breathing hard, they were barely set up when the long snout of the first Libyan T-72 nosed its way down the road and halted. A soft-skinned truck overtook it. It was a bizarre scene, the heavy tank beneath the black smoke of the battle only a couple of miles away. The smoke was thick, forming a haze overhead, softening the light and casting shadows. The tanks were real. Mackay could see them through the trees and the roadside hedge and looked across at Collier, trying to establish if the target was clearer from his vantage.

He must have been reading Mackay's mind, because he raised a hand in the air. Mackay scooped up his glasses. One stumpy finger was held aloft. He could see one. Mackay held up a hand in response. Wait.

It was a thousand yards off. To the left was a farm and its attendant outbuildings and to the right were fields, the road bordered with trees and hedges. He studied the road, the curve back away from them, the gaps in the hedges. At about 600 metres the hedge thinned out to nothing. That's it, he thought. Let them get closer. That's my killing ground. If they break west of the road then they will run into the choppers. If they come towards us, then . . . then . . . shit. He didn't want to think about four MBTs thundering towards them. Like many of those from an infantry background he had a healthy respect for tanks, but wouldn't get in one for anything. Overhead he could hear the bombers returning. That would force the tank commander to speed up. He would feel safe below the smoke, hoping that none of the jets were using thermal image equipment, but he would still want to be moving south away from the battle. He might even think that he is being attacked from above, Mackay thought. Another good reason to wait till he's side on.

The tank began to move, not tentatively, but with purpose. The truck had been the recce, clever bastard. His APC escort had been done over, but he's not moving without a scout, not venturing into the open without sending someone else to have a look. A second tank appeared and then a third. They were nervous. Didn't have the cool of their boss. They were bunching up.

'Lead tank,' Mackay said to the nearest missile team. 'You got him?'

'We have him.'

He leaned over his radio. 'Team two tank two, team three tank three. Got it?' he called.

They acknowledged, the last lad nervous, his mouth dry.

'Team four close the back door.' After that Collier could hit whatever he liked, but they had discussed this scenario. The sergeant acknowledged.

'Then reload and stand by. Fire on the command.'

Mackay, still holding the radio mike, rolled away from his radio man, who was wedged in beside him, the big Clansman radio on his back to look down the hillside.

'Whisky Papa Mike, Whisky Papa Mike. Five three, Nathan, do you read over?' The corporal on the OP.

Nothing.

'Nathan, do you read me over?'

Still nothing. Fucking radios, he thought. The PRC 320 Clansman were better than their predecessor, but for the soldiers they were still notoriously unreliable.

'Nathan if you can hear me, heads down. We are going to engage.'

Mackay dropped the mike, lifting his binoculars to his eyes. They looked so fucking big. Even at this distance they were fearsome beasts, great lumbering steel leviathans that could crush the life from anything. Just steel plate on an engine, he said to reassure himself, and a bloody great gun. Oh, but they burn, and my Milans cut through steel, blast through armour like it was plywood.

They were nearing the gap now, closing at fifteen miles an hour.

'Wait for it,' he said. He raised an arm in the air, hoping Collier was watching from the second position.

'On the command . . . Fire! Fire! Fire!' he shouted, dropping his hand. The nearest missile blasted out of the launcher half a second ahead of the other two. Mackay tore his eyes from the flight to look across at Collier's team. They had a missile in flight.

Corporal Smith snarling at one of the men. 'Don't watch it, cunt! LOAD another!'

Mackay watching the missiles searing away from them, praying for a direct hit, please Jesus.

'More tanks on the road,' someone yelled.

The first missile hit the lead tank, its armour-penetrating warhead piercing the thick steel plate and exploding on the inside. There was surprisingly little obvious damage. The tank slewed right off the road and drew to a halt, black smoke pouring from its vents. The crew were dead, cooked by the close proximity of the blast and superheated gases. The second and third Milan missiles hit their targets a second later. The second tank exploded in a spectacular fashion after the missile detonated its magazine, twelve HE rounds in the racks exploding half a second after the missile had hit. The blast of the secondary explosions lifted its turret into the air, the concussion wave rocking the ground and blasting leaves off trees sixty yards away. The third tank didn't die. The Milan had hit low, taking out the tracks on the left side, venting its power on the driving wheel and heavy steel of the rear under quarter, strengthened specifically for land mines. The crew were stunned for a couple of seconds and then the driver reacted. The offside drive wheel began to churn in reverse, the tank swivelling to the right on the one working track. Then the turret began to move, like a beast sniffing the air, hurt, but far from helpless. The barrel foreshortened as it aimed at their hillside, the image obscured for a second as Collier's second missile streaked past it and slammed into the fourth tank which exploded.

'MORE TANKS!' the voice yelled again.

'WHERE?' Mackay yelled.

'The trees!' the trooper called back. 'Eleven o'clock. One thousand yards!'

The injured tank, now the last alive in the original formation, rocked back as its cannon fired and seconds later the round seared overhead making a sound like a passing train.

'Take it!' Mackay yelled, knowing that Corporal Smith had reloads on the way, and swung his glasses up to find the new threat, the other tanks.

Two missiles streaked away and they had barely cleared the hillside when Mackay could hear Smith shouting orders to his teams, moving them to new vantage points. He felt a roll of guilt. He should have thought of that, but looking instead for the other tanks, shit where are they, there, trees, focus, oh Jesus, oh my God, a column, six or seven of them, turrets turning towards them. Below him the damaged tank, hit by two more Milans, was now on fire, palls of smoke rising into the sky. The men in the trucks had jumped out and run for cover in the ditches, but one vehicle was trying to turn on the road. Keep an eye on the ground troops. Mackay looked back to the new threat. Where is the scout, they never move without a scout, he swung the glasses to the right, there! An APC in front reversing into some trees going for cover. They have seen us. They have our position marked. Move! Not just new firing points. Get the fuck out of here.

'Corporal Smith! Withdraw to secondary positions. Move it!'

A shell roared overhead and exploded behind them somewhere and a fifty-calibre gun on one of the vehicles had opened fire, the rounds hitting the hillside below them.

Mackay snatched the radio mike from the hand that held it out.

'Whisky Papa Mike, Whisky Papa Mike, if you can hear

me, withdraw to Echo, repeat withdraw to Echo.' Mackay changed channels. 'Five one, five one, this is five three.'

'Go three.'

'One, I have four dead mike bravo tangos on Juliet. But more approaching. Company strength. I have five, repeat five Milans left. They have my position marked and we are under fire and on the move over.'

'Roger three. Confirm you have company strength tanks on Juliet?'

'Affirmative,' Mackay yelled, ducking as another tank round roared overhead, this time much nearer. T-64s and 72s. Old tanks. Crappy optical sights. They are ranging. The next one. Next one will hit. Sweet Jesus. He felt the fear but overrode it. Move the lads.

'Five three, stand by.'

Mackay pulled the radio operator to his knees. 'Let's go.'

They scrambled back up the hillside through the wet grass along the hedge line, following the last of the men carrying the heavy launchers, Corporal Smith urging them on.

Mackay pushed the radio man forward and dropped to one knee, his glasses up to his eyes, seeking out Collier's team. They had moved already.

The round hit as he began to move again. He didn't hear this one. The blast picked him up and threw him forwards and when he got to his knees, he was missing his helmet and bleeding from the ears and nose. He realized he had been out for a few seconds. Someone was screaming and Smith was bending over another figure on the ground. A few feet away a soldier sat huddled, holding his upper leg, blood oozing through his trousers while another knelt beside him, tearing the covers from a dressing.

He moved across to where Smith was.

'Move them back. NOW!'

Hands grabbed at the wounded and lifted bodily they were quickly carried over the top of the hill. In the next ten seconds another three shells hit the slope below them.

'Okay. What have we got?'

'One dead,' Smith answered looking up, 'three injured. One leg, one stomach and you.'

'I'm okay.'

'Bullshit . . . sir. You are concussed.'

'I'm okay. Get these boys moved back down there.' He pointed down the hill. 'Then set up on the brow. Two launchers only.'

The radio operator appeared and handed him the mike. He took it, one shaking hand to another. It was a new voice. His commanding officer, Major Sherin.

'Five three, move your team to Echo. I am coming across with a section. Leave a controller. Angels will be with you in three. Be ready to talk them on to the target over.'

'Roger one. We took a hit. I have one dead and two wounded. Request medivac.'

Mackay listened and then dropped the mike. 'Give me the radio.' As the operator began to shrug the heavy box off his back Mackay looked at Corporal Smith. 'Low down there for the chopper,' he said. 'Mark with blue smoke. Then get word to Collier. Set up a defensive position below the brow. Major Sherin will be coming in, so keep an eye out and for Nathan and his oppo, right?'

'Where you going?' Smith asked. Another shell slammed into the hillside a hundred feet away over the brow, showering them with clods of dirt and mud.

'FAC,' Mackay answered trying to keep his voice level. The helicopters didn't usually need a forward controller, but he knew he could bring them right in to the target with no mistakes. He was shit scared but he couldn't ask any of them to do it. Not go back over the brow.

'Dave,' Smith said softly.

'Yeah,' Mackay responded looking up. It was the first time the corporal had ever used his Christian name while they were in uniform.

'You'll do,' he said with a nod.


The Lynxes came in from the west. Three of the tank-killing helicopters advanced in the scurry and hide manner, rushing forward across the open ground at cabbage height to hide behind the next piece of cover like a stalking cat. Before them a tiny scout helicopter shuffled forward from cover to cover, its rotor mounted camera designed for seeing above the blades as it hid behind barns and houses.

Mackay lay in a new shell hole on the north-facing slope, his binoculars to his eyes, and he still hadn't seen them when they called him.

'Five three alpha kilo nine.'

'Kilo nine, five three go.'

'Three I am from your left. I have four smoke plumes visual at twelve o'clock nine hundred metres. Where is my target over.'

Mackay swung his glasses with one hand, holding the radio mike with the other, searching for the Lynxes. Another shell hit the hillside below him, deafening him for a second or two and showering him with dirt, mud and grass.

'If the smoke is to your twelve kilo nine, the target is at your ten o'clock, same distance. In the tree line beside the road,' he said, adding, 'I am on the hill at your two o'clock.'

Suddenly from behind the barn at the farm Mackay saw the little scout helicopter's rotors as it lifted enough to allow the camera to see over the roof.

'Ah . . . roger . . . five three we have the targets. Sit tight.'

Mackay settled back into the shell hole, just his head over the top, aware of the danger of another round coming in close, but not willing to miss the Lynxes' attack.

Suddenly from behind the house and tractor shed three helicopters rose as one like lethal gigantic dragonflies. The first missiles launched as one, streaking over the ground trailing white smoke and immediately the helicopters dropped down again. Mackay watched the TOW missiles hit and as the first tanks began to explode and burn he knew they would be shuffling sideways to a second vantage point for their next attack. He never saw the second salvo leave the pods, the white smoke trail coming this time from the north, hitting the tanks from the rear. Finally one of the Lynxes broke cover and gathering airspeed by flying parallel to the battle it finally turned and came in, advancing at attack speed, its thirty millimetre minigun pouring rounds into the last of the tanks and soft-skinned vehicles. The APC was on fire now, and as the Lynx moved off the field fell silent except for the dull thump of ammunition burning off in one of the wrecked tanks.

'Five three kilo nine, we count eight kills. Please confirm we have all targets over.' In spite of the professional words Mackay could hear the adrenalin in the pilot's voice. These would have been his first shots in anger, too.

'Kilo nine I only counted seven mike bravos. I think you have all of them over. Thanks.'

'You're welcome three. We are homeward bound.'

'Thanks again nine,' Mackay replied. 'It was getting hairy down here.'

'Our pleasure.'

Behind the hill the Lynx carrying the dead and wounded lifted off. The dead paratrooper was a man by the name of Bonner. The first soldier to volunteer after Queen Maeve's request for a few good men was also the first to die.

The main Celtic landing was proceeding well. The Royal Marines' perimeter was now firmly established and they

490

were handing it over to an infantry regiment and moving inland. The Chinook troop carriers, up to now moving men ashore from the fleet, had begun to ferry men from the beachhead on to the next objectives. The landing area was equipped with sufficient fuel and well defended, the huge helicopters transporting forty men at a time into the long thin line held by the battalions of the Parachute Regiment.

Stewart's command was set up in a barn a mile from the beach. His APCs and communications vehicles were under cover and a line of officers stood over radio operators, monitoring each immediate phase of the landing or the battle to the north, redeploying air assets, equipment and men.

Two miles away at 5th Airborne Brigade headquarters the OC bent over a map, one ear listening to a report from 2 Para.

'That's that one closed,' the brigadier said. He had taken the Fifth Brigade over from Stewart two years before and he had been delighted with what he had found, but expected nothing else considering who their last boss had been. This action was a classic example. Only one soldier dead for eleven of their MBTs and crews, troops in the soft-skins unknown.

'Two developing over here,' said one of the intelligence officers. He dropped a flimsy message sheet and placed two orange markers on the map. East of the first break the markers were sitting over the R188, the road into Cavan from the north.

The brigadier moved over. 'I don't want them getting anywhere near that town. Air liaison officer, please.'

The resistance had started the day with a vengeance. Cells were attacking Libyan and Palestinian forces within earshot of the battle and as far away as Kerry. Local resistance people had met up with elements of the Royal

Marines outside Ardee and Drogheda and were pinpointing positions for the Celt Force soldiers. Although most of the attacks were successful, the Libyans easy targets on the roads, fate set out to restore the odds. A clever young Palestinian fighter lured a resistance cell into an ambush outside Roscrea and a Libyan patrol, strengthened overnight, clashed with a resistance team. Four of the fighters were killed when a rocket propelled grenade exploded in the culvert they were taking cover in. The remaining three were captured.

In the Knockmealdown mountains south of Clonmel a column of armoured vehicles ventured round a road that had never seen an enemy force. The column moving to reinforce the shifting battle line at Dungarven had taken a short cut through the mountains and along the R669 and stumbled on a resistance cell moving the other way in three cars. The Libyans, commanded by a thoroughly professional officer blooded in the vicious fighting with Chadian irregulars, were alert. The first vehicle in their column pulled off the road and the troops dropped into cover on the sides. The following tank, its commander up in the turret, had his hands on the machine gun and as he shouted orders to his gunner he opened fire on the cars, the troops on the ground following suit. The Irish never stood a chance. Of the eleven resistance fighters, seven were killed in the first seconds of the engagement. An SAS adviser died with them. The remaining four were captured and shot a few minutes later, their bodies left in the ditch beside the road. In a final act demonstrating the callousness of war the cars were shunted off the road by the lead tank, a Toyota ending up on the bodies of the executed fighters.

The fourth wave of bombers came in from the north. The battlefield was now almost completely obscured by smoke and the pilots' briefings, based on battle damage assessments, were now a collection of we-thinks, this-suggests and maybes. The missions were now armed reconnaissance, the aircraft dropping down through the smoke looking for targets of opportunity, the lead aircraft spotting the target and calling its position back to the following jet in the pair. The pilots were careful, watching for the trail of heat-seeking missiles as they soared skyward. These were not the big radar-guided systems – the three the Libyans had were destroyed in the opening minutes of the battle – but hand-held, shoulder-launched SAM 7s. A Tornado pilot had become complacent on the last wave. He had gone low to make sure of his attack and ejected with his navigator after a SAM 7 had taken them straight up the jetpipe at 2000 feet.

The new mission made available air power to support the ground troops and the FAC, the lone Tornado aloft for the third time after refuelling, had moved south so he could now call the bombers in on the isolated small units still trying to break out past the Paras. Four Tornadoes now loitered 20,000 feet over Enniskillen on the British side of the border, cluster bombs on their hard points waiting to be given a target. The Harriers still pounded the northernmost elements of the battered Libyan division. With minimal fuel load they could carry extra bombs and they had now subjected the defenders to three brutal hours of attack. In their sector they had hit every target twice and now, like the Tornadoes, flew armed reconnaissance while below them engineers were already trying to clear a path through the minefield.

Two squadrons, one of Tornadoes and one of Jaguars, had now been released from the northern battle and were flying deep interdiction missions, seeking out Libyan and Palestinian positions, columns, fuel, storage, massing points and bottlenecks where they could find them. The Palestinians, long on the receiving end of ground strikes by the Israeli air force, knew the drills. Expecting the attacks from the first instant, they dispersed widely and had taken cover in barns, outbuildings, factories, wherever they could. If they were in the open they were well camouflaged and most units had shoulder-fired missiles to discourage attack from above.

Maeve stood against the canvas wall, her eyes taking in the calm, measured activity in the command centre. She was wearing camouflage uniform like everyone else, the heavy paratrooper's smock taken in at the waist with a belt. Her long hair was up at the back and pinned beneath a beret. Kiernan stood beside her, dressed as always in slacks, a woollen tie and the old shapeless jacket that had become so familiar.

'There is a group holed up in the monastery at Kells,' the intelligence officer said to Kiernan. 'That's on your list.'

'It is,' Kiernan replied. 'That monastery is part of our history. If anything were to happen . . .'

'Just checking,' the officer replied with a tight smile. Another one to cut off and come back to later. So much easier to just take them out. Every time they sealed off a group in some location for later action it meant valuable soldiers taken up to keep them there.

The Celt thrust inland was to take them west as far as Longford. There they could cut off the north, take the crossroads and push south to Athlone, taking control of the bridges over the Shannon and the roads in from the west.

Anything further to the west of Roscommon was in the US marines' sector and their gunships were already probing deep inland, attacking the enemy wherever they could. Transport helicopters had already put men into the country to the north of Longford and the men of the Royal Irish were already moving northwards to meet up with the Welsh.

\* \* \*

The Black Watch were on the ground to the south, outside Athlone. Two companies moved slowly towards the town and their rendezvous with the resistance and one company, C, were preparing to move northwards round Lough Ree when a local boy ran into their company area.

'My da told me to find you,' he said panting to the first soldier he saw. 'Can you come?'

He was delivered to an officer at their command, by now in a shed alongside a farmhouse, who was folding a map on the ground. 'What's up?' the young captain asked him.

'Don't know,' the boy answered. 'My father's found something. He wouldn't tell me. But you are to come.' He stopped for a moment. 'He's *buachailli*,' he said with pride. 'He told me to bring the truck for you. It's a few miles up the road.'

'You just drove down the road now?' Captain Dugan asked.

'Yes.'

'Any Arabs?'

'Didn't see any. There were some this morning in at Ballinasloe and of course in Athlone.'

'Who told you that?' Captain Dugan asked, looking at his map again.

'We know where they are,' the boy replied confidently. 'Today they are running,' he finished with a grin.

The farmer's wife brought in cups of tea on a tray.

'Jamie Collins, you will catch your death running round without a coat,' she said, seeing the boy. 'Have one of these.'

'You know him?' Dugan asked.

'Oh yes. Known them for years,' she replied.

He quickly explained that the boy brought a message.

'If his da says come, you go. Eamon Collins has never wasted anyone's time, let alone his own.'

Dugan studied the boy's face for a moment. He had intended a slow recce round the lake until he linked up with the Royal Irish, but this changed things. Momentum was everything. Flexibility was everything. If your objective can be met faster or better, do it. If you can exceed the objective, do it. A truck to move in and reports that the road was clear were too good to miss. Whatever his dad wanted to report could be done on the way. The major said go for it and the truck was loaded fifteen minutes later. Twenty-two men, most of his platoon, were crammed into the truck and they set off, a commandeered car in the lead with a recce element, and a man on a 'borrowed' motorbike a mile in front.

The rest of the company would follow when they had found some transport. The boy had made some calls from a phone and there were local men on their way with trucks and vans.


The young soldier couldn't believe what he was seeing. Lying in the trees looking into the clearing there were men, remnants of men, behind a fence. Thin, skeletal forms, some standing, but most sitting in the mud, crowded the small enclosure. Huddled forms, miserable, near death, literally starving.

He wiped his eyes and looked back down the sight of his rifle. Beside him his officer Captain Dugan was listening to the Irishman. On the other side another soldier lay, his weapon to the fore.

'Found it this morning. I think the guards must be in the shelter at the back there,' Collins whispered. 'I have only seen two of them.'

Captain Dugan nodded. His face was a mask of stone. He picked up his binoculars and looked down at the camp.

'Tell your men to hold their fire,' the resistance man said. 'I have my boys coming in from the north.'

A few moments later two men appeared from the trees, moving absolutely silently, using hand signals as they crossed the last few yards. They slithered into the depression where Collins waited with Captain Dugan. His glance took them in. Filthy clothing, faces camouflaged with something, but the weapons were spotlessly clean.

'There's about twelve of them in the huts and three out on the fence at the back.'

Dugan didn't doubt them; a few minutes later they moved back and he gave his orders. Fifteen minutes later the Black Watch moved in and in fifty seconds it was all over.

The prisoners, the last survivors of the officer corps of the Irish Defence Force, tried to stand as the Scots soldiers opened the gates. Most moved forward, but others too weak to move just watched, not really believing that help had at last arrived. The Scotsmen could not believe what they were seeing. One, a rock-hard lad from the wrong end of Glasgow, felt a lump in his throat when a walking skeleton, a skeleton wearing a captain's bars on his filthy coat, tried to return his salute, but was too weak to manage. He sat down in the mud. Never normally one to have much time for officers, he wrapped the Irishman in his thick warm coat, and held him in his arms.

Dugan was deploying half his men into a defensive perimeter and calling for support teams when a gaunt man, one of the prisoners, walked towards him.

'Hello, Robby,' he said.

Dugan looked at him.

'You don't recognize me, do you?' the figure said with a thin sad smile.

The Chinooks came in and forty minutes later the area was alive with medical teams, tents going up, food cooking on fires. The first soldiers had opened up their rations, held their food to the lips of the starving men, but now the professionals had arrived. The worst cases among the survivors were lifted straight into the Belfast Infirmary, but most of the remaining men had asked to remain in the Republic on principle so the British army medical teams set up in another clearing half a mile away.

Stewart and Queen Maeve, who had insisted on seeing the camp, arrived in a smaller helicopter as the transfer was commencing.

'There were two hundred and twenty-seven men interned here. The middle-rank and senior officers of the Irish Defence Forces.' The officer halted, swallowing, visibly affected by what they had found. 'There are one hundred and seventy-seven left. Many of those are very poorly. They have been denied medical care, shelter and warmth. They have been systematically starved.'

As he spoke Stewart took in the scene, desperately thin forms lost inside sleeping bags being moved on stretchers. A small group of them sat by the gate, wearing newly issued coats, one smoking a cigarette and coughing violently each time he inhaled. One who had been standing alone watching his weaker comrades carried out, a word for each of them as they passed him, finally walked across to where Stewart stood. He stumbled once and a Celt Force soldier went to assist him, but he pushed the man's hand away, his head held high.

'This chap coming,' the British officer murmured to Stewart, 'the senior survivor.'

Dugan stepped forward. 'Sir. I know him. He is Andre Hyland. I played against him in March. He is . . . was . . . the fastest centre they ever had.'

Stewart nodded, murmuring, 'Thanks, Bob.'

Hyland, the man who had watched as his colonel was shot and sworn vengeance, stopped before Stewart and brought his hand up in a salute.

'Hyland. Commandant. Irish Defence Force. Reporting for duty.' Each word was laboured, an effort.

Stewart returned the salute. 'I appreciate your devotion to duty, Commandant. Last time I saw you was chasing young Dugan here up the sideline at Lansdowne Road.'

Hyland gave a wintry smile. It all seemed so long ago.

'I want you to report to the MO,' Stewart finished.

'No, sir. I want to fight.'

'I understand that, but you need food, rest, medical care.'

'Sir. I watched the senior officer murdered. I have watched my men die. I may not be as fit as usual but I bloody insist!'

Maeve turned to look at Stewart, her eyes pleading. He gave a small smile and looked back at the gaunt weak man before him, aware that every indication suggested him to be the senior surviving officer in the entire resident Irish forces. He was thinking quickly. 'On one condition. You eat and sleep for twenty-four hours. Infantry?'

Hyland nodded.

'Good. Tomorrow you will be given command of a unit.' Stewart looked at Maeve. 'You want this officer?'

'Yes!'

'So be it.' He turned back to Hyland. 'Tomorrow you will be attached to Queen Maeve's Own. That is an amalgamation of Irish units that were abroad. This is Maeve O'Donnell,' Stewart smiled, 'your Queen and Commander in Chief. I don't suppose you heard about that.'

'We did,' Hyland replied, turning weakly to Maeve. 'Pleased to meet you.'

'Now get some food into you, Commandant.'

'Sir?'

Stewart looked back.

'I can take you to the other camps. I have been in two of them.'

'Thank you, Commandant, but we know where they are. It was you chaps we had lost.'

'I want any able-bodied men we find. Any man who can lift a rifle.'

Stewart studied him for a second, the thin, desperately weak man before him. Only his eyes were strong, they blazed with an anger Stewart had only rarely seen.

'You may have whoever you wish, and get some rest

because, Commandant, Maeve's Own will be the spear-head. You will lead the Free Irish elements of Celt Force into Dublin.'

None of the guards survived the attack. Later the captain reported that although three had surrendered an Irish soldier, never identified, misinterpreted something as an attempt to escape and shot them. They were buried immediately. No one wanted a coroner's report. No one wanted anyone to see that they had been shot in the back of the head at close quarters.

'A' company of the Black Watch were now moving through the outer limits of Athlone. Once again the flexible planning ethos was used. The battalion's objective was to seal off the roads from the north and west, but when word arrived that the town was only lightly held it seemed ridiculous not to take the town as well. With a rifle platoon and the weapons platoon holding the roads, a section of the second platoon, a recce group, were moving towards an alleyway on a small estate, a resistance member guiding them to where they had seen Libyans the night before.

The platoon sergeant, a hard, fit individual, moved at the head of the two sections with four other soldiers and the resistance man. The lieutenant, very experienced and awaiting his promotion to captain, remained in the middle of the formation with his radio operator and the medic. A piper, his pipes in a bag over his shoulder trailed along as tail-end-charlie, moving backwards covering the section's rear.

As they moved forward, a point man and the sergeant's forward group were thirty metres ahead of the fifteen men in the main body and they crossed round the corner into the alley quickly, no talking, moving from cover to cover, using doorways, down pipes, rubbish bins as they had trained to do for the troubles in Ulster.

They reached the end of the alley, crossed the road quickly and had just jumped the wall into a garden when a long burst of fire raked the street. They all dropped back into cover, the point man scurrying back.

'Fookin' 'ell,' someone said.

'Shut it,' the sergeant snapped. 'Anyone see where it came from?'

'Up the street, sarge, by the church,' a lanky young private replied. Bullets hit the wall of the next house up and ricocheted noisily off into the sky.

'Fookin' bastids.'

'Mick. Get back to Mr Meers. Let 'em know where we are. Tell 'em heads down, right? Go.' The sergeant looked across at the other soldier near him and grabbed the boy's collar. 'You show me.' They crawled forward to the edge of the wall.

A window opened above them and to the soldiers' astonishment a woman's head popped out, bright cheery eyes peering through old-fashioned glasses with horn rims.

'Well, well, the English! You took your time getting here, now then. You're all very welcome, but don't stay too long this time!'

Her accent was strong and two of the men looked at the resistance man to interpret. 'What she say?'

He explained and one of the soldiers rolled over to look up at the window. 'We're na fookin' English. We're Black Watch! Scots!' he answered indignantly. More bullets hit the wall, closer this time and the little head dropped down only to appear again a moment later.

'Tell you what. Sort out those up there at the hall and I'll make a cake, shall I?'

'Bugger this. Sarge? Can we shoot back?' someone called.

'Shut it for fuck sakes,' a corporal said. He looked up at the woman in the window. 'Are you sure they are in the hall?'

"Course I am. Been there for hours now. Palestinians. Threw Mrs Peters' flowers out into the street, they did,' she answered.

'Which building is it?'

'Sure, it's the red brick one there beside the church,' she replied pointing, as though it was obvious to anyone who cared to look.

'Did you see how many there are?'

'No. But there's a few. A lorry load. The ones in uniform left in a hurry this morning.'

'Bake the cake, darling. We'll be back,' the corporal called, then rolled on to his stomach and crawled forward. 'Sarge, the red brick building, top of the street next to the church. They're in there. Not Libyan wankers. Palestinians. A lorry load, the old biddy said.'

The sergeant rolled back to look at him.

'Is it now?' he said rhetorically. He had held a grudging respect for them for years and now they were going to mix it. The Black Watch vs PLO. No fucking contest, he thought.

'Right Corporal Lewis. You stay here with Cameron. Wait for the section. I am going round the back of the hall. Recce only. We will go and return through that gap in the houses there where the cars are. Do not, repeat do not fire at anyone coming through there unless you are fucking certain of your target. Understood?'

'Understood.'

'Right. Return fire at will. You, Chalky,' he jabbed a finger at the last private, 'come with me.'

They moved down the street through the gardens until they reached a point where parked cars offered cover and darted across. Bullets hit the ground around them and two slammed into a parked car, one shattering the windscreen. Back in the position they had left the corporal began to return the fire, measured single shots aimed at windows in the hall.

Now across the street, they moved quickly up through the gardens until they were four houses from the end and the sergeant pulled the soldier down beside him, sheltering in the back doorway of a house.

'Right. If they are clever pricks, they will have someone watching the back. Move fast and low. Like you were trained, right?'

'Right, sarge,' the soldier nodded, pulling his helmet closer, his swallow betraying his nerves.

'Me first.' The sergeant leapt from cover and jinking left and right moved forward. As he dropped into cover there was a burst of fire, bullets hitting the wall.

'You okay sarge?'

'I'm okay . . . Chalky. Did you see it?'

'Yeah. One at the back door and another I think behind the car there.'

'Which car, Chalky?' the sergeant called patiently.

'The blue Volvo there.'

'Wait for it.' The sergeant eased his rifle to his shoulder. The door was wooden. His rounds would go straight through it and then some. The car? If he was behind the engine, wheel or a pillar he might be okay, but otherwise also a bad choice of cover. The door first.

He sighted.

'GO!' he yelled.

As he heard Chalky move behind him there was a flash of movement at the door, a barrel. He fired, three rounds quickly into the door at waist height, then swung left and put a burst into the car as the person behind it fired.

Chalky dropped down beside him, panting, and somewhere off at the hall someone began to scream. Firing now from an upper window and at the front of the building.

'You hit him, sarge,' Chalky said excitedly.

'You go back. Report. I'll hold them.'

Mohammed Bassam, the leader of the fighters in the hall, watched two of his men pull the wounded man back from the door. He had been hit three times by the look of it, twice in the lower belly and once further up at the base of the chest. He moved forward and dropped down beside the wounded fighter, tearing open his shirt underneath the denim jacket he wore. Above him fighters at the high windows were firing into the street and out towards the back where the shots had come from, hot cartridge cases dropping around them.

The wounds were ugly, wood splinters in the blood and fluids that oozed out of the entry points. He slipped his hand underneath. There were two exit wounds, big gaping holes in the man's back. Someone had already stuffed a dressing down and secured it with the man's belt. He looked up into the fighter's eyes. They were flat. Shock was setting in. But before Allah he was brave. He had stopped screaming now, gritting his teeth rather than cry out. Bassam had fought with him before, in Hebron and in the filth of the Shatila in Beirut. He was brave and he knew he was dying. He knew they could no nothing here. Only a hospital would have a chance of saving him.

Assem, one of his senior men, called for a halt to the shooting and dropped to one knee beside them, an eyebrow raised in question as one of the other fighters, a girl, arrived with a medics bag.

Bassam shook his head and stood back.

'Can't see a thing,' Assem said. 'Maybe they will by-pass us.'

'They will come,' Bassam replied, reaching for his cigarettes.

'Those things will kill you, you know,' the other man said. Bassam gave a dry sardonic chuckle. They were sent to support the Libyans while they held the road junctions, but the troops had withdrawn with almost indecent haste and he could not hold the roads in the open, not with eighteen fighters. Fate had not been kind. By the time he had made the decision to move the soldiers were at the edge of town. That left them two choices. Bombshell into small groups and try and make it south, or fight. They had been running all their lives. Enough was enough. In Dublin the council had discussed this. Strong resistance would slow things down long enough for the negotiators, but Bassam didn't care. They had run enough. It was time to fight.

'Gutless pricks,' Assem said. He had been to language school in Brighton and used the English vernacular.

'We knew they wouldn't fight,' Bassam said, lighting his cigarette. 'Why are you surprised?'

'I'm not,' the other fighter replied. 'But we could have used their heavy guns.'

'We have two,' Bassam said. 'And anyway, my friend, more heavy guns would make no difference. Not facing these troops.'

'Americans?'

'No. They would have helicopters overhead and ten times the amount of men we have seen. These must be British, Australian or something. Either way they are professionals and wearing that feather thing.'

'Why couldn't they have just negotiated? We don't want this place. They must have known that.'

'We Arabs negotiate everything, Assem.' Bassam smiled and blew smoke out into the air. 'I think we assumed they would, too. We were wrong. I was with Ali Jassem a few weeks ago. We were driving through some shithole in Dublin. Rocks, bottles coming at us. He said this was their intifada. He was right. I think I knew then. There would be no negotiation. He did.'

'If they are British, then we have a fight here,' Assem said. 'I had a girlfriend when I was in Brighton.'

'You had many, I seem to remember,' Bassam said drily.

'Her brother was in the British army. Met him once in a Happy Eater near Reading. He unnerved me. A man capable of violence. Someone made a remark about Cheryl.

Kevin, that was his name, Kevin head-butted him. He said they were all like him. They called him Noddy. Had a thick Scottish accent I found difficult to understand.'

Someone called from above them. Bassam and Assem looked up. They were coming. It would be dark soon.

Stewart was relentless. Momentum. He had it and he was going to keep it and he was delivering a characteristic staccato bollocking to a senior engineering officer who had not foreseen the quantities of containment wire that would be required. Prisoners were now a problem, and the column of Irish Volunteers charged with guarding prisoners of war who were due to come through the path blasted through the minefield was late. The trucks they were to have used were, for some reason, still sitting thirty miles from the front. They had used their initiative and stolen some vehicles from a Pickfords depot, but they were hours behind schedule and Stewart had a thousand of his tiny Celt Force tied up guarding the dispirited defeated Libyan survivors of the devastatingly effective air attack.

The beaten men, shocked, hands in the air, who were arriving at northern border points during lulls in the bombing were being turned back to surrender to Celt Force or the Irish. Only the wounded were allowed to cross and they were given care. Such was the volume that Stewart had ordered no-fire zones and the air force and artillery were now actively avoiding the areas where the Libyans had been told they could wait without fear of attack.

In the UN activity had been feverish since long before dawn. In Washington one Arab diplomat, the Libyan Ambassador, had been trying to see the Secretary of State, Edwin Marsteller, but was told he was unavailable. The Libyan Ambassador to the UN and the leader of the Palestinian delegation were about to meet him in a closed door meeting at the UN building. Four telephone calls to ambassadors from wealthy influential Arab states, men who had been woken in their beds just after two A M and advised of an invasion taking place, suggested that they might like to attend. As they left their offices, a senior Foreign Office man in London, talking to Sir Huw Tristan-Carter in New York, replaced the telephone and made a call. To Moscow.

Sir Huw's efforts in China seemed to be paying off and indicators from Beijing were suggesting that there may have been a change in their position. The Security Council was due to meet in fifty minutes, and he walked the long corridor down to the meeting suite, the excitement rising.

As the Arab diplomats entered the meeting room they saw another man sitting with the US Ambassador, the Secretary of State and Sir Huw Tristan-Carter. He was the Irish Ambassador to the UN, who had based himself in London as part of the government-in-exile.

'That man does not represent the new government of Ireland,' the Libyan pointed out firmly. 'He should not be here.'

The Irishman looked across the table. 'On the contrary,' he replied. 'I bear the warrant of Her Majesty Queen Maeve and I have the mandate to represent her and her people.'

The Palestinian was thinking fast. They hadn't planned on this. News from Dublin was sketchy and he had no new instructions from Amman or Tripoli. 'Gentlemen, let us discuss this in a manner fitting . . .' he began, but one of the others waved him down.

'You were warned what would happen if you became involved in this internal issue. We will have . . .'

'Sit down please,' Sir Huw began. 'We need to talk, and threats are not the way to begin.'

'. . . no option but to . . .'

'Who is involved?' Sir Huw now stood, interrupting. He towered over them. 'This is a popular rising of Irish and Celtic people under the flag of Queen Maeve. It is a civil war. Her Britannic Majesty's Government has no official presence in the Republic of Ireland . . .'

'What?' The Arab snapped back, incredulous. 'There are . . .'

' . . . other than a few advisers,' Sir Huw overrode him, 'people, I am informed, who have taken leave of absence from their jobs to act as individuals.'

'Shit! You talk shit!' the Libyan launched in angrily, his composure gone. 'Your ships are shelling the shoreline. Your jets attack! His marines,' he jabbed a finger at Marsteller, who was sitting back, a bemused smile on his face, 'are attacking the peace-loving citizens of Ireland.'

'This is boring,' Sir Huw said. He looked at Marsteller. 'Are you bored?'

'I am. Let's get this finished. I am playing golf in an hour,' the American responded.

'You were warned,' one of them threatened.

'Ah yes. Sent home like naughty boys. Russians in. Expensive oil. Perhaps we can have the Russian Ambassador in?' Marsteller said drily. An aide nodded and stepped from the door. Almost immediately the Russian Ambassador entered. One of the Arabs went pale. Set up.

'Tell me, Mr Ambassador, what is the official position of the Russian Government on this popular rising in Ireland?'

The Russian didn't smile. 'We support any popular effort that attempts to restore democracy in any country.'

'And what of claims that the Russian standing army will be deployed in the Middle East to ensure the safe production of the world's oil?' Marsteller continued.

'Claims only. I am advised that we are not able to effectively complete any task of that nature at present. Reorganization, you understand.'

An aide passed Sir Huw a note.

'Ah,' he said. 'The Chinese have announced an intention to speak at the meeting this morning.'

In Ireland the battle continued. To the south, way out ahead of the main Celt Force air–land advance, the SAS teams had unearthed their 'pinkies', their special operations equipped hybrids on Land Rover frames, and were roaring across the countryside creating havoc. They delivered immense firepower with almost complete surprise and the retreating Libyan columns never knew if they were going to come under air assault, ground ambush by the resistance or attack by the fast mobile patrols they knew could only be special forces.

Sergeant David Kenny, the SAS man who had first met Briget Villiers, was on one such deep interdiction patrol with the three other men in his team when their vehicle slammed its belly on to a rock hidden beneath a shrub, ripping out its sump.

'Fucking great,' one of them said, 'now it's fucking hoofing it.'

They were thirty miles from their camp where their bergens and personal kit lay. With the limited space on the vehicle taken up by fuel drums, team ordnance and ammunition, there was little room for such luxuries; each man had two days' rations, a space blanket, his personal weapons and ammunition, a medical pack and a survival kit.

'Tony, stag. One minute, then back here. Grunter, you relieve him. Let's get loaded quick smart. We move in two minutes,' Kenny said. 'We take the Minimi, all the rockets, the belts, radios and battery packs.'

Kenny and the other two men began splitting up the equipment, checking it was working, throwing away anything that was suspect or superfluous, disabling whatever they were leaving behind as they worked. Two minutes later, the seventy-pound loads packed as comfortably as possible, they set off at a fast walk, tabbing, one man out ahead, the rest in a diamond formation ten metres apart, heading for a low hill and the safety of its copse of trees, careful to stay in the scrubby bush and not to skyline themselves. Every time Tony, the leading man, climbed a low rise he settled to the ground and inched forward before calling the others forward and moving on. Daylight movements in enemy territory were always risky and stealth and care were worth more than any amount of speed. Twenty minutes later and almost two miles from the wrecked pinkie, Kenny called his team to a halt in a gully so that they could reorganize and check their kit and equipment and he watched them work, quickly and efficiently.

Tony was a big, lanky New Zealander with a ludicrous Zapata moustache. Phenomenally fit, he could move fast for days on end carrying huge loads and he was never without at least three packets of Marlboro cigarettes. He called everyone 'shagger' and never completed a sentence without at least one four-letter expletive.

Grunter was a lean, wiry little Welshman, who had earned his nickname for the curious noises he made when asleep. For a small man he had a ferocious appetite, would eat anything, and had acquired, much to Kenny's envy, the ability to sleep anywhere, anytime. If he did so and began making his characteristic noises there would be shower of abuse and items thrown and he would wake up with a little cheeky grin only to fall asleep again in minutes. SAS troops, through necessity, had learnt that everything you needed for existence should be attached to your person. This had tactical reasons, in that you could be up and moving in seconds, leaving nothing for an enemy to find, and leaving nothing that you would later need. The other reason was that if it wasn't tied down or attached it would get nicked. Everything was fair game. All SAS troops had their prime eating implement, a spoon, attached by string or cord to their kit. This item, called a racing spoon and always on hand, meant they could tuck into grub, theirs or someone else's in a microsecond. The spoons were issue and heavy plastic. Not Grunter's. He had a long, oversized model in a garish pale blue that he had found in a high street shop and it was so large he could barely get it into his mouth. When someone opened a ration pack and began eating they kept a wary eye out for the Grunter lest he appear with his blue bucket scoop for 'just a mouthful'.

Moons was the square-jawed, blond-haired, last-born son of a Sussex doctor. Spurning officer selection he had opted for the Green Jackets as a grunt and, a keen mountain walker and cross-country runner, he had found the selection course easier than most. He was very good-looking and ran a string of girlfriends back in Hereford. His name was Paul but 'Moons' had stuck after he had dropped his pants one drunken evening in the West End and shown his hairy naked buttocks to the wife and daughter of a senior army officer who were leaving an exclusive club.

Kenny checked his own gear. They had had three contacts since leaving their camp and were down to two belts for the gun. Each man had ten full magazines for his M 203, six grenades each, and Tony was humping his shotgun as usual. They had five 66 disposable anti-tank rockets. Enough to rock and roll their way out of trouble.

He flicked a look down at his watch. Eight-thirty AM. They would need to lie up somewhere and decide what to do. Soft rain was beginning to fall.

'Right. We want an LUP,' he said.

They moved out and ten minutes later found what they wanted, a low rise with good visibility all round, but covered in undergrowth. At one point erosion and a small slip had created a natural hollow under the root system of a gnarled old tree.

Tony came back and guided them into it and Kenny agreed. It would do. The rain was still falling and the wind was gusty. They moved under the shelter offered by the overhang.

'Get some grub heated up and then hard routine. Tony, you take first stag. Grunter get that scaley kit out let 'em know we're tabbing it. Moons –'

'The cunts!' Grunter said looking with dismay at his huge blue racing spoon. It was cracked down one edge.

'Who?'

'Those fucking Jundies. That last bastard you slotted. He got a burst away and I thought I felt a tug at my kit. The fucker shot my spoon.' The other two laughed softly, Tony grinning as he pulled his camo net down and crawled up the side of the gully.

'That's why I slotted him,' Kenny said with a grin, but his memory closed in. He had got close. Very close. Diving for cover as the pinkie had raced through he had swung his weapon and let go a burst. To have hit Grunter's spoon the bullet was within half an inch of entry to the body. He got the hexy block burning and heated food while the other two checked and rechecked their kit.

'I'm going to complain to my MP,' Moons said. 'This food is shit.'

'It's fucking crap, innit. The sex is pretty dreary too. Mind you, I like the wet clothes. Means when you piss in your pants the others won't notice,' Grunter said, eating carefully round the shattered edge of his spoon.

'When we get back I'm going to fuck your sister.'

'You haven't seen her,' Grunter replied. 'There's a law against bestiality.'

'Not for Tony,' Moons replied knowingly, through a mouthful of something. 'They do sheep down where he comes from.'

'Oh well, that's all right then,' Grunter said. 'Mind you, she's been done by a green slime rupert.'

'Oh fuck that then. An intelligence officer!' he replied, mock-appalled at the prospect of any woman actually doing that. 'Not stirring his porridge, boyo.'

Grunter looked up at the sky, leaden and grey, the drizzle falling steadily. 'Why couldn't these pricks have invaded the Bahamas?'

'Inconsiderate bastards.'

One by one and one at a time, they would rough clean their weapons, not a field strip but making sure they were clean and oiled and ready to go, Grunter lovingly working on his Minimi light machine gun. By nine-thirty Kenny, Grunter and Moons were asleep, all still wearing full webbing, while the lanky New Zealander concealed in the bush above watched over them. At ten he woke Kenny, ate, cleaned his weapon and then he too slept. It was Moons, on stag just before two that afternoon, that pulled the length of cord that was tied to Kenny's webbing. He woke instantly and silently, nudged Grunter who was making his little noises, and woke Tony. They sat up instantly and silently and as Kenny moved to where Moons was lying the other two pulled on their gear.

Moons, his camouflage face veil down, pointed and passed Kenny the tiny binoculars. Kenny swung them up.

There moving fast below and towards them were five figures, civvies, two of them women and one young, very young. Four were armed. He could see by their movements that they were tired, on their chin straps as they said in the regiment. They were running from something. He moved the glasses up. Out only half a mile behind them a group of men were chasing, Libyans by their look, and a soft-skinned truck crawled over the ground behind them, its wheels skidding, negotiating its way across the rough ground, but going no faster than the jogging men.

'Resistance,' Kenny said. 'They aren't going to make it. How long dja reckon?'

Moons, the runner, shrugged. 'Another half a mile maybe. They're knackered. Look at 'em.'

They had met the objectives of their mission the night before and were now on their way back to their base camp. Therefore their brief was open. Interdict and harass at will. Cause havoc. Create confusion. Nothing to compromise except their own position.

'Fuckin' ragheads! Let's do it,' Kenny said.

They crossed the half-mile to an intercept point at a run, moving down the narrow depression between two rises, Moons swinging up to check on their relative position before dropping back below the skyline to stand up and run, powerful like a quarterhorse catching and overtaking the others, Grunter pounding with the Minimi gun across his chest. Finally Moons dropped back and raised a thumb, skidding to a halt in the mud beside Kenny.

'About twenty of them, closing fast now.'

'The civvies?'

'Hundred yards or so.'

Kenny deployed his team on the brow of the low, soft contoured rise. Tony had unslung one of his 66s and Grunter checked the belt in the gun, the shiny brass casings out over his arm, clear of the heather and bracken. Moons was twenty yards down, a grenade on the launcher on his 203. He had produced a floppy jungle hat from somewhere and when Kenny raised an eyebrow he raised a hand, fingers curled and flicked his wrist in the wanker signal. Moons grinned and gave him the finger back.

Just then the first of the civvies staggered into calling range.

'Oy, shagger!' Tony yelled. 'Up here. Keep coming!'

The man, dragging a young girl by the arm, was exhausted, but he raised his head, the fight still in him, swinging his weapon round.

'Keep coming! We are British. Keep coming,' Kenny yelled. The man was too tired to acknowledge but dropped his head and moved up towards them, pulling the girl, the other three following him.

Grunter pulled the last over the slope behind him and dropped back down to his Minimi gun, pulling the butt into his shoulder, flicking a look at Kenny who nodded to him. Kenny could hear him spooling up, letting the anger flow, feeling the adrenalin flow through his bloodstream. 'Fuck! Fuck! Fuck! Fuckin' bastards!' Grunter would start the contact with his machine gun, raking the Libyans at will. The others would join in as soon as he had opened fire, pouring rounds and grenades into them. Tony would take the truck with a 66. Four versus twenty or more. The aggression was everything. Come on, fuckers, come and get some!

The Libyans were still on open ground below them, running after the Irish, confident of a victory when the little Welshman opened fire. Moons and Kenny were half a second behind him, their grenades arcing upward and falling into still bewildered Libyans. As Tony's rocket left the tube the other three men were coolly firing, choosing targets, chopping the enemy patrol to pieces. As the last of them fell, Tony and Moons, totally pysched up, were up and running into the killing ground, through the cover of the smoke from the burning truck, finishing off the last of the resistance, screaming and yelling, the bloodlust and the adrenalin roaring through them.

Kenny watched from above, covering them with his rifle, Grunter beside him with the Minimi as Moons hared back up the slope.

'Tracks!' Grunter yelled.

'Where?' Kenny asked.

'Two o'clock. They've clocked the fucking smoke.'

Moons dropped down beside them. He was bleeding from his upper arm.

'You hit?' Kenny asked.

'Yeah, hurts like shit but it's flesh only,' he said pulling a dressing clear of his medic pack. 'D'you say tracks?'

Grunter nodded. 'Good 'ere, innit?' he said with a grin.

Tony arrived back up at the top lugging three AK 47s and five sets of chest webbing full of magazines. Kenny took the dressing from Moons and quickly and expertly applied it to the wound.

'Syrette?'

'Naa.' Moons didn't want the one-use disposable morphine injection. Not yet anyway.

'Right. Grab the civvies and let's gap it.'

'Fuck it,' Tony said, tapping his pockets. 'Fuck fuck fuck. This is fuckin' shit,' he roared.

'What?'

'Dropped me smokes somewhere. Full packet, too.'

'Yeah, that . . . and it's fuckin' raining,' Moons replied.

They started to laugh, all of them, the buzz of surviving a big contact welling up inside them.

They moved fast, keeping the civilian resistance people moving until they were in the trees at the base of the hill they had been moving towards. There was no other cover. It was a wide open killing ground all round them, and Kenny dropped to one knee and pulled a map clear. With a bit of luck the Jundies would have given up, or think better of attacking a group of unknown size that had just destroyed one of their sections and blown up their truck. But they may have found the pinkie and put two and two together, and they may just have been pissed off enough to keep on with the search. It wouldn't take a genius to figure where they were hiding. It was the only wooded ground for miles either side. A good reason to get the fuck out as soon as it's dark he thought. He looked at his watch. Three-forty. Dark soon.

'Move upwards,' he said, pointing up the hillside through the trees. 'We may have shaken them. Find an LUP. If we get rumbled here . . .' he left it unsaid. They would have to fight and hold until they could sneak clear, or if it was really bad try and call in some help.

Finally, settled in high on the facing slope, Kenny squatted on his haunches by the exhausted tiny group of resistance people. His team had divvied up their rations and the people were now eating from the soft foil packs with their fingers.

'Thanks,' one of the women said.

He held out a hand. 'I'm Dave Kenny.'

She introduced herself, finishing with, 'Did you say Kenny?'

He nodded. She smiled. 'Sue Villiers told me about you.'

'You with that mob? What the fuck are you doing out here?'

'What? O'Sullivan's territory?' She laughed. 'Pat's okay. We were looking for those tanks. There's two of them, you know.'

'What happened?'

'We got caught out. Looking for those tanks last night.'

He jerked a thumb at the child, a girl of thirteen or fourteen.

'We found her on the road last night,' the woman replied. 'Can't get much out of her.'

Kenny looked across at her. She was sitting silently, huddled over, rocking on her knees. He didn't like what he could see. She had been caught up in something, maybe seen relatives get killed, but there was something more, something under the shock.

As he watched her she vomited. It was weak, the sick running down her front.

'Tony?' Kenny called softly. The New Zealander was the best medic in the team and he crossed over to them.

'Check her out. She just bulked up.'

As Tony slipped over to the girl and bent down beside her, Moons, currently on stag, slid down into their position. 'Tanks, two of them, three APCs and a half a dozen soft-skinned coming this way.'

'How long?'

'Half an hour, maybe more,' Moons replied. 'There's three vehicles coming from the north-east, too.'

'Dave,' Tony called, 'give us a hand. You, shagger,' he pointed to one of the resistance men, 'your shirt and coat dry?'

'Enough,' the man said standing. 'You want them?'

'What?' Kenny asked.

'Hypothermia and dehydration. She must have been in fuckin' wet kit all night.' He looked up at the man. 'No, keep them on. Come here. Undo the front of your shirt. Hold her close. Your body warmth,' he explained.

The man sat down and pulled the girl towards him, ignoring the sick on her front.

'Come on, pet,' he said. Tony pulled a space blanket clear of his kit and wrapped it round them both, then took Kenny's from his pouch as the team leader sorted through his kit for a rehydration pack, his decision made.

'Grunter. Get on the net. We want air and evacuation. Give 'em a sitrep on that armour and advise we have one wounded, one . . .' he looked at Tony. 'How long?'

'Fuck all. Without real kit maybe two hours. She won't last the night. Not if we're in a punch-up.'

'. . . one critical with hypothermia. Five civilians. Got it?'

'Goddit.'

'Map ref on my kit there.' Kenny looked at the woman he had been speaking to. 'Make her drink this. Get some fluids into her. Light this.' He dropped a hexy block into her lap. 'Brew up. Give her something warm. You people, too. Moons, you and Tony take the 66s and tab down the hill a bit. Find somewhere near the fallen tree. Remember it?'

'Yup.'

'I'll meet you there. Grunter, give me the Minimi. You go up and keep an eye on the rear slope. Try and see an LZ somewhere.'

518

'What now?' one of the resistance men asked.

'Now we fight,' Tony replied.

'Good,' he responded, holding up his assault rifle, 'but I'm out.' Tony slung him a set of webbing he had taken from a dead Libyan. He looked at the woman now holding the rehydration pack with the sick girl. 'You want some?'

She nodded and the other woman, who had so far sat silent, gathering her strength and eating, stood up and cocked her rifle expertly.

'Jesus,' she said. 'Thanks, but that stuff in the foil was awful. I could murder a bacon sandwich.'

'Shagger, so could I. Ammo?' Tony replied, warming instantly to her.

'I'll take three mags if you got 'em.'

Libyan tanks and APCs were too good to miss and a two-ship of Jaguars on armed reconnaissance was retasked and headed south in the dying light, while a pair of Lynxes much closer but much slower turned south-west and flew at maximum speed to do the extraction.

The SAS team had destroyed one APC with a 66 rocket – it had ventured too close – but tank rounds were now landing on the hill above them as the Libyans tried to find their position. Moons, seemingly not bothered by his wound, was now on the Minimi gun keeping the enemy heads down when the patrol radio squawked. Kenny changed frequencies.

'Charlie three one,' he said.

'Charlie three papa november nine, I am six miles to your north.'

'Papa november, charlie three one actual, on your ten o'clock you will see a wooded hill, surrounded by fields and heather. Friendlies on the western slope of the hill. Your target is to the west, half a mile from the hill in the open. There is smoke from one kill over.'

'Roger, charlie three. Thank you . . . ahh . . . roger that, I have a visual. Ah . . . heads down.'

The lead Jaguar pilot corrected his approach, searing in at 500 feet and seconds later Kenny heard it. They always said that once you heard one it was too late and he watched as a pair of cluster bombs dropped from the hard points, the second fighter bomber behind covering a different angle, its bombs falling too. The flash lit the sky and the concussion wave slammed into them a millisecond before the sound reached them. The Libyan tanks and APCs grouped tightly had paid the price and all were now on fire. Nothing on the impact zone had survived. Fucking blue jobs Kenny thought. When they did it they did it right!

'Charlie three, bravo delta alpha, please,' the excitement and adrenalin thick in the pilot's voice. Battle damage assessment.

'Roger papa. All targets destroyed,' Kenny responded. 'Nice one, Rupert.'

Tony had rolled on to his back and was lighting a cigarette, a big grin on his face, but the two resistance people were riveted, watching the dying flames below them where so many men had just seen real warfare, terrible modern warfare waged, and lost.

'Thanks, charlie three. Ah . . . we have visual on hostiles to your north-east.'

'Roger papa november. Go for it. Be advised there is friendly traffic inbound in that direction.'

'Nice of him to ask,' Moons said. 'There's one blue job who I will buy a drink.'

'You've never bought a fucking drink in your life, you stingy pommy prick,' Tony said, inhaling deeply on his cigarette.

'If you two have finished gobbing off, let's go,' Kenny said. The Lynxes would be inbound in fifteen minutes and the extraction would be fast.

Without being aware of it, Celt Force had just destroyed the last operative Libyan tanks outside Dublin.

By dark, on this the first day, all objectives had been met and the flexible planning ethos had allowed elements of Celt Force to surge ahead. Stewart's division had now taken a strip of country from the coast all the way through to Longford and Athlone, taking in Drogheda, Navan, Kells, Dundalk and as far south as Balbriggan.

Two regiments of Guards were advancing on the sizeable Libyan garrison at Mullingar to support the Royal Welsh. The Royal Marines, the Gordons, the Inniskillings, the Royal Irish and Maeve's Own, the remnants of the real Irish Republic's army, were moving southwards parallel to the N2 and N3 towards Dublin. The two Para battalions, who had fought with great courage since dawn, were relieved by the Welsh Guards. Instead of standing down they were told to find what they could and move south. They commandeered tractors, trucks, anything that could move them and began, virtually racing each other. If the marines were going in then they were very pleased to engage again and competed to be first into position.

The commander of 5 Airborne made preparations to move his HQ and bet one of his juniors that 1 Para would be ready to take the N4 and 2 Para the N7, their next objective, in effect cutting off Dublin from the west by midday the following day, a full day early. This he did not divulge to the media pool as they gathered for a briefing. The gathered reporters and camera crews were carefully fed information and were tightly controlled. There was to be no repeat of the media announcing moves in advance as there had been in the Falklands. Two reporters had broken from the pack, Herbie Jackson, the *Daily Telegraph*'s defence correspondent, had somehow got himself attached to the Parachute Regiment and was travelling with them, and Martin Bell, the famous broadcaster, recalled from the former Yugoslavia, was in the thick of the action with Maeve's Own wearing his lucky white suit.

There were points of fierce resistance. The pattern that developed early in the day continued. Where the air force had pounded the ground forces they capitulated quickly. Where the Libyans were engaged they also rolled over. That had been expected. Dispirited, badly led, with low morale, they were no match for Celt Force who attacked with ferocity. There were exceptions. At times the Libyans fought bravely, and were well led, but generally, like the Iraqi army in Kuwait, they didn't want to be there and had no stomach for a real fight with a professional opposition. The surprise had been the Palestinians. With low tech weaponry they defended like people with everything to lose, using every skill they had learned in years of fighting the Israeli army. Stewart was adamant. No heroics. No risk of dead soldiers where technology could be used. No risking the lives of his men where superior training and tactics could make the difference. In each place the Palestinians made a stand, Celt Force stood back and applied modern thinking and then waged war on them.

In Navan a force of Palestinians had taken heavy casualties for several hours, beyond what any commander could be expected to put his troops through. The Celt Force officer in command offered to accept their surrender. They refused. The Royal Marines major, already with three of his men dead and reluctant to accept further casualties, brought up Milan missiles and finished the fight. When the marines finally moved into the old school building they established that of the original twenty seven-fighters, seventeen had been dead or wounded at the time they suggested surrender.

The men of Celt Force, who had never doubted that they would triumph, had not expected such results on their first day. It was not just a good first day. Except for pockets of resistance the enemy were withdrawing. Fleeing the field in disarray. It was a rout.

As darkness fell word was received in Athlone that a group of Libyans, stragglers from somewhere, had arrived at a farm near Castlerea. Five resistance people were defending a large group of people sheltering at the farm, but things were getting out of hand.

A group of Australians holding the bridge at the head of Lough Ree were given the job and in three borrowed Land Rovers they set out. As the Aussies, hackles pinned to the side of their slouch hats, raced westwards without headlights in the dark, someone at the Black Watch battalion HQ near Athlone got word to the Americans at their firebase on Inishmore and they agreed to suspend air operations in the area until first light to allow the relief column through without risk of blue on blue casualties.

The column picked up a resistance fighter on the road, a young woman packing a folding stock Kalashnikov, and she led them round the back of Roscommon where the Libyans were still entrenched, to the farm. The Aussies, in their four-wheel-drives, left the road and forded a stream to approach the attackers from the rear. Guns blazing, they drove through the Libyan ranks and, like the LRDG in the Second World War, they used their mobility to advantage, firing light machine guns suspended from the roll cages with belt webbing.

The farm relieved, they handed the surviving prisoners to the resistance people and, much slower, headed back to the bridge at Ballyclare. By some quirk of fate the lieutenant in charge of the group, an Australian army SAS officer, was a cousin of the Irish army man who had blown up the officers' hostel in Dublin, and a nephew of John Peters, the mercenary who had made a similar dash in darkness to rescue a group of nuns in the Congo thirty-odd years before.

As the Chinooks whumping through the darkness ferried guardsmen and light artillery forward towards Mullingar the fight at the hall in Athlone continued. It had been going on for six hours and the Watch had one man killed and four wounded. Captain Dugan sent the men back to the old woman's house in groups of five, where she took one look at their rations and pronounced them unnatural. She made tea and sent for her daughter who arrived with bread from the freezer and a cardboard box of various cuts of meat she had been hoarding. Neighbours came round with what they had and the meat with potatoes and carrots became a huge pot of stew steaming on the gas stove in her kitchen. In small groups the soldiers sat round her table and hurriedly ate, dipping thawed-out bread layered with fresh churned butter into the tasty gravy.

The original two sections had been reinforced by the other half of the platoon and one of the Scots soldiers had produced a Carl Gustav anti-tank weapon from somewhere.

'Willis! You thieving little prick! Where did you get that weapon from?' his sergeant bawled.

'Nicked it, sarge. Thought it might be useful.'

'Oo from?'

'Some Welsh Guards wally this morning. Eddie got three bombs too, while his mate was having a dump.' He beamed happily.

'Good man! Bring 'em here.' The sergeant grinned. They crawled forward to where the captain was with the lieutenant, rounds skimming over their heads.

'They have taken a pasting and should fold with an assault,' Captain Dugan said, looking at the resistance man, 'but I'm willing not to take more casualties if there is another way. Apparently you have a suggestion.'

'I do,' the man replied. He was a round-faced individual, heavy, with eyes that said he had seen too much in his young life. Wearing the uniform of the Garda, the Irish police, he was covered in mud and grime and had been close to the fighting all day. 'We have tear gas at the station. It's old. Hasn't ever been used here in Athlone, but it should still work. If we fire some into the hall . . . I'll bet they don't have masks.'

'Can you get it?' Dugan asked.

The policeman nodded. 'We will need to work out a way to get it in there,' he said. 'The launcher is old. Bound to be bloody inaccurate.'

'We'll worry about that when you get back,' Dugan replied.

The policeman began to crawl back through the garden as the sergeant and the soldier lugging the anti-tank weapon arrived.

'We found a Carl Gustav, sir, with three bombs.'

'What? Over there in the garden shed with the shovels and things?' Lieutenant Meers asked with a grin.

The sergeant's expression said, it's good kit so don't ask any questions and we won't tell you any lies. 'I thought it might come in handy, sir. Take that big door out, for starters.'

Captain Dugan straightened his face. Fate was a wonderful thing. From hours of impasse to tear gas and a way to get the main doors open to get the gas inside the building in five minutes. He wasn't going to look this gift horse in the mouth.

The Garda was back twenty minutes late, a bag of equipment under his arm, and Dugan redeployed his men for an assault.

Inside the besieged hall Bassam, the Palestinian leader, moved among his fighters, encouraging them with a few words here and there, reminding them to conserve their ammunition. Assem followed him, handing out the last of their magazines. Four wounded men and a woman sat on the ground floor below them, filling empty magazines with loose 7.62 intermediate rounds from the last box.

They had no more grenades and efforts by one fighter to make a molotov cocktail from some barbecue lighting fluid they had found in the kitchen had failed. The fluid was so watered down that it was barely flammable. There were seven dead at the back of the stage and six badly wounded on the floor in the centre of the hall. A barricade of chairs and trestle tables helped keep debris and glass off them, but all the medical supplies were exhausted and Bassam knew they couldn't hold out much longer.

'How many rounds have we got left?' he asked Assem quietly.

'That's the last box there now. A magazine per man and a few loose rounds, perhaps.'

Bassam nodded. Half his small force was now dead or wounded, and even some defending at the windows were hurt in some way. He lit his last cigarette. 'They will come soon. They will use the darkness. Bring something up.'

As he spoke the sound of the pipes carried across to the hall, memories flooding through his mind, hooded pipers of the PLO, dusk in Gaza. They seemed louder than before.

'What are you saying?'

Bassam looked at his old friend. 'I am saying that I have to make a decision. We can't win this fight. Half my people are down. If we hold we lose more. For what? Is this going to give us Palestine? I think not.'

'But we agreed. All of us. We have run enough.'

'We have. But look around you. Perhaps we have also fought enough. Our people. Those out there. All of us. If we carry . . .'

A blast cut him off, the shock wave throwing him back for a second. The main doors, made of hardwood, blew inwards, one door coming off its hinges and landing in among the seats and tables that protected the wounded. A fighter who had been wedged into the window above the door was killed instantly, his body dropping into the dust and rubble. As he hit the floor a canister arced past him and then a second, landing on the floor and spinning as they began to release a cloud of gas. Someone screamed in pain and as Bassam, with long experience of tear gas, jumped forward to try and pick up the canister a second blast blew him off his feet.

Twenty seconds later soldiers with gas masks entered the hall. Moving fast and going for cover, they sprayed gunfire to suppress whatever resistance was left. The last survivors choking on the gas, tears streaming down their faces, began to lower their weapons.

# 15

The beaches between Dunamy Point and Clogher Head were crowded with men and equipment, and barges and LCs were still arriving. In the Falklands it had taken three days to transfer the forces' needs ashore, but here, with a force almost three times the size, the planning had paid off. Everything was where it should be and no ships had been sunk with valuable supplies. The breach through the minefield to the north had allowed the transports through, but before they arrived help came from another source.

As the Libyan garrison at Dundalk surrendered, ships moved into Dundalk harbour to unload direct on to the hard and the people of County Louth, in their thousands, came to help the landing at both the small harbour and the beach. The atmosphere was electric. Anything that could carry equipment off the waterline was pressed into service, and tons of supplies and gear were moved up into staging areas by people driving tractors, four-wheel-drive vehicles and trucks. Those that weren't needed to drive lifted and carried, shouted and sang. Queen Maeve, arriving back in the area after her visit to the prison camp, received a riotous reception and Stewart, already the subject of rumour and a hundred stories, larger than life with his tartan tam o'shanter and Maeve's Celtic tricolour hackle, was held in awe.

As the Libyans in the north-east retreated before Stewart's advance the tableau changed. Discipline broke down completely in many areas and the resistance attacked with savage intent. People who had sullenly co-operated with the occupiers now were openly defiant and as the defeated, leaderless men moved southwards away from the fighting, the pent-up anger unleashed itself again and again. A woman who had been watching occupiers steal her greenhouse vegetables for weeks found three Libyans walking through her garden and opened fire with her dead husband's shotgun. A man not many miles away, a man who had never harmed a living thing in his life, snapped when a Libyan soldier, cold, wet and separated from his comrades demanded the coat he was wearing. He had had enough. He swung the shovel he was using. The soldier fell to the ground and the man swung again and again. Finally, without change of expression, he began to shovel dirt over the corpse.

The US Marine contingent of Celt Force under the command of General Murphy had advanced far beyond their first day objectives. Murphy, barely waiting for sanction from Dark Rose Command, had moved inland at a furious pace, his first firebases providing staging areas for the leapfrogging advance. His western area command had established three smaller bases at Loughrea, Nenagh and Newcastle West, the heavy lift helicopters flying men, light artillery, fuel and supplies on to the bases within minutes of the arrival of the first marines. This was no Vietnam where the locals were hiding the enemy. Within minutes of their arrival the people living nearby were arriving to tell them where the Libyans and Palestinians could be found. The southern area had also expanded its theatre of operations with firebases at Macroom, Clonmel and Kilkenny, where they landed to be welcomed by flag-waving children. The Clonmel base was established at the airfield where Scott had first found the Libyans, the defenders falling prey to a sudden devastating attack by the marines' Cobra gunships. The attack, just after dark, had allowed the marine pilots to utilize their thermal imaging equipment after the base's only anti-aircraft system had been taken out by a special forces Pavelow Blackhawk.

The air defence down, the marine pilots stood off and attacked at range before moving in to over-fly the camp, their cannons and rockets finding their targets among the flames, smoke and confusion.

By 2200 hours on day one Murphy had men on the ground at the Clonmel base and reported that he could now control from the sky central, south and western Ireland. There were pockets of resistance and there were still dozens of small units of Libyans and Palestinians at large, but only three large concentrations of enemy forces remained intact and ready to fight: Limerick, Mullingar and Dublin itself.

As the British and Irish elements of Celt Force advanced on Mullingar, the Libyans, for the first time under an effective battlefield commander and at brigade strength, prepared to slug it out. The brigadier was short on options. His original deployment was to be able to reinforce the northern elements in case the expected massed attack over the border broke through somewhere. Aside from his new orders to hold and engage, he knew that all routes west were sealed off and that helicopters controlled the south. Even if he could break out, it would only give his force a day's respite at most. There was nowhere to run to. They had to make a stand.

The brigade intelligence team had established that although the invading forces in their theatre were without doubt comprised primarily of elements of the British standing army, they had no armour and only light guns. They had also established that the force advancing on them could only be half brigade strength, two or possibly three battalions. But although they lacked armour and heavy artillery they had air. The Libyans dug in. Deep.

In Dublin, General Saad was confident that the Celts would have to advance on Mullingar. They could not leave a mechanized brigade intact in the field, especially not on the flank of any advance on his headquarters in Dublin. He was also confident that his brigade could hold the Celtic forces long enough for everyone to agree that discussion was an option. Suddenly he was very keen to discuss things. If that failed then it also gave him time to hatch his own survival plan.

## Day 2

The Libyans were spread in a brigade front, their western flank at Mullingar across to where the N4 crossed the River Boyne. For the Libyan brigadier it was a defensive nightmare. Undulating low country of farms and hedgerows, it was wet and drained badly into streams and bogs. His only comfort was the Royal Canal which ran along half of his front. His men were dug in behind the canal, using it like a natural moat, and he had moved his eastern flank as far as the Blackwater Bridge to protect the route to Dublin. The bog to the south was a double-edged sword. His rear was safe, but it also meant he could not withdraw to regroup there. He silently cursed Saad for the tenth time that day. Only an idiot would have picked this place to fight with mechanized infantry. He had spread his force as far as he dared and hidden it to make it as difficult to hit from the air as possible and they were dug in. Now he had to wait, wait to see his opponent's intent.

The SAS had been watching the Libyan preparations all night, so when just before first light the Celt Force light guns opened up the fire was accurate. Shells dropping into the Libyan positions forced them into their hastily dug bunkers and masked the approach of the real punch of the attack. Two squadrons of aircraft, most of what Celt Force now had attached to them, attacked with every hard point loaded. Coming in at medium level, 18,000 feet, the Tornadoes delivered smart bombs with murderous accuracy at anything which could hide an APC, while the Jaguars came in lower and faster using rockets and cluster

531

bombs. One of the first Tornadoes dropped a thousand-pounder on the Leinster Bridge and then dropped its second on the smaller bridge where the N4 crossed the Royal Canal between Coralstown and The Downs. They had effectively cut the Libyan force into three elements unable to support or reinforce each other.

The Royal Welsh, the Scots Guards and the Welsh Guards were in position, the Royal Welsh at the eastern end ready to prevent the Libyan brigade from attempting a breakout to Dublin. The guards regiments were sitting to the north, holding for the moment while the sparse artillery alongside them fired round after round into the Libyan positions, forward observers monitoring the drop of shells. Some eight miles to the rear of the guards, a farmer was helping engineers to clear his hard-surfaced yard of implements, creating a forward base for the twelve army Lynxes that were due any minute. A Chinook was inbound with fuel supplies slung underneath while a second carried in ordnance, spares and ground crews. Four miles to the east just outside Trim, a crossroads town now jammed with the advancing Inniskillings in their Warriors, other vehicles carrying Celt Force troops, and military police trying to sort out the confusion, a second hard site had been found. Feverish activity was under way preparing it for the Harriers now flying south with hard points loaded to join the battle. After they had attacked their targets, they would fly on to the new forward base to refuel and rearm.

All the while the Tornadoes and Jaguars crossed overhead. One Jaguar pilot, adrenalin pumping through his blood after a successful sortie, came low over Trim, flicking his aircraft into a snappy aileron roll over the troops on the ground. Pilots, cocky now they owned the skies, were relaxed. A pair of GR3 Tornadoes, the air defence variant, patrolling over County Dublin handed over the patrol to a second pair, and as they left Irish airspace they overflew Dublin itself. The first did a leisurely victory roll over the city and didn't see anti-aircraft fire that arced up into the sky. The second pilot did and with almost reckless bravado he too did a victory roll, this time very low and with afterburners on. The Dubliners loved it.

The squadron boss didn't. They were roundly bollocked when they got back and reported the new anti-aircraft positions.

Stewart's headquarters had moved twice during the night, Queen Maeve's alongside, her radio link to the Voice of Free Ireland giving the engineers continual problems. She broadcast almost hourly, and their new and final location, after a special request from Kiernan, was at Tara. It was immaterial to Stewart who moved with his men, three special Warrior fighting vehicles transporting his communications gear and tiny staff. His chief of staff, a colonel, was now his link with the bigger divisional headquarters team spread over their maps and radios in the command and control bunker.

Stewart, a paratrooper's waterproof poncho over his camouflage, stood in the falling rain watching as his gunners worked their craft. The artillery pieces were deployed in three small groups beneath camouflage netting, the gun crews feeding the rounds into the breeches with practised perfection. Forward with the infantry he was supporting the battery commander, a major, standing over a map in a hastily completed dugout, listened to his forward observers via a radio headset and directed the fire himself. Behind the main battery were four other guns also under netting, but they were silent, waiting to begin their duel. His only regret that morning was that he had none of the multiple rocket launchers that the Americans favoured – they were over the border in Ulster – but he did have the tracking unit. His job was to pound the Libyan forces, wear them down with attrition.

Stewart had the momentum, but he wasn't a fool. There was no way he was going to throw 3000 of his men against

5000 mechanized troops that had had all night to dig in. He was going to break the enemy force into three, pound each with air and artillery and then, if necessary, let the western echelons of Celt Force loose at each in turn, using classic military doctrine. A small unit well focused could deliver overwhelming force and overwhelming firepower at any given point in a much larger formation. Focus. Morale. Momentum. The holy trinity of modern air–land combat.

Come on, you buggers, let's be having you, the major thought. Behind the battery and two miles off to the right was the tracking unit. A radar scanner sat atop a small tracked vehicle, its scanners pointing to the south, engine running. The Celt artillery was exposed and they knew that the Libyan brigade would have an artillery unit and it would reply. At the first incoming shell the scanner would illuminate, track the next rounds for two or three seconds, take a fix and immediately shut down the radar, in case it attracted anti-radiation ordnance, and scuttle half a mile. The information would be flashed to the battery, the four silent guns behind the main unit would be zeroed on the enemy battery and the duel would commence. Counter-battery fire was best left to rockets, but Celt Force had none. This would be gun to gun over ten miles of the Irish countryside. The four 155mm howitzers would lay down counter-battery fire until the real punch arrived, a three-ship of anti-tank Lynx helicopters that were now sitting on the ground, rotors turning, three miles to the rear.

The first incoming were three minutes later, forty minutes after the Celtic guns had first started their barrage. The first round hit a quarter of a mile in front of them, the second closer.

'Incoming!' someone yelled.

The crews at the forward guns dropped into their fox-holes while the rear crews jumped to position. The radio crackled and the major looked down at the tiny green glowing display on his unit. He called the co-ordinates and seven seconds later his rear battery opened fire, the crews loading and firing each piece as fast as they could, this tiny action a classic artillery duel.

To the north the Lynxes took off in close formation and began to sweep to the east. When they crossed into hostile country they were flying at 140 miles an hour, thirty feet over the ground, their scout out in front.

Fourteen minutes later they bled off their power and right down at what the pilots call cabbage height they shuffled forward, moving from cover to cover, till the scout helicopter spotted the exploding ingoing Celtic rounds. The boss called back to lift the fire and forty seconds later the Lynxes attacked. Using missiles, rockets and their miniguns they destroyed what was left of the Libyan artillery battery. Mission completed, the helicopters turned for base, moving slower now, with one of the aircraft trailing smoke from its engine after being hit by small arms fire.

The Celtic artillery continued to fire for the next seven hours and all the while the two and a half Royal Air Force squadrons under their Free Irish Airforce colours pounded the Libyans from the air. By three o'clock the Scots Guards had punched a gap across the N4 and had formed a defensive line between the Libyans and Mullingar town, still full of civilians, Lynxes with DAT mine dispensers giving them a protective barrier half a mile deep.

The Libyan brigade was now hemmed in, by the bogs to the south and the Celt Force to the east, west and north. It could now be broken down and killed at leisure. At four o'clock in the afternoon, after a last sustained daylight bombing run and as the light faded, a lone Jaguar did a pass over the battlefield, its underbelly container spilling leaflets over the battered and bleeding defenders. The leaflets offered to accept the surrender of any soldiers who wished to lay down their arms.

*　　　*　　　*

In Dublin the Libyans were in a state approaching desperation. Feverish defensive preparations were abandoned when someone in the higher echelons suggested commandeering the three ships that were in the harbour and simply sailing out under the cover of darkness. Surely no one would sink an unarmed merchant ship, they reasoned. This thought was scuppered when HMS *Nottingham* and HMS *Southampton* moved closer in, visibly tightening the blockade, *Nottingham* actually firing two shells into the harbour to prove their point. Accompanying the two British warships was the problem. The *Kathleen*, the last of the Irish Navy still free, now prowled the waters of Dublin Bay, her masts festooned with Irish flags, moving very close to shore every now and then, firing her light gun at enemy vehicles and positions on the shoreline and harbour edge, before scuttling back to deep water and the protective screen of her heavier consorts.

The British ships would not fire on a merchantman without very good cause, but there was no doubt that the little Irish ship would, and she would have been re-equipped, they thought, with torpedoes. In the last weeks she had attacked without cessation anything she could reach. Her captain, the Libyans said in their infrequent communications to the world's press, was little more than a deserter, a man who had refused to return to his base as ordered by the legitimate authorities, a freebooting buccaneer and a bloodthirsty pirate. To the Irish he was a national hero and there were already songs about him and his true love, the pride of the south-east, none other than Briget Villiers herself.

Scott, who had been in Dublin since the Celtic invasion, was now watching the Libyan and Palestinian preparations and movements in the city and reporting through a tiny satellite transmitter through Cheltenham, which in turn flashed the reports to the intelligence officers with Stewart's command. There were now thousands of extra troops in Dublin and although some seemed to have reason to be where they were, or moving on the roads, many were waiting for orders, their vehicles pulled off to the side. Some, obvious by the damage, had been in action and everywhere the men were sullen, tired, hungry, huddled against the cold in wet trench coats and, thought Scott, not far from throwing in the towel. They were nervous, skittish, and every time one of the patrolling Free Irish Airforce jets broke through the low cloud they scrambled for cover.

Wearing a workman's coat and flat cap he was with a group of other men who had been pulled off the street to fill sandbags that they were now stacking against the outside wall of a building. He had positioned himself carefully to be in the scoop of men for this job and had failed. They had to actually walk past before being ordered to help, and now two resistance men filled bags beside him, one always with his eyes on the back gates. This was Saad's new headquarters, the main post office on O'Connell Street. The Libyan general had moved into the building, almost a shrine to Irish nationalists, after the pair of smart bombs had destroyed his last headquarters the day before.

'If they think that they are safe in here they are wrong,' one man, not *buachailli*, muttered, digging his shovel into the dirt on the pavement.

Scott ignored him and lifted his own loaded shovel for the man holding the bag in front of him. So far it was rumour. They needed a sighting, a confirmed visual of the APCs that Saad had taken to using, arriving at this building and then they could do something about it. The sighting yesterday had put three stars and a small green pennant on the radio aerial on one of the three vehicles. Saad's arrogance had worked against him. He wanted the protection of an armoured vehicle, but he also wanted the world to know that he was a three-star general, a man of importance.

It was well after dark, the sandbag wall now eight feet high, when they were told to stop and they dawdled over clearing up. Then, just as they were about to give up hope, three APCs roared round the corner and turned into the back gates, a little pennant snapping out from an aerial, clearly visible under the softened gate lights that were momentarily turned on.

Scott allowed himself a small tight smile and threw his shovel on to the pile before taking a curfew pass from one of the guards and walking away, following the two resistance men up the street. Sitting nestled uppermost, just below the hessian, in a sandbag in the top layer was a tiny but powerful transmitter.

Scott was pleased. They had found Saad, located an aimer in his HQ, and now had genuine curfew passes, complete with the ubiquitous rubber 'stamp of the day' after saying they lived in Ballyfermot, a good few miles away and there were no buses as usual.

Scott's rendezvous with two section heads was interrupted when Morris arrived looking worse than ever, unshaven and exhausted. Scott had watched Morris grow, change in the last weeks. He was stronger now, decisive, altogether less theoretical and in spite of the effects of his fast dissolving marriage, he remained focused. They had left Millie and Aisling at the farm and now both took some comfort that they were in a liberated area, Scott aware that Morris was also pleased that he wasn't under the same roof as his wife.

'Something's on,' he began, accepting the mug of tea passed to him. They were in the kitchen of a terrace house, the woman who lived there sitting in her front room watching the street, just a candle burning, while she knitted and listened to the radio.

'Roads closed heading south along the coast. They have done a round-up. Buses are going in. Nothing coming out.'

'Now what's down there?' one of the men asked, thinking out loud.

'Lots,' Morris replied. 'No traffic, even with passes, from UCD down past the ferry terminal at Dun Laoghaire.'

'Get it flashed through,' Scott said. 'The cloud base is still low but it might lift enough for a recce flight. We move on tonight's jobs anyway.'

'Done. There's more,' Morris said. 'One of our groups got caught this afternoon. Three taken alive, including one of your people.'

'Which group?' Scott asked.

'Five of Eddie Jason's.' Jason had a big cell on the North Side. Fifteen or sixteen fighters, with one of Scott's men attached to them. James Cantor. Sergeant, parent regiment the Royal Green Jackets, three years in SAS. Married, three children, the youngest with spina bifida, a little golden-haired angel. Scott shook it off.

'What time?'

'Just before four.'

Four and a half hours ago. Jesus.

'So I want everybody out of here now,' Morris said. 'Move the old lady somewhere. I have got word to Jason. Made sure his cell have followed procedures and closed up any safe houses any of that group have been in.'

'Do you think they will talk?' someone asked.

'They will talk.' Scott stood up. 'Just how soon depends what they do to them.'

'Tonight?' Morris started.

'Your decision,' Scott replied, 'but it's . . .'

'I know,' Morris interrupted, 'no choice really. We go ahead. Jason's cell is suspended from all operations till further notice and they go to ground. Everything that was planned will go ahead.' He paused for a moment, both of them standing by the door. 'What do you think? Tomorrow?'

Scott smiled. The question was inevitable and had been asked of him four times that night by various people. When will Stewart reach Dublin?

At that moment Stewart was considering the same question. The lightning pace was now stressing resources, but he was determined not to halt his advance or even slow the momentum. He paced the floor, consulting, agreeing or disagreeing with his senior commanders and then, decisions made, the men left for their units and he asked his communications people to put him through to the NATO command at High Wycombe. Air Marshal Williams, Stewart's four-star joint commander, could now earn his money and do what he was there to do, liaise with the MoD and Whitehall, harry them, convince them and support his commander in the field. There was no rest.

Stewart's mobile HQ was now in the centre of a fluid wheeling action that stretched halfway across the country. His APCs were parked up in a roadside Volvo dealer's showroom near Pike Corner, the guards and the Welsh to the west holding the Libyan brigade, and the bulk of Celt Force to the east and advancing with whatever transport was available, the marines and the Parachute Regiment in the vanguard. There were no helicopters available.

Of the thirty Chinooks that had been flying at the start of the campaign, only nineteen were operational. Eight were temporarily in the workshops with double crews working to get them back into the field, one was badly damaged after taking a hit from a missile and two were lying on the bottom of Dundalk Bay after colliding in appalling weather that afternoon. Luckily they were returning to the fleet and only had crews on board. Three men survived, plucked from the water by a Sea King helicopter launched from a warship, but the remainder perished.

The Chinooks that were flying were committed carrying

ordnance and fuel to the artillery and air bases behind the Mullingar battlefield, or delivering Celt Forces to create a new southern front. The men of the Royal Irish Regiment were dropped on to their next objective and closed the N7, the main road to the south-west, at Nass. The Irish Guards, the Gordon Highlanders and Maeve's Own went in even closer, the Chinooks dropping them into positions marked by the SAS on the outskirts of Bray, not a dozen miles from Dublin city centre.

The guards were in first but it was Maeve's Own, the real Irish army units, that had the first contact with the Dublin garrison when a company strength column of Libyans in vehicles ventured into their zone, heading down the N11 towards Wicklow, their headlights off so as not to attract attention from the air.

The Irish, who couldn't believe their luck, opened fire and the hail of bullets ripped into the oncoming trucks. The lead vehicle careered off the road, the second stopped, its engine electrics destroyed, and the third slammed into the back of it. The fifth and sixth vehicles were trapped when the seventh and last truck blew into flames as tracer rounds ripped its fuel tank open. The Irish moved in through the smoke and the confusion and the action turned from a classic road ambush into a vicious rolling fire-fight through the chest-high vegetation at the roadside. In the darkness it was the sheer terror of close combat. Muzzle flashes lit the scene, screams, shouts and the sounds of men dying. The Irish who had waited months to avenge their country were merciless, racing through to finish the fight with bayonets and trenching tools. For many their Celtic blood was up. This was no objective modern military effort, cold-blooded and precise. This was rage unleashed, berserkers, like throwbacks to ancient Viking genes, one with a Gurkha knife, his rifle used as a club, his shirt torn, hacking and battering into the last terrified group of the enemy. Their officer,

Commandant Hyland, who only thirty-four hours before had been in the concentration camp at Loughrea, finally called for a cessation and then while his men secured the area he sat down in a ditch, down on his haunches and as the adrenalin surge faded away he began to shake like a leaf. A reinforced platoon, some forty-eight men, had just engaged a company. In the Irish ranks ten had died and twenty-six were wounded. There were 168 Libyan dead. There were no wounded. There were no prisoners.

Stewart, standing beneath a darkened sign that extolled the virtues of genuine Volvo parts, had spent the last twenty minutes on the line waiting to hear if Williams had been successful. The air marshal, after first pleading his case, had moved on to cajoling and finally threatening everybody he could find in the MoD, the general staff. Even Downing Street had been in the equation. At last his own service's willingness to assist and the prime minister's desire for minimal British casualties overcame the MoD's reluctance to recommit resources that had already been withdrawn. Williams's requests were met and he was able to give Stewart two further squadrons of night capable Tornadoes that were thrown into the Mullingar battle. The first aircraft, already on standby, were airborne less than two hours later. Libyan soldiers were surrendering, but not in sufficient numbers to make an infantry attack unnecessary, and Stewart was not prepared to throw one infantryman into an action that could be decided from the air with less risk and more chance of success.

Most of the Tornadoes had cluster bombs in their racks, but the MoD, now committed and somewhat embarrassed by their earlier reluctance, also authorized the use of something new for the RAF. Two Tornadoes that had so far been sitting idle lifted off from their base. On the specially converted hard points on each aircraft was one weapon, its existence hitherto classified. The bombers dropped their single loads from 18,000 feet using every available piece of technology to ensure accurate delivery. The airburst fuel bombs exploded 400 feet above the ground, the detonation, needing oxygen, sucking the air in for one mile each side, stripping trees of leaves, exploding windows as pressure dropped, and ripping the air from the lungs of the men below. The blast, milliseconds later, reversed the effect, a huge orange fireball in the sky as 2000 pounds of high octane racing fuel with accelerants exploded, the superheated gases following the concussion wave that destroyed everything for a mile each side of ground zero. Ten minutes later a third aircraft followed through, dropping leaflets over the survivors as the Jaguar had done ten hours earlier. The message was simple: surrender and be fairly treated or it's your turn next. The Libyan brigadier, without air cover, artillery or hope of withdrawal, had had enough of seeing his men die for a cause they couldn't win. He authorized surrender. The trickle of men crossing over, their hands in the air, became a flood. The battle of Mullingar was over.

They were crowded into the truck, Moira Kelly, David, Sarah, Alan and their children, Simon's wife and children, and sixty others. It was like a scene from the television, ethnic cleansing in Bosnia. No possessions, just coats David had snatched for them as they were herded from the house, herded back at bayonet point, people crying, calling out the names of loved ones. Troops moved from house to house, searching rooms, pushing the occupants on to the street, into the trucks. The images were powerful. Next to them a man, wearing bedroom slippers, was bleeding from the face. He had taken a heavy blow to the nose and through the blood that was congealing, a thin tendril of mucus, creamy yellow in the darkening red. A frightened young woman holding a baby close to her breast, her tear-streaked face now angry, defiant. An old woman confused, her hair in rollers, looking around and saying, but we haven't done anything wrong, nothing. You have to do something wrong don't you?

David looked back to his own group. His responsibility. 'We stay together,' he said. 'No matter what. We stay together. Don't allow yourself to be separated. Understand?' They nodded. Moira stood holding her coat closed over her chest, the little hand of Simon's son in hers.

'Don't worry, Ma, we will get out of this okay.' A woman fell beside him and he reached down and pulled her to her feet. It was a neighbour, a women they knew well. 'You stay close to us, Mrs Davis, so I can keep an eye on you,' he said with a grin, hoping he looked as confident as he sounded. The truck was full, jammed with people, and it began to move away, some people falling over as the driver jerkily changed gears. Got to get us out of this one, he thought. Think, man, think! His group was all women and children and Alan, who was fuck all good to anyone. Think now.

'So that's it, then. In a nutshell, they advance from the north and west and they have cut the roads south.' The intelligence officer leaned back against the wall, her windbreaker undone, the bandage across her shoulder just visible. The heating had gone off last night and had not come on again and it was cold, but she didn't seem to notice.

'And what are our brave friends doing?' Ali Jassem asked. 'The round-up continues?'

The girl just smiled and nodded. The question was almost rhetorical. He knew. They had moved into some defensive positions in the city, Saad still hoping that he could halt the advance long enough to negotiate at least something. It wasn't going to happen. He knew that. Anyone with half a brain knew that. His instincts had been right. The drunken rabble had turned out to be someone

544

else. A huge ruse and their command had fallen for it. It was time to halt the killing. Time to admit that although they could have held the Irish they couldn't hold this invader. Not in a million years. Further resistance would not get them Palestine. Only death for his people as what little world support they had left finally trickled away. But Saad was crazy. He was going to try and pull something out of the bag, something that involved hostages. Maybe another lunatic action like Saddam's infamous human shield. He stood up, a decision made. There were others who thought as he did. He had seen it in their faces and not just his people, Libyans as well. He had seen it. They all knew they were commanded by either an idiot or a madman. Khalil Ashrawi was dead, as was most of the Palestinian Council, killed by falling masonry when the headquarters was hit. His old friend would have known what to do.

'So they want a parley, do they?' Stewart barked. Since the battle for Ireland had commenced there had been requests for discussions from the Palestinians but Maeve had refused. This was for field commanders and she believed that the Palestinians no longer, if ever, had control over the Libyan commanders, in particular Saad. Her general would only dictate surrender terms and only with field commanders. There would be no discussion. No negotiation.

'This time it's Saad,' Kiernan said. 'This is it.'

Stewart's face was a mask of fury. He had just returned from a prison camp where four thousand Irish Defence Force people had been interned without medical care, adequate protection from the elements or food. He had been appalled, seeing again that his opponents had no skill, no honour and no humanitarian qualities he could grasp and respect.

'I'll not talk terms with a barbarian. At this minute he is still taking hostages! I will continue my campaign!' he snapped.

'Just see what he wants. It will give us time, surely,' Maeve said soothingly, slipping her arm through his as a daughter might, 'and he is the barbarian, not us,' her tone hardening then, using her mandate like a steel fist beneath the velvet glove of her femininity. 'Let it not be said that we continued to fight after their commander in chief had asked for a cessation.'

He turned to face her. 'You wish this meeting?'

'Yes. I want an end to it. We all do.'

Stewart turned back to the staff officer who had delivered the message.

'Tell the buggers I'll meet 'em. Fifteen hundred hours.'

'Where, sir?'

'This is Dublin,' he barked, now with a laugh. 'Trinity gate. Where else?'

Stewart's staff moved straight into action. A small group were given the meeting to 'arrange'. His instructions were simple. 'I want to be seen, I want to be heard, I do not want to be seen as co-operating. I do want the people of Dublin to know we are close. No secrets, no closed doors, everything out in the open.'

They were tacticians, men trained and paid to second-guess events, see every eventuality and make contingency plans. As the morning wore on, Celt Force tightened its grip on County Dublin while the Americans bludgeoned isolated units and closed their hold on the besieged force of Libyans in Limerick.

The staff group pulled in air liaison, the SAS and the officer commanding the Lynx squadrons to offer Stewart as much protection as they could and present the defenders with a glimpse of what was to come.

The communications people finished the little black box just before noon, and in a tent not far from Stewart's Warrior a small group of men at one end cleaned their kit until it was gleaming. A drum major, two pipers, one of them Stewart's personal piper, and two men with side

546

drums made up the group. The tartan was Celt Force, but shoulder flashes identified each man's parent regiment and showed the small group to be representative of most of the Scots regiments. The second group at the other end didn't bother. They didn't have any clean gear and so remained in the camouflage fatigues they had been wearing since they arrived in Ireland. They cleaned their weapons and took advantage of the fact they were out of the line to eat properly, shave and wash. Even so they still looked like what they were – soldiers fresh out of battle. Stewart didn't want parade ground creases and shiny boots. This was his bodyguard and like the pipers they were representative. A sergeant major, forty-three years old, a giant fearless man, ex-Royal Irish Rangers and now Royal Irish Regiment, cleaned his rifle alongside a corporal from the Gordon Highlanders who had opted to wear a kilt he had found somewhere. The corporal was cleaning a belt-fed machine gun. A Welsh sergeant, back with his unit after three years in the SAS and a man who knew Dublin well, would drive Stewart's Land Rover. The second escort vehicle would follow with the sergeant major, the corporal and the last man, Commandant Hyland, who would meet them on the road.

Each had been selected by their officers for one ingredient. Nerve.

Stewart, his long scrambled conversation with High Wycombe over, had arrived with Colonel Browning, his senior intelligence officer, and looked them over. His face was like stone. He had it all the way from Downing Street. No negotiating. Accept an unconditional surrender only.

'You know what you have to do?'

The men nodded.

'Right then, let's get on with it.'

The Libyan escort met them at Athgoe Castle and with much saluting, fluttering of flags and revving of engines, they set off down the N7 towards the city. Once in the built-up area, Stewart nodded to his driver. The Welshman pulled over. He was also operating the radio, and he wore headphones, one earpiece pulled back so that he could hear Stewart. The Libyans raced back and indicated that they should follow, but the Welshman ignored them and simply set off his own way, followed by the escort vehicle. There was a mad dash by the Libyans and again they got in front and tried to get Stewart's driver to follow them. Again he refused and finally he showed them where he was going. They set off again, this time going the way that Stewart's driver had determined, Colonel Browning trying to smother his grin in the backseat.

The streets were quiet, almost no traffic venturing out, but every now and then a pedestrian would look at the vehicles as they moved past, utter disbelief on their faces. Twenty minutes later on the edge of St Stephen's Green he pulled over.

'But sirs,' the Libyan officer pointed out, more than a little embarrassed, 'General Saad is expecting you from the other direction. He has allowed the people of Dublin out to witness this historic day, when we can finally begin negotiations.'

Hyland, filthy from his night ambush, said it for them, his voice low and threatening.

'We will enter the city any bloody way we please.'

'As you like.' The officer, not wanting to offend and desperate to see a surrender so he could go home in one piece, crossed to his radio.

At three o'clock exactly, an excited crowd gathering, and the Libyans working to keep them back, Stewart nodded to the drum major. The man, impressive in his full regalia, his huge bearskin hat giving him seven and a half feet of height, raised his heavy baton and set off, the pipes and drums in step behind him, General Stewart twenty feet back, his small leather stick under his arm, across St Stephen's Green, the skirl of the pipes carrying the 'Rose of Tralee' out ahead of them.

The two vehicles followed, bright green and orange Celt Force bunting across the bonnets. In the escort, the Gordons corporal stood up at the pedestal mounted machine gun with the sergeant major in the front seat, his hand on the shotgun he favoured, his issue rifle against the seat beside him.

As they reached the edge of the green, people in Grafton Street stopped and stood and, knowing they were seeing history in the making, initially kept their silence as pipers and the strange procession crossed the road from the green and began to move down past them towards the Trinity gate. It couldn't last. Someone began clapping, someone else followed and everyone joined in, buskers picking up the tune and people cheering, falling in behind the vehicles, like the children of Hamelin, regardless of the Libyan soldiers who were pouring up from the Nassau Street end to keep order.

Scott, his breathing at last under control, eased forward to the edge of the parapet. Beside him was the United States Marines sniper whom he had worked with to execute the officer who had killed Sinead Kelly. They had just arrived, the security cordons like never before. From here, atop the building several hundred yards up Dame Street, they could sight on the gates. The Libyans had men on nearer buildings and an entire platoon on the roof of the Bank of Ireland building opposite the gate, but here was near enough and the water tank above their heads with its supporting legs and beams gave them a nice confusing background to blend into. They were Stewart's ace card. No promises made, they would do their best to get into position in time. Now they were here, each with a sniper rifle with a big telescopic sight and, mounted underneath, a sighting laser. When turned on the beam threw a red dot of light on to the spot the bullet would hit, and as the sound of the pipes drew closer Scott and the sniper very carefully slid their weapons forward and looked through the sights at the crowd of soldiers, dignitaries and people down the street at the Trinity gate. There were rows of troops, lined up, almost for an inspection, and behind the soldiers civilians in their hundreds. The corner opposite the Bank of Ireland was civilians only, held back by a cordon of soldiers, and up on the famous gates they had put screens of some kind. In front of the screen a small knot of senior Libyan officers stood. No sign yet of Saad. He would only appear after Stewart arrived, the oneupmanship important.

Stewart moved behind his pipers, eyes to the front, his tam o'shanter square on his head, the hackle bright as the sunlight broke through the cloud, not acknowledging the now silent crowds. In spite of pleas on the Voice of Free Ireland for people to stay at home they had turned out in their hundreds. The cheering had stopped, the menace of so many armed soldiers having quashed the mood, made it tense, and the pipers had risen to it, the happier Irish tune having given way to something far more martial.

Behind him in his Land Rover and in the escort vehicle the handful of soldiers felt the same, the corporal, a picture of Celtic aggression in his kilt, his hands on the gun. Hyland, moving down familiar streets he had wondered if he would ever see again, seemed to take strength from the surroundings and people close to their route who could see his Irish Defence Force insignia attached to a filthy dirt and blood encrusted uniform, looked at the thin, wasted man and understood where he had been. Some even recognized him and called his name, memories of happier times.

The drum major stopped and the pipes fell silent. They were now just thirty yards from the gate, Libyan troops holding back the silent, expectant crowd. Stewart stopped and turned back to the vehicle.

'Brownie, Andre, would you join me, please?'

The thin Irishman and the British officer climbed from

the vehicles and the three of them moved forward past the pipers and down towards the famous gate, the escort vehicle pulling out and following.

A Libyan officer, young, good-looking and immaculately turned out, stepped forward to try to prevent the vehicle going any further and found himself looking down the barrel of not only the machine gun, the little corporal's face without expression, but the sergeant major's shotgun, too, inches from his chest.

'We are with the general, sonny,' he said sweetly. 'Step aside.'

The officer hesitated, but the big sergeant's eyes didn't waver for a second. He stepped back and the Land Rover rolled forward again.

Stewart stood in the open area facing the gates and the cadre of Libyans, his hands behind his back, his stick under his arm. The two officers and pipers stood behind him, the two vehicles off to one side. The crowd was silent, eerily so. He waited for a minute and then pointedly looked at his watch before looking up at the Libyan officers and crooking a finger at one.

The man walked forward nervously.

'Do you customarily salute senior officers in your army?'

The man came to attention and saluted and Stewart returned it.

'Where is General Saad?' Stewart asked genially.

'He will come after five minutes, sir,' the Libyan replied, adding, 'Inshallah,' as an afterthought.

'Go to him. Tell him if he is not out here in sixty seconds I am leaving.'

The man nodded, saluted, marched away and again the silence fell, the crowd and the troops watching Stewart who stood stock still, holding almost unblinking eye contact with the senior Libyan officer he could identify in the line-up opposite.

The tension was palpable. Finally there was movement

at the back of the group and three uniformed men made their way through.

Stewart recognized him from the many intelligence photographs he had seen. Short, barrel-chested, iron grey hair cut close to the skull, florid-faced, too much of the good life slightly mocking the ribbons on his dress uniform. His eyes were flat, black and angry but otherwise his expression gave away nothing.

'You have already used up four of the ten minutes you are getting. You wanted to talk,' Stewart said. 'I suggest you get on with it.'

Saad's face coloured as blood rose, but he controlled his anger and began with what he intended to say. 'We are both professional soldiers, both have the welfare of our men at heart. Further battle will simply bring more death. It is time to negotiate. We are men of the world, we can . . .'

'I don't negotiate with terrorists or butchers,' Stewart interrupted in a staccato burst. 'Besides, negotiations are for parties with equal needs and equal opportunities. You seem to have forgotten that my men are at the city walls!'

'Your men,' Saad began, spittle across his lips, 'your British men, your Americans! They are not Irish!' he yelled. 'None of them are Irish! You! You are a British man. You have no authority to represent Ireland. This is not your country! This is . . .'

Stewart stepped forward again interrupting the Libyan. 'It certainly is not yours, General.' His voice was low with menace. 'I am here because you attacked a friend. You attack one and you attack all. And you are wrong. I am Irish. I was born on this island. I am also a Celt. We are family! I hold the royal warrant from Queen Maeve and represent her and her people.' Saad was furious and it was obvious, so Stewart kept the initiative. 'I repeat, I will not negotiate. You have twenty-four hours to withdraw your forces to the north where I will accept your unconditional surrender.'

'Unconditional is it?' Saad snapped. 'I think not.' He snarled, his eyes tinged with something not quite sane. 'I have something you will want back. I have a few of your *family*.' He almost spat the word. 'Several thousand of them, and if you think I won't use them you are wrong.'

He held up his hand and as he did so Stewart slipped one hand into his pocket, his fingers grasping the little black transmitter.

The screens in front of the gates slipped back and as the group of officers moved to the left a moan rose from the crowd. There, high up on the heavy wooden gates hung the bodies of three men. They had been nailed up by their hands.

'Here's the first three. The middle one is one of yours,' Saad said. 'A spy.'

Stewart stepped to the left, pressed the little button once and almost instantly two red dots danced across Saad's chest.

'The middle one?' Stewart responded evenly, his voice laced with sadness. 'No. They are all mine . . .' he looked back at Saad. 'Look down, see the red dots? Laser sights on sniper rifles.'

Saad looked down, a flash of fear across his face. This wasn't how he had planned it.

'One wrong move, by any of your people, and I mean any of them, General, and they will shoot you. You will die here.'

Saad yelled something in Arabic, repeating it twice.

'Don't know the lingo,' Stewart continued, his voice rasping and soft. 'I hope you told them the form.' He raised his hand. 'I have a helicopter or two coming in. Tell your people to keep the peace or you know what will happen. You? You stand very still indeed.' He stepped round the Libyan general, walked forward past the officers and stood beneath the gates.

They had been tortured. Fingers were crusted with dried

blood and Stewart guessed that they had pulled their nails out. One had burns on his chest and the centre figure had obviously been cut repeatedly with a razor or sharp knife. Two ladders lay on the ground beside the wall. Stewart picked up one and put it against the gate between two of the figures and climbed up, the crowd absolutely silent.

He took a Celt Force hackle from his pocket and pinned it to the chest of the centre figure, then the one on the left and then finally he moved the ladder and pinned one on the last of the three. Back at the vehicle his piper unbidden, but knowing Stewart, began to blow air into the bag, so when Stewart reached the ground and turned to look at him he was ready.

He stepped forward a few feet, arranged the pipes across his shoulder and began to play. It was 'The Flowers of the Forest', the ancient Scottish lament for the fallen, the sad notes carrying over the crowd as they had done for centuries.

Saad, angry, embarrassed and frightened, could do nothing but stand back as the ritual was performed. Halfway through, a young man in the crowd who had been busking on Grafton Street when Stewart passed, took his flat bodhran drum from his bag and began to tap out a beat, a very traditional rhythm to accompany the piper. The people around him parted and others pushed him forward and finally he stood beside the piper, within yards of thousands of Libyan troops and played for the dead men on the gate.

Behind them a heavier beat intruded and suddenly from over the rooftops battle helicopters appeared. They hovered there, menacing in the extreme, their pods filled with rockets and the minigun barrels moving back and forth like snouts sniffing the air.

Finally, the lament over, Stewart looked at the crowd.

'Bring them down.'

A priest pushed his way through the soldiers and others

followed and soon the three bodies were on the ground, their faces covered.

'I shall take them.' Stewart raised his voice to the crowd. 'If any come to claim their brave, they are with Maeve O'Donnell of the Clan O'Donnell, High Queen of Ireland and Queen of the Celts.'

Then he walked back to where Saad stood, the little dots still on his chest.

'I have changed my mind,' he said. 'You no longer have twenty-four hours. You have twelve and I won't lead my men in here. He will.' Stewart pointed to Andre Hyland. 'He will be the first in. He will lead the Irish, the others from the camps, and I tell you this, General Saad, after the way they were treated they will give no quarter. This meeting is over. I shall now return to my lines. Do as I ask. Withdraw to the north, to Malahide.'

Stewart turned and walked back to his vehicle, indicating that the lad who had stepped from the crowd to play his drum should get aboard with the others. Further up Dame Street one of the helicopters settled on the roof of the building and Scott and the American sniper scrambled aboard.

The vehicles moved away, two of the helicopters overhead, and the journey out of the city went without incident until the vehicles rounded a corner and someone noticed a car had dropped in behind them. It followed for two miles and then well into no man's land on the N7 it pulled out and overtook them, pulling to a halt in front. One man climbed from the car, stepped into the middle of the road and raised a hand in the air.

Stewart told his driver to pull over and as he did so the escort vehicle moved in front of them and stopped, the corporal, who could see the figure on the road was unarmed, training his machine gun on the car. The man, young, tall and wearing a keffiyeh, the only uniform of the Palestinians, walked forward, the sergeant's shotgun trained on his chest as he did so. He ignored it.

'Let's listen,' Colonel Browning said quickly to Stewart as the man approached. 'This might be interesting.'

'My name is Ali Jassem. I think we should talk.'

The barn roof leaked and the men stepped round the puddle on the floor as they assembled. A trestle table with chairs was being erected in the centre of the room. The three men who had been in the car stood off to one side, steaming mugs of coffee in their hands. Standing with Ali Jassem were two men who wore the uniform of the Libyan regular army, the senior man a major.

'Let's get on with it,' Browning said. Stewart had told him to take the hard road. Get to the issues quickly. No negotiating.

They took seats around the table and Browning kicked off as Stewart entered, four of his staff behind him, one a slightly built major from intelligence.

'You said that you aren't changing sides. What are you doing?'

'Bringing this thing to an end, without further loss of civilian lives,' Ali began, rubbing his eyes, his exhaustion apparent as he spoke, 'ours, yours, it's over.'

'General Saad doesn't seem to think so,' Browning said.

'Saad is . . .' the Libyan major began, ' . . . well. Let us say, out of touch with the realities. We are not all like him. We came here to help our Arab brothers. We did not come here to see people held before guns.'

'What are you offering?'

'Saad thinks he has a final way out. He has taken hostages. They are in a football ground, a stadium,' Ali began, pulling a tourist map of Dublin from his pocket and spreading it out on the table. 'Here. Lansdowne Road.'

'We know that already. If that's all you have got then . . .' Browning responded, standing up.

'What you don't know, Colonel,' Ali retaliated, also rising

556

to his feet, 'is how to behave. I command five thousand fighters, the equivalent of one of your brigades, and I suggest that if we are to be of assistance to each other, that you show me some respect! You also don't know which gates are locked, how many guards there are, where they are, when they change, how to get in or when your best chance of success lies. This man,' he jabbed a finger at the major who sat beside him, 'worked on the plans for this. He has just ended his career and put his life in jeopardy to prevent a tragedy. So do we work together or shall we just leave?'

'Date of birth?' the slightly built British major snapped.

'What?'

'Date of birth!' he barked.

'June 5th 1958.'

'Mother's name?'

'Yasmin.'

'Your tutor at UCLA. Underwear colour?'

'But what . . .'

'You were bonking her,' the major shouted. 'You would know.'

'Pink!' Jassem yelled back. 'It was always pink.'

The major looked at Stewart and gave a nod. Across the table Stewart acknowledged and Browning grinned. 'Sorry about that. Wasn't sure, you see. Needed to know if you are the real Ali Jassem. We work together.'

It was midnight. The team had been working with the two Libyan officers for five hours and, the base plan laid, Ali Jassem and one of the Libyans had left to make their way back into Dublin. They took with them Aiden Scott and five other SAS soldiers, all now dressed in jeans and windbreakers and the ubiquitous keffiyeh of the Fatah fighters. The SAS men had been chosen for their dark swarthy looks, and carrying Kalashnikovs and Russian-made sniper rifles they looked the part. Jassem had given them the nod of approval and now they were about to link up with seventeen real Palestinian fighters, twelve of whom were to be dressed in Libyan kit and driving a Libyan truck.

Stewart had moved units forward and 1 Para waited with fast vehicles half a mile back from where the Gordon Highlanders and the Irish Guards were going to punch through the Libyan lines. The Libyan defence had been tested already and the Celt Force men were going to smash their way through with Milan missiles, supported by a squadron of Lynxes. Two Chinooks were ready to lift in eighty men of 2 Para and in England a pair of Tornadoes were being readied on the flight line.

The stadium at Lansdowne Road was crowded with people. David had kept his little band together and had shepherded them to one edge of the pitch. He had taken two coats, the one he was wearing and the second an old folding plastic mackintosh that now covered the children's heads as they sat close to their grandmother. At least they would stay dry. There had been only stale bread, but buckets of water had been positioned round the grass. They were now empty and someone had said there was a drum in the centre. Off to the south he could hear the muted sounds of a battle and he willed them closer, but dreading what the Libyans had in mind once their backs were truly to the wall. He was watching the guards, looking for a way, any way he could tip the odds. As he watched a guard slipped from his post, walked down the tiered rows and settled on the bottom row where he lay down on the lowest level and, pulling his poncho over his head, seemed to go to sleep.

The other hostages sat or stood in groups around the pitch, their coats wrapped round them, those with waterproofs lucky, some sharing their raincoats by making little tents over their heads, children and the old huddled beneath. The guards were at strategic points midway up the stands, their guns pointing downwards. In the centre of the pitch a raised platform allowed a handful of troops to see over the heads of their charges as they handed out bread and allowed people to come forward to the drum of freezing water if they wanted to drink. A taped-off path led back into the changing rooms below the stands, where other soldiers took refuge from the rain. Outside other guards were posted and a small group of men, there to crew the four tanks that were parked in the car-park, stood beneath a canvas awning that had been stretched between two trucks, drinking tea and warming their hands over a brazier.

Jassem sat in the front with the Libyan major and the driver, one of Jassem's men. The remaining men were crammed in the back and as the truck turned into the gates, even Scott who liked bold, simple plans was nervous. Now dressed in Libyan kit, they were committed.

A few moments later the truck stopped briefly as the major spoke to the gate guards. They were nervous and jittery because away to the south everyone could hear the sounds of a fierce battle, the Gordons and the Guards hitting the Libyan lines. Then the gears churned and they were off, the truck stopping by the players' entrance to the stands. The plan was simple. Nine of Jassem's fighters would remain in the changing area and hold any Libyans who tried to react to the events on the pitch. Jassem, the Libyan officer, the seven Palestinians and Scott and his men would enter the stadium. Scott and his men would slowly make their way forward down the taped path to the centre platform, while the Palestinians, two to each side, would make their way up closer to the groups of guards. Heads down under issued helmets they would not be challenged.

The Libyan officer moved forward, stopping every now and then to point something out to Jassem who nodded intelligently. Some hostages near the tapes watched, hopeful that this might be a reprieve, others more resigned just watched, and some with real anger burning in their eyes looked as if they might tear Scott's men limb from limb if given the chance.

Scott, like the others, had his rifle beneath his poncho, the big telescopic sight and nine inches of American-made silencer adding bulk and length that was difficult to conceal. He looked at his target as he approached. He was to take the western side, the three men on the machine gun. Falling rain. Unlike the others he didn't have a scope hood, the inch long plastic visor that kept rain off the lens, so he would have to work fast. The light from the stadium's floodlights was harsh with deep shadows. But at least there was plenty of it. They were nearer. The four men on the centre platform were watching them, wondering what this officer was doing out here in the rain. They were at the steps now, and Scott moved round the side to give himself a clear field of fire. He had five rounds in the magazine. Any more than that and he would need to reload and by then the silencer would have given up, its baffles compressed by one shot more than it was intended to ever deliver silently.

Above him Jassem stepped in front of the major and took the last step to the platform, pulling a machine pistol from under his poncho.

'Everybody. Weapons down. Sit down and shut up. One mistake and I kill all of you.' The soldiers, absolutely baffled, looked twice at the gun and then at the major.

'Do it,' he said.

They did. Scott watching from the corner of his eye, pressed the bleep on his wrist and lifted his poncho, the rifle rising in one smooth motion, safety off, finding the first man in his sights and squeezing the trigger.

The rifle recoiled back, a low thud the only sound, his hand worked the action in a blur, sighting on the second man as the first began to fall, other thuds behind him, a woman in front of him, her mouth opening to scream, squeeze, work the action, re-sight, the second man falling, the third leaning forward, squeeze, the recoil slamming back, the thud more of a muted bang now, the third man falling, the woman's scream loud as it reached him.

'Four,' from the other side as one of his men reported success.

'Two.' Another bang, someone letting go a fourth bullet. A burst of fire from the south side as one of the Palestinians opened up. 'Three.' That was it. All guards down. Firing suddenly from the changing areas. 'Report it,' Scott called and with one of his men raced back down the path to support the Palestinians under the stands as one of the remaining two men began talking into a radio mike.

A Libyan soldier, the one who had been asleep, sat up bewildered for only a second, then reached for his rifle.

David Kelly had seen the men enter the stadium and the moment he had seen them start to shoot he had dropped down over his mother and the children, but realized that the shots were aimed at the guards. He came to his feet in a snatched burst of energy, turning to face the lone guard they would not have seen. He saw the rifle coming up, the guard trying to make sense of what was happening, trying to cock his rifle, and he moved. He covered the twenty yards like a hurdler, over the heads of confused, frightened, screaming people trying to take cover, like a big cat hunting. He cleared the lower barrier and crashed into the soldier, the weeks of frustration bursting from him in a rage.

The SAS soldier on that flank saw the movement in his peripheral vision and swung his scope-sighted weapon one foot to the right. There in the harsh lights he took it in in a moment, and then watched, with ten-power magnification as the young Irishman's fists hammered into the guard who was now down. Finally he reached down, snatched up the man's rifle, and began to batter the form below him, brutal blows with the steel butt plate, blood splattering up at him.

Three miles to the south Lynxes were hammering houses and shops either side of the road where the Libyans had settled in. Milan missiles fired by infantry poured into their positions as two Chinooks that had been hovering behind the lines passed overhead. In front of them, lower and faster, four Lynxes raced out in front. Two were crammed with SAS men and two were anti-tank gunships.

At the stadium, one of the SAS men took the megaphone at the platform and began telling people to move into the stands, to clear an area for the helicopters, and once there to lie down behind the seats. The people could hear the fighting in the changing area and knew it wasn't over yet reacted instantly, gathering up children and running to the edge of the grass to climb into the stands as asked, the area by the players' entrance clearing like the waters of the Red Sea before Moses.

Two minutes later, two of the tanks now turned and facing the stadium while their crews waited for orders, the pair of anti-tank Lynxes engaged and the other two settled down inside the stadium. Sixteen further SAS men jumped from the doors, their officer, a major, settling on one knee to receive a report from one of the original five. He immediately sent half his team to support Scott beneath the stands. Scott was wounded, two bullets having passed through his lower left arm, and three of the Palestinian fighters were dead, but they held.

When they arrived in the tunnel, there alongside Scott's group was a young Irishman, his face and chest covered in blood splatters, firing measured bursts with the best of them. When he ran out of ammunition David Kelly slumped back against the wall, breathing great draughts of air into his lungs. He didn't reload. He didn't have any fresh magazines and he didn't know how to change a magazine anyway.

The major led the other half past a dead guard and out through a public gate to engage whoever was left in the car-park and secure the area for the Chinooks. Above them the Lynxes they had arrived in prowled the area round the stadium to the north while their two sisters finished off the tanks in the south car-park.

Eighteen thousand feet above them two Tornadoes had

let their bombs go. Running down a radio signal, the four bombs would hit their targets within half a second of each other. Two would hit the Post Office in O'Connell Street and two would hit Saad's residence, only isolated that afternoon by the Libyan major who was now being called by Scott to ask his countrymen to surrender beneath the stadium.

As the first of the Chinooks settled on the surface of the car-park between two of the burning tanks, in the centre of Dublin the bombs hit, destroying the new Libyan HQ, its command and control centre and Saad's residence behind the Shelbourne Hotel.

No one there was left alive to hear the reports that the Celtic Forces had broken through in the south and the west, and that Limerick had fallen to the US Marines. As the forward elements of Maeve's Own fought a series of skirmishes towards the Dáil, the word spread among the dispirited soldiers in the city and they began laying down their arms.

When the troops arrived at the Dáil they found the resistance was there already, John La Touche and Mary Kelly and their rat-hole fighters sitting on the steps happily eating apples, their weapons around them, the lights somehow having survived the fighting.

'What took ya?' she asked cheekily when Andre Hyland walked up the steps. 'Nice haircut. Suits ya,' her accent the North Side parody she had used all those months ago when he had stood in her studio. She held out the apple. 'Want one?' she asked.

He suddenly remembered. 'Mary bloody Kelly,' he said, a grin spreading across his face for the first time in days.

At 5.17 AM Maeve's flag flew over the Dáil and the Senate. Operation Dark Rose, the Battle for Ireland, was over.

# EPILOGUE

Maeve O'Donnell of the Clan O'Donnell was asked to perform one more function. She had seen her Celts arrive and she was asked to see them go and to hand over constitutional power in the same ceremony. Stewart's people transferred the prisoners to the Irish Defence Force and arriving, hastily assembled UN observers and quietly made preparations to leave.

The 176 Celt Force dead were scattered all over the country. Some bodies were flown home, but most were to be buried in Ireland. There were no mass graves. Each body had been identified and they were moved to Phoenix Park in Dublin where a special cemetery had been created. A simple monument was commissioned for the centre of the area and a second to be erected in memory of the people of Ireland who died in the struggle, resistance or otherwise, but that was for the future. Now there were just the graves, fresh mounds of earth in ordered rows.

It was suggested that representative companies of each regiment parade at Phoenix Park, but the Irish would have none of it. They insisted that every man and woman who had served, without exception, would have the right to attend.

The Kelly family had all gone except Moira. The family would all be there for a meal afterwards and she stood, apron on, peeling vegetables. The soda bread was in the oven and Simon had found a huge joint of beef from somewhere. Food had been flooding into Ireland since VI day, shiploads of it from Liverpool, to keep people going until the local infrastructure was back in working order.

Mary was back, her hippie artist alternative Mary who was now a national hero, and people spoke of her with affection and awe. She had changed, grown, found stature somewhere and was less concerned with the way she looked than ever. There was a new fellow somewhere. She was her Mum and she knew these things.

At Phoenix Park, Simon, his family, Sue, David Sarah and her children watched from behind a rope barrier. Directly opposite was a contingent of ex-resistance fighters, sheepishly sitting on portable tiered seating, each wearing the royal hackle for the first time. The thirty-yard gap between them was part of the parade route and as Mary looked across she saw a man she knew standing on the ground beside the ex-resistance members in the stands. He smiled and her heart skipped a beat and then he lifted the rope and walked across the gap with all the confidence of a man who could go anywhere he pleased on this day.

He presented his hand to Simon. 'I'm John La Touche. Would you mind if I steal Mary from you?'

'Go ahead,' her brother grinned.

John lifted the rope barrier and gallantly offered Mary his arm. 'Would you join me?'

'Where?' she asked.

'Over there,' he said.

She knew it wasn't because she was *buachailli* and had earned the right, but because he wanted her there, with him.

She smiled, took his arm and walked across the gap, the raucous cheering from the rat-hole fighters in the stand bringing a blush to her face. The crowd nearby picked up on it and began clapping and yelling and wolf whistling. Some who knew who she was began the chant and others picked it up, ' Ooh . . . Aah . . . Maree . . . Korbaa', and she blushed, the colour rising as John La Touche publicly and proudly took her hand in his and claimed ownership as young men do.

Scott, in civilian clothing, his arm bandaged, watched from the sidelines forty yards further up with a grin on his face. Aisling was at his side, her arm hooked through his, as the day's events began. The pipes of the Black Watch cut through the hubbub of the crowd noise and the regiments wheeled and passed in review before the dais where Maeve, Mary Johnson and Colin Mahoney stood. Stewart was below them at ground level and before the mass departure he gave the order. The field fell silent as an honour guard of Irish Defence Force and the Royal Army of Queen Maeve presented arms to the lines of fresh graves and fired three volleys into the sky. After battle honours were presented and led by the band, half a million Irish people lining the route, Stewart and his Celts would march to the docks and the ferries home.

Opposite the royal dais was another and viewing from there were Kiernan, Morris, O'Sullivan, O'Malley, Briget Villiers, McMahon and O'Reilly, some very self-conscious and in suits for the first time in years.

Scott smiled at Rory McMahon's discomfort and pointed it out to Aisling. Her parents had offered to lease them the farm, but there was talk of making it a museum, leaving the tunnels and radio room in the attic intact. Scott wasn't concerned either way. He was taking leave and as long as he was with Aisling he didn't mind where they were. It would be interesting times ahead as the new emerging political parties confronted the issues of neutrality, the constitution and laws that had allowed it all to happen. The old parties of Fianna Fáil, Fine Gael and Labour had failed the people. It was time for a change, Scott mused, and as Maeve, in her penultimate act as queen, presented battle honours to the regiments of Celt Force, they stood together, Scott holding an umbrella as the soft Irish rain fell.